HoW
TO BE
DEAD

LAUREL SCHMIDT

HoW TO BE DEAD

A LOVE STORY

atmosphere press

To Durnford King---thanks for this spectacular reunion,
And Ray Frerking, who helped me write from the other side.

CHAPTER 1

It wasn't her idea to die with "Fuck!" on her lips. It wasn't her idea to die at all. She just wanted to get home and give her aching feet a rest. Kick off her shoes, collapse with a mug of wine and put on her favorite ear balm—Albinoni's concerto for violin and oboe. It had been a long day and now it was rush hour on Madison Avenue. Home seemed very far away.

Navigating the sidewalks of New York was an urban sport that required a unique set of skills coupled with intense focus. With her elbows tucked in and a short stride, she'd zig-zag like a footballer going for the end zone. Yet on most days she loved it. The fleeting brush with a handsome stranger and a hastily mumbled "Sorry." The cheerful compression of excited shoppers at the height of the holiday season. And the endless variety of faces drawn to this mecca from all over the world. It energized her. And there were even moments of euphoria when the first snowflakes of the season fell. But right now, she felt like a salmon struggling upstream. She pulled her coat tighter and pressed on.

Rounding a corner, she caught the sound of an angry squabble above the blare of taxi horns and the symphony of construction tools endlessly demolishing and rebuilding the city.

"Hey, I gave you a twenty! Where's my change?" a burly man demanded, thrusting out a beefy hand. His red bathrobe flapped open over a Yankees t-shirt that had seen better days.

"Twenty, my ass!" the food vendor shouted. "Get outta here! I got a business to run." He shoved an aluminum tin toward the man and bawled, "Next!"

A dozen hungry people shuffled forward, grumbling or sharing their opinions as only New Yorkers can. "Move it, buddy!" But he was planted like a tree.

It was a typical New York dispute. No telling who came out ahead at the end of the day.

The disgruntled customer grabbed the tin and spun around to confront his hecklers, delivering a sharp elbow to her shoulder as she tried to squeeze by. She flinched and was about to join the chorus of detractors, when she recognized his face from her time at the Department of Mental Health. He'd been a belligerent client. She, an overloaded case worker. But her heart leapt like he was an old friend.

Before she could speak, he cried, "Is that you, Ms. Beacon? Oh God, did I hurt you? I'm so sorry." The words tumbled out in a torrent of anxiety and relief. "Lady, you sure are a sight for sore eyes!"

"Nick? My God, it's good to see you, too." She put a sheltering arm around his shoulder and tried to ease him out of the stream of pedestrians, but he stood his ground. "That jerk cheated me." He pointed a finger toward the vendor, offering a high-volume cautionary tale to the line of potential patrons. "Ten bucks!"

The vendor stuck his head out the tiny window of the food truck, shouting "That guy's crazy. Somebody get him off my corner!"

Most people didn't bother to glance up from their phones, but a few hooted, "Beat it, man."

Nick was, in fact, unstable at the best of times and chronically off his meds, but he looked stung, as if this was his first time on the receiving end of such abuse.

"Never mind him." She eased the tin out of his hand,

fearing it might become a projectile if the situation escalated. "He's..." but she didn't get a chance to finish.

"Asshole!" Nick bellowed over his shoulder, reigniting his anger.

She knew it would take more than words to pry him away from this stinging defeat, so she reached in her purse and pressed a ten into his hand. "Now, where're you headed, honey?"

"Meeting," he grumbled. "Just down the street."

Years ago, he'd landed in one of her support groups after a painful and very public firing from his job as a sportswriter. Some days he was the life of the party, wielding a wicked sense of humor that reduced her other clients to tears. But he also had an I.Q. in the brilliant range that he weaponized to fend off emotional vulnerability. He was endearing and exasperating and never famous for regular attendance, so she thought an escort might be in order.

"Well, do you mind if I walk with you? I could use a little exercise." She took his elbow gently. "Now, tell me. How've you been?"

"Not so great." He reached down and stretched out the front of his t-shirt, exposing his belly to the cold. "The Yankees are in the cellar."

Baseball season had been over for months, so his use of the present tense was a red flag. "But what about you? Who's on your team at the Center?"

He shook his head. "Can't really say. They come and go so much I don't even bother to learn their names." He raised his shoulders up around his ears and let them drop like he'd been shot. "Nobody's ever been as good to me as you."

She felt a stab of guilt. Not a week went by that she didn't think about her old clients and wonder how they were faring since her departure. "Well, you were always special to me."

When they parted, he gave her a brotherly hug. "You take care, Ms. Beacon."

"You take care, too. And Nick?" She paused and gave his arm a gentle squeeze. "Take your meds."

He laughed and called, "Good memory!" touching a finger to his temple as he disappeared into the building. She lingered for a moment, thinking how hard he struggled to keep a tenuous grip on his life. *I should call his case worker.* But then her bladder sent a message she couldn't ignore. Time to get moving.

As she approached the corner, the light turned red. Normally she'd join the crowd of fleet-footed pedestrians darting across against the light, weaving their way through stalled traffic. But her knee was throbbing—another reminder of aging that she didn't appreciate—so she leaned against a mail box and lifted her foot an inch off the ground to relieve the pressure. Just then her nose caught the smell of salt. Somehow a molecule of ocean broth had drifted into the city, caromed off the skyscrapers, survived the assault of smoke from the chestnut vendor and arrived at the corner of Fifty-Fifth and Madison Avenue pristine and laden with memories.

She closed her eyes and surrendered. Shutting out the cacophony of the city, she remembered walking on the beach with Mac, then hurrying home to make love. Afterward, she'd sleep with her face buried in his shoulder, his beard still smelling like the sea.

An elbow jostled her out of her reverie. When she glanced up, she was looking south and saw a green light, but instinctively stepped off the curb heading west. And just like that, the game was over. Environmentally-conscious vehicle—1. Unconscious pedestrian—gone!

No, death certainly wasn't on her agenda. Not even a remote possibility. After all, she was the best-selling author of *Sex, Drugs and Social Security,* who proudly declared that she'd live to be 100. But 35 years had just been shaved off the longevity guru's life by a bright yellow New York City cab.

So, where was she? This long bright hall could have been

any number of places. A concourse in the subway, a transit tunnel between airport terminals, or the bowels of most buildings in mid-town. Just ahead, a cluster of people was looking expectantly in her direction.

They've probably been to one of my seminars or read my blog.

She still struggled with the idea of having 'fans' because, left to her own devices, she had the instincts of a hermit. But she handled it with grace and humor, bantering with the zealots who called themselves *Beaconites* and shouted her battle cry, "Geezer up", then shifting gears to listen intently to those in need. But now it felt like something was off.

Come on, girl. You can do it.

She plastered on her best what-a-lovely-surprise expression and strode toward the group. "Hello there!" Then she directed her trademark kudo, "You look fabulous!" to the oldest person in the group.

A woman with a riot of long gray curls thrust a dog-eared book toward her. "Can I have your autograph, please?" while a man in a blue denim shirt shouted, "Frances! Love your blog! It saved my sanity more than once."

"Thanks." She reached out and patted his shoulder. "I'm never quite sure about it, so I'm glad it helped."

She had a love/hate relationship with her blog, but not its faithful readers. It was an invitation to abuse by a certain segment of the population, apparently because she was old or a woman or an old woman with an opinion. She'd been called an age-denying con artist in serious need of Botox, and a godless promoter of promiscuity who should burn in hell along with her books. But hundreds of readers reached out for help, trusting her with their secrets, and she couldn't turn them away. Some nights she'd spend hours answering questions about family crack-ups, retirement blues, physical decline, sexual experiments, love, loss and longing. Other times, she simply held invisible hands as grief flowed in torrents through the dark night.

Another woman pushed forward. "Frances, do you re-member Louise from Des Moines? The lady who rescues dogs? Well, that's me!"

"Louise!" she cried and delivered a robust hug, then held the woman at arm's length and gave an approving nod. "I'm so proud of you." She'd exchanged e-mails with this dog-lover through a long and messy divorce, so this felt like a joyous reunion instead of a first encounter. She pulled out a copy of her latest book and scribbled her cell number inside. "Keep in touch, Louise."

Out of the corner of her eye she glimpsed a hand clutching a small green sign with FRANCES BEACON printed on it, like a driver waiting in the arrivals lounge at the airport. But the face was lost in the crowd.

He'll have to be more aggressive than that if he wants to get my attention.

A sign on the far wall pointed to the restrooms, so Frances blew a kiss to her little tribe and sprinted the last few yards. When she pushed open the door, she was relieved to discover it was a one-seater. Plain but private. *Perfect.* She shot the bolt in the lock and collapsed on the toilet before noticing that the back of the door was covered with graffiti, top to bottom, side to side.

Why would anyone prolong her occupancy in a cubicle the size of a phone booth to share her thoughts with the squatting world?

Normally, she'd just avert her eyes and get on with business—the hopscotch required to avoid puddles, maintain-ing minimum surface contact, and religiously shunning the fluorescent-lit reflection of her face that made her pores look as big as pennies. But something caught her eye. A small heart surrounding two black letters: FB and a plus sign. Below was a gray smear like a swath of fog where something had been erased.

"Coincidence," she mumbled. "I've got more important things on my mind. Like where am I? And how the hell'd I get here?"

But her gaze had a mind of its own, deftly scanning the mass of graffiti as if studying the Rosetta stone. Several phrases leapt out:

The universe will rearrange itself to suit your expectations.
See with your heart, not your eyes.
Live everyday like it was your last.

"How about this one?" Frances asked the empty room. "Avoid bathroom oracles." Then she sat very still as the room began to spin around her.

She clamped both hands on her cheeks, trying to steady herself as she methodically reviewed her repertoire of skills for challenging situations. *Breathe. Breathe.* Slowly, she began to tap the bony ridge above her nose with her index finger, then her cheek bone and chin as she repeated the comforting chant. "Even though I have this feeling, I deeply and completely accept myself."

Next, a few power gestures. She stood up and straightened her shoulders. As if on cue, her chin rose enough to tighten the skin on her neck back to her early forties. *Head up. Heart open.* "You can handle this. You know you can."

She closed her eyes and thrust her arms up in a wide V like the top of an hourglass and visualized energy flowing down into her body. Finally, her go-to mantra, said as often in exasperation as joy. "I love my life. I love my life."

As her arms fell, her right hand grazed something rough and tweedish, prompting a startled cry. A rumpled figure like a large pile of laundry with a face had materialized out of nowhere.

"Oh, Jesus," she whispered. Then she froze, waiting for something to happen and fearing the worst. But all she heard was a faint chuckle from somewhere amongst a tumble of curls. Laughter wasn't a good sign. Probably some kind of psychosis going on, and the smallest move, the wrong word could trigger an escalation to violence. But she was a New Yorker, where they had more muggers and lunatics per square block than any other city in the country, so by definition self-defense was in her DNA. But her pulse was pounding in her ears like a boom box, making it impossible to concentrate.

Think, Frances! The best strategy she could conjure up on short notice was borrowed from the Dog Whisperer: *Never show fear. Act like this kind of thing happens all the time.* She tried to aim for a casual tone but her voice was strained and thin when it finally emerged. "Uh, I think one of us has the wrong room."

No response. The aerosol apparition propped himself against the edge of the sink, then fumbled for a cigarette and took a long slow drag.

Frances followed the cloud up to a ceiling festooned with naked neon tubes and water stains. An asthmatic fan lured the smoke into a plastic grill. More silence except for the voice in her head shrieking like a car alarm. *How did you get yourself into this?* Struggling to block another surge of fear, she swiveled her head a millimeter at a time toward the door, measuring the distance between herself and the exit. Then she factored in the size of her opponent. It would be a close call, and who knew what she'd face outside even if she managed to escape?

He followed her glance, then eased over to slouch against the door where his body filled the whole frame.

Okay, she thought. *Now this is definitely a hostage situation.* But what were the rules? She'd had some crisis training years ago, one of those coma-inducing presentations where people guzzled cold coffee from cardboard cups just to stay awake. All she could remember was something about "use his name" and "try to establish rapport" so she decided to give it a whirl.

"I was just wondering, Mister...I assume you're a man."

He reached for his crotch.

"Stop! I'll take that as a yes."

"Grayson," he drawled and took another long drag.

"Well, Mr.—"

"No mister," he interrupted. "Just Grayson." He exhaled and Frances began to cough.

"So, what is it you do, Grayson?" she asked in her best cocktail-party voice. But she couldn't muster the bright look of interest she used to disguise her discomfort in social encounters with strangers. She was just buying time.

He reached in his pocket and pulled out the green sign with her name on it. "I'm your Transitional Trauma Specialist, Grade III."

Her next move was stupid and she regretted it the minute the words were out of her mouth. "Too many syllables."

"What?" He looked puzzled or worse. Maybe offended, like she was dissing him.

But she blundered on. "Your title. Too many syllables and...I don't know." She gave him a pained expression. "Bureaucratic?" She cringed as she heard her mother's voice spilling from her mouth like a bad smell, so she scrambled for a more positive note but missed. "You need something snappier, easier to remember."

"Never been a problem before." He straightened his shoulders and his eyes strafed her from top to bottom. She recognized that glance—the one people in authority use when they want to shut a conversation down. It never worked on Frances.

"Fine. I'm just sayin'." Her voice trailed off as she wondered why she always had to have the final word. People told her it was annoying but her new roomie just shifted his weight and gave a hint of a smile like he was enjoying a private joke. Frances blinked first.

"So, Multi-syllable Man, what do you do besides hang out in the ladies' room?"

"I told you. I'm a Shock Jock. I handle the high-profile cases. Part guide, part counselor. Compassionate probation officer with a little concierge thrown in for good measure. Grayson, Madame, at your service."

"Great!" For a split second she relaxed, convinced that this had all been a big mix-up. "In that case, Grayson, I'd like an obscenely large glass of white wine. Pronto! It's been a hell of a day."

"I know. I died once."

She staggered back as if she'd taken a fist to the gut. "Died? No-no-no-no-no!" Her words sprayed the room like machine gun fire. Then she gave a little chuckle and scanned the walls for hidden cameras and microphones. "Is this a reality show because I'm telling you right now," she waved a finger back and forth in front of his face, "you got the wrong girl. I won't sign a release. You can't use this footage."

"Not a bad idea. Should have pitched that."

She pulled out her phone and thrust it toward him, tapping the screen. "See this? I have a dinner reservation, so if we could just get on with whatever...*this*...is."

He pulled the phone close to his face. "Nice place. I ate there once."

Perfect, she thought. *Delusional, too.* She slumped down on the toilet to contemplate her predicament. She was trapped, defenseless and clueless. But thinking like a victim wouldn't help. It might even be a self-fulfilling prophecy, so she ransacked her brain for a more positive explanation. *Probably some random act of urban misfortune. I just have to play along.* She wasn't sure what came next but there had to be a way to temper this lunacy. *Even if I'm in serious trouble, there's no way I'm...*

Now his lips were moving but it was like watching TV with the volume off, as the word *dead* rumbled through her head like thunder.

He jerked his thumb toward the door. "Let's blow this

joint."

But when Frances tried to stand, her knees were jelly. And she wasn't just sweating. Her armpits felt like they'd been power-washed. The loss of composure was complete. "Fine, but I need to pee first."

"I'll be right outside."

Even sitting still, she felt lightheaded. A fragment from a Girl Scouts First Aid course staggered out of a remote corner of her brain and she blew off the dust. *Something about a bag.* She spied a sanitary disposal bag, clamped it on her face and exhaled. Now she looked like a pale, sweaty Pinocchio.

Whole minutes passed while she procrastinated, hoping to conjure up a plan. *I'll just do a few Kegels so it won't be a complete waste of time.* Inevitably, the exercises reminded her of sex, but the sharp tightening in her pelvis was cut short by a spasm of anxiety that jolted her back to full consciousness.

What the hell am I doing? I have to get out of here. I need to go home.

She screwed up her courage and snatched a quick glance in the mirror. "Dead? Impossible!"

CHAPTER 2

Grayson was slumped against a pillar in the casual trance of a dedicated smoker, so Frances glanced left and right, looking for an exit. Nothing. Just a relentlessly gray jumble, as puzzling as an Escher painting. Still, he didn't look like he could move very fast and she'd been power walking for years. But just then he looked up, his eyes bright with interest.

"How about if I show you to your room?"

"Room?" For just an instant, he sounded like a concierge and she embraced the fantasy. Next, he'd be promoting spa services or recommending a cozy little Italian restaurant in the neighborhood. But she snapped back to reality when he led her down a dull white passageway that felt like a tunnel. When she glanced up, she was staring into a patch of sky that mirrored the exact color, texture, and nothingness of the walls. A nowhere sky for this nowhere place.

She was bone weary and dying to be alone, so she followed mutely, not even trying to track their path. But the moment Grayson pushed open the door, her senses went into a frenzy. Even in her depleted state she had sufficient energy to take immediate umbrage at the décor.

"Any more bad news?" She thrust imploring hands toward the ceiling.

"Good night, Frances." Grayson closed the door.

"Not likely," she muttered.

The design was straight out of NASA or a cult that worshiped at the altar of strict simplicity. Every trace of humanity had been erased, leaving an environment so sterile that the next occupant might easily be an organ donor. She paced back and forth on the whitewashed cement floor, refusing to accept the idea that she was now in residence. But that just made her feel like a caged animal. Maybe if she stood perfectly still and concentrated, she could figure out what had happened. She squeezed her eyes shut and saw a flash of yellow that made her flinch, but then vanished like the fragment of a dream. An impression but no information.

She opened her eyes wide and surveyed the space again. The far corner featured a string of white Christmas lights hung in a vertical helix that looked cheerless but completely functional unless you wanted to read something smaller than a newspaper headline. Just then they began to blink bright colors and Frances felt a stab in her chest as she stared at this relic of a time so distant and sweet. Her head was flooded with the scent of pine, carolers singing on street corners and smiling faces clustered around a table. Pure joy, vanished long ago. She wrapped her arms protectively across her middle and rocked from side to side.

Floating in the center of the room was a double bed straight-jacketed in wrinkle-free linen pulled tight enough to banish any suggestion that this might be the perfect place to rest, read or God help you, have sex. She bent over and gave it a mighty shove, sending it flying across the cement floor into a corner.

"Dead, my ass!"

Then she untucked the linens, piled them into a big nest on top of the bed and flopped down. "I can't be dead. *Can't,*" she whispered. She grabbed the sheets and twisted them around her fists, like bandages on a boxer. *It's a mistake. Has to be. I'll figure it out,* she thought, trying to summon her inner pugilist. But he refused to answer the bell, leaving her with a profound sense of defeat. She bit down on her knuckles to stifle a sob but couldn't staunch the tears that stung her eyes.

As she mopped her face with both hands, a second glance at her fists delivered a shocking thought. *Restraints! A mental ward. Crazies tethered to their beds with cheap low-thread-count sheets.* It hit her like a meteor: "Holy shit! I'm not dead! I was committed!"

Frances was no stranger to the institutional system thanks to decades in social work. More than a few of her clients had arrived fresh off an involuntary vacation at the 72-hour Hilton. She'd even visited some of the high security lockups in New York, so she knew what to look for as she scanned the room again.

It was so clear now. No windows, no sharp objects, only one exit. She leapt up and pressed the wall. It was soft, leaving a faint handprint. "A padded cell?" Her brain tried to cut through the confusion with one question after another. *How did this happen? And why?* "I must have really pissed someone off this time," she muttered aloud, prodding her memory, groping for a clue. But she hit a blank wall. *Who did this? And why can't I remember anything?*

She checked her inner arm for bruises or needle marks, telltale signs of a Thorazine IV. That would account for the dry mouth, anxiety, and fatigue. But her arm was unblemished. *Wait a minute. He said he was a Shock Jock.* "Electro-shock! How did I miss that?" She shook her head in dismay. "No wonder my memory's shot!" She'd heard of some elaborate ruses to coax compliance from the mentally unstable during intake. But death?

She charged toward the door and stuck her head out. Nothingness in both directions. "Hey, Mr. Shock Jock!" she bellowed. "Get your ass back here right now!" She didn't really expect a response since she was clearly on the losing side of the power dynamic, but Grayson appeared within seconds. Before he could speak, she pounced. "Lock-up?"

"What?"

"Don't you *what* me. I demand a writ of *habeus corpus*!"

"Fra—'

She cut him off in mid-syllable. "I know this law, chapter and verse, so if you forgot to cross one T, I'll have you hauled in to court so fast." Her face said she relished the idea of a showdown.

"Frances—"

"I know my rights." Her whole body was shaking as she pressed her case. "Seventy-two hours and I'm out of here because—"

"Frances," he shouted, but she was undeterred.

"I'm. Not. Crazy." She drilled each word into his chest with her middle finger and the expression on her face dared him to say it wasn't so.

He winced but stood his ground. "You're right, Frances," he said softly. "You're not."

She clamped both hands over her mouth. Air wheezed out like a leaking tire as the hyperventilating slowed. Finally, she whispered, "I knew it was a mistake."

He gave her a moment to compose herself before adding, "But you *are* dead." He took a step back, as if bracing for an explosion.

"Not possible!" she insisted and scanned the empty room, like she was looking for a judge or jury to whom she could appeal. Finding no recourse, she made one last ditch effort. "It's not possible because..." She pressed her lips together until they nearly disappeared. "I loved...my life." The words shattered her defiance and she collapsed against his chest.

He stood like a statue, while her shoulders heaved. When the shaking subsided, she asked in a voice barely above a whisper, "Who took my life? I want to know who took my life."

"Come on," Grayson said, steering her toward the door. "We could both use a drink."

CHAPTER 3

Only the word *drink* got Frances moving and even that was at a snail's pace. It took whole minutes for her eyes to adjust to the relentless gloom so she proceeded like a prisoner in shackles, staring down at her feet for fear that she'd trip on the uneven stones. It was eerily quiet and when she stomped one foot, it didn't make a sound, like she'd been converted from diesel to electric.

"Well, if this is dying," she grumbled, "I'm not impressed."

"Lytton Strachey said the same thing. You know him? Bloomsbury group? The twenties?" Grayson seemed to be impervious to her distress, so she decided to brood more audibly.

"Yeah. A champagne socialist." She preferred the type who got their hands dirty but she decided to keep that to herself until she got the lay of the land.

"Yes, but a wonderful writer. Probably a little before your time," he said as he disappeared around a corner.

She scurried to catch up, eager to keep him in sight until she could get her bearings. "*Probably?*" she protested. "How old do you think I am?"

"I'm not touching that. Anyway, I'm sorry you're disappointed. But things'll get better." He picked up his pace and began to whistle quietly.

Frances was in no mood for levity. "Wouldn't take much."

They took a series of turns, always ending up in an identical street or plaza, making her disorientation complete. "How does anyone find their way around here? Breadcrumb navigation?"

"Don't worry, Frances. I won't abandon you in the woods." And with that he knocked twice on an unmarked door that slid open without a sound.

The bar inside had the quiet dignity of a private club redolent of worn leather, whiskey and cigars. The kind of room Frances loved but rarely entered without an escort. She'd always envied the way men could sit at a bar for hours without attracting attention, but just let her try for a solitary drink after a long day and it was open-season for men who were far less attractive than they imagined, even in low light. Her ass was no sooner on the stool and someone would wander over with fraternizing on his mind. It just wasn't fair.

Usually, she tried for diplomacy. "Sorry, waiting for my husband" she'd lie, and that usually did the trick. But recently when she was beyond exhausted, she leaned into a bleary face and said, "I'm sure you think your attention's been the cause of rejoicing for many a lonely woman, but now hear this. I have exactly no interest in you or your delusional aspirations. So, it's time for *Have dick—will travel.*" She'd jerked her thumb over her shoulder toward the exit. "And I'd be grateful if you'd spread the word on your way back to wherever it is that you lurk."

Bitch was the nicest thing she heard before his departure.

Grayson led the way and Frances quickened her pace, already tasting her first drink in—*how long had it been?* But the wall behind the bar looked nothing like the sparkling collection of painkillers arrayed in every watering hole in New York City. Instead, the center section was dominated by a massive mahogany chest with hundreds of tiny drawers. Mirrored walls on each side reflected glass shelves with rows of perfectly spaced jars, glass cylinders and delicate ceramic pots. It reminded her of the apothecary next to her favorite restaurant in Chinatown.

The bartender was hunched over a book with his back to the crowd, but he sprang to life when Grayson called out "Evenin', Jack."

Jack was well over six feet tall but had the permanently stooped shoulders of someone who'd spent a lifetime straining to make conversation with the shorter members of the race. His face was like a carved wax figure that had been left on a sunny window sill. Drooping lids nearly obscured his dark eyes, and wire-framed glasses perched above sagging cheeks sprinkled with freckles.

Grayson made quick work of the introductions. "Jack, this is our newest arrival. Frances."

Jack gave a slight bow as Grayson turned his attention to Frances. "What'll you have?"

She collapsed on a stool and slid her phone onto the bar. "Chardonnay," she gasped, looking at Jack with beseeching eyes. "The largest you can pour without losing your job."

Jack's eyebrows twitched toward each other, forming a patch of wrinkles just above his nose. "We have many more interesting drinks, Beacon-san."

Frances threw him a quizzical look but was undeterred. "Is this an ABC issue? Anything but Chardonnay."

"No. It's simply that," he gestured toward the wall behind, "so many elixirs at your disposal."

She gave the wall closer inspection. Dozens of jars displayed what looked like grass clippings or the dark brown morsels of canine origin that played havoc with pedestrians on the sidewalks of New York. "I appreciate the thought and I'm a big fan of novelty. Great for the brain and all that. But this is an emergency. 911. What I need is first aid, not a Zen tasting or whatever you had in mind." Then she pressed her hands together in front of her and added, "Please," in her most abject voice.

Jack bowed again to reach under the counter, revealing a faint tattoo on the crown of his head. Leaning closer, Frances saw a seagull in flight. The moment her drink hit the bar, she wrapped both hands around it like she was afraid it would sneak off when she wasn't looking. Lifting the glass toward her reflection in the mirror she announced, "I drink, therefore I am." The golden liquid was gone in an instant. "Whee-eew." She exhaled and settled back to wait for the chemical relaxation of muscles and nerve endings permanently on high alert. Then she ordered a second and stared into space.

"So, I'm dead—already." She leaned toward the mirror for a closer look.

Grayson nodded. "Pretty much."

"If I'd known I was going to die so soon..." She dropped her chin into one hand, reviewing her regrets. "I'd have eaten more bacon."

He chuckled.

"It's not funny!" She lapsed into silence. *What else would I have done differently,* she wondered. *More vacations? A pet? Maybe give God a second chance?* She jerked her head around and squinted at Grayson. "Is it because I didn't pray enough?"

"Depends," he said slowly. "What do you mean by prayer?" His voice was casually curious, but she took immediate offense.

"What is this, a pop quiz? I feel like I'm back in catechism class, which by the way, was never my finest hour." Then she took a long sip of wine and decided to put her irritation on hold. She just didn't have the energy for that level of combat. "Alright, I gave up all that rosary business because it seemed like an apprenticeship in obsessive compulsive disorder. Good way to keep your lips and fingers busy, but what did it mean?" She didn't wait for a reply. "I'll tell you. Nothing! Did you ever really listen to the words in those prayers?"

Grayson shook his head. "Not really."

"Well, lucky you!" she grumbled. "Anyway, I gave up on

organized religion but I always believed in a greater... something." She shrugged. "I don't know." She looked at him for confirmation, but he just smiled and took a sip of her wine.

"I guess spiritually speaking I was a freelancer. I practiced gratitude with the fervor of a nun although I was never quite sure who I was thanking. Tried to cultivate unconditional love." She gave a tiny chuckle. "God knows, that didn't come naturally in my clan. I sent light into the universe and finally ended up in a Wednesday night bring-your-own-God meditation group. They call it mindfulness now. Lots of rhythmic breathing. A bit of chanting and then potluck supper. It was the small still center of my week."

The recitation of her spiritual efforts seemed to exhaust her, but Grayson just stared idly in the mirror. She nudged him with her elbow. "Hey! Are you even listening?"

"Sure, sure," he said.

"So, none of that counts?"

"Did you ever learn to pray the way Auden described it?" He leaned back and threaded his arms across his chest.

"The poet, right? Pulitzer Prize for The Age of Anxiety." She shrugged. "Of course, he was anxious. What kind of achievement was that? He lived in New York. It's a requirement."

Why can I remember trivia like that but not how I got here?

"Right." Grayson nodded as if he was impressed, and she thought she was finally getting somewhere. Until he continued. "Well, Auden said the definition of prayer is paying careful and concentrated attention to something other than your own constructions."

"That's why I'm here? Because I'm self-absorbed?" Her chair tipped dangerously backward and she made a grab for the edge of the bar. "Jesus, if that's the criteria for sudden death, people should be arriving by the boatload. No, let me amend that. By bullet train and jumbo jet—especially from my zip code!" Then she seemed to deflate, resting her forehead on the edge of the bar. "Why me? Why *me*?"

"Don't whine," Grayson said quietly.

"I know. I know. I can't stand whiners either."

He eased himself off his stool, waved goodbye to Jack and said, "Let's go. Time to get some sleep. You've got a big day ahead."

"Bigger than dying?" She gave him a look of disbelief.

"Much."

CHAPTER 4

So. This is home.

Frances stood in the center of her room and surveyed the spare, uninviting space once again. *Well, at least it has a desk.* Or was it? She wandered over to have a closer look at the white plank performing a levitation act on the far wall. No hinges, no legs, no visible means of support. Its companion piece looked like a retired shopping cart enjoying a second career as a chair. It had a shiny metal handle across the back, four wheels, and no cushion, so she could already feel the tic-tac-toe pattern painfully embossed on her butt.

The desk was barren except for a colorful brochure with the heading *Guest Questionnaire* and a handwritten greeting, *Welcome Frances!* But she was just too tired. It would have to wait.

The only comforting object in the room was an old-fashioned piano stool. All battered wood and cracked red leather, it stood out like a crow in the Arctic. It wasn't much—scarcely room for her computer, phone, and a tiny silk pouch she carried like a talisman. But she dragged it over to the bed, then stood in a near stupor.

Something's missing.

Her nightstand at home looked like a shelter for homeless books. They jockeyed for space and toppled on the floor. Occasionally one managed to sneak under the covers like the literary equivalent of a dog on a winter night.

How will I survive without my books?

On the pillow she spied a large white T-shirt and shook her head in dismay. For years, the only way she could face the night was swaddled in a man's flannel shirt. She'd curl up on her side with her fist near her face and bury her nose inside a frayed cuff, inhaling the lingering scent of safety and love. So, she crawled into bed fully clothed, put the phone under her pillow and prayed that she'd awake from this nightmare, in her own bed. In her own life. Or simply descend into oblivion.

Instead, she exchanged consciousness for a night of industrious dreams. The opening scene is a crowded auditorium. Five-hundred people have paid good money for a day of high-octane motivation from the author of *Sex, Drugs and Social Security,* her unorthodox guide for boomers heading into retirement.

Frances was still amazed every time she set foot on stage and stared out at a robust crowd of eager faces jostling for seats near the front. In the early days, she'd been shocked when more than 10 people showed up at her seminars, but over time the audience swelled as people stumbled across her blog or heard from a friend that they just had to go hear the *Geezer Up!* lady.

Yes, she was a walking encyclopedia of how not to get old, but they could get that from the internet. What she brought to the game was humor and heart, so within the first half hour her seminars felt like a high school reunion and she was their big sister, favorite teacher, old flame or best friend. She mixed science with self-deprecation, told the truth about her fears and follies, and begged them to embrace the incredible opportunity of being boomers. After all, they were the kids who wanted a revolution and still harbored that rebellious longing for something new. What she understood above all was the unspoken belief that their youth was somehow still within sight. And the sheer energy of her presentation convinced them that they could tap into it and feel alive again. They just had to Geezer Up.

In her dream she was in full evangelizing mode.

I'm not against aging. We've been doing it since the day we were born. What I militantly oppose is olding. Bitching about every ache and pain. Blurting out your ailments to total strangers. Voluntarily segregating yourself in geezer ghettos with bad food, bad role models, and bad vibes.

She paused and gave a sidelong glance. *Kill me first.*

A wave of cautious laughter ripples through the audience.

But aging. That's different. Aging means curating your life to include the very best it has to offer. Delete all the bullshit. Fine-tune your passions. Blow out all your tubes. Dance, drink, fuck.

A few people in the audience stir uncomfortably. One woman grabbed her purse in one hand and her husband in the other and charged for the exit.

Perfect, she thought. A little drama to get things rolling. The rest of them will sit tight just to prove that they're proud members of the generation that made *fuck* a noun, a verb and an adjective.

Robust aging calls for staying up late and getting up early. Sucking the life out of every day. That's right. Suck to the power of ten.

Frances awoke with a start. Her clothes were stuck to her body like a decal and her pulse was racing. But it wasn't panic. It was exhilaration. "Oh, God," she moaned. "How can I live without my work? And my people?"

She didn't know most of her followers personally, but there was a palpable sense of mutual understanding, even intimacy. They'd shared the events of the last 50 years—the war, the protests, hope for a different future. Many of them still clung stubbornly to the belief that the world could be a better place. And so did she.

"But what does any of that mean now?" She gazed at the

ceiling and wondered for the hundredth time, "What the hell happened to me?" She flung her arm to the far side of the bed where it encountered nothing. Just the cool barren landscape of unwrinkled linen. She grabbed a handful, rolled over and wrapped it around herself like a shroud. "Kill me first," she whispered into the pillow.

Ping! The sound nearly stopped her heart. She dug under the pillow and squinted at her phone. R U there? shone on the screen.

"Mac! Thank God!" But his signature message blurred as tears stung her eyes. How many times had that text arrived while she was working in their study, cocooned in her single-mindedness? *But did I get off my ass and go to him? No, I'd text back—Still here.* And now she wasn't.

Ping! again.

"Yes, my darling, I'm here." She tried to reply but between the tears streaming down her face and the phone wobbling wildly in her hands, she only managed to hit one letter out of three accurately, producing the garbled reply I;n gere ny kive.

Ping! More insistent.

"Shit!" This time she opened her eyes wide and pressed her lips together to steady herself. She touched each letter with the concentration of a novice. I need U. But when she hit send, nothing happened. She was still staring at R U there?

"Screw this!" She hit the microphone and yelled "Mac, I don't know where I am! Help!"

Ping! Ping! She hit send but watched in dismay as the cursor erased her message one word at a time, leaving nothing but his query.

Ping, ping, ping! It sounded like a countdown. Her breath came in short, sharp bursts as panic gripped her chest. She stared at the screen, then slapped herself on the forehead. "It's a phone, you idiot! Call him!"

Ping, ping, ping, ping! Faster, louder, broadcasting urgency.

She scrolled down to MAC HOME but her sweaty finger slipped off the glass, so she dragged it across her pillow and made another stab. With the phone clamped to her ear, she held her breath. On the first ring she cried, "Pick up, baby. Please!"

Once, twice and then muffled static as if the sound was traveling through water. She closed her eyes, straining to make out a word here and there. "Sorry...please."

"I can't hear you." She groped for the speaker button and cranked the volume to max as the battery light blinked red. "Mac, can you hear me? I need you."

Boo-eee-ooo pierced the room and she flinched as a voice boomed, "We're sorry. You've reached a number that has been disconnected or is no longer in service. If you feel you've reached this recording in error, please check the number or try your call again."

"Impossible!" He'd had that number since he was fourteen. She jabbed the redial button viciously, clinging to the belief that her vehemence registered with this hunk of metal, glass and lithium. As if in self-defense, the screen froze on the unanswered question—R U there?

Think, Frances! She grabbed her computer and clicked the e-mail icon. "Come on! Will you hurry?" Several impatient stabs yielded nothing but a black screen with the words: Unable to connect.

"Damn wi-fi," she cried out loud.

Refusing to accept defeat, she grabbed the computer and waltzed it around the room, hoping for a hot spot. She froze when she heard a single beep and then a message popped up— ACCOUNT CLOSED.

"No, no, no!"

She slammed it shut and hurled it on the bed. Just then her stomach contracted violently, so she stumbled to the darkened bathroom and groped for the sink with both hands. With her teeth clenched, she dropped her forehead until it came to rest against the cool white edge. In the dark, her mind conjured up the image of an astronaut untethered from the mother ship, drifting off into space. That triggered a series of dry heaves, and then the dregs of her chardonnay. When the contractions stopped, she mopped her face with the back of her hand. Now her lower back began to spasm, so she stood up, flipped the light switch, and flinched.

Even on a good day, Frances was no fan of mirrors. For a start, they tended to congregate in places with forensically high levels of light. And they insisted on delivering far too many details instead of a quick update. Some mornings it seemed like she'd been enrolled in a witness protection program, so at odds was the face in the mirror with the 35-year-old image she stubbornly carried in her head. It was like the opposite of Dorian Gray.

"Jeeez!" This morning was worse than usual—Frances Beacon as if painted by Edvard Munch in his scream period. A genderless cringing zombie. And the day hadn't even begun.

Cold water was the only answer. With her head in the sink and the water blasting, she thought she heard whistling. When she stood up gasping, her groggy brain was just able to knit together the notes. *Always look on the bright side of life*—the Monty Python song she'd adopted as the signature finale of her seminars. It never failed to get people up on their feet. They'd lean on each other and sway from side to side, as they belted out the lyrics on the jumbotron. Then they'd charge out the door, determined to do battle with the grim reaper.

"Jolly rotten. You got that right."

Back in the bedroom she heard a quiet knock. "Frances?"

She wanted to pull the covers over her head and hit the Dive button, like a submarine captain evading the enemy. Descend into darkness and silence or maybe just die and get it over with. *But was that even an option?* Instead, she wrapped a blanket around her shoulders like a tent, and opened the door a crack. "You again?'

"And a good morning to you, Madame."

"Not likely."

"Time will tell."

"I'd kill for a cup of coffee." This seemed like such a simple, obvious request that she was amazed he'd arrived empty-handed. *What kind of concierge didn't deliver morning coffee?*

"Sorry. Caffeine-free zone."

Frances stared in disbelief. "Oh, my God! There really is a hell."

"Call it what you want."

She rubbed her temples where a headache was beginning to bloom. "Fine. Just cut to the chase. When can I get out of here?" She dragged her hand over her face, as if bracing for more bad news.

"That's entirely up to you."

Her head jerked up in surprise. "In that case, fifteen minutes ago would've been perfect."

"Just a few details we need to—"

She waved her hand dismissively. "Whatever. Let's get to it. I have a lot on my mind."

Grayson nodded toward the blanket. "Wardrobe malfunction?"

"Funny." She pulled the blanket closer. "Give me a minute."

She swiped an armpit with her hand and gave it the sniff test. *Lavender? That new corpse smell?* Then she smoothed the worst of the wrinkles out of her clothes, grabbed her phone, and yanked open the door. "Where to?"

"In your rush to get to the ladies' room, you skipped Customs."

Frances shrugged. "No problem since I seem to have skipped baggage." She gestured toward her outfit. "Nothing to declare."

"We'll see about that."

"That doesn't sound too good, so here's an idea. How 'bout a pharmacy?" She pointed to her temple. "Or maybe a gun so I can just blow my brains out?"

"Sorry. It's mandatory. No one's exempt."

She resented the coercive tone in the conversation, and this whistling warden hustling her into the complete unknown. She wanted to grab the front of his shirt and give him a vigorous shake but a voice in her head cautioned, *Use your words, Frances*, so she shoved her hands in her pockets and barked, "Mandatory? Says who? Who's running this place, anyway?"

"I don't think you could handle it."

"Try me," she dared.

But he was already disappearing into the gloom.

CHAPTER 5

Frances had to believe escape was possible. It was her only weapon against a mounting sense of despair, so she began to construct a mental map of the place while she sprinted to catch up with her guide.

It reminded her of Venice—elegant buildings standing shoulder to shoulder, stately colonnades and low arched bridges--but the entire scene was drained of color and water. It didn't even have the sharp edges of a black and white photograph. Just a full spectrum of somber gray alleyways, passages and lanes.

The only distinguishing marks in the labyrinth were the occasional manicules at the top of the buildings. These hand-painted fists with a single extended finger were the medieval equivalent of Post-it notes, sketched in the margins of books to highlight important ideas. But they'd evolved over the centuries into signs pointing the way to the train station or a bar. Unfortunately, the ones overhead offered exactly no help in navigating much less crafting an escape. Two or three congregated on a corner, all pointing in different directions without a single word about the destinations they were promoting.

She was so busy craning her neck in a fruitless search for an exit that she slammed into Grayson when he stopped at a door marked *Customs*. "Sorry, sorry," she mumbled in embarrassment, as if she'd been caught stalking.

"See you later, alligator." He cracked open the door and stepped aside, gesturing with his head that it was her move.

Frances crept in just far enough to assess the situation. The dim room was dominated by a clear plastic sphere like a diving bell. A tiny attendant dozed alongside, like the pensioners who guard dusty rooms in third world museums. Maybe she could sneak out. But just as she turned to go, his chair creaked and he sprang to life.

"Step in, please." He pointed toward the globe.

"Why?"

"Screening."

"More like TSA on steroids. You do realize that scanners are considered unlawful, invasive and ineffective. Not to mention a violation of the Privacy Act, the Religious Freedom Restoration Act and the Fourth Amendment."

The technician shook his head slightly. "Yep, I've been told." Then he repeated "Step in, please," with the maddening sameness of the automated message on a complaint line.

"I'd rather be patted down. That's my right. So, pull on your gloves and get busy." Frances thrust out her arms as an invitation to be frisked. "And in case no one told you, you're getting a hell of a dose of radiation every day. I'll bet you glow in the dark."

"It can't hurt you now. Honestly. We wouldn't lie."

"Really? Does Iraq ring a bell? Weapons of mass destruction? Don't talk to me about lies."

"Step in, please." No impatience. No new inflection. Only a veteran bureaucrat could exhibit such poise. She wasn't going to win this battle.

The air inside was sharp, like heavy-duty air conditioning or an early morning in autumn. Frances stuck one hand inside her blouse in a vaguely Napoleonic gesture. Shouldn't she be getting colder by the hour, more dead with every breath? But she still felt 98.6-ish. Just to be sure she exhaled and a tiny cloud formed in the chamber.

Two sets of yellow footprints were painted on a blue mat, like a diagram for learning the tango. Directly above hung the image of two overlapping human figures inscribed inside a circle and a square. It was Vitruvian Man, Leonardo da Vinci's great picture chart of the human body. He called it a *cosmografia del minor mondo*—a cosmography of the microcosm—because he believed the workings of the human body were analogous to the systems of the universe.

A voice crackled from a speaker somewhere inside the bubble. "Assume position Number One, please."

Frances stretched her arms out and up until her hands were even with the top of her head, then adjusted her feet, creating a triangle between her legs. Click. Flash.

"Now turn around and take position Number Two."

She pivoted and pulled her feet together, arms extended to the side level with her shoulders. Click. Flash. The bubble filled with blinking red lights and a line of text crawled across a screen—*Exceeding allowable limit*. The voice said, "Step out, please. Take a seat."

Frances had never been arrested but she imagined this was how it felt while waiting to be booked. Guilt flooded her body like a shot of adrenaline but a quick examination of conscience left her confused. She'd been trying to do the right thing for as long as she could remember. Granted, she wasn't an unequivocal success, but either through piety or cowardice she'd managed to avoid any major transgressions.

Her standard reaction in challenging situations was division of labor. One part of her brain sprang to her defense while another began devising ways to placate the offended— whoever that was. But without the requisite information, she was stumped.

"Of *what*?" she demanded. Silence. She wasn't sure of her rights but *what the hell?* She decided not to go quietly. "Allowable limit of *what*?"

"I can't really say. That's above my pay grade."

"Yeah, right." She jumped up and began to pace. "I want to speak to your supervisor." Then she stopped and chuckled to herself. How many times had a disgruntled client hurled that impotent threat at her?

The clerk handed her a computer print-out. "Report to Room 13. Outside and to your left."

"Outside and to the left," she repeated, then stepped into the hall and instinctively turned right.

"The other left," called the attendant.

"I know. I always get that wrong. It's a brain condition. Directional dyslexia. Freud had the same thing. No worries. It's not fatal."

She spun to the left and skidded to a halt.

"Room 13," barked a voice from out of nowhere. "Get moving!" It was a cattle-prod kind of voice and her resentment flared.

"I'm going," she shouted, lifting her fist in the general direction of the order. But her defiance vanished when she saw her entire arm shaking like a conductor dragging a crescendo from an orchestra.

Never show fear.

But fear was the only sane response as she headed for who knows what, clutching an unreadable document that could seal her fate.

CHAPTER 6

In another part of the afterlife, a door flew opened.

"I thought we had years until we'd be doing this again," muttered Cornelius Beeckman as he marched into a dark wood-paneled room. "At least that's what she led us to believe."

He looked as if he'd just stepped off the label of the Dutch Masters cigar box. His broad face was framed with a wide white collar trimmed in lace as delicate as a spider's web. But from the neck down he was a study in black. Black cloak and breeches, dark silk stockings, and black leather shoes with shining silver buckles. His head tipped slightly forward under the weight of a huge felt hat trimmed with beaver pelt that shaded intense eyes and a bristling moustache.

Glancing over his shoulder, he caught sight of a short man lounging against the wall. Swathed in a patchwork coat of motley colors, green tights and pointed shoes, he could have been a model for a line of circus clothing.

Cornelius barked, "You there, Fool." Without waiting, he flung his hat at the startled man.

"Thank you, Sire," the man replied. He snagged the hat and flipped it into the air, catching it on his head where it settled low on his brow. Just then a heavy wool cloak was launched in his direction and he staggered under the weight. "My pleasure, Sire. Anything else I can do for you? Leap, whistle or perhaps fart a tune?"

Cornelius bristled momentarily at the insolence, but he had bigger things on his mind. He threw a notebook and folder on the table, cleared his throat, and scanned the room. There were a dozen niches in the paneled wall that could have held statues of saints, portrait busts, or oil lamps. One of them was sheltering a yogi wrapped in saffron sheets, apparently deep in thought.

Cornelius studied several knots of people engrossed in quiet conversation, searching for familiar faces. But most of them were strangers. The largest cluster was presided over by a woman who seemed to be holding court. As each newcomer arrived, she offered her hand and whispered "Juliette." No last name.

She wore a high white collar cinched with a black tie. Its crisp austerity was a perfect match for hair pulled in a tight bun, not a single strand out of place. Her upright carriage and sharply turned-out toes gave her the unmistakable profile of a ballerina. Drained of what must have once been a prodigious beauty, Juliette still had drawing power. Every man in the circle leaned in, mesmerized by a siren call emanating from an aged yet ageless charmer.

Listening attentively at her side was a young man clothed in a dark leather vest pulled over a simple shirt. The sleeves were rolled up to the elbows, signaling that he was ready for a day of manual labor. His right shoulder hung lower than the left and he shifted his weight uneasily from foot to foot, as if looking for a comfortable position for his sturdy trunk.

"What the hell's going on?" Cornelius raked his hair away from his face, like he was trying to dispel a mirage. Then he turned on the Fool as if this was all his doing. "This is supposed to be an Executive Committee meeting."

The Fool gave an elaborate shrug. "I cannot say, Sire. I'm a stranger here myself."

Cornelius stomped from one group to another but no one

paid the slightest attention and he was stunned at the lack of deference. "Everyone, take your seats." His voice seemed to fall on deaf ears, so he bellowed like a four-star general commanding his troops. "I said...take...your seats!"

One by one, they moved toward a huge circular table that dominated the space, neither hurrying nor making eye contact with the imperious Dutchman. Gentlemen stood aside for the ladies, pulling out chairs and offering a hand before finding places of their own.

"Don't get too comfortable," he announced. "We just need to get this sorted out and then you'll be on your way."

Heads swiveled from side to side. The women exchanged puzzled looks while the men furrowed their eyebrows at the rude reception.

Now that he had them corralled, he shifted to a more congenial tone. "Clearly some of you are in the wrong room, but no worries. Probably not your fault. The General Assembly meets in the basement." He pointed down with one finger to illustrate his point. "This is an emergency meeting. Executive Committee members only." Then he produced a mechanical smile. "I'm sure you understand."

He paused and glanced at the Fool who dutifully pushed the door open a crack and bowed low, giving the interlopers their cue to exit in mild disgrace. No one moved. Then the silence of the room was broken by the sound of a chair scraping against the stone floor.

"There's been a change," a woman said in a cool, even voice. A cloud of light blue powdered hair sat upon her head. Curls trailed down her neck to a white scarf pulled tight to shield against drafts. Her brown eyes gazed steadily out of a face that exuded intelligence and dignity.

"Sit down," Cornelius said dismissively, as he thumbed through the file on the table, prospecting for a memo he could use to oust them.

She remained standing, her long silk gown rustling slightly

as she repeated, "There's *been* a change."

He looked up, shocked at her impudence. "You're telling me! Blacks and...*women*?" Then a chortling sound escaped from his throat. "What idiot came up with that idea?"

"The committee lacked diversity," she said.

"This isn't diversity." He threw both hands in the air. "It's...insanity." Then he sprang from his chair. "What is that god-awful smell?" He charged around the table, coming to a halt beside the man in the leather vest. Below his brown breeches were rough boots caked with manure and sprouting bits of straw like porcupine quills.

"Identify yourself," Cornelius demanded.

"Gwilym, Sire.'

"Stand when I speak to you."

Gwilym rose unsteadily, leaning on the table for support.

"Occupation?"

"I was a groom."

"Horse kick you?"

"No, Sire. My master."

Cornelius shoved the toe of his black pump against one dung-encrusted boot. Gwilym lost his balance and collapsed onto his chair. "Groom, indeed? You mean stable boy."

"As you wish, Sire."

"What I wish is to get on with my work." He clamped a lace handkerchief over his nose. "What can he possibly contribute?"

He stomped to the front of the room and paused for a moment, staring at his reflection in a large blank monitor on the wall. He smoothed his moustache and offered himself a warm smile of approval. Then he punched a button, and the screen lit up with the frozen image of Frances, standing in the dim hallway and clutching her Customs report. He flinched as if he'd been jabbed in the eye, and spun around to survey the group. Shaking his head, he muttered, "This will never work."

But it had to. He'd just have to work the room. Build a

coalition. His eyes ticked around the circle, looking for recruits. He was a man on a mission.

Just then there was the muffled sound of babbling. "Is that a *child*?" A toddler with shiny black hair and almond eyes crawled out from under the table, and Cornelius reacted as if he'd seen vermin. "Get it out of here!" He advanced on the child like a placekicker going for the point after, his elegant shoe aimed at the soft rump, intent on catapulting him toward the door.

"Stop!" A woman sprang forward and snatched the boy out of harm's way. He gurgled through a smile of tiny innocent teeth and tried to wriggled away, but she smothered him in a hug. Soon he was resting his head in her lap, and staring at Cornelius like he was an oversized crow.

"How can you be so heartless?" she demanded.

"That's rich coming from you. Correct me if I'm wrong, but didn't you abandon a child who was still hanging on your tit? Not exactly Mother-of-the-Year behavior, so spare me your outrage, Perpetua. And keep the brat quiet."

Stunned by the one-two punch of guilt and regret, she bowed her head, cowed into silence, as was his intention.

"At least there are a few familiar faces. I see the foliage master is here—not that we have much use for your particular expertise. Flowers, huh? You actually liked them, Mr. Gerard?"

"Indeed, sir." A tall, lean man with sun-kissed cheeks stood and touched his velvet vest. "They were my heart's delight."

Cornelius shook his head. "Highly perishable. Fickle market." But he was warming to the topic and seeking common ground. "Risky business, my man, but you managed to make a go of it. My hat's off to you." He let a note of admiration soften his voice, but couldn't leave it at that. "Of course, a little royal attention never hurts."

"Until it kills you," said a figure hunched over the table in a blood-spattered shirt. "Every day my life was on the line."

"Soldier?" Cornelius asked, with a look of interest. Though

he'd never been conscripted, his personal vocabulary relied heavily on images of combat. Words like *strong, dominate* and *carnage* studded his conversations. So here was a potential ally.

"No, sir. Chef," the man replied with pride.

"Good God! " Cornelius looked insulted. "They let servants in, too?"

"*Not* a servant." The man stood, revealing the muscular arms and sagging belly of one who works hard and eats well. Cornelius surveyed the bulk and retreated a step or two. "Allow me to introduce myself." The man swept one arm out in front of himself in a courtly manner. "I am Andreas, head of the royal kitchen for Louis VI, fondly known as Louis Le Gros."

"That doesn't sound so dangerous," Cornelius scoffed and began to turn away.

"Spoken like one who sits down to a fine meal without ever thinking of how it got to his plate." Andreas spat out the words and Cornelius looked stung. "With your permission, I'd like to enlighten you about life in the king's kitchen."

"If you must." Cornelius threw up a hand. He seemed to have lost control of the meeting but was at a loss about what to do next. "But make it quick."

"The demand alone was enough to kill a man. Endless meals of roast meat, swan, heron, peacock, vegetables, cheese, bread and sweets. And every meal I served, no matter how simple or lavish, was like rolling the dice. One lazy mushroom purveyor sending his children out to forage while he fucked a servant could spell disaster. Yes, a single subversive fungus popped into the pot and I could be up for treason. Every day felt like a near-death experience."

The Fool cleared his throat. "I faced death every day, too."

Heads swiveled and at least one chortle was heard.

"Don't be deceived by the stories of merriment and feasting," he continued. "Being a Fool at court was the ultimate high wire act. When you're entertaining a royal, one bad joke or a very good one on a bad day could mean a life of exile, poverty, or the rope. Why do you think comedians say *I was dying out there*?" He jerked his thumb toward Cornelius. "This gig is a lark."

"You can be replaced," Cornelius threatened, trying to regain the upper hand.

"See what I mean?"

Cornelius pointed to a man sitting apart from the rest. Wisps of gray hair sprouted from beneath a wool watchman's cap. His clothing was layered: shirt, vest, sweater, and a coat that hung to his knees, as if he was wearing everything he owned. A shovel rested against the table next to him, but his head was bent over a notebook, his pen scratching away. Surely, he'd be easier to manage.

Cornelius moved closer and tapped on the edge of the table to get his attention. "What's your story?"

The man clenched his right hand into a fist and tapped his knuckles lightly on his chin.

"What's that?" Cornelius demanded, imitating the gesture.

"He's mute," the Fool explained.

"Perfect. The disability rep." Under his breath he added, "At least that's one less opinion I'll have to hear." He returned his attention to the mute. "Well, make yourself useful. Take notes."

The mute put down his pen and his fingers flew, spelling out a reply.

"What's he saying now?" Cornelius asked.

The Fool watched carefully as the mute spelled out w-a-n-k-e-r. "I believe he's admiring your moustache."

Cornelius stroked the hair on his upper lip as he surveyed the group again, and then sighed. "If you'll excuse me for a moment."

The Fool hurried to open the door.

"Step aside, man," Cornelius snapped, reaching for his fly.

"I must relieve myself." But the moment the door was ajar, a large blond dog charged the opening, inserting himself between the Dutchman's legs. "My God, they're sending dogs, too!"

He struggled to regain his balance amidst the tangle of arms and legs. Grabbing the Fool for support, he drew back his foot, determined to give the hound a vigorous send-off. But the animal seemed to levitate as Cornelius delivered a robust kick to thin air and collapsed.

How has it come to this? he wondered. *Peasants, women and chaos. It's an affront to everything I achieved.*

The Fool averted his eyes as a dark stain spread across the Dutchman's crotch.

CHAPTER 7

"Now, what do we know about this...*Frances*?" Cornelius growled as he barged back into the Committee room. No eye-contact. No explanation for his absence. Just weapons-grade irritation that he took no pains to hide. He punched the button on the monitor and stared at the close-up of Frances clutching her Customs report.

He looked around impatiently for the Fool who was sprawled on the floor, playing peek-a-boo with the baby. Pulling his hood down low, he'd wait for the baby to pat the hidden contours of his face. Each time he cried "Boo," the baby tugged his red hair and squealed in delight.

"Can you please pay attention?" Cornelius begged.

The Fool scrambled to his feet. "Pardon, Sire." The baby scooted after him, grunting when his chubby fingers caught the toe of a pointed shoe. But the Fool soldiered on toward the front of the room, dragging the baby like an anchor.

Cornelius slung a file in his direction. "Let's get started. Read the record, please."

As the Fool flipped through the sheaf of papers, a half-dozen black and white photos fell to the floor. He gathered them up and grimaced. "Roadkill! That's disgusting," then tossed them on the table as Cornelius repeated, "Read!"

"Frances Beacon. Born in New York City. Five feet seven inches. One-hundred thirty-five pounds." The Fool snickered at what was clearly a lie. "Me thinks not since her freshman year in college. Unmarried. Social worker, writer, activist, entrepreneur, author of— "

"Stop, stop, stop! Let me rephrase the question. What do we *think* about her?" Cornelius's eyes ticked mechanically from one person to another like the hands of a clock, inviting them to speak but with an air of menace that said he had a specific outcome in mind and would brook no interference.

Andreas spoke first. "She says she loves Paris, that it feels like home. But did you ever see the way she eats? Nothing but salad, salad, salad. With iceberg lettuce. *Merde!*" He spat dramatically, a gob of phlegm landing on the Fool's shoe.

The Fool clapped his hands and cried, "Well done, Broth Meister. Shall we say two out of three?"

Cornelius fumed. "Her dietary habits are of no concern to me...us. What of her *character*?"

"She's an atheist," offered Juliette from the back of the room. Her voice was matter-of-fact so it was unclear if she was for or against the notion.

The Fool checked the file. "Says here urban agnostic."

"That's what city living will do to you," Gerard said.

"Especially that city," the Fool added.

Perpetua shifted the baby on her lap and said, "That's none of our concern."

"Well, I like her," the blue-haired woman announced with enthusiasm. "She's got a spine."

"*Spine?* My God, what are you talking about?" Juliette spluttered, leaping to her feet. "Look at that posture. The ballet master would have taken a stick to her." She drew herself up to her full height, as if to provide a model for poor miserable Frances, cowering in the hall outside the Customs Office.

"I mean grit. A mind of her own." The blue-haired woman aimed a challenging glance at Cornelius.

"Still not willing to back down, Madame?" He swanned elegantly around the room and paused directly in front of her, wearing a smug expression. "Reconsider the *what if's?*"

"Such as?" the woman countered.

He was suddenly animated as the topic moved into his arena—commerce. "What if...you'd kept your mouth shut." He paused and gave her a moment to consider the proposition, but she was unmoved. "Your clever little deception put you in tight with the elites of Paris. Wealth, power, superb business connections. You could've parlayed that phony title of yours— Olympe de Gouges, wasn't it—into a life of comfort and maybe some serious money." He lifted one hand and rubbed his fingers and thumb together with a smile. "Quite an accomplishment for...a bastard." He spat out the words and looked around to gage the effect of his slur. "Instead, you took up with the riff-raff. Rabble rousing market women. Really scraping the bottom of the barrel. And what did it get you?"

"Not all gain is personal," Olympe said.

Cornelius laughed. "Well, if it's not, it doesn't count." He wandered around the table, touching the shoulder of one, the arm of another. "Now back to the topic. We're supposed to be talking about Frances."

"She's too serious," the Fool suggested. "A good heart but she really could work on her sense of humor."

"She was dealing with the flotsam and jetsam of New York. It's a struggle just to stay sane in that city," said a woman who barely looked up from her knitting.

"Amsterdam was far worse," Cornelius declared, "but I managed to thrive."

Juliette scribbled a note to Olympe. *What do you think of her taste in men?*

Olympe rolled her eyes and wrote. *The cowboy, the ex-priest, the weight-lifting Marxist? She really knew how to pick them.*

Juliette, a veteran of many amorous but doomed encounters, scribbled: *The last one was handsome enough. Carried himself very well. But he had issues.* She glanced at Cornelius who was pointing at the frozen image of Frances and hectoring the group.

"What else do we know about her?"

Seizing the moment when his back was turned, she folded the message and handed it back to Olympe who silently mouthed: *What issues?*

"Sixty-something, healthy bank account, no strings attached," Juliette whispered.

Cornelius couldn't hide his irritation. "Ladies, either let us in on the conversation or take it outside. We're trying to get something done."

They waited until he turned again, and then Olympe wrote, *Gay? Bi?* But as she launched the note back toward the ballerina, the Fool materialized from nowhere and snatched it. His eyebrows shot up and with a look of glee, he scampered around the table and delivered it to Cornelius, who crushed it into a tight ball.

"You know nothing," he snarled, aiming his fury at the women. "Do you hear me? Nothing!" His voice was low and iron hard. "So, I'll thank you to keep quiet."

Once again, he stabbed the button on the monitor and the Committee watched as Frances fanned herself with the Customs paper and struggled to gain her composure.

"I'll tell you what I see," Cornelius continued. "A classic case of denial. Make a note of that." He gestured toward the corner where the mute formerly sat, but there was only a shovel resting against the empty chair.

"Where's Harpo?" Cornelius snapped but he was met with blank stares. "Harpocrates. The Mute. Call him what you want. Has anyone seen him?"

Again, silence reigned.

"Never mind. I doubt we'll have anything worth recording."

"Mr. Beeckman is a tad cranky today," observed the Fool. "These last years have been a torment for him."

"Mind your words, Fool," Cornelius threatened. "That's

none of their concern."

"It does appear our silent friend has made his escape," the Fool continued. "Pity he didn't invite the rest of us along. Perhaps he'll drop some breadcrumbs so we can follow."

"Let's get to work," Cornelius sighed, reaching for the file. As the group grudgingly came to order, a heavily dressed figure was making his way into the labyrinth. He paused and pressed his ear to one door after another, before disappearing into the shadows.

CHAPTER 8

Outside the Customs Office, Frances drew in a long breath and inched down an uninviting passageway that brought to mind her years in social work. For decades she'd toiled in no-name buildings with dull overhead lighting, scuffed floors, and utilitarian spaces. She'd routinely scavenged for mismatched furniture left behind by colleagues who'd found better jobs as prison counselors or *sous* chefs in failing restaurants. It was the public employee's plight—doing good deeds in bad surroundings—so she was totally unprepared for the opulence of Room 13.

"Wow! Movin' on up."

It looked like the kind of private screening room you'd find at a major movie studio or a star-studded Hollywood agency. A single chair that whispered *executive* sat expectantly in the middle of the room facing a large screen. A small pull-out table offered a set of earphones, a mouse and a bottle of designer water.

The room was overseen by a young man in a tie and lab coat which seemed incongruous until Frances spotted a stethoscope and blood pressure cuff on a low table behind him. A tank of oxygen stood discreetly in one corner.

"I'm guessing there won't be popcorn," she said.

"Welcome, Frances. I'm Danny. Retrieval technician."

"What's up with the oxygen?"

"Just a precaution. Some people need a little first aid. But you look pretty robust." Danny reached for her print-out and fed it into a tabletop scanner. "Huh."

"Huh, what?" She felt like he'd touched a raw nerve.

"Take a seat. You'll be fine."

"Fine hasn't been an option since..." Once again, she struggled to recall the details that landed her in this predicament. The precursor. The inciting incident. Dates, times, places.

God! I'm like one of those old ladies who can't remember if she had breakfast.

She straightened her shoulders and walked briskly toward the chair, trying to project a confidence she didn't feel. It was soft beige leather with generous armrests, the first inviting object she'd encountered since...*whenever*, so she sank gratefully into its depths and closed her eyes, savoring the possibility of a warm and dreamless nap.

But she jerked upright as the screen gave a slight beep and lit up with the silhouettes from the Customs office. Vetruvian Frances—front and back, side by side—her personal body atlas. The figures were dappled with shapes in a variety of brilliant colors. Shiny yellow points of light. A large purple blotch that could have been lifted from one of Monet's waterlily paintings. A cluster of seven circles caroming off each other in a minor frenzy like molecules bound together against their will. Near her heart was a green swath that reminded her of a pine bough.

Taken as a whole it looked like the work of an apprentice tattoo artist after a night of heavy drinking. Then she looked closer. Behind the random markings was a faint pattern of lip prints on her neck, shoulders, and stomach.

Danny pointed to the mouse. "One click for basic identification. Double-click for the details." Then he adjusted the earphones and she was bathed in the sound of Vivaldi's *Stabat Mater,* so perfect that it seemed to be coming from inside her skull. She longed to just sit and listen but a glance in Danny's direction told her she needed to get a move on. Probably other people were waiting for their turn.

Technology was never her strength. Left to her own devices, she'd be the only person in captivity without a cell phone. And her friends jokingly asked if her computer burned clean coal, so Room 13 clearly required a leap of faith. But what were her options?

She decided to dip her toe in the water with one of the minor shapes, a pulpy, pink blotch over her solar plexus. The Vivaldi sound track switched abruptly to Linda Ronstadt complaining about being cheated. Frances hit the mute button as the word *Betrayal* lit up on the screen.

Well, this should be fun.

Double click and it was just like being at the movies. Except—wait a minute—she was in the starring role. She hit the pause button and stared in fascination at the young-adult version of herself standing in her old apartment.

Who was I then?

But before she could begin the virtual autopsy, she was struck by a thought that was clearly the product of 21st century paranoia. *Who made this film? And how?* since this was long before at-home surveillance systems became as common as toasters. Realizing that logic wasn't the tool of choice in this situation, she took a deep breath and hit Play.

On screen a phone rang and when she answered, a woman asked to speak to her husband. Actually, she slurred—"Z'Adam there?"

Before young Frances could reply, she heard "Shhhh-orry, wrong number" and the line went dead. But was it a mistake or a deliberate drink-and-dial to speed up the inevitable? Frances watched herself hunch over and remembered the dead weight feeling in her stomach, like she'd eaten too much, too fast.

Yes, she'd felt betrayed. Wounded pride and humiliation clamored for top billing. But it took only seconds for the on-screen Frances to realize that she was pantomiming a knee-jerk reaction—how wives are supposed to feel when they discovered that until-death-do-us-part really meant until something better comes along. What she really felt was more like embarrassment at being party to such a cliché. And on the bright side, his philandering was proof that the disenchantment was mutual. Filing for divorce was simply a formality.

Frances took a deep breath, blew out her cheeks and slid down in the chair.

Well, that wasn't too bad.

But it was just the first of many images, so there could be some boobytraps ahead. *Still,* she took a moment and smiled. *That whole marriage-divorce fiasco was one of the best decisions of my life.* Things started to improve before his side of the bed was even cold. Work. Study. Travel. And with that, the pink blotch on the screen began to fade.

She yanked off the earphones and called to Danny. "So, what is this—transubstantiation therapy? Revisit the pain. Retell the story? Because I do this for a living so maybe I could just skip ahead."

"Keep going, Frances."

She nudged the mouse like a child toying with unwanted food and it grazed a mustard-colored blob that looked like a piece of paper crushed by an angry fist. It throbbed as the word *shame* lit up. "Why am I not surprised?" she said out loud.

Shame on you was the theme song of her childhood, her mother's go-to parenting strategy. Tiny infractions earned a frown, but forget to take out the trash or leave a wet towel on the floor and mom launched into the shame-on-you aria, dispensing disapproval and character assassination at full volume.

Being good was like marching in place or treading water. An exhausting survival technique that had to be repeated every day without fail just to earn your daily portion of—what?

Surely you couldn't call it love when it could be erased by a moment of inattention, a lapse from perfect to merely human.

"No, thanks. I think I'll pass."

Her eyes wandered around her body atlas, looking for something more encouraging. There was a patch of shimmering gold like the background of a Klimt painting. A tangle of threads in random paths could be Jackson Pollock's napkin doodles. But the words that flickered as she swept the mouse across the map were anything but beautiful: anxiety, fear, avoidance, insecurity. A cavalcade of traits that would mark you out as a bad bet on a first date.

"Hey, Danny. Didn't you guys save anything good?"

"We didn't do the saving. That's your domain. We're just in the retrieval business."

Her eye fell on the green swath that reminded her of the woods where her family vacationed each summer. *This could be nice.* She clicked once and the word *regret* flashed on the screen. Double click. It's Christmas night and she was giving her father a hug. "I'll see you at the end of January." His face morphed from joy to alarm.

"Gotta study. Comprehensives coming up," she reminded him.

"Right, of course. Good luck with that, honey. You'll do great."

But she could see the disappointment in his eyes as she kissed him goodnight. Then came the call. He was already dead when she arrived at the hospital. Machines kept him breathing but no one said he'd recover. She knelt by his bed and kissed his hand. "I'm sorry. I'm so sorry," Her last act had been to disappoint the man who was her favorite person in the whole world.

Frances slumped back in the chair, stunned by a cry of pain that felt utterly fresh, echoing in a bottomless well of longing. "God, this hurts."

She trained her fury on Danny. "Why can't you just let

sleeping dogs lie? Or better yet euthanize them?"

"Is that what you've been doing all these years?" His voice had the calm professionalism of a therapist, observing without judging.

"Oh, shit!" He was right. She scrubbed her hand over her face, feeling the sheer exhaustion of trying to outrun, outthink and outwork her pain.

Danny tilted his head toward the screen, nudging her back to the task. "You can do it."

Frances grabbed the mouse and dragged it over the large purple scar. Just then the DJ mixing tunes for Room 13 decided it was time to play *Feels Like Home,* triggering a compression in her chest that made her gasp. But the machine malfunctioned. No word appeared on the screen. She double clicked and jabbed compulsively to no avail. Then she gave up. "I have to get out of here!" The soft voice crooned on about loneliness, but the lyrics were lost on Frances as she ripped off the earphones and stumbled toward the door. Danny abandoned his post by the table, trying to intercept her. "Are you okay?"

Her mouth opened but no words emerged.

"Frances?"

"I'm done." Not angry, but flayed on the outside and crumpled within. Dodging his outstretched hand, she thought, *Don't touch me. I couldn't bear it.*

Danny handed her the print out and a copy of her body map. "You'll need to finish. It's a process."

Outside, she was tempted to shred the printouts and set off in search of an exit, but suddenly her balance was off and she sagged against the wall.

I need to get off my feet.

At the end of the hall, she spied a manicule that pointed left. "Why not?" She stumbled down a passage that led to a door marked *Lounge.* Not her first choice but her legs felt unreliable.

She'd never been good at lounges. She knew it was

irrational but something about the sight of people actually lounging—playing cards, gossiping or dozing over a text book in broad daylight was mildly infuriating. *There was so much work to be done and only 24 hours in each day. Didn't they know lost time is gone forever?*

This lounge was like every student union in every university she'd attended. A wide-open space littered with indestructible plastic tables surrounded by chairs that scraped noisily across a linoleum floor. Vending machines, trash cans, and a scattering of old magazines. No one even looked up and the exclusion was a relief as she collapsed at the nearest table and reflexively reached for her phone.

Once again, Grayson appeared as if out of thin air. "How'd it go?"

"Apparently I have...issues." She said it quietly, like she was sharing the news that she had herpes. Then she closed her eyes and massaged the bridge of her nose just below her eyebrows.

He chortled. "You? Nah. They must've got the wrong file."

"It's not funny." But she was desperate for a listener. Someone, anyone, and he'd pulled the short straw. "So, here's the story. Did you ever see that clear plastic model of the human body? The Visible Man? All the organs and guts on display for anatomy geeks?"

Grayson nodded.

"Well, I'm the Visible DSM-5. *Diagnostic and Statistical Manual of Mental Disorders, Cluster C.* Look at this." She stabbed a finger at her silhouettes. "Anxiety, avoidance, hyper-sensitivity to criticism, fear of rejection, insoluble regret, a fixation on orderliness with an overlay of not-good-enough-ness." Her voice rose several octaves during the recitation. Chairs scraped and heads swiveled to get a better view.

"This is none of your concern," Frances shouted at the amused onlookers. But that didn't seem to satisfy her. Leaping out of her chair she continued, "Why don't you get off your ass and find something to do?"

Grayson grabbed her arm and pulled her back down. "Get a grip, Frances!"

She felt momentarily humiliated. "Sorry. It's just that it's so pathetic." She pointed to the purple scar. "They couldn't even tell me what this was."

"That's odd."

"Stupid machine malfunctioned. Whatever. I'm a walking time bomb so I wouldn't get too close if I were you." She slid the body map across the table. "I look like the poster girl for a battered women's shelter."

"I've seen worse."

"Yeah?" she asked, dying to feel superior to someone. "Who?"

"JD Salinger and his little girl thing. Not a pretty picture. And the commie-hunter, Joe McCarthy. He just about blew out the tubes on the ol' scanner. You're actually a lightweight. And anyway, they're not permanent." He paused and tilted his head to the side before adding, "Mostly. You can get rid of them, but it's a process."

She shook her head and then leaned in close. "What if I can't?" It was a child's voice, seeking reassurance.

Just then a loudspeaker crackled. "Frances Beacon. Frances Beacon, report to Division Seven."

"What's Division Seven?" She flinched, clearly alarmed by the prospect of a new challenge when she was still in recovery from Room 13.

"Just a formality. Sort of like in-take. You know that kind of thing, right?"

"I'll say. I did it for a living. Size 'em up and set 'em straight."

"Something like that." He gave a non-committal nod.

"So where is it?" The prospect of wandering through the labyrinth again was daunting.

"Follow the line." He pointed to a pulsing black line that

appeared on the floor.

"Seems a little funereal."

"Time will tell."

Frances frowned. "Can't you give me a clue? Dress code? Sanity test? Truth serum?"

Grayson just shrugged.

"Will I at least see you at happy hour or is this *adios*?"

He opened his mouth but his voice was drowned out by the loudspeaker blasting, "Frances Beacon to Division Seven!"

The word *division* didn't sit well with her. It brought to mind crime novels and she couldn't help wondering if she was the criminal. *Don't go there*, she chided herself. Division Seven was probably just another pitiless bureaucratic gimmick specializing in petty rules and red tape.

She'd had enough surprises for the day, none of which had turned out well, so the thought of one more ordeal filled her with dread. Suddenly she longed for the comfort of her sterile room.

I wonder if I'll ever make it back.

CHAPTER 9

The docket posted outside of Division Seven displayed just one item: Number 3174 *FB Preliminary Hearing*. A husky man stationed at the entrance was a study in charcoal gray. A tailored coat that grazed his knees, matching pants and a black t-shirt that provided just the right touch of casual-chic. The pin on his lapel read MORGAN. But he had a thick neck and a dull, standing-in-line-at-the-bank expression on his face. As Frances approached, he gave a slight nod and solemnly opened the door.

"A doorman? Love it!" She tossed him a brisk "Thank you, sir," but froze the moment she stepped inside. The room had all the warmth of an igloo. White marble floor, white walls of an indistinct material, merciless over-head lighting of the variety found at the Department of Motor Vehicles. In the center of the room sat a single white chair with chrome armrests. It was gazing directly at a gleaming monitor the size of a bathmat, poised for a *tete-a-tete* in an electronic language.

Frances slid into the chair which seemed to quiver and morph, hugging her backside in an overly familiar way. "Back off," she snarled, cringing in the harsh bright silence. With her reservoir of patience dangerously low, she scanned the room for signs of life and then addressed the blank screen.

"Hello? Anybody home? I don't have all day."

The screen crackled to life.

A voice from the speakers on the monitor droned in what sounded like the Latin Mass before Vatican II brought in folk music, hand-holding, and clumsy translations read by priests utterly stripped of their magic. She strained to catch a word or two, hoping there would be an *ego te absolvo* somewhere in there. Then she could make her exit—forgiven, unburdened, and cleansed.

Finally, she heard her name and a string of words appeared on the screen in bold green letters. *Quae neglegentia vitae humanae praecipitem.*

"What the...?" Frances couldn't hide her indignation. *Latin? Who the hell reads Latin except priests and...lawyers?* Not a good sign. She whirled in her chair and hailed the bailiff idling near the door. "I haven't cracked a Latin textbook since high school, so I hope your staff includes a translator."

Silence.

"I know my rights. First and foremost is the right to understand what's going on. I quote: *Defendants in criminal proceedings are entitled to interpretation and translation services in a language they understand.* Does that ring a bell? And by the way, it's free, so don't try to slip me a bill on the way out."

Morgan shuffled through a stack of tattered cards on a small desk and handed her one with the appropriate translation: *Reckless disregard for human life.*

"Are you kidding? Do you know who I am? Frances Beacon, geriatric guru. Campaigner for longevity. *Live all you can. It's a mistake not to.* You've got the wrong file."

She rose to leave, but Morgan planted himself in front of the exit with all the authority that two-hundred-fifty pounds of muscle convey. A line of static like a lie detector crackled across the screen and the charge was repeated. *Quae neglegentia vitae humanae praecipitem.*

"Okay, okay. Let's start over." Her negotiating skills kicked in. "I'm sure we can work this out once I've filled in some of

59

the details you might have overlooked. No criticism intended. It's just that I spent my life *promoting* life. Social worker, advocate for women and seniors, union organizer, immigrant activist, blogger, speaker, writer. All with just one goal in mind. To convince people to get a grip on their lives. To help them realize what a gift it is and make the most of it." She took a deep breath and nodded with satisfaction. All things considered, not a bad accounting, which made the charge all the more ludicrous.

"So, what do you say? Can we just put this behind us? I promise not to hold a grudge."

Silence.

"Did you even hear me?" she asked.

More silence. "Disregard for human life. What a joke!" She took a step closer to the monitor, now blank and reflecting her face. She looked pale and drawn but managed to compose herself before announcing, "I demand that you dismiss that charge."

The screen lit up and flashed a single word. *Dimisit.*

Morgan cleared his throat but Frances cut him off. "I got this one." She tried without success to suppress a smirk as she strutted toward the exit. "See? I told you it was a mistake. But it was nice meeting you. And by the way, Morgan. Great outfit."

"You'll be needing this." He handed her a brochure and held the door.

Just outside she spied Grayson speaking to someone who ducked behind a pillar when she called out, "Hey, you."

"How'd it go?" he asked.

"Piece of cake," she boasted with the satisfied grin of a debate champion. "Case dismissed. They even gave me this souvenir."

Grayson took the brochure and scanned it quickly. "No Frances, *you* were dismissed—temporarily. You have to return for another hearing."

"What? Like I'm on probation? That's absurd!" She grabbed the brochure and charged back toward the court room, an out-matched but determined boxer returning to the ring.

Grayson snagged her arm. "That's not how it works."

She yanked herself free. "Then for Christ's sake, tell me how it works!" She threw the folder at him. "Isn't that your job?"

He tossed the brochure back at her. "No obligation to do the impossible is binding."

"Asshole!" she seethed under her breath as she trailed him back to her room.

CHAPTER 10

Once again Frances woke with a start from her nightly retreat to the one place where she still felt competent—on stage. In her dream she was performing for a boisterous crowd, and soaking up the love.

Let's just cut to the chase. No seminar for free-lovin' boomers would be complete without bonking. In fact, sex is a growth industry in our demographic. So, I have just two words on the subject. She paused dramatically. *HAVE IT!*

Excuse me, sir. Frances gestured toward a man in the second row who threw his arm around his partner, audibly nuzzling her neck. *Not here. But he's on the right track and here's why. Jumping into bed with your partner, lover, main squeeze, or catch-and-release can boost your immunity and lower blood pressure. It relieves pain and if done well, can supercharge your self-esteem. But honestly, there's so much more. All of us have a deep craving for flesh-on-flesh. It starts at birth and that visceral clamor never goes away.* She stopped to let her words sink in. *Think about it. Sometimes don't you want to be hugged so badly that it hurts?*

A sprinkling of sighs can be heard in the crowd. A few people reach for each other, proving her point.

Don't tell me you're too old because plenty of octogenarians are still in the game and it's not just the drugs talking, legal or otherwise. Some of them swear they're having the best sex of their lives. So, here's what I think gets in the way. She patted the little pillow of her stomach, grabbed the flesh strung between her armpit and elbow like a hammock despite her best efforts, and finally pointed to the wrinkles around her eyes. *How we look. Seriously, how many times have you thought that you'd love to have sex if only you could rent a body double?*

She lay quietly in bed, enjoying the rush she always felt during a rousing performance. She missed it. But it was more than that. She missed her Beaconites. At first, being their eponym embarrassed her, but she grew to love the image of her fans creating countless points of light as they worked to become their best selves. Now she was struck by the irony that they'd be biking, belly dancing, and bonking while their guru was marooned. She stared at the ceiling, inert and utterly dismayed with her prospects.

A knock on the door scarcely registered.

"Rise and shine," Grayson called.

Highly improbable, but she managed a feeble "Be with you in a minute." When she emerged, she was clutching the brochure from court, which featured a logo bearing the letters UAL surrounded by planets and stars.

"U-all?" she drawled as she sailed it toward Grayson like a Frisbee. "Sounds kind of southern."

"University of the Afterlife."

"Perfect. I'm a degree whore. *Was.*"

"Then you'll fit right in."

"That's never been my strength."

"People change, Frances. I have faith in you."

"That's not what you said last night." She grabbed the brochure and scanned the mission statement. Words like *untethered, acceptance* and *consciousness* jumped out. "Obviate nuance," she mumbled.

"Say what?"

"Mission statements. They're like bumper stickers for intellectuals. *Obviate nuance* was one of my favorites."

"Mine was, *It's always darkest just before it goes pitch black.*"

"Well, that's certainly encouraging." She scanned the section describing the curriculum: *The Fear Cure, The Gratitude Formula* and *Freedom Now.* She smacked the paper with the back of her hand. "There's got to be more to it than this. I could teach these classes. Hell, I have taught them!"

"Right. I heard you were pretty good." He didn't seem overly impressed.

"Are you kidding?" She bristled at his tone. "I was great. People loved me."

"I bet they did." He helped her unfolded the brochure until it was the size of a chess board and gave a low whistle. "So, you're enrolled in the A Track."

"Why are you so surprised? I was a great student."

"Right. Well, it looks like you're going to start with a writing class."

She grabbed the paper and stared in disgust. "Doesn't anybody around here pay attention? I *am* a writer."

Grayson nodded. "So, this should be easy."

"Or stupid. I don't do either well." Her face wrinkled in annoyance. "Is this really necessary? Maybe there's some kind of waiver or whatever because I'm really not feelin' this."

Grayson gave her a minute to stew. "You wanted to know how it works, right? Isn't that what you were carrying on about last night? Well, here's your answer." He waved the brochure in her face like a fan. "Get with the program or..." He paused.

"Or what?" Finally, it seemed like she was getting somewhere.

"You'll never get your Letter of Transit."

"My *what*?" It was beginning to dawn on her that being dead was a complicated proposition that got more Baroque every time he opened his mouth. *Body scans. Latin. Now letters?*

"Casablanca ring a bell?" he asked.

"Of all the gin joints in all the world?" She felt like she was losing the thread of the conversation again but begged herself to be patient. "Help me understand. What are you saying?"

"Exit papers." His shrug made it seem so obvious.

She gasped, as if he'd been transformed into Santa Claus right before her very eyes—full beard, red suit and all. "Oh, my God!" The word *exit* was all she needed to hear.

"*Now* do you want to talk about that class?" he asked.

"Hell, yes!" she cried. And starting with writing was definitely a stroke of luck. She figured she could ace the class and rack up a few units or brownie points—whatever they used to keep score in this place. Plus, writing was her haven. When it was going well, she was lost in the words, completely unaware of her body. And yet that was when she felt most alive.

"Catch you later." Grayson ushered her into a room that looked like the headquarters of a dot.com start-up or a non-profit think tank. A dozen work stations stood in precise rows, each outfitted with a computer terminal and ergonomic chair on wheels that let you glide around the room like a figure skater.

A scattering of other students pored over their keyboards, so Frances snagged a chair in the back row and scanned the room for a lecturer or a teaching assistant. Someone to get the ball rolling. But they seemed to be on their own. Not even a chaperone.

She looked left and right again, pulled out her phone and stared at R U there? in a kind of a trance. She poked it a few times just to see if there were any signs of life. "Still dead?" She shoved it back in her pocket. "That makes two of us."

Maybe she could check her e-mail just in case the system had been restored, but when she grabbed the mouse, the screen lit up.

Assignment No. 1: Write Your Own Obituary.

"Whoa! Whoa! Who's in charge here?"

The machine beeped and a line of text appeared. That would be me.

If I press zero, can I talk to a real person? she typed.

This is as real as it gets came the reply.

Fine. So why not be up front with me? Clearly this is detention hall and I need to write 'I am dead' a hundred-and-fifty times. Take it from a professional. As a behavior modification strategy, that's a non-starter. Tends to harden oppositional types. She leaned back and thrust her chin in the air to demonstrate her unequivocal membership in that group.

She'd always treated the obituary page like the sports section. It was all post-facto, so what was the point? The people who died young were tragic and the centenarians never told you how they managed to pull it off, so it was a big waste of time. Plus, she refused to think about death on the grounds that it was unhealthy—a self-fulfilling prophecy. Granted, this didn't make complete sense, but it produced some memorable sound bites that TV producers and publishers loved.

"If they want to know how old I am, they'll have to saw me in half and count the rings," she'd say and it never failed to get a laugh.

The machine gave a slight beep and a box appeared on the screen: FULL NAME. With nothing better to do, she relented and typed in Frances Anne Timothy Beacon.

Timothy? the machine instantly queried.

"Well, this should be fun. I can't even state my name without getting busted." It's my confirmation name. What of it?

It's just that…do you have issues?

Dozens. Possibly more. I haven't taken a head count lately but gender dysphoria isn't one of them.

Is Timothy even a real saint?

This supposed 'writing class' seemed to be wildly off track already. What did any of this have to do with getting her exit papers? But she typed: Minor leaguer. Loved his wine. That's probably why he's the patron saint of stomach problems. If you must know, it was defiance.

Against?

Hello? Roman collars. Patriarchy. Subjugation of women. It was a gesture.

How'd it go over?

Frances remembered that during her confirmation, the bishop administered the ritual slap on the cheek with an excess of enthusiasm. His lips said, "Bless you, my child," but his eyes telegraphed damnation, probably for all the feminist-inspired offenses he imagined she would commit in the years to come. Campaigning for the Equal Rights Amendment. Insisting on using Ms. to withhold her marital status. Voting for every woman on the ballot.

Not too well. She clicked the word DONE and the screen immediately rewarded her with a new request: OCCUPATION

This isn't writing. More like a passport application.

We don't have those here.

How about a get-out-of-jail-free card?

Is that how you see this? Jail?

Forget I mentioned it. There was probably some great computer in the sky tracking her every remark, harvesting non-compliance data that would come back to haunt her when she was hauled into court.

Is there much more to this because I'm a little uncomfortable giving my personal information to...I mean, who the hell are you, anyway? Got a name?

They call me Albert.

Like... but here she drew a blank...you know, the relativity guy?

Yes, that would be the one. Now, let's move on.

She clicked on the box and filled in Geriatric Guru. It sounded so new-age that she added motivational speaker, longevity coach and author. Her trademark was promoting the *third half*. "If you're 60 years old you could easily make it to 90, which means you have a third half of your life ahead of you. What are you going to do with it?" she'd teased. "Watch M*A*S*H reruns? Alphabetize your prescriptions? Ladies and gentlemen, that's death on the installment plan."

She clicked DONE and the next box appeared. CAUSE OF DEATH. She took a deep breath, blew it out audibly, and wrote: Failed to fulfill my longevity potential.

Red letters popped up on the screen. Try again.

Frances spun her chair a full 360 degrees. Nothing but earnest obituarians hunched over their computers. She seemed to be the only one dealing with a censorial pen pal.

Cause of death? The machine nudged her back to the task.

She closed her eyes and tried to focus. Once again there was that yellow blur but nothing more. It was like she'd stepped off the edge of the world. Try as she might, she couldn't conjure up a single image. The slate had been wiped clean. She opened her eyes and wrote: I have no goddamned idea.

You should probably leave God out of this.

You mean it's not too late to offend him? I'm so screwed.

Time to get back to work.

Frances clicked and a new box appeared. NEXT OF KIN. "Gimme a break, Albert." Her voice sounded like she was pissed, but the tension in her chest warned of another emotion lurking just below the surface. "Is this really necessary?"

They don't accept incomplete responses appeared on the screen.

That was more than a little creepy. He could hear her after all, so she demanded in an even louder voice, "Who the hell are *they* and what do they care about my kin? I'm dead, remember?"

Albert said nothing so she rubbed her hands together and hammered in the answer. None. Then she leaned back and stared at the four-letter word that summed up her life. At her age most people would have a string of survived-bys to wrap up their obituaries. *Beloved wife of, devoted mother of* followed by a list of sons and daughters. Even grandkids got into the act. She had nothing. Not even a dog.

Kids? Albert seemed to be indefatigable while Frances was already exhausted. She wanted to bang her head on the keyboard, but once again the idea of court stopped her. They were probably reading along right now.

None. A purple line spiked up and down across the screen like vampire teeth.

No kids?

"I already answered that. Try to keep up, Albert," she muttered.

There was a baby.

His words hit her like a brick. A hot flash seared her from head to foot and red caution lights flared behind her eyelids, like the warning of an on-coming train. *Block it! Block it!*

She took a long slow breath to make herself relax, and then gave a casual chuckle. Oh, she wrote, the pagan baby! That hardly counts.

She remembered a flurry of excitement in grade school when the nuns introduced the Pagan Baby project. Students brought in their allowance and dropped it with great ceremony into a small cardboard cylinder. When the class had accumulated the princely sum of five dollars, they'd vote on a name with the understanding that a child in Africa would be baptized and known forever more by Thomas, Anne, or perhaps Matthew. So, it was possible that there was at least one black Frances puzzling her way through life, saddled with a male-sounding name and no idea why.

That African Frances certainly wasn't kin, just a victim of religious colonialism at its worst. Her real name, perhaps the only thing her parents had to bestow, was erased as she was swept into the maw of the Catholic Church doing what it did best—prospecting for new souls.

Not that baby.

Frances felt trapped. Her hands slid off the keyboard and she grabbed her thighs to steady herself. Slowly she wiped her sweaty palms all the way down to her knees. Slowly. To buy time. An image flashed through her mind of a blue paper gown, cold linoleum tile and the smell of disinfectant.

The non-baby. She never regretted her decision but the subject was embargoed beyond scrutiny, and irretrievable until just now. *What if?* For the first time she allowed herself to think about the road not taken.

If I'd gone through with it, she'd be 35. I'd have someone to take care of me in my old age and perhaps insurance against being forgotten.

But there'd been no baby and there would be no old age. Her DNA had hit a brick wall. This was the end of the line.

It was an accident. A mistake. She could hear the pleading tone as she entered each word. What was she looking for? Absolution after all this time?

Be honest. You didn't want kids, did you?

Fuck it! she thought. *No sense lying now.* No, actually. I didn't. Suddenly her fingers started flying over the keyboard like she was channeling the winner in a touch-typing contest.

Here's why. I was raised in a family of four kids. My hard-working father swore that his kids were his wealth but my mom just swore, so it was hard to see the upside of repeating that experience. Alone was what I

70

wanted. Solitude. Space uncluttered with someone else's belongings. Uncluttered with someone
else. Sounds selfish, doesn't it? Which is
why I had to hide it. Girls were supposed to
want marriage and the whole kid thing. Opting
out was suspect. Unnatural. So, I found an
escape route. I married a congenial slacker
who specialized in meandering idleness and
announced on our honeymoon. "I want to be a
bum." It wasn't a marriage. It was a train
wreck. So that worked out well. I was divorced
and free in under two years.

There was just one downside to her no-kid philosophy and
here it was, staring her in the face. No child left behind. No
one would inherit her fascination with obscure words or the
big toe that seemed to be heading west when her foot was
pointing north. She wouldn't be passing on her dad's hazel
eyes and love of art. The machine beeped her back to the
present.

What about men?

This is getting a little personal. Is this
system encrypted?

Don't change the subject. Men?

No shortage there. The world was full of
unavailable, unevolved or profoundly unstable
characters who couldn't threaten my autonomy.
Let's see. There was a race track denizen. A
Rosicrucian snake-milker. And a man who brought
his mother along on our first and only date.
I thought a Ph.D. might be interesting until
he lapsed into fluent baby-talk after a double
martini. And let's not forget the two studs
who eagerly outed themselves as erectile dys-
functionaries. One said he couldn't get it up
because of his meds while the other swore that
he could but thought it was too messy. I had
my pick of the pathetic litter.

But each romantic disaster provided prime material for
entertaining her friends until they were reduced to urine-
leaking laughter. The more bizarre the stories, the greater the

proof that Frances was alone by choice, not popular demand. Of course, she joined in the chorus of women who lamented the dearth of decent partners, but just drop her into a room full of strangers and she'd invariably end up with the man with a lampshade on his head.

Her standard morning-after report to her girlfriends always began with "Step right up, ladies. There's misery aplenty but no chance of a broken heart."

Albert gave her a prod. `Something's missing. Try again.`

She stared at the empty box—NEXT OF KIN. Carefully she filled in the initials JMP and then added: `Not kin but kindred in a thousand ways.`
`Tell me more.`

She reached for the keyboard but couldn't see the screen through her tears. She mopped her face on her sleeve, hit *Save* and announced, "I've had enough of this. I'm going home."

She slammed the door behind her, then wedged her back against it, as if she could entomb the painful revelations of the morning.

But where was home now?

CHAPTER 11

"Hello?" Frances called tentatively. Her voice echoed down the passageway outside the writing room. "Anybody?"

This was the first time she'd been free to roam the labyrinth, just the opportunity she was hoping for, but now the prospect seemed daunting. In her former life she'd bragged that she was a human compass because within hours of arriving in any city she'd fill in her mental map with the major streets, landmark buildings and the best place to get an infusion of caffeine. Now it was all terra incognito.

She massaged her temples, trying to find the pressure points that would quell the throbbing.

God, I wonder if I can find that bar.

It seemed like there were two possibilities. Strike out on her own and hope to get lucky. If that didn't work, just embrace the maze for what it was—perfect for a brisk walk to nowhere.

What have I got to lose?

After hours of sitting, her legs rejoiced in simply moving, but soon the monotony of plain walls and dim light felt like the hardcore boredom of pounding a treadmill in a basement. Rounding a corner, she spied a stripe of warm yellow light spilling from a room that was teeming with life. The cocktail of color, noise and commotion was irresistible, so she poked her head in and was greeted by a gnomish man dressed all in tweed, like a miniature country squire.

"Greetings, Frances. Welcome to the Pet Shop."

She shifted into full retreat but not fast enough. The pint-sized man seized her elbow in a grip that went well beyond appropriate for a first encounter, unless she was being taken in for questioning. "Right this way."

The central feature of the room was a large open space like a dance floor festooned with water dishes, bowls of treats, and chew bones. White plastic chairs of the wedding reception variety ringed the circle.

"Have a seat," said the gnome.

"Thanks, but I'm supposed to be some place." She jerked her thumb toward the door.

"Ditching?"

Frances tugged a lock of stray hair. "Something like that."

"Who's your minder?"

"Some guy." She shrugged. "Calls himself Grayson."

The gnome whistled through his front teeth like a mechanic sizing up a steaming radiator. "Tough break. He's got a reputation. But there are no accidents."

"Unless there are. Really, I gotta go," she insisted.

"Sit!"

Frances almost laughed out loud. It was like taking orders from a Cub Scout, except that his tone said this wasn't negotiable. "Fine, but just for a minute." She chose a chair closest to the exit and gave it a precautionary swipe with her hand before sitting down to survey the situation.

Clearly this was a showroom for previously-owned pets. The potential adoptees ranged from an ungainly St. Bernard puppy to a teacup poodle, but behaviorally they were all dogs. Unabashed crotch-nuzzlers. Butt-bumpers. Droolers lavishly baptizing anyone who paused for closer inspection. Most were experts in that playfully deferential trick of getting the upper hand. They'd insert their noses into an unoccupied palm, then twist and nudge to find purchase. She actually saw one creature do a credible version of Downward Facing Dog and then transition into the Sun Salutation as he rested his paws on the chest of a delighted old man. *Yoga dogs*, she thought. *Namaste.*

"Anything catch your eye? We've got some real beauties today."

"They're dogs. They all look alike to me." She opened her mouth wide and gave a bored yawn, hoping the gnome would take a hint. Not a chance.

"No worries. We have a very liberal return policy," he announced proudly. "Take one. Give it a week or so. No questions if it doesn't work out."

"I could've used that when I got married. Took me years... never mind." She dropped both hands in her lap and began prospecting for bits of lint on her clothing, trying valiantly to project profound disinterest.

"Our dogs enjoy the same option."

"Great. That's all I need." She shook her head. "Rejection by canine."

"Then choose carefully."

"No dogs!" she shouted. "You got that? I'm not taking any fleabag home, so give it a rest!"

Her friends had encouraged her to 'rescue' and that word alone had strengthened her resolve. *If you save a life, you're responsible.* In self-defense she fine-tuned her list of excuses. Too busy. Too much travel. The poor dog would spend more time at a doggie hotel than at home. As a last resort she'd claim allergies and that usually put the topic to rest.

But in truth, she loved dogs. Especially the big ones where you could wrap your arms around them and breathe in unison. The real reason for her petless state was the love that dogs lavished on their owners. Strong but silent, content just to be with you. And a life-span of maybe ten years. She could mark her mental calendar with the time when she'd be talking euthanasia with a white-coated stranger wearing an expression to match the occasion.

Just then Frances was joined by a large dog with a creamy blond coat, a long snout, and folded ears that begged to be fondled. No attempted overtures. No casual contact. Instead, he seemed to mirror her behavior. While the other mutts busied themselves courting potential companions, he was absolutely still, staring out at the ring as if he and Frances were judges at the Westminster Dog Show.

She edged away, treating him like a hygiene-challenged person on the subway. In response he seemed to levitate and then settled down gently. Closer now. An exquisitely subtle stalker.

She gripped the seat of her chair, determined to move out of range, but was stopped by a furry paw placed squarely on her foot and a voice saying, "It's alright, Frances. We'll be fine." Then the dog descended into a resting pose like the lions in front of the library on 42nd Street, serene but still guarding the tip of her shoe.

"What's the matter?" he asked. "Cat got your tongue?"

Once again, the question of sanity crossed her mind. Hearing voices was not a good sign.

"Come on. People talk to dogs all the time."

She couldn't help herself. "Right, but dogs don't—"

"Don't be ridiculous. We talk. People just don't listen."

"Can you let me finish without interrupting?" she snapped. "Sure, they yip and howl, especially if you dangle a hunk of compressed by-products in front of them. But the Queen's English? I think not."

"Well. I'm a unique breed."

"You don't look special." That was a lie. He was a real beauty and she longed to stroke his head or fondle his ears.

"Looks can be deceiving."

"Tell me about it. Try internet dating. Deception raised to the level of an art form."

"What about *Plenty of Fish in the Sea*? That's supposed to

be a pretty good site," he said.

"What do you know? You're a dog."

Enough banter.

This was no time to let down her guard. She could barely take care of herself, so she launched a verbal offensive. "Would you look at them? Clumsy, over-bearing, twitching like a raw nerve. Just hopeless."

"They're doing the best they can."

"And *so* needy!"

"They just want to be loved."

"Do dogs worry about that?" she asked quietly, surveying the pack with newfound compassion.

"I was talking about the people."

That shut her up. Of course, he was right. She was always amazed at the way dogs brought out behaviors that humans usually kept behind closed doors. Nick names. Baby talk. Tug-o-wars over meaningless objects. Unbridled affection lavished on some of the ugliest creatures on the planet. Who was rescuing whom? That part was never clear.

She shrugged and dropped her hand, grazing the soft coat tentatively as if trying to touch a baby without waking it. The dog looked up and she glimpsed a soulful intelligence that she'd sought in so many human encounters but failed to find.

The dog sighed and she heard, "I'm glad we got that settled."

"What do you call yourself?" she asked.

"A golden retriever. And yes, we're known to smile but I try not to pander. It's undignified."

"No, I mean your *name*. You know—moniker, handle."

"Gabriel."

She nodded her head slowly. "I can live with that."

Minutes later they left the room, tenuously yoked together. The dog ambulated with a thick grace while Frances walked stiffly, as if under surveillance. By the time they reached her room, she was chafing at her unaccustomed meekness and dying to be alone. But Gabriel hovered around her feet like he'd already achieved roommate status.

Determined to reassert control, she blocked him with one knee. "I never sleep on the first date."

"That's not what I heard."

She spun around to face him. "What?"

Alarm bells rang as secret-hoarding Frances hastily inventoried the closet where she hid things about herself: the word thing, early onset incontinence, the grudges she harbored against people who didn't even remember her, a deep distrust of mid-century modern anything, and the imposter complex with its ever-present fear of exposure. This closet was also the last known address of the things she was hiding from herself.

"What did you hear?" she demanded.

"It's nothing. Well, maybe a little something." He turned his back.

"Come back," she begged. "Are you talking about that layover in Chicago? I can explain."

But Gabriel had already ambled away, wagging his fluffy tail back and forth like a scolding finger, signaling that she was out of her depth.

Frances shook her head in dismay. *What's the point of writing and soul-searching and all these phony classes if the powers-that-be already know everything about me?*

She slammed the door behind her and launched into a scorching reprimand. *Stop whining! You're supposed to be the crusader for resiliency. Always going on about Eleanor Roosevelt. "Life is what you make it. Always has been, always will be." Blah-blah-blah. Now get a grip!*

This was a classic Frances lecture, guaranteed to straighten her spine and catapult her back into the saddle. But it would only work if she could find the reins. *What if UAL is just an elaborate charade? An amusing diversion for a clandestine fraternity watching me fling myself against the maze?*

CHAPTER 12

Frances compulsively tidied up her room as if it was a barracks and inspection could come at any time. Then she pulled out the UAL brochure and scanned the curriculum again. "What bullshit!" She wadded up the paper and fired it across the room in disgust. Bullshit or not, based on her recent performance, it seemed unlikely that she'd be donning a cap and gown any time soon.

Her typical cure for frustration was work, but her stint in the obit room had soured her appetite for writing.

How about a little yoga?

She reached down and massaged her lower back, the most vulnerable point in her skeleton. Years of chiropractic appointments had taught her that the best defense against chronic pain was a series of stretches, faithfully executed each day. Sometimes in her bedroom, occasionally in airports or on a subway platform if the crowd was thin.

Start with something simple. Uttanasana.

She dropped her head toward her feet slowly. Slowly was the key to the standing forward fold. She clasped her hands behind her back, palms together and let gravity pull them forward over her head.

Inhale. Exhale.

The hurts-so-good release of muscles wound too tight produced a grateful moan. Now on to the warrior pose. But she stood up too quickly and the room spun like a carousel. Thrusting out her hand to steady herself, she got a shock that instantly cleared her head. The wall yielded ever so slightly and when Frances pressed with both hands like a fireman feeling for heat, she discovered a door-sized crack. "Oh, my G..." but she clamped a hand over her mouth to mute her scream of joy.

An exit!

This had all been a test and now she'd found the rabbit hole that would take her back to reality. She braced her legs and shouldered the wall until it surrendered, and then crept into the unknown like a burglar.

As her eyes adjusted to the dim light, she surveyed a space the size of the waiting room in a rural doctor's office. Wainscoting covered the lower half of soft blue walls that rose up at least ten feet. The ceiling was like a Tiepolo painting, with clouds blushing at sunset against a star-spangled sky. A window no bigger than an i-Pad framed nothing but darkness.

As she tiptoed farther in, it was like trespassing in another century. The air was layered with the scent of wood, linen and dust. She closed her eyes and inhaled, each sigh deeper and longer. Then her nose picked up the familiar aroma of turpentine and the bitter tang of linseed oil, the signature smell of empty pockets and disappointment.

This was clearly a painter's domain. An antique easel filled one corner. The walls were covered with small paintings hanging slightly askew, like they'd registered a distant tremor. Rough sketches were pinned in layers on a board, waiting for consideration.

Then she detected the faint siren call of coffee. Like a bloodhound, she tracked it to a low wooden desk where a mug with a brown lip print sat forgotten amongst a clutter of pens and paper. Her hands shook as she stroked the dark spot with her tongue and savored the memory of coffee in all its glory.

Robust and scalding hot, the first true sensation each muddled morning. Inside the cup she spied more residual treasure so she licked her finger and dragged it around, slowly gathering up the grainy dregs. She held it to her nose, trying to inhale its life-giving caffeine and then placed it on her tongue with all the reverence of someone taking Sunday communion.

Her ecstasy was cut short when the door gave a slight creak.

What if it slammed and I'm trapped? On second thought, would that be so bad?

But caution won. She wedged an old boot in the doorway, and then set out to explore the room inch by inch. Pots of paint brushes, carefully groomed and standing at attention, scissors and putty knives, all waiting to serve. She touched a disused palette dappled with bright colors and remembered getting her first easel when she was just three. It was a Christmas gift, handmade by her father, which led to a childhood of picture-making. She never tired of hearing her father exclaim, "Beautiful. Just beautiful," as she wielded her brush.

This was the life she'd imagined when she was young, but grown-up Frances was a realist. It took courage to be an artist, especially for women. Even the successful ones spent decades in poverty and anonymity before achieving minor recognition, while young male hustlers were treated like rock stars, with every new canvas a cause for celebration and profit. And in all honesty, Frances knew she lacked the vision to create a unique body of work, so she'd taken up social work. Full employment in the Misery Industrial Complex, Public Service Sector.

But art was her first love, so while her job drained her by day, she studied art history at night, eventually earning a Master's degree. To the inevitable question, "What are you going to do with *that*?" she'd answer, "Nourish myself."

A single bed with an antique iron headboard beckoned from the far wall, and she couldn't resist. She ran her hand across the rumpled sheets and found they were invitingly warm, as if they'd just emerged from the dryer or bid their occupant a recent goodbye. All she wanted was to curl up in the cozy linen and let the peace of the room wash over her like an incoming tide. She cradled her aching head on a pillow that exhaled a feather and the image of a seagull drifted through her mind.

But instinct told her this was folly. Surely the comforts of this sanctuary were a violation of the rules, punishable by a stint in the maximum-security ward. The thought of losing this refuge terrified her, so she mustn't be discovered.

But just for a moment? Her mind protested, but her body won.

CHAPTER 13

"Oh, damn!" Frances sat bolt upright. She'd only meant to close her eyes for a second, but she'd spent the whole night in her secret room. Now it was like waking into a dream instead of from one.

As if to make amends, she sprinted for the door. But sprinting was a mistake. Her stomach roiled and she pitched forward, clutching her temples which mercilessly pounded out her body's Skinnerian demand for caffeine.

I have to call for help.

She inched toward the desk, wincing at the effort to make her eyes focus. Far too much light, so she covered her left eye with one hand and groped in the approximate direction of a phone. No luck. "What kind of place doesn't have a phone? What if there's an emergency?"

Then her hand grazed the Guest Questionnaire. Plan B? Maybe she could plead a medical condition. ACDS—advanced caffeine deficiency syndrome—and a cup of espresso was the only thing standing between her and who knows? Murder, mayhem. It wouldn't be pretty.

What the hell? It's worth a try.

She eased herself into the chair and was surprised to find that the pain in her ass was nothing to that in her head, which felt like a sack of bricks each time she made the slightest move. Carefully, she lay her cheek on the cool surface of the desk, determined to tackle the arduous task of scanning from left to right.

The first sentence was encouraging. *To help us accommodate you better, please respond to the following.* Still expecting dietary preferences, she balked at the first question.

1. When was the last time you were kind to your inner child?

Frances started to laugh out loud but her throbbing head vetoed the idea. The questionnaire no longer seemed like a direct route to a caffeine injection, but maybe if she played along, she could curry favor with whoever was running this joint. She grabbed a pen with the UAL logo and scribbled: *Some time during the Eisenhower administration. And BTW, my inner child is prone to tantrums without regular infusions of coffee.* Then it occurred to her that this was actually a test. *But for what? Compliance? Confession? It doesn't matter. Just do it,* she ordered herself.

2. Can you give yourself permission to express your feelings in appropriate ways?

This is really none of their business, she thought, but she pressed on, prodded by the siren call of caffeine and the fear of offending whoever might be dispensing the life-saving brew. She responded: *Not yet. Still working my way through the inappropriate ways. Excessive caffeine consumption. Midnight cognac. And of course, a liberal use of the f-word. Did I mention coffee?* She looked ahead. Two more questions to go.

3. Do you have a right to be angry?

The jury is still out on that, but right now I'm beginning to feel pissed at whoever wrote these questions. Does that count? She was clammy, pale and covered in goosebumps, so she decided it was time for a little break. *No wonder people quit therapy,* she thought. Self-scrutiny was exhausting at the best of times. In her cold-turkey state, it was a nightmare.

Shoulder into it, girl. You're not a quitter.

4. What do you want?

The simplicity of this question was so startling that she almost wrote *Coffee, for fuck's sake!* But something stopped her. *Want* was not in her operating vocabulary. At Christmas when other children clambered onto Santa's knee and reeled off a list of requests that ranged from a puppy to a rocket launcher, she'd always been tongue-tied. Instead of reviewing the items she coveted and making a quick bid for happiness, she'd busily examine her behavior over the past year, wondering exactly where Santa drew the line between naughty and nice.

The word *want* smacked of personal indulgence. Selfishness. But it was also a naked word that made her feel exposed. Asking anyone for anything was an invitation to be told, "You don't deserve it." Wanting was risky. But desperation overwhelmed caution as Frances wrote: *Right now, I just want someone to show up and say, "There's been a mistake," so I can wake up in my old life.* Then she threw the pen at the wall.

"Time to face the mirror, lady," she announced, dreading what she might see.

CHAPTER 14

"You're no beauty, that's for sure." Frances winced at the sight of dark circles hanging under her eyes like crescent moons rising over sunken cheeks. It was a face only Kathe Kollwitz could love. Kollwitz distilled the horror of war into portraits with haunted eyes and faces lined with grief.

But looks don't seem to matter here, she thought. Actually, it felt like a relief after a lifetime of needing to care about her appearance. *Maybe I can pack on a few pounds and stop policing my upper lip for hairs that seem to sprout as fast as my head sheds them.*

The fantasy of unkempt overfed splendor vanished as Constant Comment, the Mother Superior renting space in her head barked, "For God's sake, Frances, pull yourself together."

There was only one sure way to restore her equilibrium. She needed a gym the way a junkie needs a fix. Exertion, repetitive motion, counting. The smell of rubber mats, fresh towels and sweat. There had to be one here.

She wasn't a natural athlete. Even after years of regular workouts she thought of herself as practicing fitness without a license. It was a mind-body duality problem that she'd never quite resolved. Early in life she'd declared herself not-good-at-body-things and the library became her default address.

Thereafter, she treated her mind like a visiting dignitary. Catered to it like an only child. Collected books and read as if her life depended on it. Enrolled in graduate classes and stalked people with high IQs. Her motto: *I learn, therefore I am.*

But she drove her body like a rented mule. Food, sleep and exercise were doled out grudgingly and over the years it began to show. Eventually, the simple act of taking out the trash felt like extreme aerobics and it didn't take much to imagine herself trapped in a body the size of a shipping hazard. So, she'd succumbed to a post-New-Year's-penance-for-overindulging sale at her local gym and now she was hooked.

What kind of university wouldn't have a gym?

She was determined to find one if it took all day, so she yanked open her door and nearly tumbled over Gabe, snoozing across the threshold. "You're a sight for sore eyes," she cried and plowed her hand through the fur under his chin.

"That's not what you said last time." But he leaned into her hand, guiding it to the perfect spot.

"Sorry. I was having a bad day."

"And?"

"Still am." She blew out both lips.

"What seems to be the problem?"

"Gabe, if I don't get to a gym, I'm going to kill myself."

"That option's off the table."

Her hand began to shake and tears stung her eyes.

"Killing. No can do," he said. "But there *is* a gym."

She kissed him on the top of his head and might have enlarged her appreciation, but he squirmed away and trotted into the labyrinth. Within minutes she heard the distinctive metallic clank and hearty grunting of a weight room in full swing.

"Yes!" She sprinted for the door but skidded to a halt and threw Gabe a kiss before dashing inside.

The walls in the lobby were festooned with cheerful if slightly metaphysical workout slogans. *It's your mind that you have to convince. Everything you want is outside your comfort zone.* And inexplicably, *Weak is the new strong.* A small sign on the counter read Check-in, so Frances placed her index finger on a scanner the size of an extra thick brownie, which wasn't exactly a helpful thought before a workout. Her name flashed, followed by a quiet beep.

"Take a seat, please. Someone will be with you shortly," the receptionist said.

This was *not* a good start. Frances didn't want help, so she skipped the chair and paced up and down, occasionally glaring at the receptionist until she called, "Frances Bacon."

"That's Beacon."

"I'm so sorry. We'll get it right next time."

"Don't worry. Happens all the time." She actually enjoyed being mistaken, if only nominally, for the Elizabethan philosopher who said "I will never be an old man. To me, old age is always 15 years older than I am." The other option was the twentieth-century Francis Bacon, a British painter famous for portraits so emotionally charged and raw that seeing his work *en masse* was like visiting a charnel house.

A man with *Personal Trainer* embroidered on his shirt walked briskly up to the counter. "Hello, Ms. Beacon. I'm Charles. I'll be working with you today."

"Thanks, but that won't be necessary." In all her years of faithful five-days-a-week workouts, she'd never hired a trainer. Her exercise strategy was straightforward and strict. No talking. No eye-contact. No queuing up for her favorite equipment. Just use any unoccupied device and sprint to the next vacancy.

"What's the problem?" he asked.

"No problem." She sounded almost mystified. "But I've been counting without assistance since I was two, so I don't exactly fit in the trainer-needing demographic."

He smiled and leaned in closer, precisely the opposite reaction she wanted.

"Listen, Charlie. No offense, but having a trainer seems

like renting a human stop-watch to escort me through my workout."

"We don't think of it that way." He reached for a clipboard on the counter.

Her hand shot out and pinned the clipboard in place, escalating her resistance. "Then try this. Outsourcing discipline. Like paying someone to watch me take my vitamins or tackle that black mold under the rim of the toilet bowl."

Charles frowned and she could see the bathroom image was a bridge too far. Maybe a shot of self-deprecation would placate him.

"Look, I know I seem stubborn and unmodern but it's more...pragmatism. What I'd want from a trainer is something I can't do for myself. For example, can you handle numbers *out* of sequence, like 9-1-1 if I keel over? Will you recognize anaphylaxis brought on by overexposure to testosterone and shoot me up before my head swells like a balloon in the Macy's parade?"

"That doesn't happen here." Charles paused and then continued. "Can I ask you something, Frances?"

"No. Please. Just leave me alone and I promise next visit I'll...be sure to look you up," she lied.

She didn't wait for his answer but pushed past the receptionist, grabbed a towel, and sprinted to the first row of machines.

God, this feels good!

Nothing like her first fitness outing when she suffered from the see-and-be-seen fear factor. Like most gym-virgins, she'd imagined standing on the sidelines watching a carousel of perfect bodies in skimpy outfits glide by. Worse, they'd be looking at her, fifty-something and straining to hoist a ten-pound weight with both hands.

But it was nothing like that. Just a bunch of average looking people with exactly no interest in her. They were hooked up to i-pods, staring at themselves in the mirrors or grunting through a solitary routine as quickly as possible so they could get back to their lives. It was like a monastery for fitness buffs.

An hour later, sweaty but satisfied, she emerged to the sight of Grayson and Charlie in conversation. Probably the Brotherhood Network exchanging notes on her need for a serious attitude adjustment. A quick stint in caffeine rehab. Maybe cranial implants remotely triggered. Thought reform. Anal probes. Kool-Aid. Her imagination galloped toward annihilation.

But was it imagination?

The watchers were circling. She had to be on guard.

CHAPTER 15

Frances planted one foot inside her room and was hit by a nearly undetectable scent that set off alarms. "Sweat." *Had the room been searched?* She sniffed audibly, imagining a burly thug pawing through her belongings, but it took just seconds to survey the spare white space. Everything seemed to be in order. *Probably planted a bug.*

"Oh, no!" She sprinted toward the far wall, cringing at the thought of her hideout pillaged, stripped bare or sealed like a vault. She fell on all fours to study the tiny crack at the bottom of the secret door, but the strand of hair she'd plastered in place with saliva was still there. Her refuge was safe.

Thank you, James Bond!

She rose to her knees but began to sway from the combination of adrenaline and relief. Collapsing against the wall, she closed her eyes and sighed. But there it was again. *Not sweat.* A momentary whiff of salt air. Then it vanished and the atmosphere was anonymous.

She gave the door a quick kiss and slipped inside, determined to explore the rest of her sanctuary. First stop, a boxy shape draped in a dustcover, like you'd find in a shut-up house. She gathered it into her arms and yanked, revealing a cabinet that exhaled a sweet musky smell that could only mean one thing.

"Books!" she cried, as tears of joy stung her eyes. She

extended her arms and hugged the cache like a long-awaited lover returning from the war. The shelves were crammed with dozens of volumes standing vertically, reclining horizontally, stuffed in with no apparent system except to make room for one more and one more. A Tom Clancy thriller rubbed shoulders with Shakespeare's *Midsummer Night's Dream*. She spied *One Hundred Years of Solitude*, which sounded like the autobiography of a previous guest.

Then she pulled out a small red volume with gilded edges and stroked its cover like a newborn's head. *A Christmas Carol* by Charles Dickens. She'd read it a dozen times, but never tired of the moment when Scrooge awakened, a new man. Opening the pages at random she read, "He was conscious of a thousand odors floating in the air, each one connected with a thousand thoughts, and hopes, and joys, and cares, long, long, forgotten."

She pressed her nose gently into the crease and felt the soft pages caress her cheeks, triggering an avalanche of memories. The house full of books where each night four kids vied for prime spots in and around her father's huge chair, while he read dramatically, creating all the voices. One chapter, two, then three. When they begged for overtime, as they always did, he'd carry on until their mother called a halt on account of bed time or unfinished chores. The rest of the world dropped away during story time in her father's chair.

His death was like being mugged in broad daylight. No hint that it was coming. No idea that calamity was seconds away. No time to prepare for the irreparable event that would strike like an ax, cleaving her existence in two, forever a *before* and *after*. *Before* when she was loved unconditionally and returned that love without reservation. *And after.* A life tinged with longing. This was the great stone she'd carried in her heart for over thirty years, the perpetual task of how to stop missing her father.

What's the point? What did I expect to get from it? An immediate return of my dad in full working order?

She'd channeled her abundant grief into her work, dedicating herself to keeping people alive, guarding them like a shepherd with her flock. Day and night, in writing and in person, she raged against the dying of the light, a Dylan Thomas poster girl determined to get revenge on the Grim Reaper.

The old clock in the room ticked with a comforting tempo like a heartbeat. She lay on the bed and synchronized her breathing to its sound, and then opened *A Christmas Carol* and began to read aloud. "Old Marley was as dead as a doornail."

But suddenly she'd had enough of death for one night, so she returned to the bookshelf for a more congenial diversion. *The Wizard of Oz?* As she pictured the crazy old imposter cowering behind a curtain, cranking away at levers to intimidate poor Dorothy, she couldn't help thinking of the courtroom in Division Seven. The unseen judge, the opaque pronouncements, and being sent off to complete meaningless tasks. She and Dorothy had a lot in common. Frances slowly tapped her heels together. "There's no place like home. There's no place like home." But nothing happened.

Maybe The Hitchhikers Guide to the Galaxy? She could certainly identify with Arthur Dent, struggling to navigate the universe after his home was abruptly vaporized. *Too bad Douglas Adams didn't write a guide to the afterlife.*

A ragged ear of brown paper peeked out of *Death in Venice,* folded small enough to fit in a back pocket. When she tugged on it, she heard the brittle sound of old paper, so she pried open the first fold with the care of an archivist. But her hands began to shake when she realized that it was a map. Throwing caution aside she peeled back the second fold and ironed the paper smooth with her hands. The surface was covered with finely drawn images, like a visitor's map of an antique theme park.

But first things first. Her eyes darted around the edge of

the paper, searching for an exit, but all she found was a tiny arrow pointing to a ragged edge where the map had been torn. Her heart sank. What had been lost?

Still, there may be a clue in what remained, so she decided to make a careful inventory of the images. A red swan, a nautilus shell, and a balance scale. Then her hand grazed a yellow chalk circle and the words *You are here,* like a personal message from the previous refugee. She drew her hand back as if it had been scorched and a trace of golden dust clung to her palm. But the message was intact and for a second it felt like she wasn't alone. But was that a comfort or caution?

She needed more information so she leaned in closer, determined not to miss a clue. For the next few minutes, she poured over every inch of the map, trying to make sense of the bits of architecture, footprints and cherub faces. Then her eyes fell upon a symbol so familiar that it sent an electric shock through her fingers. A blue circle with the letters MTA.

Could it be real? The New York subway?

"Home!"

CHAPTER 16

Frances was outside in seconds, holding the map in front of her like a dousing stick. A series of left turns deposited her in front of a doorway as plain and uninviting as a janitorial closet. But every New Yorker had heard about unmarked portals in mid-town leading to subway tunnels repurposed as graffiti academies or havens for the homeless.

Glancing over her shoulder to see if she'd been tailed, she yanked the door open and descended a flight of concrete stairs worn smooth by millions of shoes, boots and flipflops hurrying to catch the trains. Instantly, she recognized her favorite station, 42nd and Bryant Park, her destination-of-choice in every season. Above ground, the park hosted outdoor films on summer nights and in winter, a Christmas Market pedaling high-calorie nostalgia, but the biggest draw was the four-season trove of books just steps away in the main library.

Maybe this is the way home.

Instinctively she dug in her pocket for her transit pass, a futile gesture since her only possession of any value was a phone permanently asking R U there? Undaunted, she approached the turnstile, determined to vault over if necessary, like legions of scofflaws. But when she shoved the metal arm, it yielded easily and she strolled out on to the deserted platform.

A half-dozen vendors near the entrance were shuttered behind metal security panels decorated with graffiti. An unlit neon sign announced the Strong Silent Coffee Bar, and she impulsively banged on the metal. "Anyone in there? Please!" In desperation she peeked through the gap, and then shoved her nose in to catch a whiff of the java-scented heaven just beyond her reach.

Undaunted, she parked herself on a wooden bench to drink in the familiar atmosphere. Gritty asphalt underfoot and discolored walls that collected and stored oily memories of every passing train. On the ground, there were heat-proof sleeves from Starbucks, a ticket stub from *The Lion King,* now in its twentieth year on Broadway, and discarded water bottles. City workers tried to keep ahead of the litter, hoovering up thousands of pounds every night, but Frances remembered a discarded gum wrapper that wintered under a bench for three full months. Taken as a whole, the underground sprawl of tunnels, machines and the endless flow of humanity was the exact opposite of the afterlife—dark, dirty, crowded, noisy, baking in summer, and freezing in winter.

"God, this feels so good!"

From her bench she had an unobstructed view of the opposite platform which had a sprinkling of commuters. As she watched, two former colleagues ambled down the steps. Jake, tall and graying, carried the unmistakable signs of stress-eating between clients. Emily was built like a bird, so slight that she was often mistaken for a student intern, despite her years on the job. Both were industrious and committed to social work, but not kidding themselves about the odds against them.

Emily turned to Jake. "Did you hear what happened to Frances?"

"Pretty shocking."

"I'll say. Who would have thought she'd end up like that?"

Jake shrugged. "I guess we just missed the signs."

Frances recognized those words as professional code for

something serious. Something you'd report or slap into therapy if you'd seen it coming. She jumped up and charged toward the edge of the platform, demanding, "What signs? Tell me what happened!" But just then a train roared into the station and her colleagues were whisked away as she mouthed the words "What happened?" She stared at the empty tunnel, and then stomped across the deserted platform toward the glowing green letters. E-X-I-T.

You let me down, pal.

But somehow, the visit to the subway had revived her. She refused to accept the afterlife as a closed loop, a mobius strip of misery that would exhaust and vanquish her. She spied a bright poster that read *"Thank you for riding. Come back soon."* With one last look at the coffee bar she shouted, "I will!"

CHAPTER 17

"Time to get rolling, Frances. Class in ten minutes," Grayson announced in a sonorous voice.

No response. He tapped lightly on her door.

"Oh, shit! Morning already?" Frances moaned. Ever since discovering the secret room, she'd been keeping bartender's hours, gorging on books most of the night to catch up after years of portioning out her recreational reading like a dietician dispensing Ben & Jerry's at a fat farm. She plowed through one novel after another, like a cocaine lab rat pressing the reload lever.

Now she opened one eye slowly, trying to decide if she could drift off for a few more minutes. She sure as hell didn't feel rested, but then sleeping was never her strength. Just a life-shortening obligation she fought until her body cried "Uncle!"

Another knock. This time with feeling.

"Coming," she growled, deciding to skip the showdown in the mirror and cut to the chase. She cracked open the door.

"Good morn..." Grayson's voice trailed off as Gabe squeezed out between her legs, looking like a four-legged bedhead. He shook himself to advertise his disheveled state, then rested on his haunches, eyeing his genitals.

Grayson recoiled as if the dog was radioactive. "I didn't know you were a pet lover."

"More like a one-night stand," she insisted, but shot a quick wink in Gabe's direction.

Grayson looked from one to the other, and then shoved a pink enrollment card toward Frances. Capital letters across the top read MISANTHROPY 101.

She took a quick look and shoved it back. "You're slipping, buddy. I think this was meant for someone else. Maybe D.H. Lawrence. He hated people. Or Oscar Wilde. He said *the only possible society is oneself.* I loved that."

Grayson chuckled. "See what I mean."

"I'm kidding. Besides." She gave him a satisfied smile. "People love me."

"It's not the same. You've got work to do."

A frown replaced her smile and a defiant tone crept into her voice. "I've been told, several times. But just let me remind you that I toiled for decades as a social worker. My misspent youth. And I was good at it." She paused and her voice was wistful. "I could do wonders with bleakness." Then she switched in to bargaining mode. "So, in a way you could say that I gave at the office."

"What happened with that?"

"One day I was sitting in the break room and I had an epiphany."

"Mine always come in the shower."

She ignored him. "Suddenly I saw my colleagues for what they were—addicted to misery. Each new file slung on their desk was a fix that got them through another day. But did they shine with the joy of altruism? Hell, no! They were irritable, grouchy, bad-tempered and cantankerous. As messed up as their clients except that they got a small paycheck at the end of the month."

Grayson nodded but turned his back and ambled down a passageway toward a set of double doors.

"So, yes." She lengthened her stride to catch up. "I left social work. But I wasn't a misanthrope. I knocked myself out, but I was also a realist. On the whole, the people who got saved were the ones with survival in their DNA. I helped, no doubt about it, and it felt good. But there were times when the job just seemed like pitching food pellets to a gerbil on a wheel. Eventually, my pitching arm gave out."

He stared at her like a Parisian ignoring a helpless tourist, but didn't budge.

"Fine." She'd exhausted her arsenal of objections. "So, what's the story here?" She jerked her head toward the doors.

"Think of it as an informal get-together." He reached toward the door but she blocked his arm.

"No, please!" Her voice inched toward full whine. "Just kill me now."

"We've been over that. Anyway, you might find it amusing."

"I wish I could believe you. Honestly. But your track record hasn't been great so far." She looked down, avoiding his eyes. "But then...neither has mine."

It wasn't that Frances didn't like people. She found them fascinating from a distance, when she was the watcher. And there were individuals for whom she'd gladly take a bullet. Her problem was that she was a social worker who was bad at socializing. As a result, she dreaded the kind of gatherings that delighted most other people—baby showers, bridal showers, welcome receptions, retirement lunches, leaving-because-I-got-a-better-job parties, leaving-because-my-therapy-finally-kicked-in bashes. It was agony—all of it. The effort to pretend this was a great idea, the swift conversational descent into small talk, the rictus displayed by the guest of honor during obligatory remarks, and the twitching facial muscles in the crowd after half an hour of de rigueur smiling. Inevitably, there was the disappointment that people never turned out to be more interesting than they appeared at first glance—sometimes less. Finally, the covert maneuvering for a place near an exit, and the resolve to find and punish the person who'd issued the invitation.

So, Frances would huddle with one or two like-minded loners trading acerbic remarks under their breath, a talent they'd honed at happy hour. Now *that* was a social function she could get behind. Happy hour! Where the withdrawn and morose fit right in. When it came to groups, she was at her best when they were seated, eyes riveted on her, ears on high alert, applauding enthusiastically in all the right places.

Her hand reached for the heavy door in slow-motion and then paused in mid-air. "Seismic, pettifogger, neurogenesis, ruckus, finagle, erection."

"Frances?" Grayson's voice was a mixture of confusion and concern.

She felt the scorch of humiliation as she realized she'd been talking out loud. *God, where to start?*

"It's just a thing I...do," she stammered. "I have this... condition."

She'd always suspected she had a trace of rabbit mixed in with her mongrel DNA—French, German, Irish, Neanderthal and *lepus*--because when confused, frightened or so overwhelmed that she didn't know what to do next, she froze. At least, her brain did. The soft gray matter that held a hundred ideas for solving other people's problems solidified into a doltish mass.

When she first noticed it, she thought it was her own idiopathic quirk, unnamed and best unrevealed. Or maybe it was a disability that other people were treating with a drug she couldn't pronounce or afford. Then one Saturday afternoon in the Argosy Bookstore, she flipped open a copy of *The End of the Road* by John Barth and the answer jumped off the page. *Cosmopsis: the inability to choose a course of action from all the possibilities*. The main character's cosmopsis left him stranded in the train station, overwhelmed by his choices. Finally, she had a name for her mystery condition. And somehow that was a comfort.

Cosmopsis could strike anywhere, but her office seemed to

be its favorite playground, when the demands of the job achieved critical mass. She'd stand as still as a statue staring at the growing tower of files on her desk, and the blinking light on her phone. She knew without checking that at least three digits worth of e-mails had landed in her box since the last time she gave it her full attention.

"They call it cosmopsis," she explained to Grayson. "It's like something flips the switch in my brain and I go from high gear to paralysis."

Barth's character repeated the Pepsi Cola jingle to get himself unstuck, but for Frances the solution was words. At the first sign that her brain was shutting down, she began to recite words picked at random from who knows where. It wasn't free association because they had exactly nothing in common except that they waited somewhere in her head like first responders, until called to her rescue.

"So, I say words. Any words. I'm not exactly sure why it works. My theory is that because it's a simple task, no right or wrong, no judgment, no failure, my brain begins to feel confident again. By the time I switch back to the problem at hand, it's got its act together."

Grayson just stared at her.

"I sound insane, don't I?" She winced in dismay.

"No." He gave her a fraction of a smile. "Intriguing."

And she thought there was an outside chance he meant it. "So...?" She raised her eyebrows in a hopeful expression as she glanced toward the door.

"Nope. Still on the agenda."

She scanned the pink enrollment card once more. Well, at least it said 101—the starter course. Maybe a compassionate instructor would take pity on her. Maybe dead people would be more fun. Who knows? She might even fit in now that she was post-mortem. Plan B—stay close to the exit.

CHAPTER 18

"Right this way, Miss."

Frances had scarcely set foot inside the cavernous auditorium when she was intercepted by a husky usher. "That's Ms. to you," she snapped, thereby proving that her enrollment was no mistake.

"Whatever," he replied, stepping close enough to block most of her view.

Over his left shoulder Frances spied a stage. To his right, rows of red velvet chairs that would be right at home in a down-at-heel theater showing classic films. Now if she could just snag a seat on the aisle.

She plastered on a smile. "I'll just sit over there," she whispered, pointing toward the back row. But things were not falling her way.

"Those are reserved."

"But they're all empty," she observed, as if he hadn't noticed.

The usher made a minimalist gesture with his head as he stood aside. "You need to join a group." She flinched at the word *group* but his body language said, "Get moving."

Just give them a uniform and the next thing you know they're embracing their inner bully.

She turned reluctantly and surveyed her options. There were three distinct clusters of activity at the front of the auditorium. To the left was a huddle of people, each cradling a book. The center group had a minister at the helm and even from a distance he radiated piety. The right-hand crew was arranged in a semi-circle, texting and shouting comments at a large white screen.

The choice was obvious. The book-people. She looked closer and sure enough, they were all armed with identical volumes.

This could work.

Not that she'd ever belonged to a book group, but she'd appeared by Skype to hundreds of her readers. The discussions were always lively, sprinkled with anecdotes her editor had axed. It made her fans feel like insiders to hear her joke and swear, which inevitably led to quotes in someone's blog and more invitations.

She strode confidently toward the circle but froze as their apparel came in to focus. Hats, t-shirts, hoodies, vests and visors all brought to you by *The Lord of the Rings*.

Oh, God, it's a coven!

She took a few steps back, reviewing her choices. *Tolkien geeks, Jesus freaks and trolls.* "The wacko trifecta," she muttered out loud. *And to think I believed all that BS about, 'You'll be fine, Frances. Nothing can hurt you now.'* This was definitely going to hurt.

A violent case of book-group flight seized her, a yearning like a physical ache to find a well-lit corner where she could read in solitude, but the usher blocked her path. "Sit!" he growled, suggesting he'd apprenticed with a dog trainer.

She dropped obediently into an empty chair next to a woman wearing a t-shirt that announced, *I am in fact a Hobbit in all but size.* Strewn down the front of the shirt were the telltale signs of serious doughnut consumption.

You are in fact, a pudgy denialist taking shelter in a fantasy world, aka mentally ill. Put that on your t-shirt.

She didn't have to wait long for the first signs of cult behavior to emerge. The in-group language, as she must have heard the word *elvish* a half-dozen times. And the way they referred to the main character in intimate tones, like they were sleeping together. A gray-haired man crowed, "I adored *The Lord of the Rings*. Read it so many times when I was younger, I can quote verbatim from any page in the trilogy and I'm not even obsessive-compulsive."

I'll be the judge of that, thought Frances. Then her critique was interrupted by a sobering thought. The Number One Rule of book groups is that you have to read the text. No fair coming and nodding in agreement while others carried the conversation. But that was a minor offense compared to her dark secret.

She was that rare bird—a Tolkien-shunner. She'd always been a voracious reader but with a contrary streak that made her avoid literary blockbusters. She didn't hate Tolkien, just the craven deference to popular opinion. Every other person you met was spellbound by a short creature with hairy feet. All that fanfare made it common, something she refused to be. Consequently, she'd never bothered with any of Tolkien's works.

But actions have consequences. She was an outsider in some conversations, missing literary references that made her seem like a philistine. God knows what these groupies would do when she was outed. If she could just snag an extra copy and do a bit of speed-reading, there was a chance she could fend off their wrath.

But they didn't look angry or hostile. Every one of them had a kind face and their hands reverently clutched a well-thumbed, dog-eared book. These were honest to goodness pulp-people. Not a Kindle in sight.

A shy woman on the far side of the circle said, "I love this part. *Death is just another path, one that we all must take. The grey rain-curtain of this world rolls back, and all turns to silver glass.*"

"Wow!" Frances said. Here was someone who appreciated the daunting effort of sitting as still as a bird-watcher waiting for an idea to arrive. And then the Rubik's Cube ritual of testing and replacing word after word until she heard that satisfying click. Or the purer moments of inspiration when entire sentences tumbled from her brain in such a rush that it made her heart pound. It felt more like midwifery, catching phrases fired through a chute as fast as she could grab them.

The conversation shifted to the differences between *The Hobbit* and *The Lord of the Rings* with regard to Gandalf and the Elves. It still felt cultish but at least they weren't calling for the deportation of all non-Tolkienites or blaming nonfiction writers for the fall of Western Civilization. They simply found the comfort and companionship in books they'd been denied in the wider world.

Frances opened a purloined copy at random and her eyes fell on the sentence, "All we have to decide is what to do with the time that is given us."

I thought I had so much more.

She considered making an observation about Tolkien but was distracted by a boisterous chorus of "Amens" that rose from the group in the middle of the room. Dozens of arms reached for the sky, like children greeting the first snowflakes of the season. Frances shuddered and slid down in her chair, diving back into the text. Just as she was crafting a comment about Mordor, she felt a light tap on her shoulder. The usher tipped his head toward the Jesus crew. "It's time," he whispered.

The image of a guard floated through her head. A lumbering guy, like a side of meat with clothes on, letting the condemned know that "the executioner will see you now."

"I'm just getting into it," she said, pointing to the book on her lap. "Have you read this? It's not bad, really."

"Course I've read it. Who hasn't? Now move!"

CHAPTER 19

"Amen" rang out to greet Frances as she idled her way toward the God Gang's tight circle of chairs. A spindly vicar was poised in front like an orchestra conductor. Black pants, black jacket, with just a touch of white circling a pale neck. His flock wore the expectant faces of people waiting for a bus or the doctor.

She guessed that this was the Q&A portion of the meeting because the cleric wore a you've-got-questions-I've-got-answers expression as he patted his bible like a baby's ass. Something about that gesture set her off, provoking a visceral wave of skepticism. But she didn't chide herself, figuring that she'd come by it honestly. When asked his religion, her father always replied "Pedestrian" and left other people to figure it out. But after years of mental arm wrestling with priests who laid down the law from the pulpit, Frances had settled on a more aggressive moniker—Urban Agnostic and proud of it.

Maybe this time will be different, she thought as she slid down in a chair at the edge of the circle. But then she saw a t-shirt that said *Jesus is the answer,* and just like that, her Socratic instinct kicked in. *Excuse me. What was the question?* But she knew it was futile. Like asking someone to explain exactly what they meant by "personal" as in *Jesus is my personal lord and savior.* What did that even mean? Would he pick up your dry cleaning or remind you to send a birthday card to your mother?

Zen, she told herself. *Ohm, god dammit! Ohm. Just breathe and get through it.*

"Now, any questions?" the minister asked.

A woman raised her hand and announced, "It's about recycling. I prayed on it and God told me I don't have to recycle because Armageddon is coming soon."

A puzzled look rippled the pulpiteer's forehead.

Frances couldn't hear the answer as more questions popped into her head. *How is it that you merit private communications from a conversationalist god? And why do you get to duck the responsibility of making decisions that the less-connected among us have to shoulder? Oh, and one more thing. Just out of curiosity—why didn't God tell you that horizontal stripes on a Size 18 ass are a bad idea?*

This wasn't her first encounter with God-based nonsense. She'd heard most of it before. *Homosexuality is an abomination. I have to stay in my abusive marriage because it's the wife's job to lead her husband to God. Faith can fix anything.* But she could never inoculate herself against its provocative power. While she fumed, a woman who looked like a kindergarten teacher or a crossing guard tentatively raised her hand, as if she was afraid that an innocent query might endanger her membership in the group.

The minister said, "Yes, Janie?"

"I'm having a hard time praying ever since my husband died. I'm lonely and scared. The bills are piling up. I'm not sure I can go on without him."

The churchman reached into his spiritual first aid kit and brought out the flimsiest band-aid Frances could imagine. "God never gives you more than you can handle." Then he pressed his lips firmly together, like a bank teller declaring that his line was closed.

Frances sprang to her feet. "So, what you're telling..." she paused. "Excuse me, what was your name again?"

The startled woman replied, "Jane."

Frances returned to the field of battle. "You're telling Jane, not *Janie,* that God decided to heap this tragedy on her because she can *take* it?" She used two fingers on each hand to make air quotes around the word take. "And what about people who can't?" Her voice broke with frustration and pain but she struggled on. "Iraq War veterans committing suicide at a rate of twenty-two per day because of untreated trauma. People who drink themselves into an early grave to escape the ghosts of priest abuse?" She stared at the man of God who clutched his bible like a life preserver. He lifted his eyes heavenward, probably to avoid the stunned faces avid to hear his answer. "Well?" she goaded.

A hint of excitement rippled through the group as their eyes shifted from the reverend to the heathen who'd wandered into their midst.

"It's God's plan," he announced solemnly.

She turned to the group. "Raise your hand if hearing that ever made *you* feel better. When your family was evicted the week before Christmas or your mother was diagnosed with early onset Alzheimer's?" She looked from face to face, letting the silence sink in before she said under her breath, "I didn't think so."

Once again, she trained her eyes on the minister who'd taken several steps backward, as if her words were stones. "His plan? To take her husband and leave her destitute. To take...my..." She choked and had to stop. Her voice dropped. "What about grace and love and compassion? Why can't you just say I'm sorry it's so hard. How can I help you?" She thrust both arms up in supplication and her voice dropped to a near whisper. "Would it kill you to be human just once, you insufferable moral narcissist?"

Silence. Then slow applause from a single pair of hands fractured the air. More joined in but Frances lifted her hands to still the clapping. "I'd like to talk about a different kind of plan. Jane here needs help now and you look like a resourceful crowd. What do you say?"

The woman next to Jane reached over and squeezed her hand. "Let's have dinner."

Another volunteered, "I'm looking for a companion for my mom. She's sweet but a little feeble."

Frances looked at Jane and said, "You're among friends now. You'll be fine." She turned to leave but paused and spun around. "And Reverend, the next time you're talking to God, let him know he can take the rest of the week off. We've got this covered."

"Timothy 2:12! Timothy 2:12!" sputtered the man of the cloth but Frances didn't wait for the punch line. As she shoved aside the chairs cluttering her exit, people reached out to shake her hand or offer a whispered thank you.

"Misanthrope, my ass," she swore. "I love people."

"Not so fast, Beacon," the usher barked, clamping his hand on her shoulder.

"What?" she snapped.

He pointed toward the knot of bloggers, yelling and laughing in the far corner.

"You're kidding! Did you see what I just did? That must count for something," she pleaded. The usher shook his head slowly but Frances couldn't ignore the adrenaline pumping through her system. She leaned in close enough to notice a slight twitch in his left eyelid and a cluster of dark hair peeking out of one nostril. "Trust me. This is *not* a good idea."

The floor around the bloggers was a sticky, malodorous carpet littered with the evidence of serious junk food addiction coupled with a high S.Q.—sedentary quotient. Sure enough, she spied a bulging calf sporting a Stadium Pal, the ultimate portable urinal allowing the wearer to sit for hours, ignoring bladder demands in favor of slot machines, football or in this case, varsity level trolling.

Each person was clutching an identical device. Not a book

or bible but a version of the phone Frances kept at her side like a policeman guards his gun. But clearly their contraptions were several generations beyond her simple unit. Above each keyboard was a large mirror in which the users' features were magnified to Godzilla scale, an ever-present selfie. Oversized headphones, like scientists might wear to eavesdrop on Mars, completed the package.

Sealed in their electronic bubbles, all the bloggers performed the identical routine. Their fingers flew over their keyboards, and then they hit Send and glanced up to see their statements in bright letters on a large white screen. Each new post was greeted with sounds that might issue from a herd of large animals in distress. Then their heads dropped down, like ducks feeding in a pond, to repeat the process. These weren't your garden variety bloggers, but trolls whose sole purpose was to sow discord on the internet. Some specialized in provocation with the goal of starting arguments. Others were flamethrowers, verbally scorching their victims for their own entertainment. Boors. Bigots. Mouth-breathers.

Frances had been attacked online more times than she could remember, misogyny being a favorite sport among trolls, though they probably couldn't spell it at gunpoint. But she never fought back because she'd been warned: "If you want to survive in the blogosphere—don't feed the trolls."

The white screen already had a choice array of current topics: politics, science, health and other rubbish of the highest order.

- *Every damn year we learn about the hollow cost in school. I'm tired of this shit.*
- *Most women after 35 stop taking care of their shapes and let's not forget mental pause at 45.*
- *Overpopulation is causing the planet to get so heavy from too many people that it will fall into the Sun.*
- *Gay couples shouldn't adopt because they can't make babies and we'd all go extinct.*

- *What's the problem with taxing tampons? Women should just hold it in until they go to the bathroom.*

Once again, the usher motioned toward the chairs but Frances was at the end of her rope. She spun around, determined to escape even if it meant resorting to violence. "Do you have the powers of arrest? If not, you'd be well advised to back off." She looked pointedly at his genitals. "I studied self-defense, and I promise you it won't be pretty."

"Whatever. My shift's over anyway." He shrugged and ambled off.

Too bad. She was dying to punish someone, so she vented her frustration on the doors which seemed to be stuck shut. She pounded on the cold metal release bar. "Get me out of here." But her cries were barely audible over the cacophony of the bloggers. Finally, the door surrendered and she burst into the hallway, spoiling for a fight.

CHAPTER 20

"Who takes that much anger to the grave?" asked a bespectacled man, gazing at furious Frances on the monitor in the Committee room.

"Rhetorical, *n'est pas*?" Olympe asked, rising from her chair.

"No, seriously." He gave her a look of innocent wonder. "I don't get it."

"I'm sorry, Monsieur. I missed your name," she said politely, like a concierge apologizing for an oversight. She approached him with the grace of a lion stalking a gazelle.

"Ronald," he replied hesitantly, then looked around as if searching for a way to escape the conversation.

"A fine name." She took his chin in her hand and brought his gaze back to her. "Now, Ronald, you have the face of an intelligent man, so I will give you one guess. Who could possibly take that much anger to the grave?"

He elevated his shoulders until they nearly grazed his ears and looked utterly mystified. His lips opened and closed but no answer emerged.

"*Non*?" Her French accent was round and soft, almost a caress, but what came next was not. "Then allow me to enlighten you." In a single breath she unleashed a torrent of nouns: "Gentlewomen, blue stockings, virgins, whores, scullery maids, nuns, ladies-in-waiting, widows, wet nurses, witches, confectioners and countesses, midwives and warriors, milk-maids, mothers, wives and daughters." She narrowed her eyes and inhaled audibly, signaling that the list wasn't nearly complete when the Fool stepped in.

"AKA, the fairer sex," he said.

"But never fairly treated," Olympe said. She began to pace as she delivered her indictment of the system. "Talented, visionary women have spent their entire lives trying to make sense of a social order in which competition and self-interest were celebrated, with wealth and power the only hallmarks of success. How could they possibly compete, much less excel when their strengths—relationships, intimacy, nurturing, intuition, resilience and concern for the common good—were dismissed as inferior currency?"

She took a step toward the startled man and observed with some satisfaction tiny drops of sweat forming on his upper lip. "Granted, my knowledge of the status of women in the 21st century is less than exhaustive, but I can tell you that in my day, Ronald, anger was the coin of the female realm."

She watched his Adam's apple bob up and down like a fishing float with a trout on the hook below. "Do you think even one alpha male ever stopped to ask *Where would I be without the care of women?*"

"You have to understand..." he stammered.

"*I* have to understand?!" she demanded. She grabbed his necktie and pulled his face closer to hers. His eyes semaphored a rapid SOS, hoping for someone to save him. But help was not on the way.

"It's rather simple, really. Men are..." he babbled on in vain.

"*Do not* lecture me on what men are." She dropped his tie and stepped away in disgust.

"I just meant..."

The Fool launched his body into the gap as Olympe's hand sliced through the air, destined for Ronald's terrified face. He ducked and let out a whimper of disbelief.

"Forgive him, Madame," the Fool begged. "He's afflicted. An ancient condition, but I believe it's currently known as *mansplaining*."

"Perhaps he should seek medical treatment," she said without a trace of sympathy.

"More like psychological. Some men still assume women are less capable of comprehension, despite all the evidence to the contrary."

Olympe shook her head in disgust. "Then I fear that my death was in vain."

"When was that?" the Fool asked.

"November 3, 1793 was my last day on earth, but it seems that little has changed."

"No!" he protested. "It's not so. Women have made great strides!"

"And men are miserable," Andreas interjected. He threw a smile at Cornelius who was watching this encounter with dismay. Every time that woman opened her mouth, his agenda went up in smoke.

"Must we *always* talk about men?" Olympe fumed.

"Right. Let's stick to the topic," the Fool said, "and there's plenty to celebrate. Junko Tabei, the first woman to summit Everest. Sirivarno Bandaranaike, first woman head of a country. Fifty-one Nobel Prize winners in skirts. Scores of Pulitzer Prize winners! Women are pilots, inventors, rappers."

"And look at Frances," Juliette added brightly.

"You look," Andreas smirked, lighting another cigarette and blowing the smoke in her direction.

"Spare me," Cornelius groaned and flopped into a chair at the front of the room, abandoning all hope of regaining control.

Olympe strafed both men with a withering glare, then turned to the Fool. "You see what I mean?"

"You're right," he conceded.

"Nothing's really changed," Juliette agreed.

"It's tragic." Olympe tightened her scarf around her neck. "The revolution failed us, and Frances will pay the price."

CHAPTER 21

"Hey! Watch it, lady!" Grayson yelled as he dodged the flying door. The shouts of the bloggers roiled into the hall, carrying along one very agitated Frances. She was certain that he'd set her up to fail, maybe even watched from the sidelines while she'd done so in spectacular fashion. Another black mark on her academic record.

"Let me guess." She threw her hands up in surrender and her face had a look of dismay. "Was that your idea of a joke?"

"Not at all," he said calmly, but wisely kept his distance. "How'd it go?"

"About as well as you'd expect," she sighed. "I was a stranger in a strange land. You may as well have dropped me in Botswana or Liechtenstein."

"That rough, huh?"

"Jeeze, those trolls. That was a really low blow." She surprised herself as tears stung her eyes but she swiped them away with the back of her hand. "Do you have any idea how those idiots tormented me? For years! Opening my e-mail was like picking through a minefield."

"Yeah, they're some crazy motherfuckers," Grayson agreed.

Her face registered relief at his unexpected solidarity and she sagged against the wall. "It's not the crazy part that gets to me. I worked with crazies all my life and some of them were the brightest, most interesting people I ever knew. I'm good with crazy," she insisted, tapping a forefinger on her sternum. "It's ignorance I can't stand. People not literate enough to express a sin-gle-com-pre-hen-sive thought." She hit each syllable like a drum beat. "In fact, thinking is optional. They've got just enough brain power to fire off mind-bending, gram-mar-offending sentence fragments. Imbeciles, bigots, anarch-ists bent on destroying civil society thanks to talk-radio and the internet. It makes me, a pacifist, want to go for a gun."

"How 'bout if we just go for a drink?"

"I thought you'd never ask."

She hoisted herself onto a bar stool, nodded to Jack and pressed her lips together, struggling to pantomime the de-meanor of a semi-normal person. "Actually, the book people weren't so bad. Don't get me wrong. They're clannish as hell, and socially speaking, some of them shouldn't be out without a keeper."

Grayson nodded. "But you have to admit, they do like books."

"*Like?* They're passionate and opinionated with a few borderline fanatics thrown in just to keep it interesting." She paused. "Other than that," she cleared her throat, "they're a lot like...me." The last part of her confession was delivered just above a whisper.

"Wow, where's your t-shirt, girl?" No longer the target of her fury, he was clearly enjoying the upturn in the conversation.

"You have to make fun?" She squinted at him and then glanced in the mirror. *Well, why not?* Even she had to admit that some of her behavior bordered on strange.

"Sorry. Bad habit. Go on." He took a long sip of her wine.

"The minister..."

Her voice trailed off and her body stiffened as she caught sight of a man reflected in the mirror behind the bar. But not just any man. Leaning in the doorway was the tall, gangly figure of Graham, an old lover. Hands shoved deep in the pockets of jeans that had worn patches before shabbiness was chic. Thinning hair. Glasses perched on a long nose. Mustache like a thatched roof that obscured a pair of the Size 12 lips on a Size 10 mouth. Too flabby to produce a robust smile. He wasn't a beauty by any stretch of the imagination. Not even marginally handsome. But he radiated bad-boy magnetism to the power of ten.

Even from a distance of thirty feet the attraction still felt strong enough to pull satellites out of orbit and truthfully, weak enough to escape. It had always been that way. The agony of the decision was part of the thrill. And now the bad boy fixed Frances with his gaze, like a champion in a staring contest.

She tore her eyes away and reached for her glass but missed, sloshing a puddle of wine on the bar. Struggling to recover, she took a huge gulp and held it in her mouth for a moment to steal time to think.

Grayson put his hand on top of her glass. "Maybe you better slow down. I think that stuffs getting to you."

"I'm fine. Fine." She waved a hand dismissively then adopted a cheery voice to cover her rattled state. "Sorry, where was I?"

"The minister."

"Oh, yeah, the minister." She straightened her shoulders and threw herself into the conversation, trying to broadcast the impression that she was having a marvelous time, impervious to Graham's sudden intrusion. "I swear he didn't know whether to shit or go blind when I lit in to him. It was a real scene." She laughed just a little too loud and several bar patrons glanced her way. "Actually, I quite enjoyed it."

Grayson nodded. "He's a piece of work, but he gets the job done."

She felt instantly betrayed, like he was the mastermind behind a curriculum personally designed to frustrate and humiliate her. "What do you mean—*job*?"

"You tell me."

"God, I'm so sick of this game." She started to slide off her stool, but Grayson grabbed her arm and pulled her back in place.

"It's not a game." His voice was dead serious. "Didn't you get anything out of that?"

"I don't know. Something like the value of being curious about people whose ideas are repellant instead of caucusing exclusively with kindred spirits who share my deeply held beliefs?"

"Something like that. Yeats said that quarrel is essential," Grayson added.

"I used to think quarreling about religion was pointless because those people were all zombies. And some of them are. Don't get me started on the snake handlers or the ones who speak in tongues."

She locked eyes with Grayson to defy the laser scorching her back with a barrage of vivid memories—hotel rooms, dark corners in bars, irrational longing and the pain of never getting enough. And she couldn't deny it. The thought of an encore crossed her mind. She reached for a napkin, ostensibly to mop up the wine. But with a slight rotation, she managed to catch a glimpse of Graham exiting the bar with a twenty-something blonde in tow. She felt like she'd been stabbed.

"Quarreling zombies?" Grayson prompted.

"Right." She struggled to refocus. "The truth is, most of them just want their lives to mean something. The problem is that they're not sure that their love and work, the way they care for their families—that all of that constitutes meaning. And you can't really blame them. The church has done a pretty thorough job of convincing humans that they're damaged goods and the only hope of salvation is to hook their existence to a greater...something. I still feel like they came up with the wrong answer, but at least they struggled with the right question."

"Damn, Frances. Keep this up and you'll make the Dean's List!" He sounded genuinely impressed and called for a second glass of wine.

"I doubt it. In case you didn't notice, I'm a dropout."

"It doesn't work that way. The only way out is through."

In a moment of undeniable regression, her eyes took a spin around their sockets. She hated being on the receiving end of advice she was always giving her readers. "Right. Through." But what did through actually mean when there was no telling what came next?

"I'm tired of being so bad at this," she confided to him and clamped her hands around her glass.

"This?"

"Death. I really suck."

"There's only one person who can change that."

Not the answer she wanted but at least the battle lines were clear. It was Frances against the system. And herself.

CHAPTER 22

"Jesus, Mary and Joseph!"

Frances awoke channeling the oldest nun in her grade school, which was a bizarre choice given the situation—a stunning commotion in her southern hemisphere. Full arousal without any idea how she got there. Her t-shirt was twisted around her torso, the rough underarm seam stretched across one nipple. A slight move, the brush of the fabric, and the involuntary contractions began. She pressed her hand between her legs and tightened her thighs, determined to catch the wave of energy before her brain barged in and tried to explain away this craving in a world without her man. A world without her world.

Afterward, she lay exhausted in a tangle of phantom limbs. "Well, that was refreshing. Not." It wasn't good sex—more like the past pleading to be heard—and it left her with a residue of sadness and rebellion.

I need to get out of here!

Map in hand, she found her way back to the subway, yanked open the door and stopped dead in her tracks. Like most people, she'd had the experience of returning to a childhood haunt where everything—the schoolroom, the front porch, the kitchen table—seemed to have shrunk. This was the exact opposite. She was the one who'd shrunk back to childsize.

Now the arms of the turnstile were chest-high and it took both hands to budge them. She craned her neck to read the signs and hoisted herself up on a bench where her legs dangled, barely grazing the pavement. Her feet began to swing back and forth, marking time like a metronome and releasing a flood of memories.

She remembered sitting in church holding her father's hand, following his gaze up the columns and past the arches to the vault. They'd smile at each other, relishing their shared disinterest in the mechanical rituals of the priest and the pantomimed piety of the families crowded in the pews. Her mother was the believer in the family. Then Frances would lean a bit closer to him and pump her legs as they waited for the final "Amen" that released them to enjoy the remains of their Sunday.

Sporadic knots of people arrived on the opposite platform as if dumped from a fleet of tour buses. They loitered in front of a patchwork of cracked mirrors on the wall, the creation of an artist who thought urban density could use a little help. She scanned the faces, a favorite pastime in times past and spotted one that looked like it had been plucked from a medieval altarpiece. An expectant face, as though waiting for an angel to come down and explain the wandering star or the three kings visiting a simple family in a cowshed. Another face had the serene detachment of a Buddha but that was probably the effect of earbuds muting the chaos.

With a jolt, she watched her mother and sister file in and take up separate stations, each in her own cocoon. As one turned to make conversation, the other peered down the tracks or stared at the pavement.

Then her sister, Veronica, crept to the edge of the platform, stood stock still and stared across the gap. Frances stared back at her big sister, her first friend, the cat rescuer and voracious consumer of presidential history. The big-hearted loner who could hold center stage in a conversation for hours. The prolific painter. *She got the talent in the family.* By turns funny and distressing, Veronica tugged to the breaking point at the heart she swore Frances never had.

Frances loved her sister but none of that got through. Not then. Not now. *Small wonder* she thought as she caught a glimpse of herself in the mirrored sculpture beyond. All her sister could see was the Franny of their childhood—her immobile face, distant and cold. Then the old accusations flew across the gap like darts hurled by an angry pub denizen.

"Unfeeling! Perfection-obsessed! Boastful bitch! So busy helping other people but what did you ever do for *me,* Franny?"

No surprise that their phone calls felt like obligatory rituals performed on holidays and birthdays.

Now Veronica began to pace, a jittery tentative dance. She circled their mother and then stepped beyond the yellow safety line, her toes hugging the edge of the platform like a bird on a wire. Frances watched transfixed with the frightened eyes of a little sister wondering what would happen next and the practiced eye of a social worker calculating the odds.

Jumper or pusher?

If her sibling was true to form, the next act could be tragic.

Frances stepped forward and suddenly the rigid train tracks became sinuous ripples of silver, like snakes slithering through the tunnel. The gap narrowed to an arm's length. She could jump across. Hold her sister's hand. Hug her mother. And then what? Return to the fold. Take up her role as mediator suturing together the fissures in the family. She thrust out her arm, responding to the gravitational pull of history and belonging, but it was instantly repelled by the superior anti-magnetism of like poles avoiding each other.

A horn blared, rattling the entire station and the train swept through as if driverless and out of control. Then it darted into the dark hole at the far end, sucking bits of trash into its frantic wake. Frances squinted and felt a few strands of her hair try to follow. When she opened her eyes, the opposite platform was bare except for a panhandler clearly off his meds.

Instantly, she remembered honing the urban talent for avoidance. No eye-contact. No sudden moves. Definitely no conversation. She'd convinced herself that it was simply an act of protective invisibility. Besides, she'd told herself, *I gave at the office.* Now that strategy seemed like calloused indifference, so she looked straight into his eyes and saw the desperate, unrelenting pain of suffering in public, unable to touch or be touched by a single soul. She stretched her empty hands toward the man, as if asking for understanding or forgiveness.

But he'd seen that move before. "Say my name," he shouted. "Say my name."

She stammered, "I don't know it. Tell me."

But he'd run out of patience. "Hypocrite. Coward. Heartless cunt!" Then he wandered down the platform to a trash can, rummaged for recycles and disappeared.

The spell was broken by the sound of a metal security door rolling up, and Frances hurried over in time to see a woman duck into the Strong Silent Coffee Bar. The neon sign buzzed to life and lights filled a space no bigger than an elevator. Bustling behind the counter, Antoinette, caffeine maven to throngs of sleepy commuters, hit the button on an industrial-size grinder, dumped in a scoop of beans and set out a pitcher of fresh cream. A sign behind the bar read *Strong Silent Rules:*

- *No politics.*
- *No proselytizing.*
- *No soliciting of any kind.*
- *Yes, I know who I'm voting for.*
- *No, I haven't found Jesus.*
- *So unless you're selling Thin Mints, drink up and shut up.*
- *Hours: When the spirit moves me.*

Frances stared mutely while Antoinette worked, not sure if "Good morning" qualified as excess talk that would send her back into the decaffeinated wilderness. Maybe she should just blurt out "double espresso" and hope for the best but before she could speak, Antoinette broke the silence.

"How ya doin' today, Frances?"

"Better now that you're here."

"You got that right. We women have to stick together. Ain't no hashtag can change the fact that it's still a man's world. Double espresso, comin' up."

"Oh, my God, thank you so much." Seized with anticipation and gratitude, she felt a momentary wave of compassion for every sufferer in the world and blurted out, "But you know, it's not easy for men, either."

"Say what?" Antoinette snatched the tiny cup from under the spigot and reached for the switch.

"Wait! Wait!" Frances cried as her magic potion morphed into a mirage right before her eyes. "Don't get me wrong. There are some first-class assholes out there."

"Now you're talkin'." Antionette slid the cup back in place and pressed the button. "They act like they won the lottery just because they have a set of balls. Opinionated, unreliable, controlling, self-absorbed." She paused and removed the steaming cup. It sat on the counter in a no-man's land between them until Frances summoned the courage to pounce.

It was gone in a single gulp. "Thank you so much!" Eyes closed, she sighed deeply. "Perfect!" Then she looked beseechingly. "Encore?"

Antoinette prepped another double and resumed her monologue. "And thick? The social and emotional intelligence of a bus bench but egos as fragile as Baccarat crystal. Why do you think I put up that sign? If one more guy tried to tell me how to make *his* coffee—*180 degrees, long pull, two extra shots cold brewed*—I would have thrown him under the next train. Not good for business."

"I hear you," Frances said. "But those balls come with chains. Bread-winning, any kind of winning for that matter.

Constantly eyeing the competition. Not enough money. Never enough sex. Lots of energy devoted to policing their anger. Lots of pain if they don't. And they're the first to be picked off when the grim reaper comes to town. I'm just saying, life's hard for men, too."

Antoinette shook her head. "What are you—a shrink or something? Get a grip, Frances. Women are superior humans. Believe me. I've been both."

"Really?" She tried to use her social worker voice, calm and non-judgmental but it didn't work.

"Yeah." Nothing more from the barista.

Of course, Frances knew people switched genders in the real world, but this was the afterlife. "Are we talking past lives or...?" she cautiously prompted.

Antoinette shook her head. "First trans barista in Queens and proud of it."

"So, how'd you end up here?"

"They couldn't figure out where to put me. What's new? So I offered my services to new arrivals and outliers. By the way, a guy came by looking for you."

"Probably my handler. He gets nervous when I'm off the leash."

"No, it wasn't Grayson but this guy definitely had handling on his mind. And I'm pretty sure he'd know all the right moves."

"Really?" *Graham.* As she replayed the scene in the bar, she felt her temperature rising.

"Yeah. Tall guy. Not a beauty, but there's something about a lanky slouch that's pure sex." Antoinette leaned over the counter, whispering to Frances like a bookie sharing an insider tip. "I'd bet a caramel macchiato that he likes his pleasures with a bit of a slant, if you know what I mean."

"Uh-huh," Frances mumbled, hoping to head off an open-air conversation that could lead God-knows-where once Antionette was on a roll.

"If I was a few years younger..." Antoinette mused.

"Age has nothing to do with it. Passion is what counts and you've got that in spades."

"Anyway, he left this for you." Antionette handed over a matchbook with a phone number scrawled inside.

Frances jammed it in her pocket like it was contraband and drained the last drop from her cup. "Thanks, Antoinette. It was great to meet you."

"Come by anytime. I know things."

"Well, that makes one of us." The caffeine had definitely kicked in, microscopically lifting the perma-fog that had settle in her brain, but the enhanced view of her predicament did nothing to revive her spirits. On the contrary, it was painfully clear that she had no idea what she was doing. All the tools she'd relied on in the past—patience, persistence, logic, diplomacy—were like blunt instruments.

"What seems to be the problem?" Antoinette asked.

"I don't know shit." She folded her arms on the edge of the counter and lowered her head, pounding her forehead slowly, rhythmically, trying to loosen the gridlock inside her head.

"Don't be ridiculous. You have a great brain." She patted Frances on the top of her head. "A little too good some times."

"Had. It seems to have gone AWOL. I can't even remember how I got here."

Antoinette pointed to the torn map Frances was still clutching in her hand. "Could be a clue."

"Not here!" she cried in exasperation, slamming her hand on the counter and making the espresso cup dance. "Here!" She flung her hands in a wide arc as if to encompass the entire universe of the afterlife. Then she tapped her forehead with a clenched fist, like she was trying to rouse a determined sleeper barricaded behind a locked door.

"Nobody's home," she announced. "I can't put two coherent thoughts together."

"It's not about thinking."

"Great! Then I'm really fucked." She looked like she was on the verge of tears.

Antionette swiped the counter top with a damp towel to erase the handprint. Then she stepped back and eyed Frances, letting her brood. Finally, she relented. "Fine. What do you want to know?"

"How it works. The rules."

"Fuck the rules!"

"Easy for you to say," she groused, pointing at the sign overhead. "You get to make your own. But I'm flying blind. Grayson's hovering like a warden. The dog's probably wearing a wire. And did I mention that I have a call back date with the court at which time the rules, regulations, criminal codes, civil codes, bar codes, bar tabs, sell-by dates, finger prints and probably the last time I changed my underwear—which is another thing I can't remember—will be scrutinized by some Latin-spouting Judge Judy or Judas who doesn't even have the courage to make a personal appearance?" She massaged her temples and blew out a long breath. "I'm doomed."

She fixed Antoinette with imploring eyes. "Got any ideas?"

"I can't change the rules."

"And I can't change myself."

Antoinette drew back, pantomiming disbelief. "You are Frances Beacon, right? The great evangelist of self-help?"

Frances winced and felt a wave of shame wash over her.

Antoinette continued to press her point. "Do you even hear yourself?" Then she lowered her voice to a near whisper. "What the hell are you so afraid of?"

CHAPTER 23

Frances awoke in her secret nest and struggled to get her bearings but only the book beside her pillow felt familiar. The light was dim and the ornate hands on the clock were frozen at 9:15, so she had no clue to the actual time or even what day it was. This was how she imagined it felt to be retired, something she'd vigorously eschewed on the grounds that it would kill her.

And now here I am. Stuck in the Central Nowhere Time Zone.

She was loath to put tally marks on the wall like a prisoner but she had to find a way to fight her disorientation, so each morning she constructed a To Do list from a narrow range of choices: read, walk, write, do yoga, and with any luck, workout. She had to have something to show for her day.

But she'd been so excited the first time Gabe led her to the gym that she forgot to memorize the route. She tried to recreate the trip on her own, but each time it was like searching for the lost continent of Lemuria. Her frustration tolerance got a vigorous workout but little else. And no amount of nagging could convince Gabriel to play scout. He insisted it wasn't in his job description.

"Well, too bad," she muttered. "This is an emergency." The gym meant control in her out-of-control existence. Not to mention the endorphins, dopamine and norepinephrine—those feel-good chemicals that worked like a charm in her other life.

I could use a vat of them right now.

So, she grabbed a stick of red chalk from a box next to the easel, dropped it in her pocket, and slipped out of her secret room. She tiptoed to the corner where the big dog occasionally had a sleepover. Channeling her most abject client, she whined, "Please? Please, Gabe." For a big finish she massaged his ears from skull to tip, begging until he relented.

"A little to the left," he groaned with pleasure and finally added, "This is it. Last time." He took a leisurely approach to getting on his feet as she pelted him with "Good dog, good dog."

The passageways were so narrow that it didn't seem suspicious when she dropped a few steps behind. By extending her arm at a forty-five-degree angle, she managed to leave a faint red chalk line on the walls.

The next day she set out for the gym again in a state of mild excitement, thrilled to be speed-walking through alleys where she'd formerly stumbled without direction or hope. She kept a close eye on the red line and just as she was nearing the first corner, she noticed tiny yellow scribbles perched on top of her scratches, like canaries on a wire. *Yellow chalk?* She was certain those marks hadn't been there the day before.

She tried to quell her excitement, telling herself that it might just be *For a Good Time Call,* but she nearly lost her balance when she bent over and read: *Had we but world enough, and time.* The words stabbed deep in her chest. Pain and then anger at this ruthless ambush. Unable to stifle the impulse, she watched as her hand shot out and scrubbed the text until it was a yellow blur like the sky at dawn. Then she leaned against the wall to consider the situation.

Her immediate reaction was to feel exposed, which seemed to come naturally these days. But on second thought, it could be just the plaintive scribblings of another lost soul. Then a more constructive thought took hold. *Be curious. Keep an eye out for the next dispatch. Or even better, propose a dialogue.*

She pulled the red chalk from her pocket, crouched and wrote *There could never be enough.* Just as she stood up, Grayson rounded the corner. She gave a startled cry but managed to hoist her cheeks in a facsimile of a smile as she tucked her yellow-stained palm behind her back.

"Where you going?"

"I have an appointment." She was deliberately vague, hoping he'd take the hint and leave.

"With?"

"Myself." Her voice had a no-room-at-the-inn-move-along-please quality. He ignored it and stared, his brow telegraphing the inevitable next question. Finally, she relented. "If you must know, I'm going to the gym."

"Mind if I walk along?"

Mind? Do I mind? My first few minutes of freedom and you show up with your choke chain. Yes, I mind!

"No problem. Lead on." She fell in behind him, keeping an eye out for more graffiti.

"Weren't you some kind of fitness freak?" he asked.

"Freak? Because I can still hold a fork and have the use of both legs? That's not exactly freak material. Although now that you mention it, a lot people my age live in their bathrobes with a death grip on the remote, except when they're prospecting in the refrigerator." How many times had she scoffed at people who retired and let their lives deteriorate in a vertiginous, sneakerized downward spiral? *But at least they were alive!*

"I hate to exercise," he said.

"Everybody does. That doesn't make you special. And if you don't mind me saying, you really should hit the gym. Get rid of some of that..." She patted her stomach.

"Yeah, I've put on a few pounds, but..."

"Anyway, physical fitness wasn't the point." She'd quickly discovered that preaching about exercise-for-exercise's sake wasn't likely to sell books, fill her seminars or catapult her fans out of their La-Z-Boys and into the gym. Nope, she was pedaling longevity. Extra years, even decades, filled with adventures, purpose and hot sex.

Her strategy was simple. Do an end run around the exercise issue and hit them right where it hurt—in the brain. While many of her followers had made peace with their borderline obesity, the idea of being mentally adrift and helpless tapped into a vulnerability they couldn't ignore. Her opening line was "If you think exercise is inconvenient, try senility."

"The leg bone's connected to the think bone," she said to Grayson and gave her forehead a light tap.

"What the hell are you talking about?" He couldn't suppress a laugh.

"It's true. Exercise does a body good, but it's even better for your brain."

"That's not what I heard," he protested. "I distinctly remember being told that 100,000 brain cells up and disappear every day except on Friday when alcohol consumption accelerates mental deterioration to supersonic rates. From what I could tell, my mental wattage would dim to the point that I'd need the help of a minimum-wage minder just to operate a toaster."

Frances had heard all of that before but she couldn't help laughing before she proceeded to set him straight. "You know what, Shock Jock? That's crap. Your brain is like a construction project. You can build and rebuild mental capacity as long as there's breath in your body. But you gotta do the work. Sweat equity." She looked around at the endless samescape. "Are we almost there?"

"Few more minutes. Got any other words of wisdom?"

But Frances had gone radio silent. She was thinking how confidently she'd joked with the people in her seminars. *"You need to stop moaning about the state of your brain because there aren't any others available, for sale or rent. Believe me,*

I've done the research." She'd point to her temples. *"This is it and it's got to last if we're going to make the most of the 85 years that longevity researchers are promising us."*

Eighty-five, she thought in dismay. *I was cheated.* She'd never signed up for Medicare or got a discount at her favorite museums. Never took a mid-week excursion with a gaggle of gray-headed adventurers. At 65, she'd announced, "I'm just coming of age!" Now she longed to go back and slap the confidence right off her smug face.

Shortly before reaching the gym, she spotted another yellow message but didn't dare pause for inspection.

"We're here," Grayson announced.

"Great!" She sprinted toward the gym. "See you later."

"Maybe after we can—" he said to her back.

Frances checked his move. "Gotta go," she called over her shoulder. But when she reached the door, a sign the size of a postage stamp said CLOSED.

"God damn it, let me in. I need to work out!" She kicked the door in time with her outbursts until her knee twisted and let out an audible popping sound. "Shit, shit!"

Grayson stood back and waited for her tantrum to subside. "Are you okay?"

She took a tentative step and winced. "Yeah, great."

"Frances, can I ask you a question?" His voice was so gentle that she momentarily dropped her defenses.

"Why is the gym so important?" He paused, seeing her confusion. "Let me put it another way. Why now, post-mortem and all?"

"If you must know, I'm trading one pain for another."

"How about a little pain killer? Looks like you could use some," he pointed to her knee. "If we hurry, we can catch the end of happy hour."

"That would be a miracle." She took a tentative step and flinched.

"No, it's right around the corner." He gestured to an

intersection festooned with a half dozen manicules, all pointing in different directions.

"I mean the happy part," she grumbled.

"How so?"

"I haven't been happy since I landed in this place." Her voice was forlorn when she added, "And maybe not for years before that."

"Well, they're not checking attitudes at the door so, let's give it a shot."

Frances limped to the entrance of the club and made her way slowly toward the bar.

"So, Beacon-san, how do you like the afterlife so far?" Jack turned his left ear toward Frances to catch her tone more than the actual words.

"I'm waiting for the book to come out." Her voice made it clear that the conversational welcome mat was definitely not out.

Jack nodded. "Low *shen*."

"Translation?"

"Low spirit."

"You got that right," she confessed.

He reached for her hand. "May I?" When she nodded, he slid his thumb to the inside of her wrist, searching for her pulse.

"In case you haven't heard, they say I'm dead. Or dead adjacent, so that may not be your best bet."

Jack turned away, idling in front of the wooden drawers as if in meditation before opening one and then another. Frances stared at Grayson in the mirror.

What a pair! We look like Manet's absinthe drinkers but at least they had Paris.

Jack handed Frances a bag of ice for her knee and slid a tall frosty glass across the bar. It looked like a cruise-ship cocktail but tasted like lime juice strained through her gym togs. "God, that's awful." She pushed it away and ordered her usual.

"It takes time."

"Well, I seem to have plenty of that." She nudged Grayson with her elbow. "So, Shock Jock, what do people do around here at night?"

"Clubs mostly."

She grunted. "I never got the club thing. The noise. The exhibitionism. All that desperation on display. Everyone trying so hard to have fun or drink enough so they wouldn't remember another night of overpriced disappointment." She drained her glass. "It was like spending New Year's Eve in the emergency room."

"Maybe you just picked the wrong clubs. Let's go."

She didn't move. Her knee throbbed. The wine had failed in its duty, and the prospect of clubbing was grim. But it was more than that. If she was honest, the clubs weren't to blame. She'd acted like a snob, bored by the mindless rabble when in reality, she was the problem. Socially wary and rhythmically challenged, she always felt like an outsider.

Grayson jostled her arm. "Come on. Let's give it a whirl."

"Trust me. It'll end badly."

CHAPTER 24

Grayson led her down a passage, identical to all the others. Frances tried to pay attention. Two lefts, one right, straight through a square but her mind kept returning to the graffiti.

Who was the author? Could they make contact and help each other? Or was it a trap set by an informant?

Without warning, a neon sign appeared out of the gloom. The After-Hours Kierkegaard Club. Over the doorway a sign read *Do you not know that there comes a midnight hour when everyone has to throw off his mask?*

"Mr. Fear and Trembling, the world's most anxious man. Some club," she huffed in disgust as Grayson held the door.

The interior was hushed and soothing, the antithesis of the cacophony that was de rigueur in most New York night-spots. Wide wooden floorboards creaked underfoot. Deep leather chairs, creased and cracked with time. Shelves stacked with books and an antique hourglass with most of its sand suspended in the top bulb. A half dozen men and women sat around a sturdy table nodding and talking quietly. One was a dead ringer for Mark Twain. Two women of the homey persuasion inclined toward each other in a private conversation. A man in lumberjack attire was earnestly knitting.

Frances looked at Grayson. "Nice place. What's the story?"

"You go to the gym. They discuss philosophy. Different ways of—"

"Coping?"

A twenty-something with a riot of red curls broke the spell with a voice that was too loud for even the chicest Manhattan bistro. He stabbed the book on his lap, bristling with irritation. "It says right here: *I have seen men in real life who so long deceived others that at last their true nature could not reveal itself.*" Then he jumped up out of his chair and continued his rant. "But I ask you. How do we reveal ourselves when our whole society is built on pretense? People relentlessly broadcasting images that have been carefully curated for public consumption, all the while bunkered in their parents' basement in their underwear. Sometimes it's like living in a mad house."

"He's got that right," Frances whispered to Grayson.

His voice rose in pitch and volume. "And why not? What would authenticity get me anyway?" He dropped down in his chair as if someone had pulled the plug.

The lumberjack put down his needles and cleared his throat. All eyes turned toward him. "But Kierkegaard gave us the answer to that, didn't he? He said, *He who cannot reveal himself cannot love, and he who cannot love is the most unhappy man of all.*"

Then they all repeated quietly, "He who cannot love."

As the words echoed in her ears, the memory of something long-buried stirred. Buried because living with it day after day was more than she could bear. But it was elusive, like a dream that's so visceral it rivals reality, but vanishes the moment you try to find words to describe it. Frances closed her eyes and willed the memory to reveal itself, but all she could taste was hubris, missed opportunities and indelible loss.

"Well, that was some fun!" she said in a mocking tone as she and Grayson stepped outside. Then a welcome wave of anger welled up inside her, blunting the pain. "Dreary little group. I must say, you really know how to pick 'em. But I've had enough. Take me home."

CHAPTER 25

"Stop!" Frances cried as they emerged from a narrow passageway. She lifted her head like a deer sensing a change in the atmosphere, something afoot. "Can you smell that?" she asked.

"What?" Grayson froze in his tracks, sampling the air around him.

"Flowers!" It seemed impossible in this barren nonscape, but she was certain that she'd caught the scent. "Gardenias. Maybe roses." Gripped by the image of a secret garden, she forgot all about her room and her throbbing knee. She seized control of the excursion, hobbling down a flight of stone steps and then another, leading with her nose. Out of the gloom she spied a huge door. No handle. No knocker. She pressed her ear against the cold metal and heard the clear shimmering strains of *Lux Aeterna,* Lauridsen's requiem to his dead mother.

"I need to get in there."

"Maybe another time. It's getting late." Anyone else would have heard the warning in Grayson's voice, but Frances was having none of it.

"Now." It was an order not a request.

He began to whistle softly.

"Remind me. What's that?" she asked.

"Procol Harum. *Whiter Shade of Pale.*"

"I loved that song. Mournful but elegant." And with that

the door creaked open, revealing a vast circular room with dozens of people in saffron-colored silk vests, looking like novice monks or first responders at an emergency. A silver samovar sat on a central counter surrounded by baskets of roses, and a vase the size of a man held a bouquet of sunflowers pointing up to a golden dome.

Frances turned her gaze to the surrounding walls. No sharp lines or shadowy corners to jangle the senses. Only a thousand hues of pink, blue and lavender, the unmistakable utopia of Monet's famous garden in Giverny. His Waterlily series. For the first time since her arrival in the afterlife, she felt completely safe. She turned slowly, inhaling the landscape of flowers, bridges, willow trees and a piece of sky floating in a pond. Then she fell to her knees.

It was beauty. It was breath. It was life itself.

Yet all this was born out of grief. For ten years Monet didn't touch a brush, so deep was his mourning for his wife. Then over 200 paintings poured forth.

Grayson touched her shoulder but she didn't budge, so he crouched beside her.

"He made these while the war was raging only a hundred miles away," she whispered.

"They also serve who only stand and paint."

Interspersed between the paintings were seven huge doors framed in marble columns. The lintel above each was inscribed with a name. *Europa, Afer, Terra Australus* and so on around the room. All the continents, present and accounted for.

As if answering an inaudible bell, the attendants moved in unison toward the doors, now open and flooded with arrivals, all in the funeral attire of their national origin. Some were wrapped in pure white winding cloths trailing the scent of roses. Others wore their best suits or prayer shawls or very little at all. A young woman had leaves tangled in her hair from an aboriginal burial, another a dusting of ashes. The guides glided through the crowd as if on casters, welcoming the arrivals in their own languages, pressing cups of tea into their hands. An old man reached into his mouth and removed a coin, eagerly exchanging it for the comfort of the steaming brew. A huddle of women chattered like chorus girls in a dressing room, while a small child ran among the forest of legs, calling for his mother.

Frances watched, stunned into silence by the panorama of death on a global scale. Even Grayson seemed transfixed by the sight.

"What's that?" She pointed to a large cluster pushing through the *Europa* door as if bound together by invisible cords.

"It's hard to say. Ferry overturned, earthquake, maybe a plane crash. We try to reduce the shock by keeping them close to the people who shared their final moments."

In the distance she heard the strains of a New Orleans jazz band, raucous and celebratory, but all she could feel was the trauma of sudden irreversible separation. She'd looked at death from both sides and knew the grief of those left behind, as well as the utter confusion of the souls crowding through the portals. As if by instinct, she plunged into the crowd, confident that years of social work had honed her skills for comforting the newly bereaved. Be present. Listen. Then listen some more. She remembered sitting with a client for an entire rainy afternoon, holding her hand while she recited a litany of traits that made her murdered son the light of her life.

But what could Frances possibly offer the newly dead, she who was still grappling with denial and staggering bouts of anger? She grabbed a handful of roses and approached a knot of old women. "Welcome. You're safe." She crouched down to comfort a young girl, and then took her over to the paintings. "Wouldn't it be lovely to play in that garden?" It was all she could do. Pat the arm of one and wipe the face of another while whispering softly.

Then her eyes fell upon a set of wide shoulders. Gray hair curled softly on a head that tilted slightly to the left, as though puzzled by an intriguing question. Her heart stopped but her eyes drilled into the silhouette, so familiar and so loved. *Look at me. Please look at me.* She willed the apparition to turn around with all her might, and he did. It was a kind face, but that of a stranger.

Disappointment and relief collided as she fought back tears. When Grayson touched her shoulder, she jumped. "Please, can we go? I can't bear it."

They slipped outside where she pressed the heels of her hands into her eyes, trying to blot out the image of the surging crowds. Then a thought occurred to her. "Grayson, I don't remember coming through that room."

"I told you. High profile case. We let you in the VIP entrance."

"The ladies room?"

"Hey, it was quiet. Private. You have to admit that. And it came with your own personal factotum." He pressed his hands together in front of his chest and gave a slight bow.

"Did I ever thank you for that?" She winced, reviewing the fiesta of bad behavior to which he'd been subjected.

"Ah, that would be a no. But you had a lot on your mind."

"Well, thanks," she offered quietly but he'd already disappeared around a corner.

"One more stop," Grayson called back to her.

"No more, please. I need my bed."

"I think it will lift your spirits."

"Impossible." But she didn't have the energy to resist as Grayson ushered her into a space that resembled the first-class cabin of an airbus. Softly contoured chairs were tucked into individual cubicles. The lights were restfully low.

A man stepped out of the shadows. Short and round. A fringe of hair like a monk. Jowls hung from his cheeks and jiggled as he greeted them in a near whisper. "Welcome to the Dawn Treaders." He pointed toward a glass enclosure like the sound booth in a recording studio with a view of the whole room. "We can talk in here without disturbing them."

The *them* to which he referred were men and women who seemed to fade in and out of consciousness, like passengers on a long-haul flight at the end of dinner service.

"What are they doing?" Frances asked, suppressing the urge to say that it looked like a snooze festival.

"They watch humans who are at risk of not making it through the night. We send light into their personal darkness, project images that can give them a reason to live or at least survive until dawn."

Frances sat down to watch as beams of violet light streamed from the watchers to a projection of the earth on the screen in each cubicle. One beam carried the image of a pre-teen girl clad in black biker boots, strumming a guitar as she called out, "Thanks, daddy, I love you." Other beams transported a patch of garden with a collie romping and a toddler taking his first steps.

"Just suicides?" she asked.

"No. Medical emergencies. Accidents. We've spotted some pretty bad ones before they occur. Can't always prevent them but sometimes we manage to cushion the blow. We've pulled a lot of people back from the brink." He nodded in satisfaction as he looked from Grayson to Frances.

"You smug bastard!" Her face was livid as she spit out the words like bullets.

Let the record show that Frances had never assaulted anyone. In all her years of living in New York, a city that boasted over thirty thousand acts of interpersonal violence every year, she'd never been assaulter or assaultee. But her fists seemed tailor-made for the job. Leaping to her feet, she pummeled his chest and shoulders, and would have gladly rearranged his nose if he hadn't shielded his face with his forearms.

"Where...were...you when..." she snarled. Then her voice choked as she landed one more blow. "Where were you?"

Grayson caught her from behind and even in her feral state she recognized this as a basket hold. He crisscrossed her arms over her chest and held on tight until she surrendered, hanging over his arms like a shawl. Regret surged through her, replacing anger with dismay.

This isn't normal. Borderline at best, heavy on the impulsivity and mood swings.

But resorting to physical abuse was a new low, and certain to show up in the court record. Maybe she could arrange for an intervention, or just take herself directly to electroshock. She wanted to howl, but that wouldn't make her less dead.

"I told you it would end badly. Now will you take me home?"

CHAPTER 26

"You're losin' it, girl," Frances muttered, throwing back the covers.

Morning was never her prime time. In truth, her salutation to the dawn often included a string of curses as she hung over the coffee pot like a gargoyle, waiting for it to dribble out the first fix of the day. But this morning slammed her with a wave of shame as she considered her behavior at the Dawn Treaders.

I guess they won't be coming to my rescue.

She hoped to hell that her lapse into *non-compos mentis* was an aberration, but the mounting evidence seemed to suggest that she wasn't adjusting well. Of course, she'd have to apologize profusely, never one of her strengths. But right now, it seemed like her best bet was compliance with a capital C. Just get to class and shut the fuck up, when all she really wanted to do was prowl the labyrinth in search of more graffiti.

The day was already shaping up to be an exercise in patience—also not a strength—when she consulted her class schedule. "*Letting Go*? More bad news." She didn't know when she'd be able to face Grayson again, so the sight of Gabe idling on her doorstep was a relief. "Just don't say anything, please," she begged, certain that word of the attempted assault and battery had spread like wild fire.

Letting Go had already left the starting gate when she

arrived. Ten desks were arranged in a half circle facing the instructor who was lounging in a large red hammock. He was in mid-sentence... "things that happened in the past that you haven't let go of still affect you, limiting your potential and stealing your happiness. This morning we're going to give that unfinished business Priority Cleanup Status. So, let's..." He paused. "Welcome, Frances. I'm Craig."

She nodded silently as she slid into a seat, determined to go through the motions and double-think before she uttered a single word.

"Now, where was I? Ah, yes, we're going to get rid of that baggage."

What a load of crap! she thought. *Just like that, Magic Man is going to eliminate traumas and neuroses that have achieved the status of a personal religion. All in one session? You'd have to be a damn wizard!*

Then she cringed, recalling that she'd made similar promises to scores of fans, though never from a hammock. She, of all people, knew how hard it was to denounce your useless, unhealthy, irrelevant, outdated, or possibly delusional beliefs. And when you did, you felt like a traitor at the McCarthy hearings, testifying against yourself.

How could you abandon the guilt, fear and shame that had shaped your behavior, even your world view, for decades? Wasn't that an admission that you'd been wrong? That you could've lived a happier, more successful life if only you'd had your head screwed on straight? No wonder success in therapy often produced a vague sense of private failure. Therapy graduates could probably pass for sane, except at family gatherings, but where was that deep interior peace, the promised joy of liberation?

I wonder if things work differently here in the afterlife. Frances took a deep breath. *Maybe I should give it a try.* Another one of her well-worn motivational quotes came back to bite her in the ass: "Whether you think you can, or you think you can't, you're right." When she checked back in, Craig was dispensing instructions to an apprehensive circle of faces.

"When I say *letting go*, I want you to write down the first word that comes to mind." Everyone in the room dutifully reached for the pen and blank cards on their desks. This was clearly the lightning round because Craig was back within seconds. "Now let's go around and share."

Frances loathed sharing. *Honestly, who could be authentic on demand and in a room full of strangers?* But she tried not to leak those tiny fuming sounds that broadcast her disgust as one by one, the students read out their words: *freedom, falling, release.* Then the buck stopped at Frances. She held up the card on which she'd scribbled *UV?*

Craig gave her a puzzled look. "Frances?"

"*Of.* Letting go...*of what*?"

"Perfect segue! Now we're getting somewhere. Thank you, Frances," and he bounded out of the hammock.

"No problem," she muttered, managing a fleeting grimace as Craig continued. "We all harbor intense residue from bad experiences that burdens us with anxiety and saps the energy we need to move on. Well, time's up!"

Again, the image of a game show host came to mind.

"You deserve to let go. And here's how we get the job done." He reached into a box under his desk and began firing rolls of toilet paper at the students. Several ducked, while others laughed nervously.

Is he kidding?

Frances hadn't seen this trick before, but immediately wondered if she could steal it for one of her talks. Obviously, it would need a bit of tailoring since she didn't have the time or the pitching arm for five-hundred deliveries. But a half-dozen strategically aimed were sure to make an impact on the crowd. *Definitely has potential.* She caught herself in mid-thought. *Right, I don't do that anymore.*

Craig's voice broke in. "Those were shitty experiences and we all know the way to get rid of shit," he announced. "Dig out that old pain, grief, humiliation, disappointment or doubt that has you in its thrall. Name it, then write it where it belongs— on toilet paper." Suddenly, Craig's cheerleading was deeply at odds with the air in the room, which felt heavy and damp, but also alive with an undercurrent of electricity like the moments before a rainstorm. Posture slumped, breathing slowed as people were thrust into the dark recesses of the past without so much as a flashlight or safety vest.

Frances watched in horror as one student started to tremble, like a seizure was in the offing, while another put her head on her desk and sobbed. Her first instinct was to leap up and comfort her fellow students, or at least pass out paper bags for the hyperventilators. Second was to shake Craig until his molars rattled, but last night's fiasco stopped her in her tracks.

When she looked back at Craig, he was staring at her pristine roll. "Time's up. Enough procrastinating."

She pulled the top off her fat blue marking pen and shocked herself as she scrawled *BROKE*. The word sat and stared at her like a lab specimen on a glass slide, waiting for intense scrutiny. As she stared back, the round edges of the B started to dissolve and bloom like a mold creeping up on the R. More blooming as tears bounced off her hand and dimpled the tissue. She blinked hard to clear her eyes, just in time to see her hand perform what seemed like a cross between automatic writing and demonic possession. In quick succession, square after square was tattooed with its own word:

Disabled
Maimed
Sidelined
Laid-up
Fractured

Damaged

She watched in helpless fascination as the pen really took to the task, each new word digging deeper into what seemed like a bottomless well of sorrow.

Wounded

Concussed

Out of commission

Crippled

Amputee

Bro

ken

Heartbroken.

Meanwhile Craig circulated and nodded, monitoring progress. When the writing had subsided, he said, "Now on the count of three, I want you to read your thoughts out loud—all of you at once. One, two, three!"

The room reverberated with the low rumble of confessions.

"My father left when I was twelve. Never heard from him again. I thought it was my fault."

Another said, "I never cried when my mother died."

Another: "I feel worthless so how can anyone love me?"

Long after the chorus of laments died down, Frances was still reciting her *a capella* epiphany. *Heartbroken* emerged barely above a whisper.

Craig switched back to cheerleading mode. "Time to say goodbye to all that shit." He herded them to a bathroom identical to the portal where Frances had made her entry. One by one, the students dumped their paper into the toilet as Craig vigorously flushed and joined them in shouting, "Good-bye!"

When it was her turn, she balled up the tissue that trailed behind her like the tail of a kite and squeezed until it was the size of a ping pong ball, oozing pale blue tears. Then she dropped it in the toilet and whispered "Good-bye." Taking that as her cue, she stumbled outside and stood for several minutes, trying to pull herself together. Then she remembered her goal for the day: locate the second cluster of graffiti.

But that was easier said than done. She took several stabs, choosing one identical alley after another without any luck. *Letting Go* had put such a dent in her energy that she stopped and slumped against a plain gray wall. But when she looked up there was a familiar sight. A deformed manicule with five fingers and no thumb that she'd noticed yesterday during Grayson's forced march to the gym. She was close!

Five more minutes and the red chalk line appeared, etched into the plaster near a corner. She hunched over like a miner entering a shaft, determined not to miss the faint yellow letters. There they were, just three words.

Don't Think...Feel.

A golden oldie! Neil Diamond's song had topped the charts in 1976, when people still listened to the radio, experiencing the latest music served up by flesh and blood DJs. Millions of people heard the same song, at the same time, instead of a soundtrack tailored to every waking moment of their existence, delivered through small bits of plastic shoved in their ears.

Don't think, feel. It wasn't exactly her anthem—then or now. She thought about her staunch reliance on brain power to help her navigate the tricky world of emotions. All her life she'd avoided the heights of ecstasy because she dreaded the inevitable depression that followed. She'd refused to trust the sloppy lies that unbridled feelings told before vanishing. But she pulled out her red chalk and wrote: *I'll try.*

Then she slumped forward and rested her head against the rough wall, the bite of the plaster suggesting that there was more pain to come. Did she, in fact, have the courage to feel? Slowly, methodically she banged her forehead on the wall.

"I'll try, I'll try."

CHAPTER 27

Cornelius sat at the table in the deserted Committee room, surrounded by black and white photos and a thick sheaf of paper that had clearly been riffled and discarded. He dragged his fingers through his hair as he trained his gaze on a small brown envelope marked Personal Effects/Frances Beacon. After stealing a glance at the door, he unwound the red string around the button that held it shut and tipped the contents out. A stack of items the size of a deck of cards slid onto the table and he pounced, hunching over like a poker player trying to hide his hand. After a quick check of his pocket watch, he removed the yellow ribbon holding the collection together and began his investigation. A New York City public library card. Another library card. And another. He threw them to one side in disgust.

Returning to the pile, he glanced at an MTA transit pass, a bookmark from Madison Books, two credit cards and a plastic hotel key wrapped in a receipt. Quietly fuming, he raced through the remaining artifacts—coupons, movie tickets, half of a cardboard nail file, thirty-nine dollars in cash, a twenty centimes coin from pre-Euro days and a customer appreciation card for Suddenly Salad—discarding each like a Vegas dealer.

The last two relics were a pristine business card with Charles Beacon, Architect, written in elegant script and a fortune from a cookie that read: *A beautiful, smart and loving person will be coming into your life.*

"That's it?" He gazed at the meaningless pile of mementos in frustration, then swept them aside and grabbed the envelope again. Turning it completely upside down, he caught his breath as a photo of Frances and Mac slid onto the table. They were bundled up in coats and gloves with the bare trees of Central Park silhouetted behind them. He snatched it up for closer inspection but his hand began to tremble so he placed it gently on the table, lowered his head and stared.

Just then the door rattled and the sound of muffled voices jerked him to attention. He scooped up the meager souvenirs of Frances Beacon's life and shoved them in the envelope, then piled the photos and papers on top, creating the impression that he'd been hard at work studying the case. Finally, he tucked the photo inside his waistcoat and smoothed his rumpled hair.

As the Committee members entered in twos and threes, it was clear they'd spent the break getting to know each other. Gerard and Gwilym were deep in conversation about the most reliable strains of barley and oats. Olympe's hand was threaded through the mute's arm and he hung on every word as she said, "In my day, Parisians sat in the cafes for hours, drinking coffee. It was quite new. All the rage. But the real excitement was the talk of revolution. It was an amazing time to be alive." The toddler napped on Perpetua's shoulder and Andreas trailed behind the others, nursing a smoke.

Cornelius levered himself out of his chair as if heavily burdened. Wobbling for a moment, he put both hands on the table to steady himself and drew in a deep breath. Before the group had even settled in their seats, he ordered the Fool to turn on the monitor. "Let's get on with this." Then he dropped his chin and mumbled, "It's taking far too long."

On screen Frances was hunched over in a gray passageway, head pressed against a gritty wall repeating, "I'll try. I'll try."

Galvanized by the scene, Cornelius pulled himself up to his

full height. "Head banging!" he said, clearly incredulous. "What good can that possibly do?"

"It's the nature of coming to terms with something," said the yogi.

"That's right. Recovery isn't linear," said a whiskered old man. "But all progress is progress."

"Is that supposed to mean something or just sound clever?" Cornelius snapped. "One of those slogans designed to fuel unreasonable optimism among those less fortunate than yourself?"

"I simply meant—"

"I haven't the slightest interest in what you meant." He spun away from the old man and directed his assessment to the entire group. "All I see in Frances is avoidance and backward steps."

"If you'll allow me, Sire," the Fool said. "A wise woman once said that no matter where you are, no matter what you did, no matter where you've come from, you can always change, become a better version of yourself."

"And that woman was...?" Cornelius feigned curiosity but couldn't disguise the mockery in his voice.

"Madonna, Sire."

"Oh, please!" he exploded. "Let's keep religion out of this!" He braced his hands on his hips, as if prepared to do battle. "The last thing we need is an excursion into the irrational."

Perpetua leapt up, determined to protest this slur against believers but the Fool cut her off. "No, Sire. She's a singer."

"Even worse!" he scoffed. He pinched the skin on the bridge of his nose and shook his head.

"Net worth, $850 million and counting." The Fool couldn't suppress a smile as gasps of admiration animated the Committee.

Cornelius was dumbstruck. "Millions? For *singing*?" He dropped into a chair and his eyes roamed around the ceiling like he was trying to picture such a fortune. After a long pause he added in a wistful tone, "I knew a singer once."

The Fool sidled up behind Cornelius, bent down and whispered in his ear, "The show must go on, Sire." Cornelius jerked back to the present. Scanning the puzzled faces around the table, he realized that the meeting was in complete disarray. "I'll try," he moaned. "I'll try."

CHAPTER 28

Fresh from a stealth visit to Strong Silent, Frances slipped into the gym, reeking of Antoinette's rocket fuel. Coffee was the new smoking and she was determined to escape detection. True, she'd yet to spot a breathalyzer or drug dog, but any staff person with a decent sniffer could tell she'd been indulging. The last thing she needed was another black mark in her book. Caffeine was probably a misdemeanor but coupled with the assault, her upcoming day in court was not looking good.

The coast was clear so she jumped on the rowing machine, certain that a half-dozen sets would put a dent in her jittery high. Eyes closed. *One, two. One, two.*

"You're good." Charlie was standing over her.

She was startled but instinctively clenched her fists above her head, assuming the classic strongman pose. "Fifteen years, five days a week. No trainers."

"Like I said, you're good at the physical part. But you know..."

Why do they always start with "you know" and then carry on as if you don't? Any minute now he'll launch into a monologue designed to help me understand how workouts work.

Her mind flashed back to a gym encounter in her pre-obit days that only amped her annoyance. She'd just started her set on the biceps machine when she was approached by a man whose physique suggested either excessive beer consumption

155

or an extraordinary scientific breakthrough. The first male to successfully reach his third trimester!

"Do you want some advice?" the human balloon had asked.

Since she'd rigorously eschewed professional coaching, why would she be interested in amateur hour, particularly with a professional glutton? But she'd declined with a polite, "No, thank you," and then watched in fascination as he'd pressed on, blissfully ignoring her disinterest.

"Move your hand a little to the left and do it slower," he said.

She couldn't help herself. She'd burst out laughing.

"What?" He'd bristled as if she'd taken a swipe at his manhood.

"I can't tell you how many times I've made that same suggestion." Then with a sly you-know-what-I-mean smile she added, "It rarely worked."

Charlie waited while Frances was mentally AWOL. When she snapped out of her reverie, wearing a slight grin, he asked, "What?"

"What?" she echoed. Her voice was the audible equivalent of batting her eyelashes. All innocence. *Must curb display of attitude. Fly under the radar or you'll never get rid of him,* the voice in her head warned. Then she noticed that his lips were moving again. *Better tune in.*

"Ever heard of mental gymnastics?" he asked.

She wasn't sure if it was the twang from the caffeine or the sheer preposterousness of his remark, but a wave of rancor nearly knocked her off the machine. Poor Charlie had ripped the lid off an archive of affronts she'd collected over the years, all sorted, catalogued and freeze-dried but instantly reconstituted, fresh as the day they were delivered.

If he starts preaching to me about mental gymnastics, I swear I'll take a kettlebell to his cranium. How does he think women have managed all these millennia?

And then the safety was off the trigger. The broadcast went live. "When it comes to mental gymnastics, Charlie, women are gold medalists in every event. Shape-shifting to seem helpless when they can bench press a Harley hog. Launching stealth ideas into meetings so any male with a room-temperature IQ can pick up the scent and claim owner-ship. Listening for the hundredth time to a man whine about how unfair life is. Feigning interest in March Madness! Faking orgasms! Is it any wonder when feminists finally drop their masks, they're ready to pick up a gun? Fuck!"

Frances had no idea how long she'd been raving but Charlie looked like he'd been standing in a stiff wind. In no mood to back down, she stared right back and barked, "What?"

"Can I ask you something?" His voice was surprisingly calm, concern mingled with curiosity. She managed a slight nod. "Did you have a bad experience with a trainer? Someone drop a weight on your toe or make fun of your jiggle?"

Her defenses collapsed. "No. It's me. I was never great with new relationships. So, I figured I'd just work on the most important one I already had—with my body. After all, without it I'd be out of luck. No ice skating at Rockefeller Center, no yoga, and no sex if this poor *corpus* gave out. I didn't need a stranger's help to grasp that."

"I'm impressed," Charlie said. "Lots of people never make that connection. But I'm talking about a different kind of workout. Maybe we could just go in and take a look?" he offered cautiously. "You might find it interesting." Then he quickly put some distance between himself and the human hand grenade.

She followed him into a space that bore exactly no resemblance to her local sweat emporium. It had a wide center aisle like the midway at a county fair. The rows of husky exercise machines had been replaced with booths on either side and the whole space had a lively air. Death had never looked so festive.

She spied a booth flying the French flag and drifted over for a closer look. A smartly-dressed woman waved her into a small enclosure like a mini-bistro complete with a classic rattan chair and a table set with a row of sparkling glasses, ready for a wine tasting. "Please, sit, madam."

Frances was already savoring the idea of a waiter displaying a bottle of *Beaujolais* for her approval when...*whoosh!* She looked up just in time to see a holographic face flying toward her like an onrushing car the moment before a head-on collision. Instinctively, she ducked and glasses flew. From her foxhole below the table, she could just make out a sign high above the booth: *Le Bureau des Provocateurs.* "Are you kidding me?"

She sat up cautiously and found herself staring directly into the face of her least favorite relative. A loud-mouthed miser whose man-breasts crept closer to his belt with every passing year. Ill-mannered and socially repellant, nonetheless he'd claimed the role of family patriarch after her father died. In fact, he was the family disgrace. Every holiday he'd arrive empty-handed and at least an hour late, but somehow, he managed to give the impression that his entrance was the signal that the party could officially begin.

After a perfunctory "Hello" he'd knock back a tumbler of wine and then begin to decant his usual tirade. "Just because the Supreme Court rules on something doesn't mean it's constitutional." All the while he shoveled in hors d'oeuvres with never a grunt of acknowledgment for the undeserved hospitality. With his mouth half-full, he'd spew bits of food and declarative sentences. "There is no global warming. Marijuana is the only vegetable that's bad for you." He pontificated shamelessly, as if speaking *ex cathedra* or addressing a room full of morons.

Inevitably he'd place himself at the head of the table. Then the moral-bankrupt would insist on saying grace before broadcasting his brand of lunacy from entrée to dessert. "The

Great Flood was an example of climate change. Try to blame that on fossil fuels. And could you pass the gravy?" For the big finish he'd announce a government conspiracy to buy up all the guns while Frances silently longed for a single bullet with his name on it. But she was raised on the importance of good manners which included being polite even when subjected to a level of rudeness so extreme that it could qualify for a scientific study. In her family you would simply blink in disbelief at the gross violation of social norms, and then out of earshot vent and fume, honing your imitation of the offender with each telling. But never to the person's face. Thus, year after year her holiday was ruined.

Now she recoiled. Anger and humiliation ripped through her like shrapnel. She narrowed her eyes in the direction of the attendant. "Thanks for the memories." A bit of glass ground audibly under her foot as she pivoted toward the exit.

Charlie put a hand on her arm. "Sit down, Frances."

"I don't like this game."

"You will once you learn the rules."

She slumped into the chair and folded her arms stoically. *What does it matter anyway? The only real family is the one you choose.* "What am I supposed to do?"

The attendant calmly explained. "You move the face telepathically. Agitation and it flies toward you. Calm yourself and it stands still. Indifference, it recedes."

Frances knew this technique. It was called Least Reinforcing Scenario, a strategy taken from animal trainers and at least one marriage manual. The theory behind LRS was that provocateurs live for the reaction—any reaction—as long as they capture your attention. But if you ignore them, stoutly, resolutely, with every fiber of your being, the behavior will fade away. The challenge was doing it without shoving your fist in your mouth up to the second knuckle or inducing a cerebral hemorrhage. It was all about self-management.

"How about if you just give me a gun and I'll blow him to

kingdom come? Or is he already here?"

"Why not give this a try?" The attendant patiently continued her pitch. "Say nothing, do nothing, display no facial expression. Imagine you're an appliance that's been suddenly unplugged."

"Got any suggestions? Crock pot? Nose-hair trimmer?"

"That's your call, madam." She waited patiently while Frances drummed her fingers on the table. "Ready?"

Frances tensed as the face was released and flew toward her like an arrow. She took a deep breath and pictured the ocean. The face downshifted into slow-motion. In her head she heard a seagull cry over the crash of the waves. Now the face crept like a reluctant tortoise on a mission to deliver bad news.

"That's the idea, Frances."

The comment broke her concentration and before she could recover, a booming voice proclaimed, "Same-sex marriage will lead to love affairs between men and animals. Pretty soon people will want to marry their golf carts."

She felt the blood rush to her head. Her carotid artery throbbed visibly as the ugly uncle resumed his jet-propelled collision course toward her forehead.

"Unplug! Unplug!" coached the attendant.

Frances focused. She pictured the tornado of her emotions colliding in a coffee grinder, bruising every nerve in her body. Then she yanked the plug.

Silence. Tranquility.

The face receded to a pinpoint and for the first time she could see him for what he truly was, a hollowed-out disappointment of a man inflating himself with second-hand vitriol to avoid utter collapse. A self-styled disaster. His menacing presence was now as flat and harmless as a movie poster, a movie she had no interest in seeing.

"Well done, Frances," said Charlie.

"Somehow I don't think congratulations are in order. Do you have any idea how many years I was consumed with dreading his arrival and then nurturing a fresh helping of anger for months afterward? And it never made a damn bit of difference. I was taking poison and waiting for him to die. What a colossal waste!"

She retrieved an unbroken glass from under the table. "God, I need a drink."

CHAPTER 29

"Grayson, I thought I spotted someone from..." Frances gestured over her shoulder with her thumb as they took up their posts at the bar.

"Your past?"

"Uh-huh." Her voice was dull and uninflected from the effort to sound casual, but it seemed to have the opposite effect as Grayson's face lit up.

"Really? Tell me more."

She immediately scrambled for an escape route. "You know what? It's probably better to let sleeping dogs lie."

"How many sleepers are we talking about here?" His voice had a teasing quality that bordered on sexy.

"On second thought..." Again, she tried to pull the emergency brake on the conversation but he was already on his feet.

"If you're in the mood for a little snoop around the past, I know just the place."

Within minutes, he'd ushered her into the Records Room. Barricaded behind a desk was a sweet-faced girl barely visible for all the folders stacked in teetering piles around her. The walls were jammed floor to ceiling with thousands of folders like a doctor's office before computerized record keeping. But the clerk seemed blissfully free of the grudging, downtrodden demeanor typical of people on the lowest level of the office food chain. Instead of the thinly veiled hostility that promised resistance no matter how simple your request, she sprang from her chair with a cheery "Hello, Grayson. Good to see you."

"It's great to see you, Miss Molly." He patted her hand and asked, "How are you?"

"I'm well, all things considered." She swept her hand across the vista of files covering every surface. "How can I help?"

He took the green paper sign from his pocket and slid it across the counter. "New arrival."

She glanced at the name and handed the paper back. "And how can I help you, Ms. Beacon?"

Frances hesitated and considered making a dash for the door. Voyeurism could be dangerous. She knew who she was looking for but what did she expect to happen after that? Her cheeks flushed at the thought of Graham and she grabbed the green sign, fanning herself furiously.

"Are you okay?" Molly asked.

"Damn menopause," she joked, grateful for the convenient lie.

Grayson gave her a quizzical look. "Well?"

"Right. Sorry. Is there any way to check on people who are, uh, I don't know? Currently enrolled? Just wondering if there's anyone I might know."

"Actually, we have rather strict confidentiality rules."

Frances felt instantly admonished. She who'd guarded thousands of people's secrets, from adoption to incarceration, had crossed the line. "Right, of course, HIPAA privacy and all that. Sorry."

"But if you're interested in your own past," Molly offered.

"How *past* are we talking because, well, there are a few bits I'd rather not revisit?"

"That's up to you."

Frances shifted her gaze from Molly to Grayson, playing

who-do-you-trust in her head. Curiosity trumped caution. "Well, why not?"

"If you'll just follow me." Molly led her down a hall to a door marked *Akashic Records.*

Frances shot Grayson a look, her face radiating skepticism. "Sounds like a Motown outfit."

"More like a library. Right up your alley." He escorted her to a row of cubicles that reminded her of the booths where inmates met their families for supervised conversations. Each space had a table and chair but was surrounded by transparent walls so the whole room could be seen at a glance.

Molly returned clutching a file the size of the Manhattan phone book, its edge festooned with dozens of tabs bearing initials. Frances pulled Grayson aside. "She's got the Welcome Wagon part of the job nailed, but you should probably tune up her office skills."

He shot her a confused expression.

"That can't be mine," she said, gesturing with her head toward the file. "I led a very dull life. Looks more like Edward Snowden's."

"You've been here before," he said.

"Meaning?"

"You know. Other lives."

She tugged the file toward her and zeroed in on a tab labeled with a double S. "SS? SS as in Nazis? I was a *Nazi*?!" She was practically screaming.

Grayson put a hand on her shoulder. "Get a grip. You weren't a Nazi. Far from it."

She folded her arms protectively over the file. "I think I'd like some privacy."

Grayson shrugged. "No problem."

"I didn't mean you. I meant...them." She jerked her head toward the empty booths around her. "What if other people come?"

"People will come, Frances." The distinctive bass voice of

164

James Earl Jones rumbled out of Grayson's mouth. "People will most definitely come."

"I loved that movie. When his dad showed up. God, that was perfect."

"Well, I can't promise there's a Field of Dreams in here," he said, giving her file a pat, "but it should be an adventure."

Frances wanted to believe that she'd been an upstanding person, or persons, consistently doing her bit for the welfare of the human race. Maybe not Mother-Teresa-good but surely no headline-grabbing offenses. Still, there was no telling what the file squatting in front of her held. Maybe all her present sorrows weren't unfair after all, but simply karmic payback for villainous deeds in the past.

Who knows what I was capable of? Lust, gluttony, greed, sloth, anger, envy, pride. The old list from Sunday school popped into her head. Possibly something more spectacular. *Murder, betrayal, exploitation.* Now she was just procrastinating, an exasperating habit she'd never fully vanquished.

There's only one way to find out.

CHAPTER 30

Frances stared at the SS tab, still gripped by the fear that she'd been part of Hitler's death machine. So, she flipped to the back of the file which was organized like a ledger with columns for dates, locations and relevant details.

Oh, my god! This is me?

She scanned the pages, fascinated by the brevity and anonymity of her many appearances on earth. She'd been a beekeeper in ancient Rome, a fisherman off the coast of Normandy, a jailer, a nun, an Ashanti weaver, a cobbler, a rice farmer in China, and an infant who died within two days of her birth.

She touched her finger to a line with the word *scribe* and jumped as a figure appeared just beyond the glass in front of her, conjured up out of thin air. Art history 101 covered the ancient world so she recognized that he was Egyptian and probably plied his trade several thousand years before Christ. His soft, pudgy body was seated cross-legged on a pillow and both hands rested in his lap next to the tools of his trade. A writing palette, papyrus scroll, and reed brush.

His face was alert and attentive, gazing at Frances as though waiting for her to dictate a letter or bill of sale, but she was too stunned to speak. Since his job was to listen, they simply stared at one another until her hand slipped off the page and he vanished.

She slumped back and exhaled loudly, realizing that she'd been holding her breath. She'd always said she believed in reincarnation, not on religious grounds but because it was the only rational explanation for those irrational events that left her shaking her head in wonder. What else explained her feeling that Paris wasn't a foreign capital but her real home, the only place where she truly belonged? Or walking into a strange room and recognizing every stick of furniture? Or that thunderstruck condition called love-at-first-sight that actually felt like a long-awaited reunion? She even had a secret fantasy about finding the graves of her former selves and leaving flowers. Now here was her hypothesis made flesh.

She surveyed all the tabs, touched one with the letter P and watched as a scene appeared beyond the glass. The space was dark and cavernous with walls of carved limestone and the sound of water echoing throughout as if a stream ran below the floor. As her eyes grew accustomed to the gloom, she peered into the depths and spied a cluster of veiled women in the deepest corner of the grotto. Then her nose caught the smell of ethylene and she knew without a doubt that she was in the presence of an oracle.

Frances had a whole apartment in her brain stuffed full of esoteric trivia, like the Oracle of Delphi in ancient Greece. Thus, she knew that for over twelve centuries a series of women, all called Pythia, dwelt in the temple of Apollo advising leaders, philosophers and commoners on everything from political intrigues to personal hygiene.

Of course, no photographs of the Oracle existed but the surviving accounts indicated that they were beautiful young virgins. Most paintings showed slender creatures, moon pale and swooning. They were seated on a tripod stool and lubricated their epiphanies with the sacred vapors that seeped through a crevice in the stones.

But oracles were no laughing matter. Those ladies predicted wars, famine and destruction, so there was a definite don't-fuck-with-her aura that still clung to the institution, though officially they'd been out of business since 86 BC.

Frances knew just enough to know that she didn't know what to do next. Bow or genuflect? Madame Oracle or Ms. Pythia? Gape in awe or risk a request? As she weighed her options, a swath of yellow caught her eye. The center of the room was dominated by a figure so incongruous that she couldn't have been more surprised if she'd stumbled upon a vintage jukebox or a power lawn mower.

This oracle took impressive to the power of ten. Swathed in yards of brilliant lemon-colored silk, her rich mahogany face was topped with dozens of braids in elaborate patterns, and golden spangles the size of a fist hung from her earlobes. She may have been seated on a tripod—it was impossible to tell. But it would have to be titanium because this Pythia was a colossus. Her arms didn't fall straight from her shoulders— they couldn't—but rested at a forty-five-degree angle, propped on her capacious hips. Her legs were splayed out in front with tiny feet overflowing her red patent leather shoes like freshly baked bread and her ample breasts flowed like lava, obliterating her waist.

The woman was as radiant as a sunflower and broadcast *Diva* at full volume. When she saw Frances, she laughed and raised her right arm like a priest elevating a host. Her chubby fingers clutched a hamburger that dwarfed her hand.

All Frances could think was *Look at her! Three-hundred pounds if she's an ounce. Keep eating like that and you'll be knocking on heaven's door in no time.* But her interior scold was cut short by a joyful noise.

"Hello, darlin'," the oracle called.

In times past, the lines of people hoping for an audience with the oracle were epic. Many supplicants were turned away repeatedly, waiting years for an audience unless money, political pull or both helped them jump the line. But Frances seemed to have the oracle all to herself.

"Where is everyone? I thought there'd be a mob."

"You caught me during my dinner break. A girl's gotta eat."

Instead of being awed, Frances felt an immediate kinship. *This poor woman sits here all day, in moderately dreary digs listening to a parade of supplicants seeking guidance, intervention or hope.* She flashed on her office at the New York City Mental Health unit, which always had an unending line of people seeking guidance, intervention or hope. The bone-weariness of it all came back in a rush. The oracle would have fit right in.

"How are you?" Frances asked with a tone of genuine compassion.

"Thanks for asking. Some days are better than others. Right now, my back's a misery. Stuck on this stool for hours. It's killing me."

"You know sitting is the new smoking."

"I never smoke. Just inhale. It helps."

"I felt the same way about wine."

"Well, New York City. Who wouldn't drink?"

Frances leaned closer. "Do you ever get tired of the job? Just leave-me-the-hell-alone exhausted?" Somehow Frances felt comfortable making this confession to a total stranger.

"Well, you know. Not so many career choices for women. Even the talented ones. You take what you can. Hopefully, it has some value." She took a serious chunk out of her burger and chewed contentedly.

"Right. Of course." Frances shook her head in wonder. "You must have seen it all, the flotsam and jetsam of humanity."

"Tell me about it." Then they both fell silent, listening to the gurgle of the water carrying away secrets and prayers, simply enjoying the peace of each other's company.

Eventually the oracle continued her assessment of the human race. "They're a mixed bag really. Some are good-hearted and sincere. Really trying to do the right thing. Lycurgus used my counsel well, building a democracy in Sparta that treated all men with respect. Others are irresponsible and selfish in equal measures. On the whole, when I look at humanity, I see perpetual dissatisfaction and pure adolescent cravings, even among the gray beards."

"That sounds about right. But what exactly do they want?"

"Solutions. After all, I'm the divine fixer. You wouldn't believe the problems they bring! Anything from empty coffers to a limp dick." She nibbled the edge of the burger and chuckled. "One of them even asked me for real estate advice. He couldn't decide between Corinth and Thebes. I told him "Honey, I live in a *cave*. How the hell would I know?"

"All part of life's colorful pageant?" said Frances, mentally reviewing her clients and marveling at how little humanity had changed.

"I wish it was that simple but the leaders really worry me. They show up, all gifts and supplication, swearing they'll do anything the Oracle commands. I tell them: Make love, not war. It sounds straightforward but they're constantly twisting the interpretation to get my blessing for carnage on a grand scale."

"Yes, we're good at that, despite the endless misery," Frances agreed.

"I tried to convince them that the most powerful secret was to know thyself. In fact, it was carved in stone at the entrance to my temple so they couldn't miss it, but I don't know if that ever caught on."

"I tried to sell that idea, too, but the closest some of them came to self-reflection was their latest posting on Facebook." The two women shook their heads and sighed.

"But tell me, Frances Beacon, what can I do for you?" The oracle gave her a motherly smile, so filled with kindness and compassion that Frances wanted to climb into those sturdy arms, bury her face in the folds of yellow silk and weep like a child. But she held back. "No. You don't need to hear my troubles."

"No trouble. Sisters gotta stick together." Again, the voice was like a soothing balm seeping into every wound and worry that she possessed.

"Well." She broke down and her words tumbled out in a torrent of ugly adjectives. "I'm a mess. Hostile, contradictory, at odds with everyone, even myself. And I feel so useless."

The oracle shook her head. "Honey, you been useful your whole life and what'd it get you? Take it from me, there's more to life than work. Red wine. Goat cheese drizzled with honey. Newborn bread still warm from the oven. Now there's a mouth full of joy." The oracle gave Frances a long look. "How 'bout you try bein' happy?"

A bell sounded somewhere inside the cavern and the oracle shifted. "Five minutes to curtain. Gotta finish up here."

Frances was instantly bereft. She wanted to wrap herself in the yellow folds and stay forever but was flooded with a wave of guilt. They'd talked all through the oracle's break, her only chance to be alone and quiet. What could she offer as a token of gratitude to a woman who sat at the center of the world, routinely accepting gifts of silver and gold? Her only possession was her phone, so she held it out, R U there? shining in the darkness.

"No, baby, you keep that. You'll need it."

The acolytes closed in as Frances took a last glance at the oracle, gulping second-hand fumes and a first-class burger. There was richness and truth in that burger and she realized with a stab of regret what she'd denied herself in the past—the pure pleasure of eating. No sausage pizza. No chocolate croissants. Definitely no burgers. Years of small daily deprivations had robbed her of the ability to gobble and gulp and stuff without the specter of a confessional hovering on the horizon.

When was the last time I ate Cherry Garcia straight out of the carton? All she could remember was an endless parade of salads. And what did it get her? There would be no prize for her sacrifices, and the jolt of that epiphany unleashed an overwhelming salivary impulse to cry out *Gimme one with everything. Next time,* she vowed, and began mentally compiling the menu for her first next meal.

But would there be a next time?

Right now, she felt like a rat in a maze. The temple bell rang once more, and she bowed to the sunflower woman who was so wide and so wise. As the scene faded, Frances heard the oracle whisper, "Courage."

That seems to be in short supply.

CHAPTER 31

Just then there was a rustling outside the door. Grayson hadn't mentioned a time limit on time travel, but just in case, Frances decided to pick up the pace. The dreaded SS tab glowed like neon. *Do one thing every day that scares you.* Wasn't that Eleanor Roosevelt's advice?

"Courage." She grazed the SS tab and a gentleman with long white hair and a full crop of whiskers came striding into the view.

"My God! Samuel Smiles!" She strained forward to get a closer look into the bright eyes of her hero and go-to inspiration when her spirits were low. But Smiles was too busy to notice her as he plunged into a restless crowd of shop keepers, railway men, fishmongers and journalists. They were all exchanging greetings or embroiled in heated debates while an assistant stationed at the back of the room did a brisk business in book sales. The air was thick with the smell of damp wool and anticipation, so the moment Smiles took the podium, the crowd settled down, eager for a dose of his compelling message delivered with unflagging enthusiasm.

"My dear friends, it is not eminent talent that is required to ensure success in any pursuit, so much as purpose and the will to labor energetically and perseveringly."

The son of a grocer, Smiles had trained as a medical doctor, then worked as a newspaper editor and railroad developer all the while writing on the side. In 1859, when several publishing houses rejected his manuscript for *Self-Help,* he found a printer, self-published, and had a huge hit on his hands. The book was an international best-seller, turning him into the nineteenth century equivalent of a literary superstar and Victorian life coach. In many homes *Self-Help* had a status second only to the bible, and when he died, his funeral cortege rivaled that of Queen Victoria.

His message was simple. Even those at the bottom of the social ladder should be able to improve themselves through self-education, tenacity, industry and endurance. "If you want to achieve anything worthwhile, it's up to you. Work, work, work."

Frances studied the weary faces in the audience, momentarily transformed by hope, awakened to their own potential and galvanized by their desire to succeed. And she was seized with the kind of longing that a mother feels for a child who's been taken by death.

Smiles was wrapping up now. "Remember this and believe me, for I know it to be true from my own experience. Life will always be to a large extent what we ourselves make of it. Lost wealth may be replaced by industry, lost knowledge by study, lost health by temperance or medicine, but lost time is gone forever."

Watching Smiles brimming with adrenaline, consumed in his work, Frances couldn't quell her yearning for all that he enjoyed—human contact, dynamism, intense purpose, and the certainty of making a difference. Everything she'd lost. But it was more than that. She was jealous! Of the crowd, the applause, the fucking fandom lavished on Smiles while she was banging around the Bardo, anonymous and useless.

"It's not fair!" She slammed the book shut. "I was cheated! I never got to finish."

She hunched over the table, with her arms wrapped

around her file like an insomniac hugging a pillow. Then she let out a muffled sob.

Molly touched her shoulder. "Frances?"

No response. Frances clutched her file even harder, feeling lonely and bereft. If this was her past, then clearly, she was devolving.

Who knows how far I might fall?

CHAPTER 32

"Wow! Worse than a Nazi?" Grayson asked as Molly hurried him in to revive Frances.

She lifted her head and wiped her face on her sleeve. "No. It's not that." She blew out a long breath. "I miss my life. I miss the Earth."

"No worries," he said. "Follow me." He led her to an unmarked door and up a staircase into a small room with an oculus like a giant port hole in the ceiling. Directly below sat two classic deck chairs of the type that cluttered the decks on the Titanic. "Ready?"

She nodded and he pressed a green button on the arm of his chair. The roof glided open to reveal the solar system and the universe beyond. He pressed another button and a silver joystick popped up. With a slight push, the view zoomed in on the Earth.

Frances responded with a deep-throated groan as the view skimmed the surface of the ocean. She could see waves and tidepools and taste the salty fog. He pressed the stick again and the image strafed a stand of giant redwoods.

"That's it!" she cried, lurching forward in her chair to get a closer look. "That's what's been bugging me about this place."

"Besides me?" He gave her a half smile but she missed it in her determination to inhale the scent of the forest stretching before her.

"Not enough wood! I haven't seen a tree since I got here."

"How's this?" The camera lingered above a dark green woodland dotted with lakes.

"I remember the first time I saw how autumn could transform a maple tree. I was nearly hysterical."

Grayson pressed a blue button and the audio track kicked in, filling the room with the sound of a mocking bird.

Frances sighed. "Those birds have a brain the size of an almond but it holds over 400 songs. I couldn't keep more than three phone numbers in my head. I'd be...was...lost without this thing." She pulled out her phone and glanced at R U there? still frozen on the screen.

Grayson smiled. "Any requests?"

"Venice. Could we see Venice?" she begged.

He hesitated a moment and then pressed the stick gently. The globe spun and the view swooped down to a boardwalk crowded with cyclists and skateboarders. Sun-dazzled tourists in cannabis-themed t-shirts lounged in outdoor patios, knocking back over-sized glasses of beer.

"Not that one. Venice, Venice. You know. Gondolas. Pigeons."

The globe spun to pitch darkness with tiny pinpoints of light and the sound of water slapping on stone. "Guess you'll have to save that for another life. That is, if you want to—"

"Are you crazy?" She reared forward in her chair. "Of course, I want to go back!"

"It's up to you."

"Well, then it's a lost cause." She flopped back, cracking her head on the wooden slats and releasing a cry of pain. "All these pathetic classes and moronic rules. Nothing but redundancy on top of repetition. It doesn't make sense." Her voice was trending toward a wail but she couldn't dial it back. "I tried so hard when I was alive. Why am I stuck here?"

"What do you mean?" He looked genuinely puzzled.

"When I was a kid, I was taught that your behavior on earth determined your fate in the afterlife. If you were good, you were rewarded. Virtuous people—you know the type? Annoying to be around for any length of time."

He nodded.

"They went straight to heaven. Big time sinners enjoyed eternal damnation among people far more interesting than I'd ever be. And then there was purgatory."

"Which is?" Grayson asked as he pulled a pack of cigarettes from his pocket. Then he lit up and leaned back, as if settling in for a long but potentially interesting lecture.

"Like detention hall for sinners. You've screwed up but you're not beyond reclamation."

"And what did people...souls...do there?" he asked.

"I'm not exactly sure. I guess some personalized brand of misery, otherwise it wouldn't be penance. Right?"

He shrugged his shoulders. "You're the expert."

"Well, in my case, penance could be a long-distance bus ride without a window seat or a good book, Casino Night in the parish hall, a conversation with a person who knows a lot about Bitcoin, daytime TV, gin on the rocks, or the after-effects of excessive kale consumption. Take your pick."

"You have a vivid imagination," he laughed.

"It comes with the territory if you're Catholic. Don't get me started on original sin and limbo." She paused for a moment to mentally review the archive of bizarre ideas she's swallowed whole as a youngster, never questioning the logic.

"Where was I? Oh, yeah. Purgatory. The only way to avoid it was to be exceedingly well-behaved. Rule-following even if it didn't make sense. I mean, really. What kind of God is gravely offended if you eat meat on Friday and then in 1966, up and changes his mind? Anyway, it all felt like a behavioral straitjacket."

"How'd you manage?" he asked.

"I was belligerent and utterly miserable." She couldn't

suppress a chuckle. "Does that sound familiar?"

He tried not to laugh but failed. "You *are* a handful."

"Anyway, with eternal damnation hanging over my head, I kept looking for an escape hatch, and eventually I found one. Indulgences."

"Now you're talkin'." He leaned eagerly toward her. "Sex, drugs, and tiramisu?"

"Wrong! All wrong." She jumped out of her chair, continuing her explanation as she paced back and forth. "Indulgences are prayers with benefits. Like a *Get out of Jail Free* card for sinners. Recite enough of those prayers and you could reduce your sentence in purgatory before you ever set foot in the place. Choose the right one and the slate was wiped clean." She swept one palm over the other and then raised both arms, like a magician at the finale of a disappearing trick.

"Sounds like some clever lawyering."

"They don't call it Canon Law for nothing. More like bookkeeping than religion. And the first indulgences were actually for sale. Absolution for a price." Her voice sounded like an auctioneer and Grayson laughed. "Major donors could even get their dead relatives out of trouble. It was a nice little money spinner for Pope Leo the Tenth."

"You know, Frances, I've learned more from you in one night than in all my years of Sunday school. You sure know a lot about a religion you don't like."

"I liked it fine for a while, and I still haven't kicked the incense and Gregorian chant addiction. But eventually I realized that they didn't like *me*. Free thinkers weren't welcome." She flopped down in her chair and her voice took on a resentful tone. "Every time I found a loophole, they'd tighten it around my neck."

"And a lovely neck it is."

She gave him a sidelong glance but his face was as blank as if he was observing the weather, so she returned to her lament.

"My quarrel wasn't just with Catholics. Even the Buddhists led me astray and they were the closest I came to spirituality. Granted, I had a limited understanding of the whole karma business, but their message seemed to be that life is where we learn our lessons. If we evolve enough, eventually we never have to return to the earth. Well, forget that! I loved the earth!"

She looked back up at the hole in the ceiling, where dawn was breaking over St. Mark's Square in Venice. Then she lay back, exhausted from a conversation that seemed to be shedding exactly no light on her predicament.

"Not that I had much to worry about." Her voice brightened. "I knew I'd screw up just enough to keep my frequent-return status. Round-trip ticket every time!" she announced with a note of triumph.

"That's not how it works," Grayson said quietly.

"What?"

"In fact, you've got it completely backward."

Her entire body registered the shock as she bolted upright and stared at him in disbelief.

"Reincarnation is the *reward* for earnest effort in the afterlife."

Frances was stunned. She'd been wrong-footed since the moment she set foot in this place, digging her grave with her mouth. "Let me get this straight. If I ever want to live again, I have to learn how to be dead?"

"Exactly."

"Now you tell me?" Her voice soared in exasperation. "What the hell were you waiting for?" She flopped back, struggling with anger, disappointment and an extra-large helping of self-pity.

"Sorry." His voice was gentle and sounded truly repentant. "I thought you understood. It's not like it's your first time." Almost as an afterthought he added, "But come to think of it, we do have something like purgatory. F.R."

Her face lit up. "France? If that's the punishment, I'd love to see where the winners go."

"Not France. *Frigus Repono*." His voice was deadly serious. "Cold storage."

Frances wasn't sure she wanted to know more but couldn't help asking. "What happens to people there?"

"Just what they want. Nothing."

"Sounds like Florida." She lay back on the lounge for a long time, homesick and confused. "Grayson, does anybody make it out of here?"

"Depends. Some get sidetracked. Others get special assignments. But in general, I'd say traffic is pretty brisk. The printers are working double shifts to keep up with the Letters of Transit and *Corpus Selecti* runs 24-7."

"Corpus what?"

"Come on." He stood up and headed for the stairs. "You deserve some fun."

Fun? So far, he'd been her guide on a non-stop misery tour. But she decided to take a chance.

CHAPTER 33

"Feels like I should whip out my rosary," Frances said as Grayson led her into a circular cloister like those found in monastic settings, where meditating monks could pace for hours without ever leaving home.

"Save it. This is for shopping, not praying. The latest models on display for the soon-to-be-reincarnated. Have a look."

The inner wall of the ambulatory was pierced with a series of glass doors framing cubicles the size of a shower stall. Inside each was a nude figure. Frances has seen a similar set-up in Amsterdam, where scantily-clad prostitutes tempted potential customers from small, dimly lit nooks.

Eye-contact was out of the question, so Frances confined herself to inspecting legs, feet and hands, avoiding the more coveted physical attributes—generous breasts and cocks standing at attention. But eventually, she realized these were just holograms. Male and female models of all ages and races, representing every color and texture in the human catalogue. A Charlie Chaplin look-alike, tall elegant figures with purple black skin stretched over high cheekbones. Shivas and shoguns. Beauties and beasts. The variety reminded her of the crowds in the subway at rush hour.

"Ready?" Grayson cocked his head toward a door. Inside, the monastic architecture was replaced with an arena surrounded by bleachers. A dozen people jostled for space along a low railing padded in crimson velvet, like the standing room section in a New York theater. A vendor roamed the stands hawking red and white boxes of popcorn.

"I used to love this stuff," Frances said, taking a warm, salty sniff. An image flashed through her head, more visceral than visual. A soft hand grazing hers in a darkened theater.

A bell rang and the models glided into the ring as if suspended on invisible wires. White paddles with black numbers flew into the air as eager bidders competed to secure upgrades from the last life or take a chance on something completely new.

Frances watched in fascination, trying to fathom the logic that would prompt someone to choose a face that only a mother could love. She was so engrossed that she jumped when Grayson asked, "Do you want to come back as a man or woman?"

"I told you. I don't want to *come* back. I want to *go* back. To my old life." She shook her head like she was dealing with a low I.Q. situation. "I want to be me again."

He gave her a nod. "Right."

"But if I had to choose, I'd be a woman. After all the work we did for the Equal Rights Amendment, I'd like a chance to enjoy it."

"Not interested in playing for the other team?" he asked.

"I don't know. Plenty of built-in perks." She scanned the room, noting the crowd of men muscling each other at the railing, each exuding confidence and unapologetic self-concern. "It looks tempting."

"But looks can be deceiving."

"Well, that's true. Most men are yoked to invisible burdens or slapped in emotional shackles before they're even out of diapers."

"So, you think biology is destiny? We're just slaves to our genes?"

"I'm not talking about genetics. I mean the environment and cultural influences. And family! That alone can put such a warp on a person that it totally wipes out their genetic potential." She sighed. "Don't even get me started."

"Hey, this was supposed to be fun, not a Darwin seminar. Pass over that popcorn." He paused and gave her a sideways look. "So, what kind of body do you want for your next lover?"

She was stunned by the intimacy of the question, then walloped by the memory of long showers when she traced the outline of muscles in cedar-scented soap before ladling hot water over the slippery patterns.

Grayson watched her face soften in the silence.

"Sorry." She flushed in embarrassment and then hurried to pick up the thread of the conversation. "Hypothetically." She underlined the word with an emphatic tone. "Hypothetically, masculine but not macho. Solid, not just physically but a person of substance. Character. And smart."

"Brains and brawn."

"Not just IQ but interested in everything. Politics, metaphysics, the really out-there ideas." She looked away. "I was never bored."

They sat in silence as the auction wound down. Successful bidders high-fived each other before heading for the exit. Then she asked in a near whisper, "Grayson, do you think I'll ever get out of here?" The odds seemed monumental and the clock was ticking down.

"I already told you. It's up to you. But you have to do the work. Can't pick and choose." He clapped her on the shoulder like a coach encouraging a rookie. "So, I'll see you bright and early tomorrow. Room 13 is back on the agenda."

Her postured stiffened as she pictured her body atlas covered with painful memories. She'd fled Room 13 once and didn't think she could muster the courage to face it again, especially the throbbing purple scar that still haunted her.

"Room 13 is bullshit!"

CHAPTER 34

"*Now* what?" Frances sighed in exasperation when she opened the door to her room and found a turquoise envelope lying on the floor. She tore it open, fully expecting a citation for violating some obscure UAL rule or point of afterlife etiquette. Defacing walls. Ditching class. And there was that unfortunate assault incident.

But no. She was invited to an evening event at PUBlic Domain. The capital letters caught her attention. "Clever. Sounds like a watering hole. Can't hurt." She fanned two complimentary tickets in front of Gabe. "Want to tag along?"

"Does that mean I'm GPSing, or are you requesting the pleasure of my company?"

"Both. Let's go take a look."

At first glance, the club wasn't promising. "Are you sure you got the right place?" she asked Gabe as she surveyed the scene. No blazing neon or line of eager patrons chatting up a bouncer. Just a dingy staircase leading to a subterranean hole in the wall with a deserted bar the size of a coat closet. No clink of ice punctuating boisterous conversations. So much for the PUB.

Most of the space was dedicated to rows of audience seats facing a stage that had seen better times. Tired red curtains framed a floor that couldn't hide the scuff patterns of nervous first timers and wannabes. A microphone hung overhead like a noose.

Frances guessed it was a dive where aspiring stand-ups could fine-tune their material and build up scar tissue through nightly rejection. Except there was an electronic scoreboard with sections for points earned and time elapsed. The only other prop was a pulchritudinous blonde in a skimpy costume holding aloft a hand-printed sign like a demonstrator in The Women's March. It bore a single word—FRUIT.

Low-budget game show. Man versus clock.

The guy on stage was floundering. "Did I say banana already? Grapefruit? Those fuzzy little green things. Does that count? Damn! Kiwi. That's it, kiwi!" He glanced at the clock. "Uh, coconut." When the gong sounded, he'd scored less than a dozen points.

Frances couldn't restrain herself. "Ten points!" she yelled. "Are you kidding? It's not like he asked you to name every country in NATO or put the Holy Roman emperors in chronological order. It's fruit, for God's sake! How about carambola, cherimoya, clementine, durian, guava, plantain, lychee?"

The game show host took center stage and grabbed the mic. "Well, you seem to have a lot to say, little lady. What's your name?"

She cringed. *Another unseemly outburst.* But she couldn't ignore the lure of the stage, the buzz from the faces craning in her direction. And there was the lingering image of Samuel Smiles in all his glory. *You're pathetic, you know that?* said Constant Comment as Frances slid down in her seat.

"No need to be shy. You're among friends. Come on. Tell us your name."

"Frances Beacon," she muttered.

"Well, Frances, you're our next contestant. Step right up."

And she did. Yes, it was a moronic game, but she was dying to feel competent again, if only through the energetic recitation of edibles. Most of all, she needed a fix of applause.

The host gave her a quick hug around the waist before his hand drifted south into prime groping territory. "Ready?"

She squirmed away, eager to have the spotlight to herself. "Ready!"

"Remember, when the gong sounds, name as many items as you can in the next category. You have two minutes."

The competitor in her was instantly on the bit. She grabbed the mic and thought triumphantly *Get a load of this, Samuel.* But just as her eyes were adjusting to the lights, the host threw down the gauntlet. "Okay, Ms. Beacon, let's see if you can shed some light on this topic." Once again, the human prop in high heels appeared with her sign. This time it bore the question: *What do you wish we never knew about you?*

Frances wanted to vanish. Dive into her secret room and never be seen again. As the gong sounded, she realized her colossal folly.

What was I thinking?

She had two strikes against her before she ever opened her mouth. First, the structure of the game was the complete antithesis of her communication style. She loved to cram dozens of words into every sentence and then lash them together into robust paragraphs. But the time limit meant she'd have to rely on phrases or even better, words, preferably monosyllabic.

Second, there was the inevitable humiliation that any such disclosures would cause. Playing to win was the road to disgrace. Nonetheless, when the audience broke into rhythmic clapping, "Frances, Frances," she took the bait.

I can do this, she told herself. *Condense each idea. Trim it to the bone and then spit out a few key words. Nothing too revealing.* With her strategy in place, she started broadcasting revelations like the neighborhood gossip on truth serum.

"I resent the hegemony of kale on every damn menu. Whose idea was that?"

"I think Facebook is a waste of time."

"I never read the Harry Potter books. It's that Tolkien thing. Never mind."

After each disclosure the scoreboard gave off a shrill *ding*, fueling her efforts. "I still can't find airplane mode on my phone so I just ignore the flight attendants when they give those safety warnings." Several people in the audience gasped at her cavalier attitude, but she was on a roll and impervious.

"Fantasy football. I don't get it."

"Ditto reality TV."

"I wake up annoyed. Positivity is like caffeine. I have to shoot up every morning." She made a vicious gesture toward a vein in her arm.

"I can't stand the sound of Ronald Reagan's voice even though he's been officially dead for ages and God knows how long before that."

Now she was picking up speed, egged on by hoots or occasional booing from the audience. "I swear at politicians on television. *Stupid motherfucker* is the go-to phrase these days."

Suddenly her brain had a mind of its own. *Give 'em the good stuff!* Before she knew it, she was heading into the vault.

"I got fired once and was unemployed for six months. Me! Unemployed!"

"I didn't talk to my mother for a whole year after my father died." She gave a casual shrug and then added, "I didn't like her." She shielded her eyes from the lights and scanned the darkness. "Whoever is keeping score, those were two separate items." She thrust out two fingers like a peace sign to underscore her demand. "Two. So, don't try to cheat me."

Ding. Ding.

Her brain shouldered its way back into the competition. *Here's another gem.* "Oh, yeah. I failed the placement test before my freshman year in college so I had to take Dumbbell English."

She felt her throat tighten around the unmistakable taste

of shame. *Jesus, is that still here after all those years.* She'd earned a full scholarship to the college of her choice but was forced to enroll in Dumbbell English. That's what everyone called it and that's how she felt. Dumb as she reported three mornings a week to her hall of shame. She'd worked her ass off and ultimately the professor said, "Must have been some kind of mistake." But the damage was done.

Three books published. God knows how many blog posts and magazine articles but it still stings like a first-degree burn.

"New item. Which is why I'm a thief. That's right. I steal from non-dumbbell writers. Ideas, phrases, whatever works. And no, I don't give them credit. Their stuff probably wasn't original anyway. Everyone steals."

"New item: I used to be fat. Still am in my head."

Ding.

"I cultivated eccentricity which was mistaken for confidence. In truth, I was a bundle of insecurity."

Ding.

"Still am some days." She waited for the sound of another point and said a quick "thank you" before plunging on.

"I'm not nearly as nice as I seem or seemed. You wouldn't believe the crap I'd say about people waiting in the TSA line, but only in my head. I was always careful in public and especially in print, but that's not the same as being kind."

When she stopped to draw a breath, a woman in the audience shouted, "What about sex and drugs?"

"May as well come clean about that, too. Drugs, yes. Never snorted or injected. Nothing exotic. Just the recreational stuff which, by the way, often failed to deliver any recreation at all."

Ding.

"About sex..." Her voice dropped. It was so low and confidential that it had the audience straining forward to hear more. "Well, the truth is that everything I know about sex." She paused for dramatic effect. "I learned while standing in line at the supermarket."

A sprinkling of laughter rippled through the audience.

God, that feels good!

"No, seriously..."

Frances didn't know if it was the heat from the stage lights or the thought of sex but she reached for the buttons on her shirt. "There were long spells of no sex followed by sex so empty that it was like an out-of-body experience."

Now she stepped out of her pants and kicked them aside. "I had to invent reactions because I had no spontaneous feelings. None whatsoever."

Several women in the audience weighed in on the subject, nodding and clapping. "Amen, sister. Tell it like it is." The men around them slid down in their seats, anxious to distance themselves from this tale of deception and failure to deliver.

"In the end," Frances continued, "I'd just lie there thinking *I shaved my legs for this?*"

The sheer energy of her performance and the ego-pumping effect of the applause lifted her up and up, like she was tethered to a helium balloon. But when the gong sounded, the string slipped from her fingers and she collapsed, birth-naked, in the glare of the spotlight.

The audience gaped.

The game show host crowed, "Twenty-two points! A new record!"

Frances pleaded, "Someone call an exorcist!"

CHAPTER 35

"Is she insane?" gasped Cornelius. "I've heard that people in the helping professions need the most help, but this?" He swiveled his head away from the image of naked Frances, frozen on the monitor.

"Insane may be a bit of an exaggeration," the Fool said. "Let's just say she has a broad repertoire of unusual behaviors."

"Looks more like she's flying her freak flag," Andreas sneered.

"She needs to be put out of her misery," Cornelius concluded.

"I think she's *magnifique*," Olympe said. "Which of you has that kind of courage?" Her eyes ticked deliberately from one face to another, interrogating the entire group.

"Spare us, Olympe." Andreas grimaced and clapped his hands over his ears.

Olympe circled the table in a flash and yanked his hands down. "And what does that mean?" she demanded.

"Only that some things are better left unsaid. And unseen." He snickered and cast a glance at Cornelius, who nodded in obvious agreement.

"Are you talking about her body?" Olympe couldn't contain her indignation. Now all the members of the Committee were on the edge of their seats, eyes riveted to the duel unfolding before them.

"Well, you have to admit she is a bit over the hill for—" But his words were cut short as Olympe pressed her interrogation.

"For what? Passion? Sex? Love?"

He lit a cigarette and exhaled a long stream of smoke before replying. "She can have whatever she wants, or can get. I'm just saying that I prefer younger women, that's all." His voice was all innocence, as if he was simply stating the obvious, challenging her undue agitation. "The body of a 25-year-old is extraordinary. The body of a woman of 50, not." He took another mouthful of smoke, then looked pointedly around the room. "And 65, well."

Another voice joined the debate. "You mean I'm *unfuck-able*?" Juliette approached Andreas with the imperious grace of a Prima Ballerina after a star performance in Swan Lake. "That I have no chance with a man of your obvious distinction?"

Drawing closer, like they were partners in a *pas de deux,* she began to tick off his abundant attractions. "Thinning hair, filthy nails, puffy eyelids and..." Patting his ample paunch in an overly familiar way, "too much of this." Then her hand slid down between his legs and probed as if sizing up an animal at auction. "Not so much here." She lowered her face so close that she could hear a faint whistling from his nostrils. "*Je suis devaste.*"

"The Fempire strikes back," the Fool observed.

Andreas attempted a scoffing snort that couldn't disguise the effort to suck in his gut, but before he could speak the Fool continued, "She's got a point, Mate. Have you looked in a mirror lately?"

"Never mind that." Olympe returned to the arena. "He's an imbecile!" She tossed her head, contempt and pity replacing her anger. "You don't know what you're missing. Nor will you ever because I can assure you that women over 50 are breathing a collective sigh of relief."

"Right. Feminists." Andreas spat out the words.

"Indeed. We'd be fools not to be on our own side." Olympe drew herself up to her full height and noticed every woman in the room nodding vigorously.

"Just what you'd expect from a female mind," he countered.

"You poor, sad man." She drew each word out in an exaggerated show of sympathy. "For your information, there is no such thing as a female mind. It makes as much sense to speak of a female kidney." She put her hand under his chin and tilted it up toward her. "But in your case, better not to speak at all."

Cornelius banged on the table for order and then glared at Olympe. "May I make the same suggestion to you?"

"Are you trying to stifle debate?" she shouted, training her fury on him.

"I'm trying to point out the utter futility of your behavior. Your protests are impotent, your cause hopeless. Has history taught you nothing? Biology trumps biography."

"Bravo, sir! A woman's place and all that," Andreas stood and gave Cornelius a solitary round of applause.

"A woman's place is in your face," Olympe snapped back.

"She's a one-woman rebellion," the Fool whispered with a note of admiration.

"You, sirs, are proof positive that Frances can never get a fair hearing in this room," Olympe said.

"And you, Madame, are wasting our time, of which we have precious little," Cornelius replied.

Olympe shook her head in disgust. "Even in the afterlife, the cards are stacked against her."

CHAPTER 36

"Miss your off-ramp?"

Grayson's voice was the antithesis of jocular when he discovered Frances barricaded behind a pile of books in the library. She gave him a look that was the visual equivalent of her middle finger but didn't say a word. "What's up?" he demanded, waving the note she'd left on her door. It read: *I need a library. Gabe offered to show me the way.*

"Nothing. I just need a break. Time to rethink this whole program or at least find something more enlightened than that Room 13 business." She patted a teetering stack of books. "Besides, I can learn everything I need right here." She grabbed a book on horticulture and thrust it toward him like a shield. "Even Cicero agrees with me. I quote, *If you have a garden and a library you have everything you need.*"

"Right. He also said, *Any man can make mistakes, but only an idiot persists in his error.*"

"Only an idiot pimps for the University of the Afterlife. What a joke! It's more like junior high!" She turned back to her books, hoping he'd relent or just leave. But he stood his ground so she added, "And any fool knows that therapy only works if people want it to." As soon as the words were out of her mouth, she knew it was a mistake but hoped it might slip by without comment. No such luck.

"So, you're saying you don't. Now we're getting somewhere."

"I'm not saying anything, especially to you. Come to think of it, why are you still in the netherworld? Miss *your* off-ramp? Get stuck?"

"I have work to do."

"No shit." She leaned back and gave a little laugh. "So why don't you get on with it and leave me alone? And while you're at it, you could use a bit of a tune-up. Shock Jock 101?"

Grayson took it on the chin and returned fire. "Cicero to the rescue. I quote, *When you have no basis for an argument, abuse the plaintiff.*"

"Gladly," she snapped, as he turned his back to leave.

But in truth, she wasn't glad. Things were getting exponentially worse. Bouts of hyperactivity followed by bewildering torpor. A fog in her brain so thick you could lose solid objects in it. And the gnawing suspicion that she was the author of all her sorrows.

Overwhelmed by the bleak contemplation of her future, she called out, "Grayson," but it was a feeble, woeful sound, rather like something a lost kitten might produce. Part cry for help, part apology, but it failed on both scores. He didn't pause or glance back over his shoulder, but simply lifted his hand in a one-finger salute and disappeared.

As she watched him retreat down the tunnel of books, a siren began to wail in her head.

Could he really quit? So many people had been snatched from her, leaving a fear of abandonment etched deep in her psyche.

I have to stop him.

She leapt from her chair, sending a cascade of books tumbling onto the floor. Then she picked her way through the rubble, grabbing the shelves to steady herself, but by the time she'd reached the exit, he was gone.

CHAPTER 37

"Watch it, buddy!" Gabe yipped as Grayson burst from a passageway and collided with him, treading on his front paw.

"Thanks a lot," Grayson snapped.

"For?" Gabe gave his injured foot a quick lick and waited attentively.

"For nothing." Grayson jammed both hands in his pockets and kicked the ground in frustration, "I'm busting my ass trying to keep her on track and you take her to the library?" He thrust out his hands in a *what-gives?* gesture.

"Hey! Don't blame me. She would have found her way there eventually."

"You realize she was ditching," Grayson said. "Again." In that single word, his tone shifted from exasperation to a hint of personal failure.

"Sorry." The big dog hung his head, making himself a bit smaller. "She said she had a free period." Then a note of concern crept into his voice. "So, it's not going well?"

"It's...uh, uneven." He gave a half-hearted laugh. "Sometimes you win..."

"Sometimes you learn," Gabe said gently and then got back to business. "But then, I guess you have to expect this, the rate of relapse being what it is."

"But I'm supposed to help her. That's my job."

"I understand. Believe me, I do. But no obligation to do the

196

impossible is binding. Your man, Cicero."

"Big help." Grayson collapsed against a wall and got down to some serious brooding.

"Bro. I'm just saying. Maybe you need a little break. Get yourself some R & R." The dog leaped up and pressed his front paws on the wall where he could almost meet Grayson eye-to-eye. "What about that little red head who was so crazy about you in Venice?" He panted audibly. "I think I saw her somewhere around here."

"Venice? Remind me."

"Yeah, right after the plague."

Grayson nodded and a look of fondness crossed his face. "Lucrezia. God, she was gorgeous and what a brilliant writer. But, nah. We tried it again during the Enlightenment. Couldn't make it work."

"What about Amina?"

"All armor. No amour. That was a disaster. Never again."

Gabe returned to a sitting position and gave Grayson a long, thoughtful look. "What seemed to be the problem?" he asked with genuine concern.

"Same old, same old." The words slipped reluctantly out, barely above a whisper.

"Pussy-whipped?"

Grayson looked stung. "What do you know? You're a *dog*." He started to walk away but Gabe placed a paw on the toe of his shoe. There was such kindness in the gesture that he couldn't move.

"I know *you*," Gabe said softly. "Fifteen lifetimes and counting."

"I thought angels didn't have a memory. They said that in *Barbarella.*"

Gabe gave him a tiny dog smile. "Old sci-fi movies? That's where you got your metaphysical education?"

"Hey, don't knock Jane Fonda," Grayson protested, not yet ready to return the smile.

"I'm not. She's awesome, although she'd be a handful as a client. I'm just trying to point out that I'd be useless if I couldn't remember the good, the bad and the ugly. And there's been plenty of that, so you have to admit I'm loyal."

Grayson abandoned his defensive posture and reached for a spot behind Gabe's ears which was prime scratching territory. "And you have to admit that some of it's been fun."

"True. But you've also had some pretty tough lives. God knows, I tried my best to protect you. That's my job, isn't it?"

Grayson patted Gabe again. "Don't beat yourself up. I know you're doing your best."

"Thanks," Gabe sighed and then continued. "This last time around it seemed like we were on the right track, but now I don't know. Something's off. We're out of sync and, honestly, I'm worried." He shook his head until his ears made a flapping sound. "Fifteen lives. Could be time for a change."

"Am I that hopeless?" Grayson asked.

"It's not just you, buddy. It's humans! I love 'em, but they don't make it easy."

"You're right. Dogs are easy," Grayson said. "You can read a dog at ten paces and generally, what you see is what you get. And most of that's good—loyalty, companionship."

"A warm body on a cold night," Gabe added. "Don't forget that." He yawned and slumped down on all fours. "And we expect so little in return."

Grayson was suddenly filled with guilt for treating this magnificent hound so shabbily. "Sorry. I'm really sorry."

But Gabe pressed on with his assessment of the human condition. "With you people, it's like the surface is almost a mirage. The stuff that really matters is buried in a deep, dark maze."

"Sounds like underground parking."

"More like a toxic hazmat stew." He was clearly warming to the role of amateur psychologist. "Under even the sweetest face, there's a Calcutta of beliefs and passions and scars all struggling for dominance. But they're completely hidden from the unsuspecting host. In fact, most humans are on auto-pilot. They just feel an impulse and act. Say outlandish things they can never take back. Make snap decisions with no idea why. One minute they seem perfectly normal. The next they're punching out a total stranger whose beer-breath triggered a childhood trauma. Or weeping uncontrollably during a pathetic rom-com that only got 28 percent on Rotten Tomatoes."

"No wonder there's mayhem." Grayson rubbed a finger up and down the center of his forehead.

"But wait. There's more." Gabe chuckled at his imitation of a cheap, late-night infomercial. "When people set out to love and be loved, that subliminal throng is riding shotgun. Only the brave survive."

"And you think...." Grayson paused.

"I'm just sayin'." Gabe tipped his head back as if contemplating a long howl then turned, scratching the ground with his hind feet like he was washing his hands of the topic. But he wasn't quite done. "Word of advice. Tie yourself to the mast."

Grayson shook his head. "I can't keep doing this."

CHAPTER 38

"You just missed her," Antoinette announced before Grayson could inquire.

He flopped in the corner of Strong Silent and stared across the deserted platform. "Any idea where she went?"

"I'm a barista, not a P.I. What's going on?"

"I have no idea, but it ain't good."

She jerked her chin toward the espresso machine.

"Yes, ma'am. I could really use a jolt." He waited while she measured out the grounds and applied the tamper. They put the conversation on hold, content to simply listen to the soothing sound of water being changed into the precious elixir.

"Here you go—hot and black. Just the way Jesus wants you to drink it."

He sipped in silence, and then toyed with his empty cup. "She's a tough case."

"Frances? You gotta be kiddin'. She's a cupcake!" Antoinette strode up and down in the tiny space, putting on her best New York swagger. "You ain't seen tough."

Grayson was staring at his hands in his lap and missed the show. "I swear, I'm trying so hard but she's actually getting worse." He rubbed the back of his neck and swiveled his head until it released a tiny cracking noise.

Antoinette winced at the sound but continued. "That's your problem right there. Take it from a recovering doormat.

You can't change other people."

"*You?* A doormat?" That got his attention. He sat up in surprise.

"Was. I didn't just let people walk over me. I licked their shoes. All I got was a dirty tongue. So, here's the bottom line. There's only one person you can change." She grabbed the shiny metal tips plate on the counter and held it up to his face.

He stared at his reflection for a long time and then shrugged. "Seems like a long shot."

"It may be your only shot. Speaking of which, do you want another?" Antoinette asked, reaching for his cup.

"No, better get moving. But leave the light on. I'll be back."

"Anytime. But think about what I said. Lives are hanging in the balance." She leaned on the counter and watched him disappear, then realized that she'd had enough for one day. "Time to go home."

But first she had to tuck Strong Silent in for the night. Her ritual was always the same: wash the cups, check the supply of beans, remove every last fingerprint and stray granule from the espresso machine. When she was finished, the cafe looked as shiny as the day it opened, a small serene island of sustenance in an ever-shifting landscape. Be it ever so humble, she thought of her mission as Chaucerian. She stayed put and served while people passed through, each on the way to his or her own private Canterbury.

She closed her eyes and sighed with satisfaction, but her mood was abruptly broken by the rustle of shopping bags. "With you in a minute," she grumbled over her shoulder. When she turned around, she was staring at the top of a woman's head. Thinning hair with pale roots and small pink patches of skin where the follicles had called it quits. The woman seemed to be conducting a comprehensive inventory of her bags, prospecting for God-knows-what with none of the urgency that animated most of Antoinette's patrons. This seemed to go on for whole minutes until her patience, already thin, gave out. *At this rate we'll be here 'til midnight. Enough already.*

But a customer is a customer so perhaps a guttural nudge would move the proceedings along. She cleared her throat. "Uh-hmmm."

No response.

"Is there anything I can do for you, ma'am?"

The woman's head rose slowly, as if being cranked manually like an ancient drawbridge. Her eyes scanned Antoinette from waist to chin, mouth to nose and finally, cautiously gazed into her eyes. Suddenly the air between them felt thick and dangerous, as though a lit match would blow them both sky high.

"Is there anything I can do for you...mom?"

"Tony?"

"Antoinette."

"Right. I knew that."

"What are you doing here?"

"Depends on where *here* is. The last thing I remember was a priest." She touched a dab of oil on her forehead. "So, I'm either dead, or this is Queens. Isn't that where you ended up?"

"I mean what are you doing *here*? You promised I'd never see or speak to you again and frankly, that's one promise I hoped you'd keep." Antoinette stepped back as far as she could until she was pressed up against the espresso machine, her body as rigid as a board.

"You missed my funeral." Same old mom. Change the subject. Find or manufacture a position from which she could indulge in her favorite sport—guilt mongering. The total absence of logic never seemed to bother her.

"I seem to recall you missed mine, too," Antionette snapped.

"But we're here now." The woman looked around as if she was going to comment on the décor.

Antoinette held nothing back. "That's *it*? That's all you have to say for yourself! We're here now?"

"What?" She stared with a look of innocence so flimsy you could see light through it. But there was no light. Simply a hollow gray facsimile of the person she might have been.

"Forget about it. What do you want to drink?" Antoinette tossed her head toward the menu board, hoping to wrap things up as quickly as possible.

"Do you have that George Clooney kind? I love him." Her voice was sweet and syrupy, like she was talking about a favorite grandchild.

"That's instant coffee, mom." Antionette pointed emphatically toward her chest and shouted, "I'm a barista."

"I can never do anything right with you, can I?"

"All you had to do was love me." The enormity of that statement seemed to sack Antoinette. She sagged against the counter. "I was your son. You made me!"

"But I did...do...love you."

Antoinette struggled to regain control. Her voice cracked as she gave a small laugh that doubled as a sneer. "Must be some kind of deathbed epiphany because the last thing I recall you were screaming that I was a disgrace and throwing my books and clothes out the back door."

"You don't understand. First, I lost my only son. Then I lost my only child." She touched her chest with her fingers splayed. "How much pain can a mother's heart take?"

"*Lost?* You didn't *lose* me." Antoinette's voice dropped to a whisper. "You threw me away. Banished me. Or have you forgotten?"

The old lady dropped her head, begging, "Please don't hate me."

"Hate? Huh! You're not worth the energy. But if I was looking for lessons in loathing, you'd be a fantastic mentor."

"But I didn't ha—"

"Save it. You were the only one I could talk to—thought I could—and you turned on me. I hoped you'd understand or at least show some compassion. But you were vicious. *Why?* Just tell me why, mom?" Her voice boomed through the tunnel, rattling the metal security doors.

Her mother slumped against the counter, bracing herself. But she was no match for the secret she'd been keeping from herself for decades. "I was trying to protect you. I didn't want you to get hurt." She lay her head down and wept.

The words were almost paralytic in their effect. Antoinette stood in stunned silence. Finally, she rallied enough to say, "That may be the greatest revelation since they broke the Enigma code." Then she turned away and took a deep breath.

Closing her eyes, she folded her hands over her solar plexus and began the ritual that sutured her emotions back together after every shattering event. *Picture a spark of white light beneath your hands and watch it grow to fill your whole body.* In a whisper she said, "I am perfect and loveable just as I am." Again, she repeated it with more conviction, waiting for the calm after the storm. Instead, she heard the rattle of shopping bags.

Is she still here?

The sound reignited her fury, but just as it was approaching hurricane force, a hand cautiously stroked the back of her head and a tearful voice said, "Yes, you are, my darling. Perfect. Now can I have that coffee?"

CHAPTER 39

"Ladies and gentlemen, step right up!" cried a barker, waving Frances toward the spidery skeleton of a trapeze rig in the corner of a square.

Wow! I remember these guys, she thought. *The Trapeze School of New York.* The school set up shop on the pier in Hudson River Park every summer. From morning to night, gawkers crowded around to enjoy the vicarious thrill of seeing people fling themselves into mid-air when they were already high above the water, a double remove from solid ground.

The school's founder said he wanted to give people a renewed sense of possibility and transform their outlook on life. *High wire psych services disguised as entertainment,* she thought. He also adopted the motto: "Forget fear. Worry about the addiction." *Clever. I should have used that in my sex talks.*

The barker nudged Frances on the elbow and gestured toward a line of excited patrons. "Ready?"

She jumped like he was a mugger but quickly recovered with a little laugh. "Cold turkey? Forget about it. I'm not that kind of girl."

He gave her a quizzical look. "Meaning?"

"You know. Spontaneous, devil-may-care. I'm definitely the look-before-you-leap type. I'd need the details, preferably in writing."

He handed her a brochure entitled *What You Need to*

Know. It started with the right clothing. Comfortable but close fitting for maximum movement and no tragic wardrobe malfunctions that could leave a flyer hopelessly tangled in the ropes. It ended with the confident statement that *All you need to bring is your enthusiasm and willingness to learn!*

Frances turned the brochure over and then frowned. "There's got to be more to it than this. For a start, there's nothing about grip, which is odd since I've seen people lose control of a leash when pitted against a determined dachshund prospecting for trash."

"That doesn't happen here," he said and tried to nudge her toward the growing line of daredevils.

She stepped back and asked, "What about upper body strength?" Could she rely on her biceps once she'd flung herself into thin air and gravity got its first real shot at her?

The barker gave her upper arm a familiar squeeze. "Feels pretty good to me."

"Hey!" She slapped his hand away, but he just laughed.

There were other omissions. Not a word about eyesight, coordination or bladder control. Her mind raced through an entire catalog of conditions that might disqualify a trapeze virgin like herself but the brochure was largely mute, so she continued her interrogation. "What about maximum weight? Somehow I can't picture a person the size of a refrigerator scaling a twenty-three-foot ladder."

"But you're not fat."

"My guess is that you're counting on the law of natural selection. That people who have trouble squeezing into a theater seat rarely imagine they can fly." She put finger quotes around the last word.

The barker cocked his head to one side. "What's a mattah? You scared?"

Frances bristled. *Damn right I'm scared.* But he'd have to beat it out of her. She moved closer to study the situation.

Looking up she saw a woman perched on a platform the size of a beach towel.

"Jane!"

The widow from Misanthropy 101 was strapped into a harness with belay ropes to insure a safe landing in a net the size of a basketball court. Two coaches were stationed next to her like bookends, reciting a steady stream of instructions and encouragement.

Despite their assurances, Jane was working up a good panic. Each time they handed her the bar she recoiled like it was molten. Then she'd repeat, "I'm scared" and shrink into the nether reaches of the platform. Frances could hear her pain from forty feet away.

"What's she doing up there?" she asked.

"Said someone named Frances told her to face her fears. Somethin' like that."

"What?" Frances shook her head. "I didn't..."

"So that's you?" He pointed at her and gave a chuckle.

Frances winced and nodded.

"What, you some kind of shrink?"

"Sort of. Was."

A half-dozen gawkers shouted to Jane, "You can do it! You can!" But each volley of support was like a bucket of cold water, freezing her in place.

"Ya betta give her a hand, lady, cause she's causing gridlock. I got a business to run."

"It's just that..."

"Oh, I get it. Do what I say, not what I do. S'what I always heard. You guys are crazier than your patients." He turned to the people waiting in line. "She can't do it."

Frances had no appetite for more humiliation after her performance at PUBlic Domain, so she crept toward the ladder and started her ascent with the caution of a novice on Everest. When she reached the top of the ladder, she was hyperventilating but covered her distress with a quick, "Nice view. I think

I can see the Brooklyn Bridge."

Jane managed a muffled laugh and then, "I can't do it."

"Right, but what if you could?" Frances asked almost casually.

"I don't get it?" Jane was confused by the question and momentarily distracted from her fear.

"How do think you'd feel if you could?" The simple restatement seemed to clear Jane's mind.

"Brave." She bit her lower lip. "Proud of myself." She glanced down at the net and nodded up and down. "Proud."

"You got that right. Now hear this, Jane. I get scared all the time," Frances announced like it was a medal of honor.

"You're kidding? The way you took on that minister?"

"That wasn't courage, darling. Just a surplus of anger. Truth is, I can get a knot in my stomach just sitting in my study trying to write my blog." She thought about all the evenings when her fingers hovered over the keyboard like a water-diviner in the Sahara. "Yep. I sit there but nothing comes out. Scares the shit out of me."

"I loved that blog," Jane said.

"Me, too." She gave Jane a quick hug. "Now tell me this. What else have you done that scared you?" The word *else* was deliberate, subtly asserting that the trapeze was just the next in a long list of triumphs.

"Learned to jet ski on Lake Superior."

"Scarier," Frances urged.

"I was a substitute teacher for ten years. Chicago. Inner-city. Junior high English."

"Wow! That is tough. Got anything scarier?" Frances asked, prospecting for something to convince Jane that she was already a champ.

"Signed the Do Not Resuscitate order for my husband." Jane closed her eyes and winced, as if reliving the deed.

The words hit Frances like a hammer. Her mind flashed on a hospital room where life support machines kept a up steady beat but there was no life to support. She shook away the memory. "My God, Jane! Fear should be afraid of *you*. You're amazing."

She gave Frances a tentative smile. "You think so?"

"Definitely. So just one more tweak and I think you'll be on your way. Look at that trapeze. Really stare it down." She paused and gave Jane a moment to focus. "Okay, do you feel that in your chest?" She spread her hand wide just below her throat and could feel her own pulse pounding.

Jane nodded. "Tight. Nerves in a big knot."

"That's right. Now let's call a spade a spade, girl. That's not fear. It's excitement. Every molecule in your body is twanging with aliveness." Then she gently released Jane from her grip. "So? What do you say?"

Jane straightened up and asked for the ropes. The buckles snapped noisily onto her harness and this time the trapeze fit snugly in her hands. Posing like an Olympic diver on the tip of the board, she leapt. The ropes followed and she swung like a rubbery pendulum. Back and forth, back and forth—laughing.

"Nice work, Frances," the coach said. "You're pretty good at that stuff."

"Was." She tried not to glance down at the ground as she edged toward the ladder.

"Hey, not so fast." He stuck out his arm like a turnstile.

Her instinct was to recoil but she feared that a sudden move would catapult her off the tiny platform in a spectacular freefall, giving the crowd a thrill they'd be talking about for days. "What?" she snapped.

"Your turn." He held out the harness.

Her fists were clenched so tight she could feel her nails digging into her palms. "Uh, nah...not today." She aimed for casual disinterest.

"So that was all BS?"

"Excuse me?" His remark stung and she retaliated. "You're just a rope jockey. What do you know?"

"Then?" he taunted, thrusting the harness toward her.

She tried to open her hands but the paralysis grew and the muscles in her jaw joined in the fun, twitching as she clenched her teeth. How could she explain? Letting go couldn't be selective. It was all or nothing and right now, every fiber of her being was holding on. The surrender of a single muscle could unleash a tsunami of emotions. She was certain she'd be engulfed. Or worse.

"What's it gonna be?" he nudged again.

She gave her head a microscopic shake, then stepped to the back of the platform. A more adventurous patron cut in front of her and she watched in dismay while he leapt into the air, as if into the arms of a lover.

Defeated, she started her descent, unswung. Backing down the ladder, she groped for each step with her toe, as if she'd even lost the confidence to retreat. Once she was safely on the ground, she skirted the line where Jane waited for another turn, hoping her failure would go unnoticed. Breathless and baffled, she scurried in the direction of the gym.

I used to help the living. I can even help the dead. Why can't I help myself?

CHAPTER 40

The gym was busier than usual, teeming with dozens of hardbodies skimmed off the younger end of the NFL demographic. One man clutched a metal disk the size of a spare tire and executed knee bends that would put a ballet dancer to shame. Another performed a set of crucifixion impressions on a cross-cable machine while a pale Santa Claus of a man grimaced through a dozen sit-ups. The usual sound track was amplified by a he-man who vocalized so lavishly after each bench press that he could have done voice overs for Enhanced Interrogation training films.

Presiding over the room was an old beauty queen, as delicate as a China teacup, who swanned in a stately circuit from one conversation to another.

"Hey, Liz. You're lookin' great today."

The old lady smiled. "Thanks, Danny. It's the Pilates."

"Whatever. It's workin' for you."

Frances gave them all a wide berth since she'd rather take a bullet than chat. The gym had always been her library with benefits. She could knock out thirty minutes of moderate pain without a whimper if she had her Kindle or the Sunday book review for company. But this gym was a no-print zone. Not even a discarded Grisham legal thriller, so she was reduced to reading the club rules while using the biceps pull, and then scanning the warning stickers on the equipment. But instead of *Keep hands clear of moving parts,* the cautionary label on the rowing machine read: *Nothing ever works out as you wanted, so give up all your schemes and ambitions. If you have to think about something, make it the uncertainty of the hour of your death.*

No shit, Frances thought. She recognized the source of the quote as *The Tibetan Book of Living and Dying,* a text she'd visited more than once and discarded in frustration. She switched to the chest press machine where she was greeted with: *The world can seem like an utterly convincing place until death collapses the illusion and evicts us from our hiding place.*

"Really?" She deliberately dropped the arms of the machine. Metal slammed on metal, echoing through the gym. Then she surveyed the room, looking for a supervisor. *They're never around when you need one.* Maybe she could crowd-source some support for her irritation. "Any chance we can change the narrative?" But no one took any notice.

On it went, each machine having its say, like fortunes without the cookies. The last message—*happiness is up to you*—was scrawled in yellow chalk.

"Give it a rest." She closed her eyes and concentrated on her buttocks, clenching her gluteal muscles with a vengeance and wondering, *Can you get a charley horse in your butt?* When she opened her eyes, the beauty queen was planted in front of her.

Oh, God. Not her.

Frances pre-empted any socializing with a hasty, "Do you want this machine? Here, you can have it. I'm done."

Liz made no reply but stepped closer, blocking her exit. "Wrong muscle group, Frances."

"Sorry?" She tried once more to dismount, but the China cup wasn't going anywhere.

"Wrong muscle group," she repeated.

"I'll be the judge of that," Frances snapped.

"Suit yourself." Liz turned to walk away. "I'm just sayin'."

"Christ!" Frances exploded. "Anyone else have an opinion about how I should live my life?" The last word was nearly inaudible, as she was struck for the umpteenth time by the irony of trying to fine-tune a life that no longer was.

"Stupid cow," Frances muttered as she pictured a dumb-bell-shaped dent in the old white head. But just then something caught her attention.

Nothing wrong with that ass!

The beauty queen was a looker from behind. Her buttocks rode like two melons in a sack, high and firm as a teenage gymnast's. She floated down the aisle and seated herself on a bench, looking majestically around as if expecting a waiter to appear with a tray of champagne flutes.

Frances just sat, paralyzed by the blind arrogance of her words. Liz was 85 if she was a day—thin, graceful, erect, mobile, togged up in fashionable work-out gear, socializing comfortably with people half her age, *in a gym!* Everything Frances had hoped to be and failed.

But it was more than that. She realized that she was staring at a walking, talking billboard for a concept she'd endlessly flogged from the stage in her seminars.

"Ladies, gentlemen, non-binaries, non-sectarians, vegans, carnivores and all the ships at sea. Now hear this! You're smart, energetic, healthy, curious and fresh off the 40-hour-week treadmill. You have an abundance of experience, time and unspent passion."

She knew perfectly well it had been decades since some of her listeners had seriously exercised their arousal muscles, so her goal was to deliver a wake-up call like a car alarm to their dormant aspirations. More than a few leaned forward in their seats, hoping to hear something juicy. She paused and lowered her voice, as if sharing a secret.

"You're ready for prehab."

The audience stirred. At least a dozen touched their ears

and asked a companion, "Did she say *rehab*?" They weren't sure if their impairment had kicked in, but were clearly put off by a word that smacked of drugs gone wrong. Not that they had anything against drugs, legal or otherwise, but rehab meant rules and confinement. They could just kiss their precious freedom goodbye.

"You heard me. It's not enough to simply stave off decline. Prehab seizes the incredible opportunity of this moment to build on your peak instead of letting it slip away. Yes, you'll have to exercise. And chuck those old habits that even you can't explain anymore. Then go find something in this world that truly needs you and give it your all. And one more thing. Pull the plug on the damn TV." There were a few groans from the ESPN set.

She paused to let them consider the proposition, then plunged back in. *"So, what do you get in the bargain?"*

A woman in the third row shouted out a boisterous, "More sex?"

"Yes, madame. That's definitely on the menu because as you boost your metabolism, you'll reconnect with the person you always wanted to be."

Sitting there in the gym, inescapably post-mortem, Frances was staggered by the ghost of her old self, peddling freedom and growth while she was well and truly stuck. Her cheeks flushed with shame. She wanted to grab that dumbbell and clobber herself where it would do the most good. Instead, she walked over to Liz and whispered, "Slide over."

Then she slumped down and put her head in her hands, overwhelmed by a sense of desolation so heavy you could measure it in metric tons. "Help me. What can I do?"

Liz gently reached out to Frances and began to massage the ring finger on her left hand. A current of warmth flowed up her arm, directly into her chest where it swirled for a moment, and then swaddled her heart.

"That's it," Liz whispered.

Slowly, Frances felt the great Gordian knot in her chest loosen. Her lungs discovered whole new territories for expansion. Then her heart hammered against her ribs like a pick-up drummer, rusty but determined to show how much it could still feel, despite the years in solitary confinement.

But what good was an eager throbbing heart here in this afterscape? And why try to revive a dead woman walking? As her heart beat, beat, beat, all she could think was, *Where were you when I needed you?*

CHAPTER 41

"Unfinished business," Grayson announced. "Room 13."

"Right. Tattoo removal," Frances mumbled.

"No. Gilead." He began to hum a few notes and then sang, "The-ere is a balm."

But Frances cut him off. "Don't give up your day job."

Rough start. They trudged on in silence until they reached Room 13. Grayson didn't actually shove her through the door, but something about her entrance suggested that her attitude could use some work.

"Welcome back," Danny said.

She threw him a glance that said, *Don't push it.*

"Do you remember how this works?" He pointed to the mouse. "One click for basic identification. Double-click for the details."

Frances refused to sit down. "Thanks for the refresher but I'm going to need more than that."

"No, really. It's that simple." He gave her a smile. "I've heard you're really smart. You can do it."

His enthusiasm had the effect of an irritant and she demanded, "But *why*? What's the point here?" She recognized this argumentative streak, her go-to strategy to block unwanted emotions.

"It's about memory," he said patiently.

"Nothing wrong with my memory, except for the bit about

how I died." Of course, this was nowhere near the truth. Every day the glitches were increasing, the connections jumbled.

What is a person but the sum of her memories? And who will I be when they're gone?

"And liberation," Danny added.

"Too vague." She was determined to thwart him at every turn. "Try again." And damned if he didn't. She had to hand it to him, the guy had patience.

"It's the idea that there's no true forgetting. Every experience leaves a discoverable trace. That's why the past and the present manage to co-exist in your emotions." He watched as her face lit up.

"So, like PTSD?" Now she was on more solid footing and hoped she could think her way out of this predicament.

"Something like that." He nodded and folded his arms across his chest, waiting while she processed the information.

"I get it. Remove the old scars so I can move forward."

"Exactly. To be freed from the wounds that were your primary source of suffering."

She'd done this work a thousand times with her clients and knew that the road to healing was paved with pain. "Don't suppose you have a shot of Dutch courage around here?" Her eyes prowled the table, hoping for a row of sparkling bottles. Anything would do at this point, even gin, but a nice expense-account Bordeaux would be perfect.

"Sorry." Danny handed her the headphones and waited.

She perched on the edge of the seat, reluctant to sink into its welcoming folds for fear she'd never escape. The mouse lay meekly on its pad but she approached as if expecting an electric shock. Music leaked from the earphones. As she slid them on, she heard the opening chords and then a single voice, warm and low. "There is a balm in Gilead."

A piercing *z-z-z-z-z-z* like an enraged mosquito cancelled out the hymn when she swept the mouse over a small gray patch, like a tangle of dust you might extract from the bag of a vacuum cleaner. Dense and uninviting. The word guilt popped up.

Time for a visit with mom.

Her stomach issued a warning as she prepared to confront the small bundle of perpetual motion that had parented her with exquisite subtlety. The woman specialized in mime-like signals that semaphored slackers to get moving. Her pursed lips and a laser-like stare could stop you in your tracks. Anger was silent, too. Her mother would fly around the house dusting with such intensity that even the furniture was in a panic. In the worst of times, it was a quiet, busy household. In the best of times, there was a facsimile of love but it was usually delivered on the fly.

The best defense is a good offense.

"I was a good daughter," she declared, as if testifying under oath, and mentally began to prepare the evidence that could counter her lifelong sense that nothing she did was good enough.

But instead of her childhood nemesis, the screen framed a small, gray woman, her back hunched over like a question mark. Smiling and warm, with a twinkle in her blue eyes and not a trace of anger, despite the fact that she'd lived for thirty years without her husband, the man they both adored. Her mother's devotion never diminished right up to the day she died, when she firmly believed she would be reunited with her sweetheart.

Frances felt a stab of remorse, realizing that her mother was a model of how to go on with half a heart but not live half-heartedly. *I gave her so little credit for her courage. All I could feel was my own loss and the disappointment of being left with the parent who was harder to love.* She wished with all her heart that she could hug her mother one more time and say, "I'm so sorry you lost your true love."

The scene changed to a sunny room. A body lay under a flowered duvet, motionless yet emitting a steady rasp. Outside, the sun was brilliant on a snowy landscape. Frances sat at the side of the bed and asked, "Is there anything I can do for you, mom?" Then she reached for a worn prayer book on the nightstand, the pages so soft from her mother's nightly visits that they turned without a sound, as if sensing the gravity of the moment.

Frances couldn't stomach the thought of rattling off empty words like a rented eulogist, so she searched for just the right prayers. For a mother. For a teacher. For the nearly deceased. Then she inserted her mother's name and details from her life to personalize the prose.

"Lord, welcome your faithful servant Elizabeth, after a long and exhausting life raising four rascals and some pretty annoying dogs, cooking dinner every night even when she wasn't hungry and having plenty of sex with my dad who adored her. She could use a good rest."

She nearly chuckled aloud. *Me, a self-proclaimed urban agnostic, keeping up my end of the conversation with a script I jettisoned decades ago.* But now repeating the familiar words that she unthinkingly recited as a child—*May she rest in peace*—seemed perfect. The greatest comfort she could offer since she'd run out of words of her own.

Then she left the room to answer the phone and in those few minutes her mother slipped away. It was like staring at the horizon, determined to witness the exact moment when the sun disappears, sparking that mysterious flash of green. But somehow you blink or are distracted by a flight of birds against the brilliant colors and when you look back, it's all over. She bent and kissed her mother goodbye. "Say hi to Daddy."

The spidery gray image on the screen dissolved. Frances slumped back in the chair and exhaled a long, slow breath, as if expelling a lifetime of doubt. "I was a good daughter."

Danny touched her shoulder lightly. "You certainly were." He gave her a moment to compose herself. "Let's finish up.

Just one more and then your debriefing."

She knew without asking which one he meant. The large purple scar. Her throat tightened and her head began to throb, so she parked the mouse and stared at the blotch. As her eyes crept around the shape looking for a clue or a warning, she noticed again that it was floating on a background of lip prints like Valentine wrapping paper. Kisses like dozens of love tattoos. Like persuasion. Souvenirs so embedded in her very being that she could never forget. And why would she want to? Intuition or raw hope told her that finally she'd found the indelible GPS that would guide her back home. It hurt like hell but without it she's be lost in this netherworld forever.

She jumped up and tore the earphones from her head but the cord tangled around her neck and the earphones trailed behind, bouncing across the deep carpet as she charged for the door. She glanced from Danny to the exit, expecting resistance, but he didn't move. Didn't race to bar the door or call for security but simply said, "You have to face it eventually. It's part of the process."

"Yeah, well, screw you and your process. I can do whatever I want." She shoved the door open, cringing in the light.

But what do I want?

She closed her eyes and a snippet of a dream surfaced. Something essential that felt like warmth and safety. Yearning and deliverance. Her mind tried to snatch it and hold it up to the light but it slipped through her fingers like water.

Any time now Grayson would turn up looking for her. The cage was closing in.

CHAPTER 42

The direction of flight was inconsequential. Frances just needed to put some serious yardage between herself and her latest failure. She was a fugitive bent on escaping herself.

Once again, she surrendered to the maze until she stumbled into a deserted square, desperate for somewhere to hide. A bunker, an abandoned basement, or one of those little mom-and-pop stores that survived the ravages of internet merchandizing, where she could soothe her fractured nerves with a dose of remarkably bad coffee. Maybe a bag of Fritos, the original version that left a shine on your fingertips while your arteries silently harvested the grease for future calamities.

But the square wasn't completely deserted. In the far corner stood a London phone booth, bright red and inviting. A haven where she could catch her breath and think. As if to welcome her, the door inched open at her approach. And what to her wondering eyes should appear but Graham, her ex-lover. He was sporting his classic slouch and a sardonic look that turned to mild amusement when she stopped dead in her tracks and then continued toward him. She didn't know what to expect or what she wanted besides distraction from the pounding in her head.

With a nearly imperceptible nod, he invited her in and pulled the door closed. The light clicked on revealing her reflection in the glass all around. Of course, this would be his venue of choice—public but confined and efficient. Titillating, but no room for much foreplay or the obligation to stick around afterwards.

He touched her chin and she found herself staring into eyes like a pond that had frozen over in winter. As his mouth dipped toward her, his familiar scent ferried memories of hungry lips and the soul patch that left her chin scraped and red for days after each encounter. Her badge of dishonor. But no kiss of welcome was forthcoming. Instead, he spun her around and pushed her against the glass. One hand buried itself between her legs while the other tugged at her blouse and then expertly massaged her breast. She shuddered and a small cloud of warm breath formed on the glass, erasing her reflection.

"That's my Frances, easily startled nipples."

She swayed and felt his dick plowing the groove between her buttocks, arousing despite the layers of clothing. At that very moment, Frances realized that she knew exactly what would come next because it was always the same. Sex with this man was like fucking a piece of gym equipment. There was only one way to make it work. The equipment didn't notice your mood or sense your vulnerability. It didn't care about you at all. You were just the element that triggered its function. She couldn't really call it empty sex. Empty would have been an improvement over the remorse that engulfed her whenever they'd met. But she'd returned again and again, ignoring the invisible CAUTION sign hanging around his neck. Because it was safe.

She arched her back and executed an ungainly pivot, her bare breast kissing the cold glass. Amidst the tangle of feet and arms, her hand grazed rough denim and fumbled for the awkward metal button and zipper. As if choreographed and rehearsed a dozen times, he bent his knees in a demi-plie. It would've looked like a swoon on anyone else but this man was no swooner. He was simply improving access.

She shifted just enough to free her other arm and reach for the phone. With his face burrowed in her neck, he couldn't see her lift the receiver and press it to her ear for a moment before she whispered, "Here. It's your *wife*."

His aloofness shattered as she yanked open his jeans and shoved the receiver home. "What the fuck?" was the last thing she heard as she dashed from the booth.

Across the square, Grayson staggered to the back of an alcove. His legs quaked as they fought to carry the shuddering load of a man gone limp. From a distance, he looked like a garden variety drunk or the victim of bad luck in the fast-food lottery. He pitched forward and grabbed his knees, as the pavement rushed toward him. Then a dry heaving sound echoed in the tiny space. When he looked up, the phone booth was empty and Frances was gone.

CHAPTER 43

"What in God's name is she doing now?" Cornelius exploded.

The monitor in the Committee room beeped but the scene on the screen seemed to be obscured by fog. Slowly the image expanded to reveal the exterior of the red telephone booth.

"It looks like hot sex with no strings attached," the Fool offered.

"Stupid woman. Has she learned nothing?" Cornelius was incensed.

"*Stupid?*" Juliette objected. "That's the smartest thing she's done since she landed in this place!"

"Really? Empty sex?" Cornelius was incredulous and turned his back on her, intent on returning to the business at hand. "Now if we can just..." but she cut him off.

"On the contrary, if I recall correctly, it's filled to the brim." She arched her neck exposing an expanse of soft white flesh, and then sighed. "Electric attraction like your nerve endings discovered magnetic north made flesh. Visceral longing that borders on possession and a ravenous desire that feeds upon itself. Pure experience that blotted out everything—pain, loneliness, despair. The only emptiness, my dear Cornelius, was the absence of petty notions like ownership and longevity."

He spun around. "Of course, I get it. Good sex, but you couldn't make it last," he taunted. He looked around at the

Committee members, searching for nods of agreement but all eyes were riveted on Juliette.

"Actually, the sex wasn't always that good, despite the promises." She walked to the front of the room before sharing the rest of her tale. "The ballet world was full of men who claimed prodigious talents. The dancers! They were the worst! All ego, like they were doing me a favor!" She gave the women in the room a can-you-believe-it look, and Olympe nodded in a gesture of camaraderie. "And the patrons? Pathetic! Well-dressed hangers-on, wealth-ruined fops all hinting at Nirvana between the sheets. But get them in bed?" After a dramatic pause she chortled, "Most of them were rubbish!"

The Fool chuckled and nodded in agreement. "Under promise, over perform. Men never seem to grasp that notion."

"Still," Juliette went on soberly, "I was haunted by the thought that one of those times would be my last. It wouldn't announce itself or be memorable in any way, but with the passage of time it would become precious. So, I reveled in each encounter."

"I wasn't looking for a treatise on promiscuity, Ms. Cross-Dresser." Cornelius gave her a jaundiced glance and shuffled the papers in front of him, as if dismissing the entire conversation.

Juliette approached him and slammed her hand on the papers. "It wasn't just about the sex," she objected. "I loved men!" She clapped one hand over her heart. "Even when they drove me crazy or broke my heart. Loved to burrow my face into a stout neck, inhaling the scent of sweat and a recent meal. To feel a few strands of beard or the fibers of a worn collar caress my nose." Then she looked directly at Cornelius. "The thrill of being scooped into a man's arms, compressed to the brink of breathlessness but feeling utterly sheltered and safe."

Cornelius flinched as if he'd been stabbed, and several members of the Committee exchanged puzzled looks.

Now Juliette was really warming to the topic, ignoring his discomfort. She reached up and straightened her tie. "It was the differences that made them so intriguing. Their clothes. The way they filled up a room without even trying. Their curt logic and rumbling laughter. I adored that rich low resonance when they sang and their uncontrollable gasps, even tears, when they came."

The Fool snatched the folder from the table and fanned himself in mock surprise, then leaned in closer, eager to hear every last detail of her story.

She stopped for a moment and then sighed. "I once had a lover who hummed Greensleeves just before he'd climax. God, I loved that man!" She walked over and pointed to the monitor. "That's why I pity Frances, growing up in a man-hating era. She didn't hate men. Just the misogyny they'd all inherited."

"God knows, I tried to change that," Olympe protested.

"Me, too," added a mournful voice.

Cornelius roused himself. "It's too late for your pity and pontificating." He touched the pocket of his waistcoat. "Frances had her chance. Behavior has consequences. As she will discover."

CHAPTER 44

For once Frances was grateful for the labyrinth, where pursued and pursuer had an equal shot at getting hopelessly lost. She sprinted across the square and ran for whole minutes, surprised at how far the adrenalin carried her. By the time Graham was upright and zipped, she could be anywhere.

Rounding a corner at top speed, she collided with a sandwich board jutting out into the narrow lane, as much a hazard as an invitation. But who could refuse a hideout called The Serenity Salon?

She slid off her shoes and tip-toed through the door, drawn by the sound of a low rolling *ohm* as if exhaled by a hundred far-off voices. The Salon's interior was in perfect harmony with its purpose. Blank colorless walls offered exactly no distraction for the eye. The air was body temperature and completely still. Yoga mats in various shades of sand, ash and inner thigh dotted the floor. A set of tiny bells but no percussionist. Not another living soul.

Perfect.

In her former incarnation, Frances had promoted meditation like a monk with an MBA. Not a seminar went by without her extolling the health benefits, polling the audience for Zen versus transcendentalists, even offering optional mindfulness sessions during the lunch break. But could *she* do it? No way. Her brain was a free-range creature, as busy as Grand Central

Station at rush hour. She didn't just have intrusive thoughts. They barged in and set up shop.

Meditation Challenge #1:

Her faltering word retrieval function, so often and inconveniently AWOL, would kick in to high gear. Just as the little bell rang, signaling that she should empty her mind, here came a noisy delivery of nouns, verbs and adjectives that had been rounded up, too late to help. A word like *havoc* would pop into her head when just hours before she'd sniffed around it like a dog on the scent, but was forced to use a lackluster synonym like *disruption*.

Each of these bouts of brain freeze caused panic as she pictured a future in which she could feel and taste fugitive words in her mouth while they danced just out of reach, mocking her. *You used to know all those big words, Frances. Tongue like lightning. Now look at you.*

Meditation Challenge #2:

The bits of conversations that drifted in while she was hard at work concentrating on nothing. She remembered eavesdropping on two men admiring a de Kooning portrait at the Whitney Museum. "It gets me right here," one man said, thumping his chest just below his throat. His companion nodded solemnly. "Yeah. It's probably that second row of teeth around the vagina."

Meditation Challenge #3:

Her To-Do list would scroll out like those receipts at the drug store where a two-item sale produced three feet of coupons to lure you back. *Take vitamins. Replace toothbrush. Root job. Astragalus. Floss. Compression socks. Drink more water. Meditate.* The items metastasized at a rate that would make cancer sit up and take notice. Eventually, she'd throw in the towel.

Way too much going on to sit on my ass pretending to be calm.

In desperation she'd even tried the Smiling Technique.

Close your eyes and put a faint smile on your face. It was supposed to send a message to her brain that all was well, but the minute she curled the edges of her mouth, her brain demanded: *What's she smiling about? Did I miss something?* Then it would root around for smile-inducing memories. A dirty water hotdog with all the fixings from Sabrett's. Leaf-peeping in October. With the arrival of each thought, she began to feel better. And better.

But that's not meditating! Constant Comment would scold. *It's daydreaming!* So, Frances would clamp her mental sphincter even tighter but with no observable effect on the tug-o-war between ideas and inhalation.

A tiny bell rang somewhere deep in the Serenity Salon and Frances yanked her attention back to the present, if only to give her frayed nerves a moment of rest. *Remember that thing called oxygen? Now focus. Only. On. Breathing.* She drew in the sort of breath you'd use to converse with the hard of hearing, then exhaled slowly as she began to count.

One, two, three, four.

She pictured Jasper Johns' colorful number paintings, which led directly to his Target series and it was only a short hop to the certainty that she was wearing a giant target on her back. When she finally wrangled her focus back to her breathing, she was hyperventilating.

"Frances?" Grayson bellowed. "You in here?"

The door of the meditation room banged open but Frances didn't say a word. Lepus instinct at the ready—freeze. Grayson stormed in and planted himself in front of her.

Instantly, she achieved the kind of in-the-moment aware-ness that yogis tout, but without a shred of the promised serenity. Her body tingled from head to toe with her least favorite feelings—guilt, scorching shame, the helplessness of being caught out. Out of class, out of line, and out of luck.

"You're just in time," she said quietly, patting the floor beside her. "Grab a pillow. You look like you could use a few *ohms.*" Then she rearranged her hands in her lap and let her eyelids droop until a sharp nudge jostled her thigh.

"Hey, I'm trying to meditate here. It's in my curriculum, remember?"

"Get up!" His sentence landed like a smack from a two-by-four.

She scrambled to her feet, surreptitiously checking her buttons and tucking in her blouse. "What?" she asked, feigning an innocence she didn't feel.

He grabbed her elbow and stomped toward the door. "Where have you been?" he demanded when they were out on the street.

Bristling at the inquisition, she ducked the question. "Why are you so upset?"

"Because I'm supposed to be helping you." His face was just inches from hers when he finished, causing her to recoil.

"Oh, that's it. Performance anxiety. Worried about how you'll look?" She patted him on the shoulder and gave him a smile that said she'd be happy to cover for him. "No problem. If anyone asks, I'll say you're doing a *great* job. *Fan-tas-tic.* So how 'bout if you just chill?"

"Chill? Chill?" He grabbed her by the shoulders and shook her until she pulled away, clearly shocked by the violence. "Don't you get it? This isn't some kind of game. You're under court surveillance, 24-7! And this court isn't known for its patience."

Her head swiveled sharply as her eyes searched the rooftops for snipers with binoculars. "Court! Fuck that court!"

CHAPTER 45

The Committee stared at the monitor like people watching a car crash, unable to look away as Frances fled down the passageway and then paused at the first intersection. "Left," Grayson shouted. She took a hard right and disappeared.

"He's going to blow it," Juliette warned. "She has to do this by herself."

Just then the door creaked open and a dignified man stepped in, wearing only a simple white kilt.

Cornelius cursed under his breath, "*Godverdomme!* Another black?" He narrowed his eyes in the direction of the Fool. "I told you to watch the door."

"The door has been duly watched, Sire." He made an elaborate show of swiveling his head away from Cornelius. "Yea, I have my eyes upon it still. Perhaps the fault lies in the clarity of your request. 'Bar the door against those with more pigment than myself.' That might have covered the situation to your satisfaction."

Cornelius ignored the barb and returned his attention to the newcomer. "And what may I do for you?" he asked in a tone of mocking deference.

"*Je suis* Frances," the man declared.

Cornelius looked puzzled. "French? In that getup? I would have guessed Egyptian."

"Correct, Sire. A scribe in the dynasty of Rameses the First.

I specialized in the preparation of wills."

"I don't care if you did quadratic equations. Cover that bare chest! There are ladies present." He flung one hand out, as if dismissing the scribe when Olympe slammed her fist on the table and seized the conversation.

"Jesus! Would you let him talk?" she demanded.

"Jesus? You're a believer, too?" Perpetua asked, letting the baby slide from her lap and reaching for a cross around her neck.

"What?" Olympe frowned, clearly annoyed at the momentary distraction.

"Jesus. I'm a follower," Perpetua said with pride.

"Can you do your proselytizing elsewhere?" Cornelius snarled. "This is no time for a theological seminar." The interruption seemed to leave him confused. "Now, where was I?" He stared at the darkened monitor, running his hands through his hair and smoothing his moustache. When he turned around, he seemed surprised that the scribe was still waiting to be heard. "Go on," he grumbled.

"I belong on this committee," the scribe announced calmly as he placed a scroll on the table at the front of the room. "I know things. And I understand Frances better than any of you. After all, I sat day after day for a lifetime, listening to people's concerns."

"Sounds pathetic," Cornelius said. "With your skills you could have done much better." He shook his head in disgust at the obvious waste of opportunity.

"I was a *slave*, Sire. An educated slave," the scribe protested.

"Then you're to be pitied. But misfortune doesn't qualify you for membership on this committee." Cornelius turned away as if the subject was closed.

An old man sprang out of his chair and declared in a stentorian voice, "Mr. Beeckman, the greatest slave is not he who is ruled by a despot but he who is in the thrall of his own moral ignorance, selfishness and vice."

The Fool clapped his hands and cried, "Bravo!" then ducked as Cornelius took a swing at him but missed.

"And who might you be?" Cornelius sneered at the old man.

"Samuel Smiles, at your service. Now let the scribe speak." His voice was thick with an air of authority that even Cornelius couldn't ignore.

"Fine. Get on with it," he said to the scribe. Then he pulled a gold pocket watch out of his vest and frowned. "But make it quick. I have work to do."

The scribe pulled himself up to his full height. "Stop attacking Frances. Instead of judging, we need to help."

Andreas chortled. "Why? My brother's keeper and all that bullshit? Besides, have you seen how she treats people who try to help?"

Olympe jumped to her feet, determined to keep the focus on Frances. "Speak your mind, monsieur, s'il vous plait,"

"We made her," the scribe said. He spread his arms to encompass the whole Committee, and watched as they gave him puzzled looks or checked with the others to see if there was something they'd missed.

Andreas shrugged. "Don't look at me," and lit another cigarette, visibly bored with the topic.

"Wake up, people! Don't you understand?" the scribe pleaded. "We're the ultimate recycling project. Frances is our latest reincarnation." He grabbed the scroll from the table and unfurled it, revealing yards of parchment covered with careful lines of writing from top to bottom. The room fell silent. Even the baby watched in fascination. "I know. I've been keeping the record."

He gestured to the Fool for assistance. "If you please, hold it up high for all to see." Then he ran his finger down the list of names. "Here you are, Gerard. And our friend the yogi. And here's little Chaghatai." The toddler crawled toward the scribe at the sound of his name, as if expecting the arrival of a long-lost parent. "Died in Mongolia at the age of 15 months. Thrown from his father's horse. It broke his mother's heart."

Perpetua scooped up the baby and repeated his name over and over. "Chaghatai, Chaghatai."

"And my brother scribbler, over in the corner. Pierre, isn't it?" continued the scribe.

The man looked up at the sound of his name and nodded.

"Pierre was a gravedigger at Pere Lachaise Cemetery in Paris. An illiterate, stigmatized for his work and shunned by society. But he learned the alphabet by studying the head-stones, tracing the letters with his fingers. The local priest took notice and tutored him. Said he never had such an avid student. Books were Pierre's escape from an uncaring world."

Pierre touched his heart.

"Sadly, disease took his voice and eventually his life."

The scribe paused. "Surely you can see it! The evidence is staring you right in the face! Before Frances was Frances, she was you," he charged, pointing at Andreas, "with your cynical attitude and awesome palate." He pivoted, pointing an ink-stained finger at Gwilym, who cringed at the unwelcome attention. "And you, gentle sage of the stables." His hand strafed the room like a machine gun, "And you and you and you."

"You're saying she's the sum of the parts?" Olympe asked.

"Or maybe greater than the sum, despite all your criti-cisms," the scribe replied. "What do you think made her such a good social worker? Empathy born out of memory."

"A hybrid carrying strains of each of us. Is that what you're saying?" Gerard inquired.

"The pilgrimage of a soul," whispered the yogi.

"Precisely. We made her, so we're responsible," concluded the scribe.

Cornelius bristled at the word responsible, and reared up out of his chair. "I'm in charge of this committee and I'll tell you where the responsibility lies! Squarely on that woman!"

He fairly spat out the words as he pointed toward the monitor. "Don't you dare say otherwise."

CHAPTER 46

The Committee room was silent for a long time, each member subdued by the gravity of the scribe's words. "It seems like she took the best from each of us and tried to put it to good use," Olympe said, looking pointedly at Cornelius. "Good for the world."

Smiles leaned back and nodded. "That was my contribution."

Whispers and grumbles rippled around the table as the Committee members turned nervously from one to another. Each had played a role in the Frances drama, but it was anyone's guess about who'd claim her virtues or be stuck with the blame.

"Maybe that's so, but let's be realistic," Cornelius said. "Not all contributions are created equal." He looked disdainfully around the table.

Olympe stood and leaned over the table toward him. "Meaning?"

"Well," he said, pointing to Juliette. "We all know she was a bit of a slut."

Olympe looked offended but Juliette swiped back, as quick as a cat, "You object to free love?"

"I object to free anything. After all, I'm a business man." His smug face said that anything else was a waste.

"Translation: robber baron," Olympe interjected, and sat

back down. "Tulips, I think." That got his attention.

Cornelius flew out of his chair, not in a rage this time, but swaggering across the front of the room like a Shakespearian actor taking center stage. "Tulips were the least of it," he crowed. "I was a golden boy in the Golden Age."

"You don't seem like the flower-type," Gwilym observed in a quiet voice from one side of the room.

"Well, well. Smarter than you look." He patted Gwilym on the shoulder and began to make a full circuit around the table. "You're right. I couldn't care less about them. It was all about the bulbs." He looked from face to face, searching for a spark of recognition, and then shifted his gaze back to the groom. "Did you ever see a tulip bulb? No, of course you wouldn't. Looks like a lump of desiccated turd. That would be more in your line of work."

He returned to the front of the room, hungry for an audience. "I was dealing in futures and it was all done on paper. You wouldn't understand. Most people didn't." But that didn't dampen his enthusiasm for the chance to tell his story. "At any rate, that only lasted for one wild and glorious year. Got out before the crash with a tidy sum." His face lit up in a professional gloat. "I have to say it was a personal best, but I had plenty of other irons in the fire. The United East India Company, The Exchange Bank, insurance, spices." He tapped his bulbous nose. "This guy can smell money."

"Looks like it could smell the back side of the moon," Andreas sniped.

Unfazed, Cornelius boasted, "Where do you think Frances got her head for business—best-seller list and all? I saved her from a life of low-wage anonymity."

"Now wait just a minute, Mister Beeckman!" Smiles protested. "I was the one with the best-seller."

Cornelius pressed on, unashamed of his grab for credit. "Have it your way. Perhaps it was a two-step process. I bequeathed you the business acumen, then you passed it along.

And my hat's off to you, Samuel. You epitomized the entrepreneurial spirit of the time. But you, Madame de Gouges." He turned back to Olympe. "What did you contribute?"

Olympe rose and stood with the dignity of a queen. Slowly, she turned her back to him, addressing the Committee with pride. "I taught her how to fight." Then she spun around toward Cornelius and spat, "Revolutions don't happen on paper, sir. You have to get your hands dirty and Louis XVI obliged me with plenty of opportunities."

"And would you like to tell the good folks how that worked out?" he sneered.

"I...we...had a great life," Olympe said in a voice filled with wonder. "Once I learned the power of the pen, I brandished it with all my might. Wrote until my fingers were numb. They called me a one-woman publishing company. Forty essays, treatises, God knows how many pamphlets. So perhaps, Mr. Smiles, I contributed something to you." She curtsied toward him, her long silk gown rustling in the silent room.

Smiles stood and made a deep bow. "Many thanks, Madame. I believe we had much in common. Our stand against slavery and the death penalty. Our insistence on the rights of women."

"I also called for taxing those elites of whom you spoke, Cornelius, in order to redistribute wealth and eradicate poverty," Olympe continued. "If the King had listened to me, he wouldn't have lost his throne."

"Probably couldn't hear her above the rabble," the Fool said.

"But I soon realized that plays were the most powerful weapon of all. Tell your truth through a story and you'll find your audience."

"Took a leaf out of Shakespeare's book, did you?" the Fool asked.

"Why not?" Olympe said. "My first play was performed at the *Comedie Francaise*. What an amazing night!" She paused for a moment, staring into space with a slight smile, as if watching the performance in her head. "Fist fights broke out in the aisles. Abolitionists and supporters pummeling each other while the startled actors soldiered on above the fray. Of course, the run was cancelled but I thought it a great success. My one-night wonder."

She gave a sigh filled with regret. "I was trying to save the revolution from itself."

"And?" Cornelius prompted, his voice dripping with venom.

"And...I was sent to the guillotine." She loosened her scarf, exposing a deep gash that ran from ear to ear. "Unjustly accused. Imprisoned. Denied a lawyer. I was only forty-five. In the prime of life. But the rights of women and the poor were on my lips until the very end."

The women gave her a round of applause.

Cornelius banged on the table. "Silence! You will come to order!" When the clapping stopped, he grabbed a stack of papers in front of him and cleared his throat. "As much as I've enjoyed this little trip down memory lane, we have a job to do here."

Gwilym shifted in his chair. Unaccustomed to sitting so long, he seemed to be searching for a comfortable position.

"Don't tell me." Cornelius winced. "You want your moment in the spotlight, too?"

"Indeed not, Sire. I have no story to tell. I was no one. Just a simple groom who slipped in and out of the world unnoticed. Born on a kitchen table. Buried in a pauper's grave." He stared down at his hands. "What happened in between would be of no interest to you."

"Try us," Smiles said gently. "Please."

"Mine was a humble life, but worth more to me than all my master's possessions," Gwilym said with sudden fervor. "Every season brought a new gift. The fragrance of fresh hay at the end of summer. The warm breath of a mare in the crisp autumn air. Even on the coldest night in winter I slept in the stalls. Burrowed in the hay, listening to the horses chewing, I felt safe because they could sense the slightest sound or smell or movement, warning me of danger." He paused. "They were magnificent."

"Go on," prompted Gerard.

"War ravaged the countryside nearby, but there was peace in the stables. The same set of chores each day, rain or shine, in sickness and in health. Sweep the aisle, fill the water, clean the stalls. In return I enjoyed acceptance. Perhaps love. In the spring the new foals that arrived were like children to me."

Andreas sighed. "Now that was a good life."

"*Good?*" Cornelius cried. "Are you mad? He was an anonymous link in the human impulse to breed. Nothing more."

"That's true, Sire," the groom said. "But what does it matter? What did any of us do that truly mattered? We all... died. We died and we're nobody now. The only thing that matters is Frances, and if she fails or quits..."

"She won't fail," Smiles protested, jumping to his feet. "I know her. She never gives up. No matter how difficult things get, she keeps trying." He beamed like a proud father. "She took *Self-Help* to heart."

"Give it a rest, Smiles," Andreas sighed. "Yes, you worked hard enough for all of us. But look at poor Frances. She's a slave to your DNA. How much discipline can a single soul take?"

There was a rustle of saffron robes and the yogi spoke slowly and haltingly, as if his voice was emerging from hibernation. "Even here in the land of RIP, she can't seem to rest or find peace. She never took that message to heart."

"That's not the only message she didn't get," Cornelius insisted. "She's stubborn and arrogant and refuses to learn, even when the lessons are staring her in the face. As I've said, we can't be responsible for what happens next."

CHAPTER 47

One by one the Committee members began to stir, stiff from sitting for hours, weary of the tirade that seemed to gain velocity as Cornelius pursued his crusade against Frances.

Gerard leaned over to Smiles. "Would you care to join me outside?"

"I could certainly do with a change of scenery. We seem to be getting nowhere."

Gerard led the way down a dim hall and shoved open a stout door. Inside they were greeted by a cozy sitting room. Two generous chairs warmed themselves in front of a peat fire, inviting the men to join them for a spell. As they settled in, Gerard reached into his coat pocket and pulled out a pipe. He lit up and after a long pull, offered it to Smiles.

"That was a bit after your time, wasn't it?" Smiles asked.

"It's not tobacco. Another herb. A gift from my brother gardeners in France. They had a Society of Smokers. Very esoteric stuff. I think you'll appreciate it. At any rate, it can't hurt you now."

"Well, why not?" Smiles reached for the pipe and took an exploratory drag, and then coughed violently. "A warning would have been the gentlemanly thing to do."

"Apologies, my good man. I'd almost forgotten that it's an acquired skill, but I think you'll find it's worth the effort." With that, the men burrowed deeper into their chairs and stared at the flames in silence.

"So, what do you think of our little group?" Smiles asked.

"I thought we'd have more in common," Gerard said.

More silence and then Smiles sighed wistfully. "I thought we'd like each other more."

"It is odd, isn't it? The antagonism. As if we can disown the parts of ourselves that we don't like. May as well blame the mirror for what we see."

"It does seem at times that we're all wishing we could be anywhere else, and anyone else."

"But we're here and we're us. Must make the best of it. And you have to admit, taken as a whole, we're an impressive lot. You in particular, Samuel. I've heard that your books were translated into every European language. Even made it to Japan."

"And to think my school master said, 'Smiles, you will never be fit for anything but sweeping the streets of your native borough.'"

"Well, I hope he lived long enough to see the error of his ways. You had such fame!"

"And you had Queen Elizabeth! My God, what an adventure that must have been." Smiles didn't even try to hide the envy in his voice.

"Indeed, it was," said Gerard. He smoothed his pointed beard and his face lit up with pleasure.

"Tell me about her." Smiles was like a child begging for a fairy story.

"She was everything that you've read and more, but I like to think I saw her at her best. Away from court. Surrounded by nature. One morning she came out at dawn. No makeup. No entourage. Like a young girl wandering in her enchanted garden. I ducked behind a column and watched her gambol down the path like a colt, then she paused, as still as a statue with her face to the rising sun. God's brilliant creation gracing mine. It's my most cherished memory."

"I read about your magnificent garden at Theobalds," Smiles said. "How I wished I could have seen it but sadly, I was born too late."

"Yes, it scarcely lasted a hundred years. It would have killed me to see it demolished. And for what? A war that no one can remember." Smiles patted his arm in sympathy and they stared at the fire in silence. Suddenly Gerard jumped from his chair. "I have an idea." He sprinted down the hall, bounding into the Committee room which was deserted except for the Fool who was dozing in an alcove.

"You there, bright fellow. You seem to have mastered this machine." Gerard pointed to the monitor.

The Fool shook himself awake. "Indeed, I have. It's like a wondrous gazing ball." He chuckled for a moment before adding, "I dare not tell you *what* I've seen. And *whom*."

"Well, we should like to see a garden. Can you conjure up Theobalds?"

"A pleasure, Sire." He pressed the button on the monitor and there was Gerard, gladiator in the great horticultural battle for the affection of Queen Elizabeth, striding through the grounds of a massive country estate with William Cecil, Lord Burghley.

"A fourteen-foot-high marigold, my Lord, also known as a sunflower. Very rare, indeed," Gerard said, describing his latest trophy.

The queen's chief minister gazed out across the acres of exotic plants, canals, reflecting pools, and a maze garden.

The Fool filled in the details. "What Mr. Gerard isn't saying is that he was considered the best gardener in England, commissioned by Cecil to create an oasis that would dazzle the Queen, ensuring return visits and continued influence at court."

"Robert Dudley was playing the same game at Kenilworth," Gerard added. "Spent a fortune building a tower and wooed Elizabeth for three straight weeks with plays, fireworks, music, paintings, the garden and of course, his besotted face.

It was a last-ditch effort to pry a matrimonial *yes* out of her."
He shook his head. "A dismal failure."

"Political one-upsmanship waged with shovel and rake,"
observed the Fool.

On the screen Cecil clapped Gerard on the back and said,
"Elizabeth was never in any place better pleased. The house,
garden and walks may compare with any delicate place in
Italy." Then the two disappeared into a shady bower.

"That was a good life," Smiles sighed.

"Indeed, it was. A dream come true in every way and I
loved it," Gerard declared with intense passion. "But you make
me feel a bit ashamed, Samuel, for I can think of nothing I
contributed to Frances."

"Come now, John. You're too modest."

"Perhaps curiosity?" Gerard wondered. "She does seem to
have a restless, inquisitive mind. An appreciation of nature?
The capacity for joy? Is that something one can pass along?"

"Why not?" the Fool chirped. "What would life be without
a bit of joy? Trust me. I'm in the business."

"But Samuel, Frances seems so unhappy now," Gerard
continued. "It pains me to watch her struggle."

"We often discover what will work by finding out what will
not. He who never made a mistake, never made a discovery."
Smiles gave him a reassuring smile.

"Still, I wish we could help."

"It won't be easy."

CHAPTER 48

Two huge files lay open side-by-side on the counter in the Records Room and Molly was hunched over like a Talmudic scholar, flipping from page to page as she compared entries. Pausing, she made careful notations in a small notebook, and then hammered numbers into a calculator before returning to the columns of words and numbers set out like a medieval ledger.

She was so lost in thought that she jumped like she'd been caught perusing *Playgirl* when Grayson lurched through the door. She slammed the books shut and shoved them out of sight, then made an elaborate show of rearranging the pens on her blotter.

Grayson flung himself into a chair at the end of the counter, oblivious. Molly gave him time for a good, long sulk, then tilted her head ever so slightly, wordlessly asking, *Do you want to talk?*

He responded with a look of despair. "I don't think she's going to make it."

"Really?" She furrowed her brow as if this was news. "It seemed to be going so well."

"Are you kidding? Misanthropy was a disaster. It took us a week to talk the Reverend back in from the ledge," Grayson sputtered.

"Yes, but that was early on. It takes time."

"No! This is different. She's got issues," he insisted.

Molly just stared at him wearing her *observe-don't-judge* face, but he pressed on. "She won't take direction."

"You've handled tough cases before," she reminded him.

"Not like this." He seemed determined to parry and thrust his way through their chat. "So defensive and she's got a mouth on her."

"Spirited."

"Try combative. Make that self-destructive. I'm knocking myself out," he complained, his voice rising.

"I can see you're concerned." Her tone was soothing but it didn't work.

"Yeah. Lot of good it's done me." He slumped back in a funk.

"*You?* I thought this was about Frances." Her tone was even, but it stung.

"Whose side are you on?" he snapped but was instantly contrite. "Right. You're right." He gave his head a vigorous scratch, as if he was trying to make contact with his brain. "Maybe she needs another handler."

Molly reached toward him and patted his arm. "Maybe she just needs more time. It's a process."

He gave her a ruptured grunt. "A process. So I'm told."

"Hold on a minute," she said. "I'll be right back." She returned to the room clutching a huge file and placed it in front of him.

"Mine?"

She nodded. "Shall we?"

"Why not?" he shrugged. "Remind me again. What are the red tabs?"

"EEs." Seeing his puzzled look, she added, "Early Exits."

"Dropouts?" He winced. "So, this won't be pretty."

"We don't think of it that way." Then she flipped through the file. "Number 18. You left early and ended up on the wrong side of the battle at Trasimene. One of Hannibal's many casualties."

"And I didn't even get to see the elephants. Well, clearly I was confused," he said dismissively and returned to his preoccupation with Frances. "She's opinionated. And you wouldn't believe what she said to Gabe."

"Gabriel can take care of himself." She quietly flipped to a new section. "Number 128. Early Exit. England. 1568," she said as if it was last Wednesday. "That was a short one. You decided to speak out against Queen Elizabeth. I believe you suggested in print that she was too old to be making marriage plans. Lost your head. Literally."

"But you have to admit, I did have a point. Now Frances, she has this huge investment in being right, even when it's clear she's wrong. Talk about stubborn."

"Let's try another one," said Molly, ignoring his litany of complaints. "Ah, yes. You were doing brilliantly. We actually thought you'd finish ahead of schedule. Then you started skipping classes. Not showing up for appointments. You left without giving notice in the company of a soul soon-to-be-called Trotsky, raving about a permanent revolution and the need to learn Spanish."

"We thought we were on to something. And we were. Just a little ahead of our time." He shrugged his shoulders. "The Ninety-Nine Percent crowd would've loved us."

"You've certainly had some interesting returns. I told you, it just takes time." Her voice was reassuring as she closed his file.

"Time. I'm afraid it might have run out."

"That doesn't happen here." She reached over and patted his hand. "But remember what Trotsky said: *Life is not an easy matter*. That includes the afterlife."

"Tell me about it," he sighed. "Maybe you're right. I could cut her some slack or try a different approach. I don't know. But here's the problem. One of these days the court will issue a summons and I can tell you right now, it's not looking good."

His voice was beyond bleak. "I'm at a bit of a loss."

"When was the last time you went to a meeting?"

"You're saying I fell off the wagon?" he snapped. Molly didn't have to say a word. Her face announced that he'd wandered into asshole territory. He reached across the counter and gave her hand a repentant squeeze. "Thanks, Moll. I needed that."

As his soft whistle disappeared down the hall, Molly reached down to retrieve the files. Her brow wrinkled, her eyes leapt from one page to another, then she pounced on her calculator and noisily doubled checked a column of numbers. With that, she bent forward and planted a kiss on the ledger. "Yes!"

CHAPTER 49

Grayson reached for the handle on a tall wooden door, then performed a brief approach-avoidance ballet, trying to decide if he should enter or head for Jack's bar where he could sulk over an industrial-strength painkiller. The decision was made for him when Max, a portly bundle of energy, appeared. He called out, "How you been, man?" and threw his arm around Grayson, pulling him through the door.

"Don't ask. How 'bout you?" Grayson replied, delaying the inevitable admission a bit longer.

"Can't complain. But seriously, what's going on?" Max gave his friend a look of concern.

"Same old same old. Why else would I be here?" Grayson mumbled. A dozen chairs waited attentively in a circle. A dozen people loitered in small groups, exchanging news. He nodded to a few of them, then flopped down, as if conserving his energy.

Max joined him. "Need a tune up?"

"Try a kick in the ass. It would go perfectly with the kick in the balls she delivered."

Max winced. "Ouch! You want to talk?"

Grayson's posture stiffened. "What's there to say? I can't handle things? I'm a failure?" He watched Max recoil but decided to finish what he'd started. "Fine, I said it."

"Whoa, man!" Max thrust out his hands like a mime hitting

an invisible wall. "You got it all wrong. You took a risk with Frances. That takes courage."

"News flash! Courage is over-rated." He massaged the stubble on his chin. "She's gone rogue."

"And you think you're responsible?" Max challenged.

"Hello?" It was a classic are-you-completely-clueless response. "Job description? I'm supposed to be the specialist. You know, facilitate acclimation, watch for self-destructive behavior, focus on growth, keep her eye on the goal. Isn't that what the training manual said?" He rubbed the back of his neck.

"And?" Max prompted.

"So far, I'm either her drinking buddy or a punching bag. It sucks."

Just then Bill, the group leader, slid into a chair at the center of the circle and surveyed the gathering. "Good to see all of you. How about if we go around the circle and focus on progress."

Bill's job, as far as Grayson could tell, was to reduce their sense of isolation and failure by helping them see that their intensely personal hang-ups were identical to everyone else in the room.

Max led the way. "I had a breakthrough last week. Put my foot down about ditching class and it actually worked. I shocked myself."

Mild murmurs of admiration rippled through the group.

"I'm Alex. New here. I've been getting a lot of flak from my client. He was charming at first but lately he tears into me every chance he gets. Carping, bitching, sneering. Actually called me an incompetent dick. I was so stunned I just stood there thinking *he did not just say that.* By the time I came up with a decent retort, he'd moved on. What am I doing wrong?" He reared back in his chair and drummed his fingers on the metal arms.

"Narcissist?" Bill asked.

"You got that right." Alex nodded and surveyed the group, finding sympathetic faces all around.

"Never forget," Bill said. "He doesn't see you. He doesn't hear you. You don't exist outside of his own needs."

"Sometimes I want to kill him." Alex scrubbed his hand over his face.

"Someone already did," Bill said, then added, "Same reason. I get it that you're frustrated and I'm sorry, but try thinking of it as batting practice. Each time he acts up is a chance to take better care of yourself."

"Killing sounds like more fun," Grayson said and threw Alex a sympathetic thumbs-up.

"I keep thinking I should try some version of tough love," Gary volunteered. "Then I remember that my dad perfected tough but never got around to the love. It just seems cruel. So much for progress. I'm stuck."

"What about you, Angus?" Bill asked.

"I sit on my ass for hours, waiting for her to get her act together. The woman has a million excuses. And talk about too much information. By the time she explains in relentless detail why she was late or completely AWOL, my word-processing center is flat-lining. I just want her to shut up."

Bill jumped in. "Interrupt, interrupt, interrupt. Think of it as ping pong. The minute she lobs an alibi in your direction, smack it back. Don't let her get anywhere near the end of a sentence. Then see who gets exhausted."

When the conversation finally came around to Grayson, there was a long pause. "This last while has been rough. I've tried to set limits and push back. It's tough, finding the balance between doormat and dictator. So, if you're looking for progress, I'd say I'm making spectacular strides with my frustration tolerance."

"Well, Grayson," Bill said with a chuckle, "sounds like it's time to take Carl's advice."

There was an uncomfortable shifting in the group as they

looked around in vain for someone named Carl. But there was no Carl and never had been, so what were they to think? Perhaps their fearless leader was losing his grip or simply burning out without leaving a trail of smoke.

"Jung. Carl Jung, the Swiss analyst. Does that name ring a bell?" Bill laughed. "Whenever someone announced bad news or a challenging situation, Jung would say, *Let us open a bottle of wine. Something good will come of this.*"

"I'm not feelin' it," Grayson said, refusing to embrace Bill's optimism.

"I have faith in you." Max said.

"Thanks. I needed that."

Bill leapt from his chair and motioned toward a door tucked out of sight at the back of the room. "First round's on me."

Grayson snagged a glass of wine, knocked it back like a dose of medicine and wandered over to a shiny black Yamaha piano standing against the far wall. It had been a while but he couldn't resist running his fingers over the keys. It was perfectly tuned without a speck of dust. He tried a few chords almost by instinct, but after shouts of encouragement from Bill and the others, he sat down and gave his fingers and wrists a quick massage. Swaying from side to side, he opened with *New York, New York,* followed by a dozen piano-bar favorites.

"More, more," his colleagues chanted when he paused, calling out popular tunes and topping off his wine to lubricate the performance. *Sweet Caroline* and *Bye-Bye Blackbird* lured even the most timid crooners to join the impromptu chorus.

Somewhere in the swirl of music and voices and wine, Grayson found an escape from his woes.

Frances is no one.

I am free.

This is enlightenment.

As he hit the last notes of *Don't Stop Believing,* his fingers flew off the end of the keyboard and the room swallowed him.

CHAPTER 50

"Hangover?"

Grayson nodded wordlessly from his perch on a wooden stool, looking like a gargoyle on the balcony at Notre Dame. His hands were clamped around his skull like he was trying to prevent an explosion.

Antoinette brewed a triple espresso strong enough to earn a warning from the Surgeon General, but when she slid it across the counter, he thrust out his forearm. "Forget the cup. Just shoot me up."

She gave his arm a quick pat.

"Help me out here," he said.

"Hold it up to your lips?" She shook her head. "No way."

"I'm serious. You seem to be so smart about this stuff." He threw up both arms in a hapless floundering gesture that said 'Help me' but omitted the specifics about what.

"Stuff?" Antoinette cocked her head and waited, sweeping a few grains of coffee off the counter. "Doesn't give me a lot to go on."

"Humans. What makes them tick." He stared at her with imploring eyes. "How'd you figure that out?"

"Years of observing. You wouldn't believe what people reveal when they're jonesing for caffeine." She paused, as if weighing the wisdom of sharing her next words. "And of course, there was the Jackhammer School of Consciousness.

I've got the scars to prove it."

He drained his cup. "Sounds like serious business."

"You got that right. And painful." She turned and dusted the espresso machine, signaling that the conversation was closed.

"Hey, you got my attention." He slid off his chair and leaned over the counter, touching her lightly on the arm. "Don't fail me now."

Antoinette gave him a long look, like she was sizing him up as a potential acolyte. Then she continued, "You have to smash through the crap that people have been laying on you. Especially the ones who say they love you. Then dig like hell to get to the real stuff. In my case there were a few extra layers, with the gender thing and all."

"How was that?" His voice softened as he looked at his friend.

"Rough. Lost most everyone I loved in the process." Her eyes stared out at the empty train platform, like it was the landscape of her personal life. "But it was the only way I could find myself."

"To thine own self be true?" he asked.

"More like be your own cause. I'm pretty sure it's the answer you're looking for. That and a little more espresso." She moved slowly, giving him time to think.

"Where do I start?" he asked.

"Try loving yourself. Get that right and you won't need to change other people. They'll do it for you. And believe me, there's plenty there to love." She polished the tips plate and held it in front of his face. "Don't forget, I knew you when."

He gave her a wistful expression. "That was a good life."

"It was. But a trip down memory lane won't help you now. Your problem is you're afraid to accept what a great person you are. You're soulful. A real beauty."

"Feels like something I should have figured out long ago." His voice lost power as he hung his head.

"Doesn't matter." Antoinette reached over the counter and lifted his chin until she was looking directly into his eyes. "It's never too late to be what you might have been."

He blinked hard and bit his lower lip. "I'll try. I'll try."

CHAPTER 51

"Stick out your tongue," Jack said.

"Excuse me?" Frances was perched next to Grayson, watching the drinks master handle incoming orders like an air traffic controller at JFK. The demand for libations was particularly brisk.

"Tongue," Jack repeated, pointing to his mouth in one of those pantomimes that help floundering tourists navigate a language divide.

"Drink," she said, imitating his gesture, but it failed to amuse. *Grayson probably gave him an earful before I arrived.* She directed a pleading glance at Grayson to no avail. Hunched posture, face like a storm brewing. No question. He was here under duress.

She hated to ask for anything. Doing so more than once felt like begging, but what were her options? "Grayson, I could really use a drink." She looked up and down the bar with envy. Nothing but sparkling glasses as far as the eye could see.

"He's the boss," he said with a shrug.

She looked back as Jack's tongue darted out, revealing another small tattoo of a bird in flight. Try as she might to comply, she balked at what seemed like a cross between rudeness and intimacy. So, she visualized the covert battles her siblings waged at the dinner table, extending just a quarter inch of tongue when their mother's back was turned. This time she felt cool air caressing a crescent of flesh resting on her lower lip.

Jack narrowed his eyes and touched his chest. "Heart problems, Beacon-san."

"Well, at least it's too late to be fatal." She gave a hollow chuckle.

He patted her hand and turned to his cabinet. Soon he was assembling a collection of mugwort, cinnamon bark, strange creature-like pieces of ginseng, with just a pinch of what looked like fire-starter. Lifting a balance scale, he sprinkled bits of one ingredient then another in the brass pan, dumped them in a stone bowl, and ground them to a fine powder.

While waiting for her tonic, Frances took a peek at herself in the mirror, half-expecting another expressionist portrait. Something frantic and defiant. Instead, she was greeted with Frances Beacon, the mugshot version.

All I need is a number across my chest. God, could I even pick my face out of a line-up?

Her mind wandered. *What was it about bureaucratic cameras?* The DMV, border control, even liquor store TVs all managed to capture you at your absolute worst. Was it just cheap equipment and tragic lighting, or had they developed some high-tech software to forecast how you'll look at the moment you've been apprehended for a crime?

What was my crime anyway?

Reckless disregard for humanity didn't give her much to go on. Did she forget to vote in a presidential election? Skip the annual Red Cross blood drive? Maybe it was that measly 401(k) that claimed to invest in clean energy, which really meant fracking. But she'd dumped it as soon as the deception was revealed. Once again, she entertained the notion that it was all a big mistake.

They got the wrong file.

But just as she was about to launch into another diatribe against the deficiencies of UAL, she caught another glimpse of herself in the mirror and the words *tiresome bitch* sprang to mind. *Seems like my natural octave since I landed here.*

"Grayson, I'm feeling like a bit of a..." There was no way to soften the next word, so she took a deep breath and finished her thought. "Narcissist. All I do is talk about me."

"And give me a hard time. Don't forget that part." He turned away, as if prospecting for a more congenial conversation, and several patrons threw him sympathetic looks.

"I do, don't I?" Her voice dropped off at the end as she gave a slow nod. No sense fighting over that one.

"Seems to be your style."

"But it's not, really," she protested. "I used to be nice!" But it seemed like so long ago that she wasn't sure if that was true or simply how she wanted to remember herself.

"So I've heard," he grumbled.

"What does that mean?" Instantly, she was back in fighting mode. Was this just the Adjacent Factor at work here? Lash out at the closest person, no matter how innocent, as a proxy for all your troubles? She looked at Grayson and fought the surge of guilt. What had he done but try to play crossing guard and counselor in her hapless drama?

It's a wonder he shows up at all.

She shut her mouth so emphatically that she could hear her molars collide. Then she auditioned a semblance of a smile and chirped, "So, enough about me." Leaning toward him, she lowered her voice. "Let's talk about you."

The change of topic was so sudden it nearly gave him whiplash. "What?" His eyebrows collided in surprise.

"Your story. How'd you end up here, stuck with me?"

Grayson leaned back and stared at the ceiling, as if he didn't quite trust this invitation for disclosure. "You really want to hear?"

"Just keep whatever this is coming." She frowned into her glass and added, "I'm all ears."

"It's not really much of a story. More like déjà vu all over again. I just kept getting it wrong."

"It?" she asked. "Could you be a little more specific?" After a tiny sip, she slid the tonic back across the bar and signaled Jack for her usual tumbler of ice-cold Chardonnay.

"Life," he said. Full stop.

Frances could feel her frustration rising as he delivered one monosyllable after another. It felt like pulling teeth but she took a slug of wine and persisted. "You mean what's important in life?"

"That's the problem. It's not *what*. It's *who*."

"Now we're getting somewhere." Her voice took on a cheerleading quality as she added, "Tell me more."

"I tried to get close to people but it never worked out." He closed his eyes and pressed his fingers to his temples, then massaged his forehead until it was a mass of rumpled folds. "Signals crossed. Bad timing. Bad vibes. Or just flat-out rejection."

"Well, pal, that's your mistake right there." Frances gave his forearm a friendly squeeze before she continued. "I hate to say this, but intimacy is a recipe for pain."

"I thought that pain was the evidence of love—even if it was lost."

"Pain is pain. It can unhinge you."

Grayson slumped back in his chair and shoved his hands in his pockets. Finally, he leaned forward on the bar. "You had a better strategy?"

"Sure. You can be among them, but keep your distance."

He shook his head. "You lost me."

"There are plenty of ways to look normal, even successful, without getting involved. Up close, but not personal. That was my motto." She took a healthy sip of wine and glanced at herself in the mirror, but couldn't meet her own gaze as a carousel of faces, clients from years or even decades ago, whirled through her head, each one tugging at her heart. And what about all her faithful Beaconites now that she was dearly departed? They were a lingering worry.

"But, wait a minute!" She shifted in her chair, trying to dislodge the ache in the pit of her stomach. "We're supposed to be talking about you."

Once again, his face registered surprise at her sudden interest but he soldiered on. "I finally decided that I didn't have the right stuff," he said.

"Meaning?" Her face took on an expectant expression.

"The courage to be fully human. I just gave up and buried myself in other passions. Art, music, beauty from another age. The more remote, the better."

"That's funny because Van Gogh said that there's nothing more truly artistic than to love people."

"And look how he ended up." He touched his temple with his index finger, telegraphing *crazy, weapon* and *suicide* in a single gesture. Then he licked his forefinger and made an invisible mark on a scoreboard.

"Yeah, well," she mumbled. "But back to the art thing? How did that work out?"

"It had its moments, but I always felt like a bit of a failure, convinced it was my fault when a relationship hit the skids. And I never stopped longing for something..."

"Great," they both whispered, almost in one voice. She put one hand on his shoulder and they sat in silence, like mourners at a grave.

Frances recovered first and shook herself out of her reverie. "Listen, I don't think you should be so hard on yourself." He glanced up and gave her a quizzical look. "What if the defects are stamped on the soul in perpetuity?" Her voice rose as she pressed her point. "Maybe we're not meant to get better at life because there's some cosmic quota out there, and it's our job to furnish the world with an endless supply of recluses, misanthropes, tricksters, psychopaths, neurotics, victims, gluttons, loudmouths and losers." She turned and looked straight into his eyes. "Maybe," she whispered, "just a handful of lucky ones get to be the lovers."

"No, Frances." He straightened his back and his voice took on a confident tone. "People change."

"How?" she pleaded. Once again, she was back at square one.

"I told you. Earnest effort."

"You forget. I'm a remedial dead person. Probably could use a copy of *Afterlife for Dummies*." The word dumb stung and her funk deepened.

"I didn't say it was easy." The conversation seemed to have reached a stalemate, so he folded his arms across his chest and watched her brood.

She toyed with her empty glass, lifting it and pressing it down, stenciling the bar with a circle of wet rings. Finally, she broke the silence. "Well, how'd you manage? And don't tell me 'it's a process' because that won't cut it."

He chuckled. "That process business pissed me off, too."

This was news! She leaned back to reassess the Shock Jock and her personal prospects. *Maybe there's hope for me after all.*

"Anyway," he continued, "a few trips ago I landed back here and had a complete meltdown. Careened from fetal position to full on tantrum, railing against the futility of rein- carnating since all it got me was another round of grief. I was done with life *and* the afterlife. What I wanted—demanded— was death. The real thing. So, I burned through two handlers. Nice chaps doing their best, but I wasn't having any of it. The third one was a real bastard, but I have to say, he got the job done."

"Just checking." Her face registered a slight cringe before she asked, "Are you my bastard?"

His reply was pre-empted by a commotion near the back of the room. Glasses hit the floor and shattered. Drinks chris- tened everyone within a three-foot radius. A woman leapt from her seat mopping herself and a waiter, apologizing all around. "If I could just learn to talk without waving my hands. Probably too late now."

The voice pierced Frances. Not the words but something like a vibration echoing through a tunnel, arriving in sections, each bearing a distinct image. A young girl dressed in her Sunday best. A teenager pounding out *Golliwog's Cakewalk* on a piano. An artist up to her elbows in clay. Then nothing. A void where something cherished had been.

Frances rose and walked toward the voice, as if in a trance. "Gillespie?"

"Beacon? My God, Beacon!" They fell into each other's arms and then drew back. For a long moment they stared into young faces disguised by time, creating the double illusion of familiarity and strangeness. But the eyes were unchanged.

The two had been inseparable in high school and enrolled in the same college. While Frances was studious and solitary, Gillespie was socially intrepid, utterly attuned to the revolutionary zeitgeist of the times. She seemed to occupy advanced outposts in philosophy, art and literature, dashing around in her brand-new sports car trailing the telltale aroma of sex and drugs. Russell, her sideman, exuded the confidence of daddy's money, certain that he'd be pulled out of one scrape after another unscathed.

Then they'd vanished without a word.

"Where the hell did you go?" Frances shocked herself, barking out the question like a probation officer dealing with a recalcitrant. But without waiting for Gillespie's answer, she added a painful confession. "I thought I'd failed—as a friend. Maybe done something to offend or just didn't fit in anymore."

"God no, it wasn't you," Gillespie said, pulling Frances into a booth and giving her a hug. "It was my family. My father kept tightening the financial leash to keep me in line. My mother's anger was volcanic. When I couldn't take it anymore, I packed two bags and fled in the middle of the night. It was the only way I could survive."

"But we didn't."

"I know. I needed a fresh start. Clean slate."

"More like a witness protection program. I never heard from you again." The words seemed to escape from a gaping hole in her chest.

Gillespie reached for her hand. "Dear friend, I'm sorry I hurt you." Then she gently changed the subject. "How are you making out in our new alma mater?"

Frances slumped down in the booth, collapsing in disgust. "Take a wild guess."

"Well, you were always the scholarship girl, so I'd say brilliantly."

"Brilliant fuck-up. They put me in Track A."

"A! That *is* a surprise. I started on D."

"It's so humiliating." Frances grabbed a half-finished drink on the table and knocked it back. "I have no idea how to do this."

"It takes time." Gillespie reached over and gently stroked Frances on the shoulders, a soothing motion that failed to deliver.

"Well, I'm a little short on that, with the bloody court breathing down my neck." She picked up a cloth napkin and began to twist it between her hands, like she wanted to wring its neck. Then she jerked upright. "Wait a minute! Weren't you some kind of fortune teller?"

"Psychic," Gillespie corrected.

"How did that work, you know, career-wise?"

"It's not exactly a choice, like being a podiatrist or pre-school teacher."

"Social worker," Frances countered.

"Right. Anyway, it's more of an inheritance. It's just there." Her eyes scanned the surrounding tables as she lowered her voice. "But it was a step up from being a witch."

Frances leaned in, momentarily excited enough to forget her woes. "Are you talking like—Salem?"

"Shh-h-h! Keep it down. But yes. Exactly." She surveyed the nearby patrons who seemed to have exchanged drinking for eavesdropping.

"You women were the real deal?" Frances whispered and gave her friend a look of newfound respect.

Gillespie nodded almost imperceptibly. "The world works in mysterious ways."

"And you think that kind of thing lingers in the soul?"

"From what I can tell, it takes a while to work it through."

"That's fantastic!" Frances thrust out her palms, eager for Gillespie to decipher the roadmap of lines that spread out like a web. "So, how about a reading or whatever it is you do?" But before Gillespie could speak, she hurriedly added, "And trust me, I could use some good news."

"Sorry." Gillespie pointed to the center of her forehead. "No longer operational. The gift didn't survive the transition."

Frances was crestfallen. "Just my luck! An out-of-order psychic. But I know what you mean." She pointed to her forehead. "My memory missed the flight, too. I don't even know how I got here."

"All I can say is don't get too comfortable."

"Big help. Maybe— "

Suddenly Gillespie's head whipped back, landing with a thud against the upholstered booth. Her eyelids fluttered and her mouth went slack.

"Are you okay?" Frances dipped her napkin in a glass of water, mopped Gillespie's forehead and patted her cheeks. Then her friend's lips began to twitch, releasing a rasping sound. "What? I couldn't hear you."

"Doesn't look good."

"Then help me," Frances begged but her plea fell on deaf ears, as Gillespie slipped into unconsciousness. Now her fear was replaced by an irrational anger as she gave the limp body a violent shake. "Come back. You owe me!" she sobbed. "You owe me!"

Gillespie's head sagged to one side as Frances shifted her weight and turned to call for help. But the room was a sea of empty chairs. Even the bar was nearly deserted. And when she turned back, Gillespie had vanished. Gone, too, was any sign of Grayson.

Oh, God! Where's my bastard? And how many more times will I have to apologize? She gave Jack a mournful wave before stumbling into the labyrinth.

CHAPTER 52

"Good night, Beacon-san. Sleep well," Jack called, giving Frances a slight bow as she departed. Then he announced, "We're closing up," and began to polish the bar with a vigor that said there'd be no more drinks on his watch. But one last patron lingered at the far end of the bar, her eyes glued to the bartender.

"You'll have to come back tomorrow or find yourself a speakeasy." His voice seemed to run out of steam. "I'm done." Still no response, so he motored wearily toward the spot where sweet Records Room Molly sat glued to her stool, ignoring his request. "Have a heart, lady. My feet are killing me."

As he leaned toward her, giving the bar a final time-to-get-moving sweep with his towel, she grabbed his shirt and yanked him toward her with a vehemence that could have put a serious dent in his dedication to pacifism. "Finally!" she crowed. "I found you!"

Jack groped under the edge of the bar, searching for the panic button. Then he struggled free and leapt back out of reach. "Your interest is flattering but totally misplaced. Must have me confused with someone else."

"Right. Like that Norwegian tough guy, who promised to return home after one last raiding voyage but pissed off some Brits, leaving me a widow with five kids?"

Jack took a quick glance around for help but the room was deserted, all the other patrons having obeyed when he sang out *closing time.* "I don't know what you're raving about but you might want to take a closer look." He pointed to his round face and almond eyes. "Does this look *Norwegian* to you?"

"Or that Bedouin who traded me for a camel?" Molly continued.

"Look, lady. You need to get a grip. I have no idea what you're talking about."

Most bartenders were instinctively equipped to handle crazies. In truth, many were doing walk-in therapy for the price of a beer and probably saving a few wives or lovers a lot of grief in the bargain. They routinely witnessed the many guises of anger—verbal abuse, passive aggression, paranoia, revenge, and self-destruction. Smashed glasses, smashed faces, yelling that occasionally drowned out the music. It was no secret that anger and its first cousin depression fueled the retail alcohol industry, so Rule Number One for mixologists was to stay out of harm's way.

The majority of these outbursts weren't personal. Just patrons venting in their off-duty hours to keep the rest of their life on track. But this attack sounded very personal, so Jack kept a close eye on the woman. When Molly reached in her pocket he flinched, ready to duck or run. But it wasn't a weapon. Just a small leather-bound notebook. Then she ran a hand through her hair, taking hold of a clump and tugging it lightly. A cogitator's ritual.

"Huh. It's you?" His voice was flat as he gave the bar another brush with the towel.

"Yes. It's me." She leaned back, waiting for his reaction. But there was no smile. No arms open wide.

"What are you doing here?" he asked, like she was a long-lost relative who'd skipped town without repaying a loan.

"I had to find you," she said, as if that was obvious. Again, she waited, but his face was blank. She propped her hands on her knees and leaned toward him. "Seems like I've spent my whole existence pursuing you."

"You'll have to remind me," he said, but his tone said, *Don't bother.*

She pressed open the cover of the notebook, revealing a page filled with words and dates in small, precise handwriting. Her finger ran down the list. "Don't suppose you remember that wedding in Lorraine? 1427?"

"Not really." He toyed with a pile of coasters. "Should I?"

"I was the bridesmaid. The plump one on the left. But you were so busy flirting with that girl Joan that I didn't stand a chance. Then the two of you disappeared and I never saw you again." As her voice rose, it seemed to trigger something in him.

"Oh, right. Joan," he mused, like he was savoring her name. "In case you're wondering, nothing ever came of it. She went off with the army and the next thing I heard she—"

"Went up in flames," Molly said.

"Tragic."

"Yes, but she got a sainthood out of it. People still talk about her."

"Thanks for the memories, but it's still closing time." He flipped the towel over his shoulder and turned toward the door.

"No wait!" she pleaded. "Please! I've been at this so long. Surely you can give me a moment of your time."

Jack folded his arms and leaned back against the bar, a professional listener at his post.

Molly drew in a breath and launched into her pitch. "I've lost count of the places I searched for you. The Isle of Man, Honduras. Chad, Vancouver, Bombay, Iran."

All that globe-trotting made for a tedious conversation that seemed to leave Jack completely unmoved, so Molly switched tactics. "I actually tried to develop an algorithm, something more scientific than just hurling darts at a map.

Unfortunately, there weren't any mathematicians willing to coach a woman with a head for numbers obsessed with reincarnation, so I had to go it alone." The loneliness in her voice spoke volumes. "But I finally nailed three key variables."

"Location, location, location?" he asked.

"Geography was certainly the big one. But that wasn't enough. Look what happened in Bhutan."

"Bhutan? You were there, too?" He leaned on the edge of the bar, momentarily warming to the topic. "How'd we miss each other?"

"Probably because I was a monk."

"Seriously?" He laughed. "A monk! How was that?"

"Lonely. They say Bhutan is known for its gross national happiness but that sure wasn't my experience. Nothing against the place, but since I'd gone there looking for you, it was a rude awakening to end up in a monastery."

"Fascinating," he said.

"Not very, but I had plenty of time to concentrate on the physics of reunions."

"You always were a nerd." She bristled but he just shrugged and picked at the cuticle on his thumb.

"Eventually I realized that it's all in the trajectory. Our lives had to intersect at a time when we weren't otherwise engaged or off limits. I came close a couple of times but..."

"No cigar?" he asked.

"One time you were Roman-collar off limits but very hot. Another time you turned up as my best friend's son.

"Too young?"

"Cradle-robbing-jail-bait young. Plus, my best friend."

"That didn't always stop us." He glanced down at his feet.

"True. We were less than heroic." She swallowed hard and looked around the empty room, as if she feared being overheard. "After that it seemed like the universe cast its Tantalus spell."

"Slipping glimpses?" he asked.

"Exactly! For a split second you'd be so close that every molecule in my body swerved toward you. There was an art gallery in Amsterdam. Beautiful old place right on the *Prinsengracht* canal. The moment I crossed the threshold, I hit this force field that reduced everyone else to a still life. I recognized you before you even turned around, and when you looked at me, I knew you knew. It was like picking up an old conversation without missing a beat. We could've walked out arm in arm, headed straight for bed and never given it a second thought."

"Then the world intervened," Jack said. "A customer wanted to see an etching by Albrecht Durer. A landscape, I think."

"And just like that, we were swept back into our separate lives. It was over in thirty seconds, maybe a minute, but it was indelible. I could feel you for days afterward, more present than the people around me, more visceral than the cobblestones beneath my feet."

Jack nodded solemnly as he listened.

"It always left me with this inexplicable sense of yearning. Sometimes I settled for a facsimile. Placeholders or karmic debt collectors. But I just kept thinking there must be more to life than this." The weight of her disappointment over the centuries was visible, as her shoulders slumped and her arms fell heavily into her lap.

"That's why it was so exciting when everything synchronized," Jack said quietly.

Molly winced. "More like miraculous." She blinked back tears and said, "Finally—"

But Jack rushed to cut her off. "So how did you find me this time?"

Molly gave him a sly smile. "Violated my solemn archivist's oath. Broke the rules."

"That sounds like you." Instead of admiration, a chill crept into his voice but Molly seemed oblivious.

"It took a huge amount of detective work, but I finally

cross-referenced your file with mine and traced you to this bar. Right under my nose!" She looked delighted. 'I could be fired like a cannon for violating the privacy act but," she leaned in, "it was worth the risk just to see your face again." She reached out but Jack straightened up and stepped out of range.

"Well, now you have. But as I said before, it's closing time," and he reached for a panel of light switches.

She was stunned. "What?"

He flipped each switch deliberately, plunging the room into darkness one section at a time, until she was sitting alone in a pool of light, like a suspect awaiting interrogation. But Jack was as silent as a sphinx.

"Can't we talk?" she pleaded, but he was already in full stride, heading for the exit where he stood like a weary door-man, signaling that the conversation was over.

"I knocked myself out to find you, stayed up God knows how many nights digging through all those records."

"I think it would be best to let bygones be bygones."

"But—"

"It's getting late."

"If I offended, at least let me make amends."

"There's nothing to be done now. Karma will take care of it." He paused. "It always does."

"Surely there's something I can do," she pleaded, reaching for his arm, but he reacted like she was a leper.

"Go help someone else, like Frances."

"Frances! Why Frances? She had it all." Her voice had the sound of a tantrum brewing, which only made things worse.

"That's not for you to say," Jack warned.

"Why do you care about her?"

"We go way back."

"So did we," she hissed, barely able to suppress her jealousy. "*You* help her."

CHAPTER 53

"I fucked up, didn't I?" Molly shouted the next evening as she torpedoed her way through the tangle of chairs and tables in the bar, without so much as a "Sorry" when she grazed elbows and overturned drinks. Heads swiveled.

Showtime!

But she was impervious. A woman on a mission. Destination: Jack. He was playing chess on the bar with one of the regulars and resolutely ignored the noisy intruder.

"Get over here," she demanded, slamming her fist on the bar.

A solitary drinker grabbed his glass. "Hey, lady! Take it easy!"

Jack turned slowly. "I said maybe we should let bygones be—"

"Absolutely not! It was England, wasn't it?"

Jack shrugged but refused to make eye contact.

She bustled down to his end of the bar, jostling patrons with abandon. "We'd finally found each other after God knows how long. Finally got it right."

He took off his glasses and massaged his forehead, as if he could block the delivery of unwanted memories. "Must we?"

"We finally got it right and then I threw it all away." No reaction. She raised her voice. "Right?"

He nodded slowly. "Right."

"How could I be such a fool?" There was a choking sound in her throat as she continued. "So many capable women, ready to sacrifice their lives for the cause. Single women, old women, lesbians, all pouring into the streets, clamoring for the vote. Christ, Emmeline Pankhurst could have handled the whole crusade herself. They didn't need me." She climbed on a stool in front of him and clenched her arms across her middle.

"Pankhurst could have handled the Kaiser," said Jack with a hint of admiration.

"Why didn't I just stick to burning mail boxes?" Several patrons reacted to the self-confessed terrorist by sliding down the bar to give her a wide berth.

"You tell me, Miss Shield Maiden." Jack said quietly.

"What's that supposed to mean?" Molly asked. "DNA?"

"Possibly. Those warrior genes have a long shelf-life." But instead of pressing his advantage, he relented. "And I have to admit, it was a noble cause. You and the other suffragettes did a lot of good."

"*Good?*" she shouted. "Wrong! I was an egotistical zealot, thinking I had to choose between my family and..." Her voice broke and she slumped forward, resting her face in her hands. "How could I leave you and our baby?"

Jack's armor of cool detachment dissolved in the torrent of her unbridled grief. "She grew up to be a real beauty, our daughter. You would have been so proud of her."

Molly looked up, her face a study in remorse. "Tell me about her."

"She got your brains. Top of her class. Graduate degree. Nothing could stop her. But she had an even bigger heart. Never met a cause she didn't love. She was my delight."

Molly sat and stared at herself in the mirror, as sober as a judge "Well, I guess karma *has* caught up with me. I'm a frumpy archivist safeguarding the stories of a thousand brilliant lives, while my own history is a cross between a clown car and a trail of tears. One moronic stunt or disaster after another."

"No, you were brave time and time again." He reached over and gently wiped her tears with a clean bar towel.

"How can you ever forgive me, when I can't forgive myself?" she asked.

"You're here now. That's all that matters and you're not a frump. You're Dreadnaught, my proud beauty." He tossed away the towel and leaned over the bar, scooping up her hands and pressing them to his lips.

Through a cascade of tears, she clamped her hands around his cheeks, drinking in his face like an elixir.

"*Tempus fugit*," he whispered and then fairly bellowed, "Closin' time," to the startled crowd. "Drink up, and I mean *now*!"

Seated at the far end of the bar, Frances was a silent witness to this reunion, staring hungrily as their hands touched, devouring them with her eyes. Her heart felt like it had been pummeled by an agricultural thresher, casting off the stalks and husks, leaving only the naked seeds of loneliness and longing.

CHAPTER 54

Frances sprinted the few steps into her secret room which she now thought of as base camp. Within its quiet blue walls, nighttime was dedicated exclusively to her books. She plowed through one after another, heedless of the passage of time. The result was a daytime ritual of falling asleep in class or disguising her lack of interest by starting arguments. All she wanted was to be alone and read.

But tonight, she began to fidget. She was fed up with the static atmosphere of the afterlife which was like living in an Edward Hopper painting. Deserted walkways, emotional isolation, and a stillness shot through with anxiety.

She craved the noisy streets of New York where you could be solitary but never alone, day or night. Even at one in the morning there were plenty of people out and about. Boisterous groups insulated in a pod of companionship and more than a little alcohol. Amorous couples holding hands or indifferent partners gravitating toward each other when they caught sight of a stranger heaving himself up from a shadowy doorway.

Frances had become a serious city-watcher when her first job in social work took her to the projects, church basements and tent cities that often had more sense of community than the surrounding metropolis. Curiosity lured her back on weekends to explore neighborhoods studded with turn-of-the-century buildings, the frayed but dignified relics of another time.

Then she'd call her father and deliver a full report on her discoveries. The Harlem Courthouse, a masterpiece of Renaissance Revival architecture. The Edward Mooney House in the Bowery, which had been a saloon, a brothel, a general store, and a Chinese club. And one night, they spent half an hour marveling over the secrets embedded in the Cathedral of St. John the Divine.

"Did you see the locomotive in the stained glass?" her father asked. "And the Titanic going under? How about that attic and the view from the roof? It could almost make me a believer." At the end of every conversation he'd say, "Now you be careful out there." But he understood her appetite for the city and cherished these vicarious adventures.

She realized she'd been pacing as she pictured block after block of Manhattan, making a virtual jail break in her head.

Back at square one.

She stopped in front of the easel. Her nemesis. Her love. She chose a wide brush and began to stroke her face along the cheekbone, across the eyebrow, down the bridge of her nose, ending with the faintest brush of her lips. Then she dug into a box crammed with tubes of paint. Cerulean blue, her father's favorite, would surely cheer up this abandoned palette. Then red and green. Soon the palette was freckled with dots of pure potential.

"Why not?" She spied a half-dozen canvases leaning behind the easel and grabbed the largest one. "What now?"

She opened and closed her fingers, like a pianist warming up. Then she remembered watching a film of Picasso drawing with a light stick, swinging his outstretched arm to outline a fleeting image in a darkened room. She pantomimed his performance, dragging a dry brush back and forth through the air, reconnecting with the gesture and hoping for an image. But nothing emerged. She just stood for a long time—frozen.

Maybe tomorrow, she thought as she put a drop of oil on

each mound of paint. "Back to the books."

She opened her copy of *Happiness* by Will Ferguson and read, "Human nature had always been based on a deep heroic restlessness, on wanting something else, something more, whether it be true love or a glimpse just beyond the horizon. It was the promise of happiness, not the attainment of it, that had driven the entire engine, the folly and glory of who we are."

The promise of happiness felt like a cruel mirage. Her past was a closed book, bits of which were disappearing from memory with every passing day. As for a glimpse beyond the horizon, every forward move increased her sense of doom. There didn't seem to be anything heroic in her restlessness, except her determination to haul her pathetic, lonely ass out of bed each morning and grope for a solution.

But the word folly rang a bell. *What folly did I pursue, landing me in this place?* She pulled out her phone and kissed the frozen screen. She was truly disconnected from any reality but herself. And that was the dilemma.

Who am I now? What will become of me?

CHAPTER 55

Frances dragged herself out of a dream in which her secret room was floating like a ship in a bottle, timeless and isolated from the world outside. As she lay there, another bottle came to mind, the kind with a message inside.

But what if the bottle was never found?

It would be like a fragment of history or a life had been erased. She sat bolt upright in bed, struck by the realization that whole sections of her past were disappearing. She had flashbacks surrounded by complete blanks, like straining to remember an old movie but only managing to recall disconnected scenes and snippets of dialogue. She'd poke around in the fog for hints but couldn't connect the dots. Was it just a matter of time before even the fragments went missing?

The thought of oblivion terrified her. *Who will I be when my autobiography goes out of print?* And thus began her quest to capture the past, if only for herself.

On one of her earliest forays into the secret room she'd discovered a blank notebook like artists and writers used to stockpile ideas that could grow with a bit of attention. Frances had kept journals more or less faithfully over forty years, chronicling the good, the bad and the ugly of her daily life, so the instinct was still fresh. She propped herself against the pillows, pressed open the cover, and scribbled the first thought that arrived.

He came.

But fatigue overwhelmed her before she could tell the tale.

* * * *

It was late Friday afternoon, the witching hour when some of the messiest cases appeared without warning. A runaway child. Eviction notices. The mounting dread of a long weekend with a demented spouse and no lifeline. Frances was picking her way through the last round of e-mails like it was a minefield, certain that at least one would detonate, when she spied *Subway Health* in the subject line.

"Now there's an oxymoron," she muttered. Even on a good day the subways were fetid, germ-circulating machines with the added attraction of being overheated or frigid depending on the season. The sender's name was unfamiliar. Two sure hints that it would be smart to hit delete and move on. Her wariness rose when a preview of the first line contained the greeting—*Hey Frances.*

"Probably selling something I can't afford," she muttered. *Delete or trust the institutional spam filter?* In her head Clint Eastwood drawled, "Do you feel lucky, punk?"

"Why not?" She clicked and read the short message.

```
Hey Frances,
Love your blog. Great content, even better
delivery. I howled at your comment about cen-
tenarians becoming so common they'll need to
run a marathon in pumps to get any attention.
I told my dad—a great guy who's getting up
there in years—and he's already shining up
his pumps. We really could use a head like
yours for our mental health poster project.
```

The note contained details about time, place and the fact that dinner would be provided in the boardroom at a midtown address. It was signed J. Macintosh Pfeiffer above the logo of the well-known Shearing & Pfeiffer advertising firm.

Frances googled the Department of Mental Health and sure enough, there was the announcement that Shearing & Pfeifer would design the poster campaign for Mental Health Month. Since these projects were usually done *pro-bono,* it made sense that they'd need volunteers to provide the content expertise.

Okay, it's not a hoax.

She checked her calendar. *Why not? Dinner on top of a skyscraper. The view alone will probably be worth the trip and they can definitely afford a decent caterer.* It was that or takeout from her local Chinese hole-in-the-wall that had a line of impatient New Yorkers queuing outside the door most nights. Plus, it would be a change from her usual solitary evenings, and research said that novelty stimulated brain growth, even in brains of her vintage.

The last reason, that she admitted only to herself, was that she was still a true believer despite the fatigue and skepticism that came with the territory in social work. Intervention could change lives in miraculous ways. Even if most days felt like déjà vu all over again, people who seemed to be impossibly broken had miraculous transformations just often enough to justify her faith.

On the day appointed, she took extra time choosing her outfit and decided to make a bit of an effort with the mascara. Her colleagues took notice. "Got a hot date, Frances? Interviewing?"

She laughed. "Hardly. Just a meeting. Work after work."

It was a doorman building with acres of marble in the lobby and a no-nonsense security routine. "Your name? Name of person you're visiting? ID, please. Sign here, then take the elevators on the left to the 52nd floor."

The elevator doors opened directly into the spacious reception area of Shearing & Pfeifer. A fresh-faced woman stepped forward, no doubt an intern but to Frances she looked like a teenager minus the private school uniform, waiting for daddy to get off work.

"Right this way." The intern gestured toward a glass-walled room but Frances had other plans.

"Ladies room?"

Ever curious about how the other half lived, she drifted down a hallway surveying the generous workspaces and immaculate carpet even now being groomed by the night crew. Then she eased open a teak door marked with a stylish L, took two steps into the room and stopped, gaping at the décor. Black marble floor, sparkling mirrors that rose to the ceiling, and the kindest, most considerate lighting she'd encountered in years. A bouquet of white tulips brightened the black marble counter like a giant dandelion puff.

Frances addressed the empty room. "People *work* here? I'd live here. Just give me that little cubicle on the end and I'll be a model tenant." She took her time, used all the amenities and then checked her face in the mirror. *That's as good as it gets*, she told herself.

People were already gathering in the boardroom. A table at the door served up monogrammed notepads and a tasteful brochure highlighting the company's projects. Inside, a long table against the wall showcased the buffet. At a glance, Frances saw a pyramid of shrimp and a mountain of sesame noodle salad on a hand-painted platter. A closer look revealed trays of delicate crostini offering just a mouthful of goat cheese, prosciutto, smoked salmon or some variation of curried chicken. And since no meeting was complete without sugar, a tray of pastries promising immediate gratification and regret in the morning.

Several people were loading their plates as if it had been days since their last meal. This was a classic sign of people toiling in a famine culture where a ream of paper and a full box of paper clips were considered luxuries.

By the time Frances approached the conference table in the center of the room, most of the seats were taken. The empty ones would sandwich her between people she didn't know, forcing her to engage when she preferred to watch. Instead, she headed for a chair at the foot of the table where she could study the group and eat with an unobstructed view of the city below. A waiter glided around the perimeter, offering generous glasses of red or white wine.

She was just finishing the last of her noodles when a tall man in a well-cut suit sailed into the room, grabbed a glass of white wine, popped a cookie in his mouth and dropped into the chair at the head of the table.

"Evening, folks. I'm J. Macintosh Pfeiffer. I hope you'll call me Mac. I really appreciate you coming tonight."

The mystery e-mailer. Easy on the eyes.

"Let's do a few quick intros and then get down to work because I know your time is valuable." He gestured to the man on his right who identified himself as Dr. Randall White, a psychiatrist in private practice. Next came a doctor of the PhD persuasion—Jeremy Hanes from the psych department at Columbia University.

Frances began to wonder what she was doing in this crowd but the next two looked like social workers, judging from the double helpings of dessert nestled beside their over-flowing dinner plates. Sure enough. Ellen and Ben, both administrators in the city bureaucracy. Now it was her turn.

"I'm Frances Beacon. Clinical social worker." She turned and looked to her right, passing the baton to the next speaker.

But Mac interjected. "Frances writes an amazing blog. You really should check it out."

Frances was very private about her writing and occasional conference presentations, as if it was an eccentric hobby like trainspotting. Most of her colleagues knew nothing of her outside projects, so she felt like she'd been outed. All she could manage was a mumbled thank you. Glancing at him, she caught the full force of his gaze and surprised herself by staring right back until she realized she wasn't breathing. Finally, the man beside her broke the silence.

"I'm Otto Bell. Retired incarceration counselor. Riker's Island."

That set off nods of admiration all around the table. Riker's was serious business. Ten-thousand inmates, forty percent of whom suffered from mental illness, so therapists on the island were doing hand-to-hand combat with the bare minimum of resources. Then the meeting moved on. Several advertising interns rounded out the group, observing the process and recording notes on a white board stationed at the head of the table.

"So, our goal is to create an ad campaign with subway posters letting people know about mental health services in the city," Mac said.

"Like we need more clients," Ben quipped.

Mac continued. "Anyway, you're the experts. So, for a start maybe you could help us out with a few basics. What makes people—"

"Nuts?" Otto broke in. A ripple of laughter went around the table.

The psychiatrist cleared his throat. "There are many reasons why people have mental health challenges." His tone veered dangerously close to lecture mode, as if somehow, he'd failed to notice that they weren't his patients or students. "For example..."

"Their mothers," Ellen muttered. "Number one reason."

"But where would we be without them?" Ben joked.

More laughter. Now that the ice was broken, everyone seemed to relax. Mac leaned back, smiled and said, "I'd love to hear more."

"Isolation," Otto offered. "Feeling alone and friendless in a teeming metropolis."

The professor from Columbia sat forward in his chair and looked directly at the ad man. "You look like a bright guy, but my guess is you stick pretty close to this platinum tower. So,

I'll tell you what drives people nuts. Traffic, noise, unemployment, beggars struggling cheek by jowl with blingified assholes obsessed with their display of affluence. Shitty schools, shitty health care, fragile relationships, poverty and the glorification of a self-centered-disposable-sport-fucking lifestyle."

"You got that right, brother," Ben agreed.

The room fell silent for a moment.

"Maybe it would help if we identified our target audience," Ellen said. "Who are the posters for exactly? The people who need help or the ones who are propping them up?"

"Both," Mac said. "Broad spectrum campaign. All 5.5 million riders a day are potential targets."

"So how about this idea?" Otto interjected. "Voice Busters: When the conversation in your head gets so loud you can't hear the TV." Laughter and a bit of envy for the retiree's freedom to say what he thought without the filter that kept his colleagues guarded but employed.

"Otto, you missed your calling," Mac said. "You'd have made a great ad man. Any other ideas?" He smiled and surveyed the group, hoping for a crop of ideas that could be pruned into an eye-catching campaign.

"Love," Frances said quietly. Ten heads swiveled like a flock of birds turning in mid-flight, displaying ten quizzical expressions. Mac stepped into the void. "Tell me more."

"When love isn't enough. You can love a schizophrenic with all your heart, but without treatment it can be tragic." She paused. "Or when love disappears. Grief over a death or even divorce can easily unhinge people."

"When love hurts," Dr. White said. "People trapped in abusive relationships. I see it every day."

"When love gives you the boot," Ellen said with a hint that she had some firsthand experience with the subject. "Broken hearts nearly destroy some of my clients. They fracture or combust."

"When love is a no-show," Ben added. "You wouldn't

believe how many people say they've never loved or been loved. Almost like they don't exist."

"So. The Love Campaign. I like it." Mac gave Frances a nod.

The conversation rolled on. Waiters circulated with pots of coffee and tea. Interns faithfully noted suggestions about services, terminology, help lines and crisis centers. And then the evening was over. J. Macintosh shepherded the group toward the elevator and at the last moment jumped in and rode down with them, repeating his thanks for a great working session.

He nodded to the security guard and held open the front door, wishing each a good night, but touched Frances on the elbow, signaling that she should wait until the others were gone. "Thanks for your input up there. It got the whole thing rolling. Can I get you a cab?"

"No. I need to walk off some of those noodles. But thanks. It was very stimulating." She turned to go. "Good luck with the campaign."

"Actually, I could use some exercise myself." He patted his middle with both hands. "Mind if I tag along and pick your brain a bit more?"

Two hours and forty blocks later they were standing on her corner after stopping to admire the lions in front of the 42nd Street library, St. Patrick's, the Plaza, the Frick and the Met along the way. The conversation kept pace with their steps, ranging from the most effective kinds of treatment to the problems inherent in the system, finally settling on the unfortunate recognition that the money was in the disease, not the cure.

Then they moved on to changes in the city. The decline of architecture, the latest blockbuster at MoMA and survival strategies for Thanksgiving when families reunite to carve up a large bird and each other.

"This is where I leave you. My street," Frances said, jerking her thumb around a corner.

"I'll grab a cab." He stepped off the curb and waved his arm, snagging a yellow taxi almost out of thin air. Opening the door, he turned back to Frances. "We'll need a consultant on the project. Any chance you could spare a few more hours to keep us on track?"

She paused so long that the taxi driver called out, "Are we doing this, buddy, or what?"

Mac gave a small shrug and raised one hand like a stop sign, as if to say, *no problem, sorry to impose.* But just as he put his foot inside the cab, she found her voice.

"Yes. I think that'll work."

"I know it will," he replied and jumped in the cab.

Frances reeled around and floated down the block toward her apartment, exhaling a long, low "Whoa!" like the whistle of a train.

Can life still do that? Turn upside down in the space of an hour?

CHAPTER 56

The next morning was cold and gray—perfect weather for a city that seemed to be raining people in crisis. When Frances arrived at her office, business was already brisk. A woman burned out of her apartment over night was now homeless as well as broke. A disabled man whose wheelchair went missing bristled at the suggestion that he might have sold or bartered it, but it wouldn't be the first time. A family of three needed food assistance.

At mid-morning, Nick, a big teddy bear of a man signed in. He'd been admitted to Gracie Square Hospital for observation the night before but wandered away. Now he stood shivering in a hospital gown, sweat pants and running shoes with no socks. Frances wrapped him in a coat from the emergency closet and stashed him in her office while she dealt with two new walk-ins who were more interested in brawling with each other than getting help.

When she stuck her head in her office to check on Nick, he was eagerly tucking in to a carton of noodle salad. On the floor was a discarded paper bag and a crumpled note.

Thanks for the best walk I've had in years.

Bon Appetit.

Mac

A week passed. She was sure it was no more but the days blurred into one another as they headed into the holiday season, when memory, family and misfortune conspired to make her clients' pain more acute.

She spent most of Friday morning in delicate negotiations between a young runaway named Teresa and her mother, with an aunt providing back-up. It had been a rocky start. The adults were clearly at their wit's end, trying to rein in a 14-year-old who was enjoying the unexpected delivery of an adult body and the misbehavior to go with it. Frances represented authority, so they hoped she'd display enough muscle to get Teresa's attention before it was too late. But she was also a card-carrying member of the establishment and by extension *the man*. As they all sat down, Teresa's aunt flashed a set of filed teeth, signaling that their visit was a last resort and Frances was far from trusted.

Come from love echoed through her head like a mantra. It was the shorthand she and her colleagues used to stay centered, reminding themselves to see their clients as people, not cases. By listening and nodding and listening some more, she gradually found the path. "Teresa, you're so lucky to have these two wise women in your life." Slowly the adults holstered their defenses. "They love you so much and they want you to have a good life. Do you want a good life?"

The penitent teen, who was really still a little girl, washed her sullen face with tears. The referral to services was a foregone conclusion. The real triumph was watching the three of them disappear down the hall with their arms linked.

Frances stood quietly gazing after them for a moment, grateful for the outcome even though it was just the first small step. Then she pivoted and slammed directly into Mac, who was deep in conversation with Mike Grasso, supervisor of the department.

"Hello!" She was surprised. He was visibly pleased.

Mike said, "Mr. Pfeiffer's here doing field research for the subway poster project. But then I guess you know all about it. Would you have time to debrief him at the end of the day? I have a supervisors' meeting." He winced. "Another epic waste of time, but I skipped the last two so a personal appearance is required. You know what I mean?"

"No problem." She tried to keep her voice even but her heart had percussion ideas of its own.

"Meet you at your office? 5:00?" Mac asked, giving her elbow a fleeting touch.

"Sure, but it could be later depending on the traffic." She raised her eyebrows, then explained, "Fridays are crunch time." But the afternoon was mercifully light and by 5:15 they were out on the street.

"Where to?" he asked.

"Not many choices in this neighborhood. I'd take you to the Decathexis Bar and Grill but we're sure to run into colleagues." She winced at the thought of awkward introductions and vigorous interrogations the next day.

"I'll take you to a secret ad man haunt if you tell me what *decathexis* means," he countered.

"Well, it's the disinvestment of mental or emotional energy from a person or idea. Ah...sorry about the jargon." She paused and started over. "It means letting go because the outcome may be grim. Get out before you get hurt. It works best with plenty of liquids."

Mac laughed. "They call it getting shit-faced in my industry."

"Well, you're the word guys." She flung her arm out in front of her. "Lead on."

They did not, in fact, get shit-faced but sat for hours in a corner booth talking about her clients. "For many of them, distress is the norm," she explained. "They struggle with addiction, outstanding warrants, fractured relationships. At first glance their lives can seem dispiriting, even impossible, but in many ways they're really a lot like us. Kids, jobs, hopes and dreams. But the proportions are all wrong, so they need help."

"And love." He looked at Frances in a way that suggested the topic was the same but the who may have shifted.

Love wasn't in her personal vocabulary. Wasn't even on the radar. But something seemed to stir. Or was it just too much wine on an empty stomach? She couldn't move a muscle. "Right. How *is* that campaign coming?" she finally managed to chirp. It was an ungainly pivot. She knew it and she knew he knew.

He leaned back to give her space. "It's great. It's all going to be great."

CHAPTER 57

"Can't she do anything but write?"

Cornelius approached the monitor in the Committee room, staring at Frances hunched over her journal. He scowled and hit pause. "Such a waste of time."

Smiles leapt to his feet and aimed his dissent directly at the group. "On the contrary, it's one of mankind's greatest achievements."

"I'll tell you about achievements," Cornelius crowed. "Insider trading, currency speculation, and a stash of gold bullion for the lean times." He grabbed the lapels of his coat and nodded with satisfaction.

Smiles was clearly unimpressed. "That's all transitory, Cornelius, but writers have lasting influence. They record our discoveries and advances, passing the real treasure—knowledge—down from one generation to the next. That's why libraries are so important."

"Another free commodity," Cornelius sneered. "What's wrong with you people?"

"Libraries are the finest institutions on earth," Smiles objected. "Equal access to information and inspiration." Cornelius rolled his eyes but Smiles pressed on. "God knows how much more advanced the human race would be if Alexandria had survived."

"Who's she?" Cornelius asked, momentarily showing mild

interest.

"The library at Alexandria, Egypt." Smiles looked at him in disbelief. "Surely, you've heard of it. A mecca for scholars. Repository of over a half million scrolls from Assyria, Greece, Persia, India and many other nations. It contained the history, literature, and learning of the ancient world."

"Reduced to ashes and gone," the Fool added.

"It was a great human tragedy." Smiles covered his face with his hands.

Cornelius couldn't suppress his amusement. He stood and approached Smiles, patting him on the shoulder with an almost paternal air. "You writers have such delusions about your importance. Humans are humans, Smiles. Narcissistic cut-throats!" He dragged his finger across his neck. "They have more in common with a lion than a librarian." He lifted his chin and threw his arms out wide. "This is as good as it gets, my man. Nothing changes, not even if a million words spill from your pen."

"You're wrong," Smiles argued. "And we're talking about Frances here. She'd be lost without her writing. It's how she struggles to understand herself."

"Well, she's failing on that score," Cornelius chuckled. "Seems like she's stuck in the rough draft stage." He searched the faces around the table in vain for a kindred sense of humor.

"But it's the effort that counts," Smiles insisted. Now he was striding back and forth, caught up in his cause. "The tiny epiphanies and the pains of conscience that emerge before the pen can censor itself. Slipping glimpses that nurture growth."

"I still say it's a waste of time, and from what I under-stand..." Cornelius reached into a pocket and dramatically pulled out the lining to display its emptiness. "It's the road to penury." He held up both hands. "No, thanks."

"For many it's not a choice." Smiles pressed on, now speaking from personal experience. "The need to write is so profound that if we can't do it, we're miserable. The Romans called it the incurable disease."

"Well, I sincerely hope it's not contagious." Cornelius pulled out a linen handkerchief and covered his nose in a protective gesture.

"Say what you want," Smiles continued defiantly. "We'd be lost without writers. They bring clarity and coherence to our daily struggles. Help us get wiser by allowing us to look back and within." Smiles planted himself in front of Cornelius and demanded, "How could we learn about the past or ourselves without them?"

Cornelius scoffed. "History is overrated, my dear friend. Insight even more so. Everything of value I learned through personal experience." He plucked at his lace collar and adjusted his velvet waistcoat. "And my experience tells me that Frances is a loser of the first order. Mark my words! She's doomed."

CHAPTER 58

The journal landed on the floor with a thud, echoing in the secret room and rousing Frances. Fumbling to retrieve it, she read the only line she'd managed before sleep claimed her. *He came.* She chuckled at the inevitability of the next sentence and scrawled: *He saw.* But again, she couldn't fend off the lure of sleep.

* * * *

How about Sunday?

Frances was surprised when Mac's text popped up on her phone. She was still groggy from dinner the night before, a "quick bite" that stretched until almost midnight. Somehow, he'd worked his way into her daybook several times a week. First the consultations on the project. Then the unveiling ceremony in Times Square where, in the pre-Disney era, crazy was king. A few follow-up phone calls about the initial stages of the roll-out led to Happy Hours that truly were, unlike the slosh festivals of five-dollar chardonnay with colleagues. Eventually dinner.

And now they were—what? Dating? It seemed like such an antique term in the era of hooking up and fuck-buddies, but she couldn't find a replacement word that didn't make her squirm.

`Dinner?` She hit send expecting a restaurant address in return. Within seconds he shot back.

`Trifecta. Breakfast, lunch and dinner. If we can still stand each other at the end of the day...`

She stifled the impulse to fire off—All day? You're kidding! Her version of a day of rest was to write until brain fog set in, then a brisk three-mile walk through Central Park, rain or shine, where she could observe the arrival of each season. Tulips, tender green foliage, scarlet leaves, snow. The natural world in miniature surrounded by concrete and glass. Energized and refreshed, she'd grab some take-out and stroll back to her cocoon to read over dinner. Only the inevitable onset of Monday Dread spoiled the perfection of her day.

Oh, shit! Whole minutes had slipped by while she'd picked through the obstacles to accepting Mac's offer. Yes, her hours of me-time were precious, but she knew that wasn't the real problem. It was the palpable mixture of caution and disbelief. *Can I trust myself? Or him?* She hadn't liked any man this way in ages, so maybe it was just menopause talking.

Her phone chimed again. `So that's a NO? Or R U ghosting me already?`

`Sorry. Someone walked in. I'll get back to you.`

"Damn!" *Lying's not a good start for a relationship.*

But on second thought, someone had walked in. Her neuroses. Practically flesh and blood, as vivid and overbearing as her most annoying clients. These long-time companions appeared when least expected, laying claim to her time and frequently her happiness. But this was a struggle for her eyes only.

On the outside, she disguised her emotional baggage with a repertoire of defenses from humor to chilly indifference. But inside the privacy of her own cranium, it felt like she was hosting open-mic night for wanna-be bullies, each neurosis vying for a bigger reaction with its can-you-top-this schtick.

There was Sister Mary Flawless who promoted insanely high standards, and then rewarded even the best effort with "I think you could have done a *lit-tle better*." The Slack Master chided "That's all you accomplished today? More cardio. Brush up on your Spanish. And did you ever finish *War and Peace*?" Mr. Mensa relentlessly pushed her most vulnerable button. "You sounded like an idiot." Not a day went by without at least one of her demons walloping her. Occasionally they staged a jamboree that reduced her to a confused seven-year-old, trying to please everyone and failing.

Then Frances had one of those epiphanies that make all the suffering worthwhile. *Wait a minute. I have a choice!* She could spend Sunday with her phantom captors or take a risk. Her brain consulted her heart and the vote was unanimous. With a surge of energy, she announced to her empty office, "I've had enough of you lot. Find someone else to torment," and she grabbed her phone.

I'm back. And yes. I'll gamble on the tri-fecta.

The wager paid off. Sundays turned into weekends exploring new neighborhoods or heading out of town. But these junkets were just the backdrop for non-stop conversations that morphed seamlessly from Plato to NATO, fueled by their mutual curiosity about almost anything. They quickly discovered they were politically compatible and non-religious but spiritual. Frances led the charge on art and psychology but marveled at the way Mac understood things about the universe that she scarcely had the imagination to take on faith. He threw in a passion for craft beers and spy thrillers with a bit of music on the side, but his primary interest was Frances Beacon.

In truth, she couldn't remember when she'd felt so important to someone who wasn't seeking free meds or a quick fuck. And at first, it didn't sit well. She'd spent most of her life fending off scrutiny, especially in social situations, by asking a string of thoughtful questions while remaining nearly anonymous. Even among her colleagues she was economical with self-exposure. But Mac met question with question and was an easy listener, giving her time to think.

When he first asked about siblings, she took evasive action. "Let's just say that unofficially I'm an orphan with a plus one."

Something in her eyes flashed *Do Not Disturb* but he leaned in. "Me, too."

That was a surprise. He seemed so comfortable with himself that she assumed he'd been raised by a brilliant child therapist or Saint Someone, with a gaggle of adoring siblings who still met regularly for brunch and reminiscing.

"There's just me and my dad.' He paused and looked away. "My mom died when I was 14."

"I'm sorry." She didn't dare touch him, knowing how fragile she was around the subject of parent loss. So, she simply said, "That must have been hard."

He nodded slowly. "Very. Especially since I was an only child, blissfully unaware of anything beyond our one-to-one relationship. Later, I knew that there'd been some miscarriages but she had a very light touch. "

"Not a helicopter mother?" she ventured, having seen her share of children immobilized by a hovering parent.

"Never. She just seemed to enjoy sharing adventures with me. *My Mac,* she called me. She was the talker, the curious one with a love of life and I was her sidekick."

"That sounds lovely—almost idyllic."

"It was. Which made the end all the more shocking. One day I came home from basketball practice and she was gone. Aneurism. Of course, there were the usual emergency inter-ventions, life support but all pointless. It was like she'd been snatched from the planet."

Frances waited quietly until he continued. He and his father had left the hospital, stunned and speechless. How could they possibly console each other when their conversational skills had never progressed beyond the how's-school-son-fine-dad level? Mostly they'd communicated by osmosis.

"My dad scarcely knew how to be a father much less fill both roles, so he became a pal. But a great one. Still is. We have season tickets for the Yankees. He likes movies with happy endings and taking walks. Calls himself a *flaneur*, the classic stroller savoring the sights of the city. He's a real character. You'll like him."

"You're so lucky to have him. Mine's gone." Her voice trailed off.

He looked at her for a long time, waiting for her to share a snapshot from her family album. This was their way of getting to know each other, wandering from one topic to another, telling their side of an old story to a new face.

Suddenly she realized that she wasn't keeping up her end of the conversational bargain. But what could she say? There had been a family, smugly clinging to the notion that they were special. Gifted at being their tiny tribe. But it was an illusion.

Frances spent her childhood sandwiched between two siblings who specialized in rebellion, with the inevitable raised voices and tension that lingered long after dinner was over. Her sister loved a good fight, preferably with an audience, and made no secret of the fact that she wished her siblings could be transferred to another family. Her brother wasn't a born pugilist. Frances sensed that he was tender underneath but had no model for dealing with complex feelings, so he staged his protests covertly and dealt with the consequences noisily.

She'd watched from the sidelines, certain that there had to be a better way to survive, so even in good times she kept her distance, as if studying the family like an anthropologist rather than taking part. The result was that she looked independent and self-sufficient but felt wary, fine-tuning her reliance on hypervigilance. Then her father died and the carefully guarded myth shattered like a China plate. They hobbled along for years, feigning a cohesion they no longer felt, circling around an empty center at holidays. Then the tribe drifted apart as gravity failed. Only one brother remained. Thereafter, Frances was more comfortable with a passport in hand heading for Prague or Paris than setting off for a family gathering. She wasn't ready to share any of that with Mac.

But eventually she felt safe enough to talk about her goals. "I love to write and I think I have something to say to my peers. You realize, there's an army of age-denying boomers out there, heading into retirement. But who brought the map? So, I started my blog." She shrugged, still uneasy when talking about herself. "It's just an adventure. Who knows what'll come of it?" But she soon realized that to an ad man, her 'adventure' looked like pure gold. Where she saw industry, he saw talent. Where she saw the commonweal, he saw a market.

"Baby, you need to take this act on the road," he said with enthusiasm. With a quick graphic facelift, her blog became a contender and then sneaked into the *Top Ten Blogs for Boomers* club. There was even a nibble from a publisher and her invitations to speak were upgraded from lunchtime talks at senior centers in the outer boroughs to professional conferences in the city and then farther afield. Twice in Texas. One afternoon as she stared at the pile of files on her desk, hope crept up on her. *If I keep this up, I just might achieve escape velocity.*

Later, Mac circled back on the topic of her family, trying to slip under the radar and get a glimpse. It was Friday night, and they'd decided to order in and relax. The wine was flowing as they swapped tales of their clients, who at times sounded interchangeable. His were just better dressed. Out of nowhere he asked, "So, you were the oldest? The rebel?"

She looked puzzled. "What the hell are you talking about?"

"In your family." Her face dropped and she pressed her lips together, but he was undaunted. "Or were you the good girl?"

"That's me. *Very* good for thirty years. Then the universe rewarded me with a cruel joke, so I decided that virtue was pointless. For the next thirty years I'd be naughty." She stood up and unbuttoned her blouse. "Take off your clothes. I'll prove it."

He was good at sex. Thanks to childhood trumpet lessons and a stint in his high school band, his embouchure made him a world-class kisser. And with a face like his, he'd probably had plenty of opportunities to practice. The first time she saw him nude she thought *old, but beautiful*. Gray pubic hair, a softening around the middle. But gracefully sculpted legs like one of Michelangelo's slaves, so that when he moved, he had a youthful vitality that she found irresistible. She could stare at him for hours.

Hours is exactly what it took to have sex.

Frances was never in to speed dating but she'd had her share of speed sex. Now wine, music and candles were as essential as setting out forks and knives for dinner. A hot shower was simply an excuse for a long slippery embrace before bed, where he was intense but never impatient.

She'd never talked much during sex, confining her remarks to the obligatory "Oh, baby" or the non-verbal equivalent that functioned as a GPS to keep things on track. So, she was intrigued and then delighted with his approach which was more like stream of consciousness lovemaking. Funny observations, kissing, obscure ideas, more kissing and laughter interspersed with touching that seemed to stoke rather than satisfy their appetite for each other. At first, it seemed like a horizontal cocktail party with a big finish, but over time it became their cherished ritual. It was an extravagance of time and sensuality that she suspected would earn a four-star rating in the *Catholic Girl's Guide to Sins and Sinners*, though she hadn't kept up with the taxonomy since Vatican II.

But how long could something this good last?

CHAPTER 59

"I get it. *Veni, vidi, vici,*" Frances said as she rubbed her eyes and read the only two lines she'd managed to capture in her journal. "He came, he saw." Then she carefully printed *He conquered.* A tear slipped down her cheek as she burrowed into the pillow, pursuing oblivion.

* * * *

Frances started to work before she opened her eyes. No matter that it was still early, that was all the more reason to rise and shine. But when she sat up, a long arm gently but firmly stopped her, like a mother cat pinning down a runaway kitten.

"Whoa! Where you goin'? It's Sunday," Mac said.

"I know. I have a lot to do." She threw back the covers.

"We, Frances. *We* have lots to do." He dragged the covers back up and then pulled her close, nuzzling her neck while she laughed.

"Don't tell me you're going back to church," she kidded.

"Nope. I'm a seventh-day loafer, just like God. Coffee, the Sunday paper in bed, wander down the block for some brunch. House rules."

"Not my house." Just for a moment she caught a glimpse of the urgency that seized her every morning and her lifelong habit of prioritizing work over pleasure. Somehow it didn't look so attractive from the vantage point of his warm embrace.

"But you're here now. And the house always wins." He held her close until she relaxed.

Eventually they'd drag themselves from bed and head for a new neighborhood, determined to have some first-time experiences despite being lifetime New Yorkers. She took him to Pomander Walk, a tiny piece of Europe surrounded by the high-rise city. He introduced her to Brazenhead Books, a former speakeasy that was still largely a secret. They admired illegal community gardens feeding whole neighborhoods in summer, and lingered in the Trinity churchyard, trying to decipher inscriptions on tombstones that dated back to the 17th century. But their favorite pastime was to track down the gypsy artists leading the migration from one down-at-heel neighborhood to another, seeking large spaces with cheap rents. As bistros and latte bars followed, rents soared and the vanguard moved on.

One Sunday during an Open Studios tour in Bushwick, they spent an hour with a young painter who seemed to have both talent and grit. "Barista in the morning. Waitress at lunch. Painter by night. I'm living my dream." Frances and Mac nodded their appreciation as she pulled out canvas after canvas inspired by her travels in Europe. Spontaneous sighs greeted a soft gray and white composition.

"Venice?" She nodded and Mac said, "Wrap it up."

They made their way back to the city by subway carrying a newspaper-wrapped package the size of a bus bench advertisement and promptly hung it in his study. When they stepped back to admire the effect, Frances said, "Let's go there next winter."

"Not Paris?"

She'd banked dozens of sick days because it never seemed like a good time to leave her colleagues in the lurch. "Both," she announced, and it was settled.

Their adventures usually ended with food followed by bed or the reverse, especially in winter when cold and dark drove them back to his place by late afternoon. The first time she entered his apartment she was gob smacked. The afternoon sun was streaming through French doors that looked out on Bryant Park. High ceilings created a cathedral feeling and each piece of tastefully chosen furniture had plenty of elbow room.

Of course, she knew people lived like this in the city. Madison Avenue was one long billboard for the good life. She just didn't know any of them personally, social workers being decidedly of the rent-controlled persuasion. Most of them felt lucky to have a bedroom with a window on an airshaft.

"Wow!"

"Ad man salary. None of the costly extras," Mac said casually.

His remark caught her up short. If this was self-deprecation, she didn't much like it. Entire families lived in spaces smaller than this and thought they were lucky. For the first time it occurred to her that she may have misjudged him. Missed a clue that someone more astute would have picked up at a glance.

He saw her body stiffen and realized his mistake. "Costly extras. Private school tuition, cello lessons, summer camp. Alimony. There's just me."

"Well, Just Me, it's lovely. One ticket for the tour, please."

Now a growing assortment of her clothes was accumulating in a spare closet. His and hers electric toothbrushes were docked in the bathroom but she still had her apartment nearby. Two or three nights a week she'd hole up there, ostensibly to check the mail or do chores. But in reality, she needed time to touch-up the growing cracks in her carapace or at least pay homage to the lingering need to be alone and unexposed.

At her most vulnerable, she'd convinced herself that this relationship was finite, its days numbered. Ancient yogis believed that each lifetime was allotted a specific, predetermined number of breaths and she'd appropriated that idea for their affair. Just so many dates and then—curtains. Nothing but thin air and regret. So, she'd decided to make it last as long as possible by taking time-outs. But week by week, the sense of safety she'd always cherished in her cozy apartment yielded to the feeling that something was missing. The algorithm was no substitute for the sound of his breathing during the night or his husky sleep-lowered voice in the morning.

During one of her mandatory time-outs, she'd cleaned every inch of her apartment, then paced from book to computer and back again, unable to settle down and work. "Focus, dammit!"

Her phone chimed the arrival of a text. R U decthecting? Dekathecting? Deca...Fuck it. My spell check is having a nervous breakdown. R U afraid?

Panic-stricken, she hammered out, Meet me at Martelli's tomorrow night? Please.

The next evening Mac strolled into their neighborhood bistro and waved to the waiter. "Evening, Michael."

"Evening, Mac." He gestured toward their usual corner where Frances sat with her arms clenched across her middle, like she was trying to staunch the flow from a bullet wound. She stared into space with a glass of wine untouched in front of her.

"Orphan Franny, what's up?" he said as he slid into the booth.

She squeezed her eyes closed and then blurted out, "Nothing this good lasts."

"Go on." His voice was calm but his face registered a hint of caution.

She took a huge gulp of wine, steeling her nerves to share the pseudo-mathematical theory that lent a rationale to her solitary nights. "I thought that maybe by insisting on little breaks I could extend the, you know, shelf-life of..." She paused.

He winced. The term cruelly reduced their relationship to a commodity that was fit for consumption, then suddenly, arbitrarily not. "Fucking ad men."

She pursed her lips as if making a final decision and then continued. "Of the best thing that ever happened to me in my entire adult life."

He relaxed, sitting quietly for a moment, and then said, "What if it doesn't work like that? What if the expiration date is already marked on a calendar we can't see?"

Her expression shattered and tears rolled down her face.

"Listen, my darling, I think about endings, too." He touched a lock of gray hair near his temple. "How could I not with this greeting me in the mirror?"

"No!" she protested. "No. You're going to be like your father. Eighty-five and still going strong. You must!"

"I'm trying, but no guarantees. Unforeseen things. Sometimes lightning strikes out of a clear sky." He waited while she sobbed. "It took a long time to wrap my head around my own mortality, that I wasn't going to be spared the fate of every other poor sucker on earth. But that's how it is. I'm going to die, and by the way, so are you."

Frances managed a little laugh and mopped her tears on a cloth napkin.

"I'm also not perfect," he continued. "It's a good bet that at some point I'm likely to screw up and make mistakes. Piss you off. Drive you crazy."

"Me, too." She nodded her head up and down, amazed at how easily this admission slipped out.

He reached across the table and took her hands. "All we have is today. I finally understand what that means, not by the size of my dread but by the ferocity of my determination to pay attention to every minute, right now. No guarantees about tomorrow. I've decided to live, simple as that. So, I guess you could say I'm a Rogerian."

"Carl?"

"No, Fred. On every show he'd croon the message that we have to make the most of life one day at a time. That's my goal. I'm grateful each morning that I wake up as *me* with another chance to work on interesting projects, a few of which actually benefit mankind, eat too much pesto pasta, enjoy another season in Central Park." Then his voice softened almost to a whisper. "And if you can see your way clear to it—love you."

"God, I'm such an idiot!" Frances practically shouted. She grabbed his hands and kissed each palm like it was a holy relic. Then she dug in her purse and threw a twenty on the table before dragging him toward the door, calling out, "We'll be back."

Thus began her conversion toward the light. It wasn't easy to give up her dark visions of the future, silently asking: *How many more times will we do this? Will it ever be enough?* But slowly he convinced her that she was staining each day with imaginary tears that she may never need to shed.

"Death on the installment plan. Isn't that what you called it in one of your blogs?"

"Yes, but I was talking about dying slowly by neglecting your physical health. You know, sitting on your ass all day, gorging on junk food, avoiding exertion until disease comes along to claim what's left of you."

"Never mind the buts. If you snuff out a little bit of joy each day instead of nurturing it, you pretty much achieve the same thing."

"How'd you get so smart?" she asked.

"Time, experience. Lots of mistakes. And a few tips from the Warrior's Path."

The word warrior was jarring because he was the gentlest man she'd ever met, so later that evening she googled *The Warrior's Path,* and it all fell into place. This was no primer on violence or oppression, but a description of the four dignities that a warrior cultivates. The first was relaxed confidence, a feeling of being at home in one's body. She certainly recognized that quality in him, but it was the second dignity that hit the nail on the head. An irrepressible joy that sprung from seeing the best in everything and avoiding cynicism. That was his secret, the thing that drew her to him like a crackling fire on a cold night. She vowed to try. She'd reach for joy.

* * * *

The journal was still tucked under her arm when she awoke. In the past, Frances loved to review her entries in the morning, jumpstarting her day with micro-epiphanies that arrived the night before. Now she stared at the three sentences: *He came. He saw. He conquered.* Their entire history in six words.

This journal was a terrible mistake, she thought. Instead of capturing her past, she'd probed an old scar that throbbed like a fresh wound, threatening her fragile grip on the present. She added a single line. *But not for long.* Then she flung the journal into a corner.

CHAPTER 60

"But not for long," Cornelius echoed.

He sat at the table in the Committee room, glued to the monitor, his face a study in naked grief. His eyes brimmed with tears threatening to spill over but he was utterly frozen, unable to blink them away or release his burden of pain.

"Not for long." Then he closed his eyes and wrapped his arms around his chest as if trying to ward off the cold, unaware of time or the room or the perplexed Committee members waiting for him to explain the shapeshifting that reduced this towering figure to a wretched heap of sorrow.

Suddenly, the baby let out a wail and Cornelius jerked out of his trance. "Whose idea was this? You, Smiles? Forever with your damn writing. Or you, Madame de Gouges? Troublemakers, both of you. I don't know why we have to waste our time talking about her. Face it. She's a lost cause."

Olympe rose, her silk gown rustling in the silence. "J'accuse."

Cornelius stiffened. The muscles in his jaws jumped and his hands tightened into menacing spheres, answering a call for violence.

"Explain yourself, sir," she demanded, placing both hands on the table and leaning toward him.

His chest swelled as he prepared to bellow her out of existence. But just in time, pride came to the rescue. Even in this tortured state, his ego cautioned that it would be unseemly to allow a mere woman to provoke a man of his stature. He reined in his outrage and exhaled slowly, but he couldn't drain the threat from his words. "Don't speak."

"I'll speak in tongues if necessary until I'm heard," Olympe replied. "Explain your irrational antagonism toward Frances. Is this simply a gender issue? Because that thinking is beyond antique. It's antediluvian. You're a throw-back, monsieur. A troglodyte. How dare you judge her?"

A round of applause went up as the women leapt to their feet. Then the groom. Then Smiles. Soon the whole room was clapping in unison, "Frances! Frances!"

"Hear me out." Cornelius raised his hands, begging for silence. "When a second chance presents itself." But his voice broke and his mouth opened like a fish to gulp another lungful of control. Then he struggled on. "When a chance for which you've longed for centuries comes and you squander it though arrogance, self-interest and pure unvarnished cowardice, you don't deserve another chance."

"A curious choice of pronouns," Olympe observed. "*You* could mean anyone in this room, including yourself. So, help me understand. Is this an accusation or a thinly veiled *mea culpa*?"

He slumped forward on the table, his arms cradling his head and shuddered convulsively like one who'd been sleeping rough on a winter night. The Fool placed a heavy woolen cloak over him like a shroud.

But Olympe stood her ground. "Look at me," she demanded. "What did Frances ever do to you?"

Cornelius turned his head to one side, struggling for air like an exhausted swimmer. "Nothing. Nothing. It's what she did to him, and us." He looked to the Fool. "Tell them."

The Fool hesitated. "Sire?"

"Do it. Leave nothing out."

The Fool dutifully pressed the button on the monitor and

stood aside. The small red light winked and the screen framed a younger Cornelius barely visible in the shadows, passionately kissing another man. Muffled voices accompanied the hurried stripping off of stockings and breeches. Then he was pressed up against a stout post in what might have been a barn or basement, his head lurching from the thrusts of the unseen partner.

Then the scene jumped to a young man playing a lute and singing. The Fool picked up the story: "One night in a tavern, Cornelius broke his cardinal rule: Never fall in love. He invited this musician, one Jan de Vries, to join him for a drink and his fate was sealed."

Cornelius whispered, "*Ultinam ne illum conspexissem.* If only I had never seen him."

"Ah, but you did," the Fool said. Then he turned to the committee members and continued. "Discretion was a matter of life and death since—you'll pardon me, ladies—sodomy was a capital crime. The briefest meeting in public, a whiff of attraction could have put Mr. Beeckman's entire career at risk, even in Amsterdam which was the world's most liberal city. But he was sick with love, fist-around-the-heart love."

Cornelius groaned as the Fool pressed the button again. On screen, Cornelius and Jan were asleep in each other's arms.

"But when the tulip craze hit, Cornelius went into a frenzy. A single bulb could change hands four or five times a day, driving up the price and promising even more." The Fool shook his head as if signaling his listeners to prepare for the worst. "From there on out, he treated Jan like shit. Simply had no time for a lowly musician while he scaled the heights of the tulip market. And just to be fair, Jan could have used some assertiveness training."

Cornelius roused himself, unable to resist a final chance to dazzle the Committee with his tale of triumph. "I sold my last bulb for more than the price of the finest canal house complete with coach and garden." He shook his head in quiet wonder at the memory of his conquest. "I was in a mood to celebrate but..."

"Apparently de Vries had found his *cojones* or a new lover," the Fool interrupted. "He was never heard from again."

Cornelius dissolved into a rumpled heap, radiating regret.

Samuel Smiles was the first to react. He rounded the table and patted Cornelius on the shoulder. "My dear man, you mustn't be disconsolate. Look at all the amazing lives we've had since then. And all the possibilities ahead." His face brightened with the thought. "Who knows what we can become?"

"You've got that right, Smiley," the Fool declared, as if delivering a royal proclamation. "Living well is the best revenge."

"It's not revenge I'm seeking," Cornelius said.

"What then?" Smiles asked.

"Redemption." He extended his hands toward the assembly, as if they were a jury of his peers. "I loved that man with all my heart, or all the heart I had to give."

"But it wasn't enough," the Fool said.

"No, it wasn't. From that moment on, the sole purpose of fortune hunting was to bury my loneliness. But it didn't work. The longing and regret never died. The truth is, I'd never let it. I cherished the pain because it was the fragile thread that bound us together through all those dead years of nothingness." He lapsed into silence and the room seemed to hold its breath.

"And?" Olympe prompted, still waiting for an explanation.

"And...she ruined it! When he finally returned—to Frances— we had a second chance. For real love. Out in the open. No hiding. No fear. But she squandered it." Through gritted teeth Cornelius snarled, "I hate her!"

Olympe bristled. "So, Frances should serve time for the mistakes you made?"

"I made. She made. What does it matter? It's in our DNA. We're doomed." He covered his face with his hands, releasing a lifetime of tears.

Smiles touched Cornelius once again, trying to comfort him. "The time has come to give up your self-loathing."

"Not possible. It's my due, my penance, the only thing that makes sense." He buried his head in his arms.

"That's where you're wrong my friend. Are you familiar with the story of King Pyrrhus?" Smiles asked.

The Fool interjected, "He was a little before your time, Sire. 280 AD. Not a good year."

Smiles continued. "Plutarch..."

"Another writer," the Fool explained. "Brace yourself."

"According to the historian Plutarch, King Pyrrhus declared: 'If we are victorious in one more battle, we shall be utterly ruined.' That's your predicament precisely. Your victory over Frances will ruin us all," Smiles concluded.

Cornelius propped his head in the palm of one hand and blotted his face with a lace cuff. "Then just tell me this." He tipped his head back and closed his eyes. The group sat in stunned silence as his pure tenor voice sang: *How many lifetimes before we get it right?*

"That's not how it works," Smiles said. "We may never get it right."

"Then what?" Cornelius asked. "What's the purpose of it all?"

"We must be satisfied to advance in life as we walk, step by step," Smiles answered. One by one, the other members of the committee rose to contribute their perspectives, trying to build a message of hope. Trying to save their collective life.

"Abhyasa, my friend," the yogi said. "Steady effort in the direction you want to go."

"Make the right mistakes," the Fool added. "Another yogi said that. Yogi Berra, the great baseball philosopher."

"To persist, even if failure seems to be our lot," Juliette added, leaning for support on Perpetua.

"Just do the best we can with what we're given," Gwilym

summarized.

"Or surrender," Andreas interjected from a deep slouch in his chair. All heads turned toward him, disheartened by his insistence on cynicism and defeat. "Simply take our place on the great mandala and endure."

"I disagree." Olympe's sturdy voice echoed through the room. "Surely with all our experience we can set our sights higher." She looked directly from face to face, broadcasting a clarion call for optimism. "I believe we're capable of *approfondissement*. Playing easily in the deep."

The yogi placed both hands on Cornelius's head to bestow a blessing. "Inhale the future. Exhale the past. Life is a gift. The appropriate response is gratitude."

CHAPTER 61

As Antoinette approached Strong Silent, she spied a rumpled something resting against the security doors, wearing a halo of graffiti. No face visible, only the top of a knit cap above a body bundled in a full winter of clothes. Wear-or-carry was the rule of life on the street, and two hands can manage only so many bundles. But the pavement around him was empty.

She froze in place on the deserted platform, ambushed by piercing memories from her last life when she'd spent a season on the street. Each night she'd bed down, not by plan or choice, but when exhaustion from a day on the move stopped her in her tracks. Her last thought before sleep was the dread of waking to the sound of a policeman's voice. If lucky, she'd just be ordered to move along. Other times the offense of being homeless earned her a string of curses or a boot in the side. She remembered taking refuge under a loading dock late one snowy night. When dawn brought the commotion of first arrivals slinging lunch pails into metal lockers, calling out a litany of jovial curses, she'd nudged a fellow sleeper, but it was like trying to jostle a boulder. Beneath his upturned collar was a face as pale as an egg.

But she also remembered the times when she'd survived through the kindness of strangers. Some days she'd awaken to restaurant leftovers, small change, or a few dollar bills rolled

HOW TO BE DEAD

like a joint and stuck in her shoe. Occasionally a cup of coffee, still steaming. Most of the offerings were left just out of reach. Good intentions deposited at arm's length. It was the rare donor who was both generous and willing to risk contact with the unwashed.

Antoinette shook her head to dislodge the painful images of the past and strode confidently toward Strong Silent, eager to offer her special brand of comfort. "Hello, my friend," she called out to the squatter, as if he was one of her regulars. To her surprise, his head rose and two bright eyes greeted her, but no words. On closer inspection she could see that he'd been reading, not dozing. His hands cradled a small book, leather-bound and worn. Gilt letters shone against a red cover in the dim light. She could just make out the author's name. *Charles Dickens.*

Dickens, tireless champion of the poor and homeless, crisscrossed his city by night, walking off insomnia and collecting vivid images to touch the hearts of Londoners. He spared no detail in his crusade for social justice, calling on those better off to have a care for "those soaked by the nightly rains, standing near the warmth of dray horses, infected with untreated disease. Children who compete for food with the dogs in the market and those so wretched and miserable that their rags fall from their body."

Antoinette released the lock and the doors crawled up, broadcasting a noisy opening of the business day. With the grace of a ballroom dancer, she flipped on the lights and eased Strong Silent into motion. When all was in order she turned and asked, "What's your pleasure?"

He tapped his chin to signal that he was mute and Antoinette quickly replied, "No worries. I talk enough for at least two people."

He smiled and held up two fingers.

"Double expresso comin' up," and she busied herself with the beans and tamper. As she turned to announce, "It'll be just a minute," her visitor reached for the tips plate, exposing the tattoo of the grave diggers' guild on the inside of his wrist. Breathing a cloud of fog on the shiny metal surface, he wrote a single word and pointed to himself.

"Pierre, welcome to Strong Silent," Antoinette said.

She handed him the tiny cup of steaming sludge and watched as he took an exploratory sip, closed his eyes, and managed a sigh that was the universal sound of deep gustatory pleasure.

"You know, Pierre, we have a lot in common." He tilted his head to one side and gave her a quizzical prompt with his eyebrows. "The dead. You tucked them in and I wake them up."

His entire body seemed to exhale relief, grateful for a sense of kinship he'd rarely known. Even the priest who'd taught him to read couldn't mask the pity in his eyes, the unmistakable message that the tutorial impulse was fueled by the obligations of a charitable profession rather than fellowship.

"Kids?" Antoinette asked. He shook his head. "Me neither. Family?" Once more the response was no. "You didn't miss much. In fact, the whole idea of family is highly overrated. They'll crush your soul if you let them."

Again, he reached for the tips plate, breathed and wrote: *Outcasts.*

"No, my friend. That's where you're wrong," she insisted. "We're true companions to ourselves. Soulmates to our own souls. Expert navigators of that fine and private place that only we inhabit." Pierre was following her words with a look of wonder. "Yeah, yeah, I know Socrates said it better—*the unexamined life is not worth living*—but how many people listen? Damned few, from what I've seen." She gave the counter a quick swipe with her towel and paused as a puzzled look transformed her face. "It's odd, isn't it? Why go to all the trouble of reincarnating if you remain a stranger to yourself?"

The Mute raised both shoulders and entertained the

faintest smile as if to say, "Beats me." Then he covered his heart with one hand before extending it toward Antoinette in offering.

Hot tears sprung to her eyes, exhuming a vein of tenderness long since buried but not forgotten. She started to turn away but paused and touched the tips of his outstretched fingers, dusted in yellow chalk. "I don't feel so lonely now that you're here," she confessed.

Then her blustery take-charge doppelganger barged back in. She swiped her cheek as if going after a mosquito, intercepting a tear before it could even reach her chin. "Anyway, where are you off to now?"

The Mute picked up the tray once again and wrote the letters FR.

"Frances," Antoinette sighed. "She can use all the help she can get." Then she made a grab for the tamper and called over her shoulder, "One for the road?" but when she looked back, he'd vanished, leaving the small red volume on the tips plate.

CHAPTER 62

As Frances struggled to emerge from the tangle of sheets, she began to triage the day but realized it was futile. As things stood, it would probably triage her. Unfinished writing assignments, Charlie's emotional steeplechase at the gym and Grayson, who seemed to be suffering from an epic case of PMS that he took no pains to suppress. She gave up and dragged herself from her cocoon.

Standing in the gloom of the bathroom, she thought *Who's in charge of makeup today?*

She glanced in the mirror and recoiled. "Jesus!" The wrinkled imprints of the sheets slashed her face. The bags under her eyes looked like they'd been mugged by a bicycle pump, and her hair was clearly trying to escape from her head. A de Kooning gargoyle in all her chaotic glory.

I think it's time to break up with my bathroom.

She reached for the light switch and saw her hand shake. There was only one possible remedy for this disaster of a morning. Antoinette's elixir!

Once inside the subway, the smell of roasting coffee beans slithered up her nostrils and quickened her steps. "Set 'em up, bartender."

Antoinette turned around and swore. "Christ! You look like hell, Frances."

"Thanks. You're only the second person today who's

noticed. Look, I'm barely sleeping. Can't concentrate. Ditching class, then running and hiding like a fugitive. Basically, I'm fucking up on all fronts."

"Welcome to the club."

"You don't understand. This is *not* my club." Her voice was beyond adamant but she managed a spit-free delivery. "*I get things done. I* produce. I'm *good* at stuff!"

"Were." Antoinette slid a double across the counter and Frances made short work of it.

"Seriously, do you have a train schedule back there because maybe I should just jump."

"If it was that easy, baby, they'd all be doin' it."

"Then what? Help me. I can't take it anymore." Frances probed the inside of her espresso cup with one finger to gather up the foam but Antionette snatched it away.

"That's disgusting! You really are in bad shape." She turned and prepped another double but wondered aloud if she shouldn't just call 911. She delivered the tiny cup and stared at Frances.

"Tell me what I need to do," Frances pleaded. She held the second cup to her lips, blew twice and downed a scalding mouthful.

"I can only tell you what worked for me. I learned to love the fool in me. The one who runs her mouth when silence would be brilliant, takes chances, and takes shit. Buttoned up and out of control, the lover, the hater. A real spectacle. Remember what Oscar Wilde said?"

"What didn't he say? Brilliant man took wit and homosexuality to new heights. I loved him."

"You would. Anyway, Oscar said: *Be yourself. Everyone else is already taken.*"

"I'm not overly fond of me right now so that's not too appealing."

"Exactly. Your problem is you have to declare amnesty for the part of yourself that you don't love very well. Forgive that

319

poor sucker or you'll never rest. I read that somewhere, but it's true."

Frances stared into her empty cup and considered the proposition. Forgiveness was a double-edged sword. True forgiveness could bring relief but first there was the thorny issue of admitting that someone was at fault. You had to say "I was wrong" or "I'm sorry" before you could get that soothing absolution. But that meant you'd screwed up. Screwing up meant potential loss of love, so it was best to argue your way out or shift the blame, justify yourself at any cost.

Down the dark rabbit hole she tumbled, lost in thought until a small wooden disk like a poker chip sailed across the counter and came to rest next to her cup. It bore the Strong Silent logo. "What's this?" she asked. "Token for a free latte?"

"Turn it over."

On the other side, delicate lines like an etching captured a Beaux-Arts bridge that she immediately recognized from the map in her room. "And...?" She waited for Antoinette to explain.

"I told you. I know things"

"Yeah? The last time you knew things, I ended up being groped in a phone booth."

"Fun, huh?" Antoinette chuckled.

Frances shook her head. "I can't believe I listen to you."

"What else have you got going for you? You're not exactly a star pupil. You said so yourself. Now get out of here." Antoinette swatted the air but couldn't suppress a crooked smile.

I know things, too, Frances thought. That another trek through the labyrinth was likely a fool's errand. That her goal seemed as remote and unattainable as ever. *Have I done a single thing right since I arrived?*

She looked at the token again. Maybe the barista had special powers. Maybe she's was just a nutjob. *What have I got to lose?*

CHAPTER 63

Map in hand, Frances set off under a darkening sky. The path was circuitous and seemed to loop back on itself, or was it simply the effect of one identical vista after another? Finally, she reached a sturdy door of highly polished zinc. A small sign like the screen on her phone displayed the word *Nepenthe*, and a circle beneath directed: *Tap for translation*. Her finger kissed the spot and the answer appeared: *Surcease of pain*.

"Impossible," she whispered.

The door glided open without a sound. Inside a cobblestone path led to a bridge adorned with cherubs and winged horses that reminded her of Paris. A small bronze plaque like an historic marker asked: *Do you deserve to let go of your pain?*

Frances crept toward the center of the bridge, making a familiar pilgrimage for a familiar ritual. How many times had she sought out a river or tidepool, any place where living water could receive her sacred offering? She pulled the small silk pouch from her pocket and removed a pinch of gray ash, then kissed her father goodbye once again and watched him drift away.

This time she'd follow.

As she stepped up on the railing, Gabe appeared out of nowhere and began to whine and pace in circles. She ignored him, so he jumped up and pawed at her feet. "Don't do it, Frances. You have so much to..."

"Live for?" she said sadly. "I've had it, Gabe."

"But people are counting on you."

"Well, I pity them. They bet on the wrong horse. I just can't take it anymore," and she gave him a gentle shove, windmilling her arms to maintain her balance.

The water looked like it was miles below, dark and ready for takers. Would she tumble like an acrobat or simply drop like a stone, smashing the surface with all the grace of a brick thrown by an angry protestor? Maybe she should try for something more dramatic. After all, this was her last hurrah. *How about a cannonball?* Just pull her knees toward her chest and hang on for dear...death. But she didn't have the strength. Easier to just step out like those cartoon characters who sprint off a cliff and realize a moment too late that they've run out of *terra firma.* Or she could simply lean forward and let gravity make the decision.

But instead, she felt her knees relax and then spring up and propel her body into a slow arc. Instantly, she was four-years-old and it was summertime. She was barefoot in a sundress that billowed up on the warm air. Her arms flew forward, hands open, fingers stretched. Reaching. This sensation was etched in her memory from the hundreds of times she'd perched half way up a staircase or on a high rock in the woods. Then she'd launch herself into space without the slightest hesitation, filled with trust. Impeccable, unassailable trust.

The air gently caught her and she floated. Her heart pounded. Her head felt light and giddy. Then came the impact for which she longed. Not death, but nepenthe. Surcease of pain. Heart-to-heart, like two halves of a single body reunited, she buried herself in her father's embrace.

"Franny! My darling Franny."

"Daddy." She inhaled and caught a whiff of Old Spice, the signature scent of safety and love. He was her nourishment, her environment, but like a fish in water or a bird in the air, she hadn't known what she had until he was gone.

Snug in the crook of his arm, one hand clutched the back of his neck while the other patted his cheek. She swiveled her head from side to side, thrilled with the novelty of seeing the world from six feet above the ground. Then her joy was replaced by remorse. "I never got to say goodbye to you. How could I let you slip away without...?" She stifled a sob.

"No, no, my darling. I never left you." He held her close and whispered in her ear. "I've been by your side every day. Surely you knew."

She raised her shoulders, suddenly ashamed of her lack of faith in him. "Sometimes I could feel you," she sobbed, "but only in my dreams. I'd be holding your hand or talking to you. Once I was carrying you on my back but somehow it wasn't a burden." She touched his face, marveling that her dream was suddenly flesh and blood. "It hurt like hell in the morning, but I was always grateful because the pain was the only way I could still feel you."

"Oh, my God. You poor child." He brushed the tears that were streaming down her face. "Can you forgive me? I just had to reach out because I was so proud of you. Your work, your books, the person you've become." He smiled and his face was full of wonder. "You're something else, Franny!"

"But..." she asked cautiously. "Did you see everything?'

"The divorce?" he asked.

"Yes." She winced as the word stuck in her throat. He nodded and she looked away. "It's so humiliating. You and mom were married for thirty-four years. I couldn't make it to thirty-four months!" She gave a ruptured laugh. "What a catastrophe *that* was."

"Forget about it, baby." He took her chin in his hand so he could look her straight in the eyes. "That guy was a jerk! You were way too good for him."

"And the parade of misfits that followed?" she asked.

He chuckled. "I have to say, you really knew how to pick

'em. But look at it this way. It wasn't failure, sweetie. It was research!"

This was one of the things she loved best about this man. Yes, he was her mentor, her protector, her hero. Always in her corner, no matter how much she screwed up. But here was his true gift. He could find the positive in almost any situation. One of his favorite punch lines was "with all this manure around, there must be a pony somewhere."

"Research," she said quietly. "That's a nice word for it."

"And it worked brilliantly because look who you ended up with." He paused and whispered in her ear. "I liked him very much."

"Me, too." His words broke her heart all over again.

Unfairly deceased. Both of them. They'd missed so much.

"Would you do something for me, Franny?" He wiped away one more tear and smoothed her hair.

"Anything. Please, just name it." she begged.

"Paint. Art is the only thing that endures."

"I know."

"And it used to make you so happy." He wrapped her in his arms once again, holding her with a tender ferocity. Then he pressed his lips to her cheek and whispered, "Courage, my love."

Frances clung to him with all her might, feeling his heart beat. Beat. Beat. And then nothing. When she opened her eyes, he was gone.

CHAPTER 64

"Courage, my love," Frances whispered, stroking the imprint of her father's last kiss on her cheek, committing every moment of the reunion to memory. She moved through the labyrinth like a sleepwalker while her heart struggled to reconcile the titanic infusion of love with the aftermath of utter desolation. Eventually she found herself in a dead-end alley that led to a tiny shop. The sign above the door read *Ars Longa, Vita Brevis Donation Center* and displayed the universal symbol for recycling.

Frances was a fan of recycling long before it had its own logo because her father routinely arrived home with rolls of discarded blueprints to keep her easel supplied. And she'd furnished more than one apartment with discards collected from the street or her local thrift shop.

"Why not?" Maybe she could find an old chair shoved in a corner because suddenly her legs had lost the will to perform. But the scene inside was nothing like the musty East Village Thrift Shop where she'd gleaned the shelves for old books. This space was hospital clean and smelled like the morning after a night of rain. Not a lumpy couch or easy chair in sight.

Brain fog was setting in as she turned back toward the exit, but she'd only managed a few steps when a white-coated attendant with an efficient stride and no-nonsense face approached. Not wishing to seem rude, Frances glanced at the woman's badge and managed, "Nice place, Ella, but I'm a little confused."

"We're in charge of recycling."

Frances leaned heavily against a counter and took a closer look, checking for crates of plastic food containers and empty wine bottles, the debris of affluent societies shipped to the third world for re-use. But the room had the orderly appearance of a nail salon. Sturdy chairs like the early bucket seats in a Pontiac stood in rows, with a shiny metal tray assigned to each. No cotton balls, files or varnish. Just a pair of glasses like the darkest celebrity accessory resting on a black iPad.

"What exactly are you recycling?"

"Talent. Our clients donate their left-over expertise back into the world." Ella made it sound so obvious but Frances was astonished.

"Are you serious?" She straightened up, completely forgetting her fatigue.

"How do you think prodigies are created? It takes more than DNA to come up with a Norman Bel Geddes or Sor Juana Inés de la Cruz."

Frances was momentarily lost. "Sorry? Those names don't ring a bell."

Ella gave a little laugh. "Norman Bel Geddes? And you call yourself a New Yorker! NBG was a genius."

Frances felt stung but decided to press on. "Any relation to RBG?"

"Only the genius part," Ella said. "The man was amazing."

"What'd he do?" Frances asked, determined to remedy this gap in her knowledge.

"Easier to say what he didn't. There's scarcely a corner of the design world, especially in New York, that he didn't touch. Started in theater design and branched out to anything that could benefit from streamlining. Futurama, driverless cars, and a gorgeous cocktail shaker. Look him up."

"I'll do that. And the other one? Sore something?"

"Sor Juana. Seventeenth century writer born in Mexico. She did it all. Poems, plays, music theory, philosophy." Ella paused and then her face lit up. "Oh, yeah, one more thing you'll appreciate. She wrote the first feminist manifesto of the New World."

"So, you're saying that they were working with borrowed brain cells?" Frances tapped lightly on her right temple. *God, I could use a few of those right now.*

"Juana seemed to think so," Ella replied. "When she was hounded by the church fathers about her unseemly scholarship, she defended herself saying: *I have this inclination to study and if it is evil, I am not the one who formed me thus. I was born with it and I shall die with it.*"

"Feisty," Frances said. "Blaming God. I like her already." She relaxed against the counter, eager for more stories and Ella seemed to be in the mood to oblige.

"And how else would you explain Mozart picking out tunes on the piano at the age of three and composing at four? Or Blaise Pascal's computer? Donations from the other side," Ella concluded.

"Pascal. Isn't he the one who made the wager about believing in God? It costs you nothing if you're wrong and wins you everything if you're right?" Once again, Frances marveled at the trivia festival her brain so enthusiastically sponsored while leaving her stumped about the details of her very existence. Make that non-existence.

"He's the one," Ella confirmed.

"I imagine the ol' UAL was a bit of a surprise to him."

"I'm not sure he was thrilled with the payoff, but he did pass his genius on to a soul who became Enrico Fermi."

Frances jerked forward in alarm. "Wait a minute! Fermi of the Manhattan project? The A-bomb!"

"The same." Ella shook her head. "I know, I know. Sometimes the outcomes are tragic."

Frances took a step back. The recycling project, so intriguing at first, now seemed like a way to prolong humanity's worst instincts. But her curiosity got the better of her and she decided to ask just one more question. "Does the talent always go to newborn souls?"

"Not at all. There are lots of the late-blooming recipients, like Grandma Moses," Ella said cheerfully. "And occasionally the gift goes to someone who just needs an emergency infusion. Captain Sully landing his plane on the Hudson River. Things like that."

"You mean helping people in crisis?" Her social worker instincts jumped as if they'd been hit with a cattle prod, eager for a chance to be useful once again.

"Absolutely," Ella said.

"So how does it actually work?" Frances ventured cautiously, picturing a needle jammed in her arm, sharp instruments at the ready, and perhaps a row of souvenir stitches in the bargain.

"Why don't you give it a try?" Ella's voice was an invitation, not a challenge, so Frances dropped into the nearest chair, grateful to be off her feet.

"It's rather straightforward. You picture a person on earth to whom you want to donate something that was left over when you died. In a way, you're creating a legacy, but posthumously."

That got her attention. Maybe this was the work-around for the no-kids brick wall that stopped her DNA dead in its tracks. She could still leave a bit of herself behind.

But what do I have to give?

Unfortunately, Constant Comment was on duty and decided to stage a filibuster. Try as she might, all Frances could think of were the talents she never had or used to have or squandered or disparaged or discounted or neglected until they disappeared.

Music? "Not a chance," Constant said. Nothing like her dear friend John, who could instantly play any tune by ear even though he couldn't read a single note of music. Now, there was a donation. As he hammered out song after song, the life of the party, Frances would stare at the display of black and white keys without a clue to the sounds they would produce, much less how you'd find them without even looking. She couldn't even play the harmonica.

Singing? "Forget about it." Her voice was so worn out from years of high-octane presentations that she was reduced to lip-synching *Happy Birthday* at parties.

Dancing was another non-starter. She loved to watch those loose-limbed people who instantly animated to any tune, but her body refused to perform in public, not even solo on a crowded, dark, we're-all-drunk-anyway dance floor. On the few occasions when she was forced to follow a partner, her jerking clumsiness quickly deteriorated into a contest of wills. Once in a while she let the music speak to her, but only in semi-darkness after a bit of over-indulgence in wishful drinking.

Dead loss at math. Ditto that Wittgensteinian philosophy that looked more like algebra than thought. *What was that called? Episiotomy?*

"There you go again," Constant said. "Close but no cigar."

Frances cringed each time her attempts at word-retrieval misfired. *Epistemology! That's it! Epistemology.*

She loved food and once upon a time had an epic collection of cookbooks from which she'd mastered coq au vin and cheesecake without a single crack. And her guacamole was so perfect in texture and heat that she had a standing invitation to at least one Super Bowl party. But in recent years her refrigerator looked more like a science experiment gone wrong. When she was busy, she'd survived on salad and eggs which, contrary to popular opinion, had a shelf life longer than salt.

"Pathetic. My cupboard is bare." She closed her eyes, trying to think of a graceful way to slide out of the chair and slink toward the exit without attracting Ella's attention. It was humbling to think that after a lifetime of striving, the only remarkable asset she had left was the ability to prowl a stage for six hours, run her mouth and cheerlead.

Then it dawned on her. *Energy!* Abundant energy. Somehow, she'd retained the vitality and stamina of her thirties. She'd eclipsed most of her friends, even the health nuts, dismissing their veiled references to mania as simple jealousy. No naps. Not even a cup of afternoon tea. She just went full throttle all day, dropped in her tracks, and then got up and did it again and again. The inspirational Post-it on her computer read*: Be the kind of woman that when your feet hit the floor each morning, the devil says, "Oh crap, she's up."*

Frances hailed the attendant. "I need a little coaching here. The only thing I have to donate is energy. Is that *something*? *Anything?*"

"Absolutely."

"Okay." She paused for a moment and added, "The problem is, I can't picture a recipient. It's like my contact list has been deleted."

"How about if we let the universe decide?" Ella helped her adjust the dark glasses and arranged her hand precisely on the center of the pad, as if taking her handprint for an official document. The pad sprang to life and glowed a soft yellow outline. "Now just relax."

She leaned back and it was like she was in a tiny theater behind the glasses, watching a woman pilot an aging Honda Civic down a two-lane road that was country dark. No neon or street lights. Just a dull white line down the middle, eroded by a long harsh winter. The woman's eyes started to droop and Frances jammed her hand on the pad until it hurt. The driver shook herself awake but Frances could see that it was only a momentary reprieve as her eyes resisted the effort to focus on the beams of the headlights.

"Whoa! Don't do that!" she barked. "Believe me, dying is a

lot harder than it looks." The eyelids sagged toward half-mast. "Jeez, lady, don't you have anything worth living for?"

Now it was a race against impending disaster. Frances put her thumb and pinky finger into her mouth and gave a cab driver whistle. "Ella, this thing isn't working!"

Ella hurried over and noticed the veins standing out on the back of her hand. "You have to focus. Not here" she said, touching the pad, "but here." Ella's finger rested lightly on the top of her skull. "Picture a point of light in the center of your head. Now send your intention out from that light."

Frances pushed down her panic enough to grope for the point. The woman in the car cracked open her window and took a hit of the cold night air. Then she reached back between the seats and gently touched two little girls, her precious cargo.

This was the nightly ritual of Alison, a single mom working at the 7-11 by day but never scheduled for enough hours to make ends meet. So, from six until midnight she looked after a failing neighbor for much needed cash. Her girls did their homework in the cramped kitchen while she made a simple dinner, did the dishes and laundry. Then she made a nest on the couch, tucking the pillows and blankets around them before she visited the bedroom one last time to change his diaper, check on his meds, and wish him a good night.

Suddenly, Frances had a bird's eye view of the road ahead. A big-rig from the quarry was coming in the opposite direction, taking its full share of the road. Back in the car, Alison's head dipped forward and Frances realized that she was locked in battle with a bone-weariness that had been years in the making. Picturing the point of light, she recruited all forty-three muscles in her face, imagining that they could squeeze her cranium tight enough to propel every last molecule of energy like a laser. Alison's head jerked up just in time to see that she'd drifted into the path of the oncoming truck. Its horn blared as she swerved back into her lane, leaving her wide awake but shaking.

"Mom, what was that noise?" came a sleepy voice from the back seat.

"It's all right, my darling. Just a lonely truck driver saying hello." Tears stung her eyes but she pounded her horn in relief. "We'll be home soon."

Frances gasped, "Oh, my God!" but kept her hand glued to the pad until she saw the car pull into a driveway and roll to a stop. Alison threw open the back door and scooped the children into her arms for a long hug. "I love you, my beautiful girls." Hand-in-hand she guided them to their beds. The last thing Frances saw was a devoted mom tenderly planting goodnight kisses on warm cheeks. "We're going to be fine. Someone's watching over us," and the screen went black.

She yanked off the glasses and wiped the tears streaming down her face. Fear, relief and anger converged and she shook with rage. "Why do their lives have to be so damn hard? We are a pitiful, pitiless society!"

Ella set a mug on the tray. "You did great. Now have a sip of tea. You need it."

Frances limped from the center feeling like she'd just given blood to an overzealous practitioner. With a faint sense of alarm, she realized that Grayson was nowhere to be seen. But she could scarcely put one foot in front of the other much less wrap her mind around the task of finding her Sherpa. "He'll just have to find me."

She rocked on her heels until her back rested against the wall, and then she slid down into a seated position like she was waiting for a yoga class to start. Her eyes sagged and just as her head drooped forward, an announcement rattled the loudspeaker. "Frances Beacon, report for mandatory debriefing." But the message fell on deaf ears as she lost her grip on consciousness and slumped to the side.

How long had she wandered in timeless time, spaceless space before a nudge roused her? Then another more insistent push.

"Grayson?"

There was no answer so she opened one eye just wide enough to see the shaggy outline of Gabriel standing over her. With a slow shake of his blond ears, he sighed. "Let's go, Frances. This is no place to sleep."

CHAPTER 65

"Dollop, doozy, bumfuzzle, crotch." Frances stood in her room like a statue, chanting the list as she tried to shake the recycling experience clouding her brain like a hangover. "Venusian, bloviate, pentimento." The blare of the big-rig's horn echoed in her head. "Linseed, sfumato, Alizarin, paint, paint, paint."

As if guided by a gentle hand, she found herself in front of the easel. The large canvas stared and the dots of paint waited patiently, still sealed under a glaze of oil. She lifted a wide brush and poked at the cerulean blue, which yielded like a baby's cheek. Then quite without warning she was channeling her five-year-old self, utterly without expectations except to see what would happen if she dipped her brush twice, one side in yellow and the other in blue.

Freed of her lifelong habit of nattering self-judgment, a padlocked chamber in her brain inched open and released a trove of images that streamed out through her arm. She worked quickly, dashing off impressions of a crowd of pedestrians and craggy rocks battered by waves. Hours crept by in a colorful daze until she surrendered her brush with a sigh of satisfied exhaustion.

But there was one more task before she could sleep. She rummaged in the corner of the room and recovered the abandoned journal. Turning to a fresh page, she printed *Last*

Will and Testament of Frances Beacon, and then laughed out loud. She, Frances Beacon, Geriatric Hell-Raiser, always the one with a decade of plans and a To Do list as long as her arm, had neglected to make a Will. All the forms were sitting on her desk, but she'd cancelled the appointment with the lawyer twice and never rescheduled. Of course, she could rattle off the usual excuses. Too busy. Too healthy. Too certain she'd live to one hundred.

The only form she'd manage to complete was a DNR—Do Not Resuscitate. The last thing she'd wanted was a lingering twilight made possible by the life-support industry. The thought of idling without control or purpose sickened her. And what kind of person would stick her friends in front row seats, forced to listen to a symphony of breathing apparatus while the metronome of beepers syncopated her performance in limbo?

DNR but no Will.

Frances dragged her pen through the words *Will and Testament.* Too late for that. But she was longing for some sense of closure so she scrawled

Final Adjustments/Remarks.

To Sylvia:

Love you, girl. You always had my back. Please check on Nick. He's a good soul. Cantankerous but easier to manage after a carton of noodle salad.

To Mr. Wilson:

You're the best morning driver on the M79 bus. An unflagging optimist dishing out good cheer to one and all, even on the dreariest day. How did you ever remember my birthday?

To My Dear Readers,

Do what I said, not what I did.

To New York City

Love and kisses to the snow angels in Central Park, the Thanksgiving balloon wranglers, the most authentic Chinese

food in the country, the early morning flower displays and late-night strollers. The best place to be alone but even better if you're in love.

To Dad:

I carved your name on our favorite rock in Central Park. Maybe we can meet up there again.

And then paint-spattered, Will-less Frances Beacon slept.

In the morning she tried to rouse herself but felt like she'd been sleeping under one of those lead aprons worn during dental x-rays. Curled on her side, she stared at the paintings propped against the opposite wall. A single oak leaf. The bone stark trees of winter in Central Park. "Not bad, but don't give up your day job."

She'd painted half the night despite the residual lassitude of the energy transfer. Now the tank was empty.

If I could just stay in bed for a while.

But hiding was rarely a good solution. "The best way around is through," she mumbled like a mantra as she shuffled toward the bathroom and the daily rogues' gallery waiting in the mirror.

Who will I be today?

She flipped on the light and was greeted by a Toulouse Lautrec depiction of her weary face. She would have fit right in with the dance hall entertainers and prostitutes made famous by the aristocratic, alcoholic dwarf. Their garish make-up couldn't hide the boredom and hopelessness of life in the Parisian demi-monde.

She took her cue from the mirror. After all, wasn't she a performer, too? Even when plagued with jet-lag and a serious throb in her lower back, once her feet hit the stage, she'd deliver an out-of-body experience that galvanized her followers and left her high. So rather than wait for Grayson's knock, she plastered a smile on her face and threw open the door, ready to go into her act. The moment she spotted him she sang out, "Greetings, Shock Jock. What new adventure awaits me today?

Algebra II? Home dentistry?"

Grayson refused eye contact. "Actually, you have another *date*."

"A date?" She tried to sound surprised and excited but her voice was shrill. "Let me guess. The *Deus Ex Machina* match-making service? Sounds intriguing, but I think I'll pass."

"It's in court."

"In that case, I'll take romance."

"It's not optional." His eyes were hooded but his voice hinted there was trouble ahead and she couldn't count on him to play human shield.

Heedless of the warning, she soldiered on, determined to thaw out the conversation. "Well, how about a sneak preview?" she said brightly. "What's on the agenda?"

"Can't say."

Her cheerful performance evaporated. "Can't or won't?" He didn't budge and she wouldn't back down. "Is this like some Code of *Omerta*? You guys all take a vow of silence. Keep Frances in the dark."

"You have a vivid imagination." But there was no admiration in his voice. He just seemed weary of the whole enterprise.

"That's not exactly an answer. I want to know what's going to happen."

"There's no telling." Again, the flat affect as he began to turn away.

Frances grabbed him by the arm and spun him around. "But you're supposed to by my guide," she taunted.

"Right." He stared off into the distance, then slowly blew air out of his cheeks like a balloon with a slow leak. "But court proceedings are personal. It's your thing."

"My thing?" Her voice rose an entire octave. "Not likely! *My thing* is to get the hell out of this place, so I'm hoping for an early release. You know, time off for good behavior."

"Good luck with that." He gave a quick snort.

What he means is you're so screwed. She put one hand on

her throat and felt her pulse racing under skin that had turned clammy. This wouldn't do. She couldn't come unglued in front of her accusers. Turning away from Grayson, she slid her hand in her pocket and clutched her phone, rubbing her thumb compulsively over its cool surface.

Courage. Courage.

CHAPTER 66

"Welcome back." Bailiff Morgan held the door and escorted Frances to the chair facing the monitor.

"Got anything else? Balcony seating?" she quipped, gazing around the room.

"You're the star. Front and center."

As she slid into the chair, a ball of blond dog hair like a dandelion floatie drifted slowly across the floor. All else was still.

"Hel-lo-o-o. I'm here." She drummed her fingers and cleared her throat. "Anybody home?"

The speakers crackled to life and once again began to drone in Latin. Lulled by the torrent of familiar yet meaningless syllables, she remembered kneeling in church with her spine straight and eyes closed tight, straining to feel fervor or piety. *Is this how St. Apolonia felt as she leapt into the flames?* she'd wondered. *Or St. Barbara right before she lost her head?* And in that moment, she'd realized that the very act of wondering proved she'd fallen short.

Her thoughts were interrupted by a string of green letters crawling across the screen. *Mortem sibi conscivit.* She jerked her head around and glared at the drowsy bailiff. "Translation, please."

He jolted upright and shuffled through the cards on his desk. As Frances narrowed her gaze, she thought he started to speak but caught himself before a single syllable could escape. Then he pursed his lips and edged toward her, extending the card as you would offer food to a caged but potentially dangerous animal.

She snatched the card and burst out laughing. "Me? A *suicide*? What a joke! That's like calling Gandhi a warmonger. Or saying Julia Child was a vegan. You're making a big mistake."

She stared at the monitor but saw only the reflection of her flushed face. A vein throbbed visibly in her forehead. Rebuttal was impossible without the facts so once again she tried to conjure up a fragment of an image that would supply a clue to her death, but all she could remember was the smell of the sea.

Another crackle as a new line of text crossed the screen. *Quid agis?*

At the back of the room, the bailiff cleared his throat. "How do you plead?"

"Not so fast, Sleepy. I demand to see the evidence. Did I leave a note? Post a good-bye on my blog? Anything? Where are the witness statements? I want to face my accusers."

Silence in the courtroom.

"I've had enough of this!" Frances shouted, kicking the chair. But even as she turned to flee, she began the instinctive examination of conscience that had been drilled into her since the age of seven. Suicide was a mortal sin, a grave matter committed with the full knowledge and consent of the sinner, so she could just forget about her clever indulgences scheme. At any moment, she'd be clamped in chains or smote with a fiery sword. Nearing the exit, she staggered, seized in the grip of fear and hopelessness.

Morgan lurched forward, reaching out to steady her but she swatted his hand away, snarling, "Don't touch me!"

Then a small, cynical voice in her head asked *Are you really surprised? Any fool could see where this was headed.*

The university was just a ruse to prolong your punishment.

Clearly the end was at hand, but this time it would be the real thing.

CHAPTER 67

"Get up!" Frances burst from court and aimed the full force of her fury at Grayson, hunched in the corner of a bench, nursing a smoke. He scowled and casually flicked the cigarette into the air.

She jerked her head toward the door. "That is one lame-ass kangaroo court in there, all dressed up in Latin. My God, what a farce! I've seen more impressive lawyering in traffic court."

"Calm down, Frances. Yelling at me won't help."

"Calm down?! They just accused me of committing suicide!"

He raised his eyebrows. "Wow! Pretty serious."

"Without a shred of evidence." Her mouth went slack.

He folded his arms across his chest.

"It doesn't make sense. Why would I kill myself?" She threw both hands into the air. "I was just getting good at life." Then she ticked off her accomplishments on her fingers. "Day book full of appointments. God knows how many Frequent Flier miles. Green light from the publisher on my next book. I finally mastered the Sun Salutation and did my first tweet. I had it all."

"Yes, you did." His voice emerged just above a whisper.

She drew in a breath, ready to press on in her own defense when she caught a wistful tone in his voice with just a touch of I-told-you-so. But searching his face for clues was impossible because he'd turned away. "Let's take a walk."

Frances followed behind him, feeling like a lamb being led to slaughter, until he stopped at the door of the Records Room. Molly shifted a stack of papers and stood up as they entered, but after a quick exchange of glances, she turned to Frances. "How can I help you?"

"I'm not sure." She jerked her head. "This was his idea."

"Show her," Grayson said flatly.

Molly left and returned moments later, placing a dark green folder on the counter. Grayson shoved it toward Frances. "See for yourself."

The challenge in his voice made her pause and take a step back.

"Go on," he goaded.

"Go on," Molly echoed, all the friendliness drained from her voice.

Frances reached for the file and opened it cautiously, as if expecting a booby-trap. Inside was a pile of black and white photos. The corner of 55th and Madison. The canyon of buildings, the ubiquitous Sabrett hot dog umbrella, a table of knock-off Gucci handbags. She worked her way through the stack, her anxiety mounting with each new image. Emergency vehicles, EMTs. Finally, a wrinkled sheet on the ground. At the edge, her fingers and her phone.

Her gaze was riveted to the scene lit like a stage play. The police. The distraught taxi driver slumped against the hood of his cab. Curiosity seekers gawking at her clumsy final bow. Then she reached for the stack of witness statements, searching for an explanation.

Taxi driver: *I had the light. Wasn't even up to speed. Right out of nowhere, the broad steps in front of me. By the time I hit the brake, it was all over. Twenty-five years I been driving a cab but this scared the shit out of me. Time to retire.*

Witness #2: *She was standing there in a kind of daze.*

Didn't seem distraught or nervous like a jumper. More like a sleepwalker. A couple people yelled to warn her. I tried to grab her arm but I was too late.

The police report concluded that a 65-year-old woman, for reasons that could not be determined, stepped off the curb into the path of an oncoming cab. Died at the scene. Frances glanced at a few more pages but the story was the same.

"Alright, fine. But it was an accident. Not suicide. I had a lot on my mind."

"What about your heart?" Grayson asked.

"Hello?" She held up the photo of her body under a cheap cotton shroud. "What's that got to do with it? I screwed up, I'm dead and now I'm screwing up some more!"

"Nobody's perfect."

"I don't even come close." She shook her head as an avalanche of black and white images crowded her brain. She finally understood the flash of yellow, but that still didn't explain *why*. All she could feel was a profound disappointment. How had she fallen so low?

"Maybe that's not the point," he said.

Frances grabbed a handful of photos off the counter and took a swing at his face. "Would you just shut up?"

"I'm not the enemy, Frances." He turned to leave.

"Listen, I just meant..." she snapped her mouth closed, as if a little silence might undo what had just been done.

He spun around, his face just inches from hers. "Forget about it, Superwoman. You're right. Of course, you're always right. The big altruist, taking care of everybody else, preaching to your huddled masses yearning to be young. What is it you always said? *Live all you can. It's a mistake not to.* Too bad you didn't read your own books."

He slammed the door behind him and ducked into a dim passageway, nearly tumbling over Gabe. "Watch it," he snarled, lunging toward the wall to regain his balance.

"Hey, man. I'm not the enemy," Gabe growled, giving

himself a vigorous shake.

"I know. I know. Sorry about that." Grayson reached down and patted the silky head in a gesture of mutual comfort.

"Hate to say I told you so, but she's not going to make it."

"You're telling *me*?" Grayson closed his eyes and blew out a long, deep breath, as if to empty every trace of Frances from his system. Then he straightened his shoulders and announced, "God, I need a drink."

"Me, too," sighed Gabe. "*Acta, non verba.*"

"Whatever. Let's get the fuck out of here."

CHAPTER 68

Grayson ducked into Strong Silent and looked all around. "I thought maybe she'd be hiding down here." Then he collapsed in his usual corner with Gabe at his feet.

Antoinette just shrugged. "I hate to say I told you so, but..." She offered him a tiny cup with a puddle of sludge, so thick you could stand a spoon in it.

"What would I do without you?" he said.

"Stagger around in a fog. Screw up. Make amends. Repeat. Some fun, huh?" Antionette chuckled. Gabe managed a tiny smile.

"It's not funny." Grayson inhaled the espresso, then stared into the bottom of the cup like he was trying to read tea leaves.

"Humor was never my strong suit. I always serve it straight," Antoinette said, removing the cup and prepping another dose.

"Okay, give it to me. I'm all ears."

"How's your Greek mythology?"

"On a par with high school calculus," Grayson said. "Probably buried in my brain, somewhere near the answer to *Which are the Shiites and which are the Sunnis?* You'll have to remind me."

"Gladly," Antoinette said with a satisfied smile. "Orpheus descended into the underworld to rescue the woman he loved. The gods said: She's yours. Just turn around and walk away.

She'll be right behind you."

"And?" He braced himself for the punch line.

"And nothing. Do I have to spell it out?"

Then the light went on. "Wait a minute. Didn't that story end in tragedy?"

"Pretty much. So, learn from his mistake." She shined the counter top with a towel and gave his hand a squeeze.

"I've been trying to tell you, mate," Gabe said. "You've been going about it all wrong."

"You're right," Grayson conceded. "I seem to be good at wrong." Then he lifted one finger at a time to illustrate each point. "My timing's wrong. My efforts are futile. And honestly, my heart's no longer in it. So enough. She's on her own."

CHAPTER 69

The monitor in the Committee room captured Frances staring at the accident photos in disbelief.

"Well, that went well." Andreas smirked, crossing his arms over his chest.

A panicked voice from the back of the room cried, "The girl's going down in flames and all of us with her."

"Everything's falling apart according to plan," the Fool announced.

"What can we do?" cried Juliette.

"Assume crash position!" the Fool advised

"Joke if you wish, but if she fails, we'll surely perish."

"So what?" said Andreas. "The world is such a fucked-up place, why would anyone want to return?" He surveyed the faces in the room, daring them to present a rosier scenario. Then he continued. "Face it. Maybe we should just throw in the towel."

"Do you even hear yourself?" Perpetua challenged. "That *would* be suicide."

"And I'm supposed to believe you never thought of suicide when you were in that stinking prison?" Andreas countered.

"Prison!" Juliette echoed. "She's a criminal?" She cast her eyes around the table to see if the others shared her surprise.

"I didn't think we sank that low," Gwilym said. "What was she in for?"

"Calm yourselves," the Fool urged. "Perpetua was a belief-criminal. Totally harmless." Olympe leaned over and put a comforting arm around her shoulders. The Fool reached for the button on the monitor but paused, looking expectantly at Cornelius. "Shall we take a look, Sire?"

"Why not?" Cornelius grumbled. "Maybe a little diversion will help because we're certainly not making any progress."

The Fool pressed the button and the screen filled with the silhouette of a young woman swathed in a blue veil, sitting in semi-darkness. Smoke from a brazier drifted toward an old man who clamped the hem of his sleeve over his nose. "What is that filthy stench?"

"Urine, sweat, feces, rotting food, menstrual blood," Perpetua explained. "And tears, father. Tears of the innocent."

"But you are noble born," he protested. "This is no place for you."

"Tell that to your Roman friends, Septimus Severus and his minions."

He shook his head in dismay. "I have no power over them. But you can save yourself. Just a few words." He reached for her hand. "Denounce this Jesus, here in private, and you'll be a free woman."

Perpetua shook her head calmly, as if declining a second cup of tea.

"Then save *me*, my daughter. Have pity on my gray hairs. Do not deliver me to the scorn of men."

She reached for his hand, the only comfort she had to offer but he pulled away in anger. "My father, you're a good man and it breaks my heart to see you consumed with fear. But here's what puzzles me. I care not who they worship. Cybele, Mithras, Dionysus. Polytheism or pantheism. It's none of my concern. So why can't they extend the same tolerance to me?"

Olympe leaned toward Smiles. "We still haven't figured that one out. That headscarf could get her in serious trouble, even if she's just lingering over a cup of coffee in the wrong neighborhood."

Smiles nodded. "Different guru. Same issue. Power by othering."

On the screen a prison guard touched Perpetua's shoulder. "It's time." Her robes rippled and a drape slipped down to reveal a nursing infant. She fondled his head and gently began to remove him from the cradle of her arms. There was a sharp pop as his mouth gave up her breast and he let out a bleating sound that she hushed with a kiss. Then she handed the tiny bundle to her father and reached inside her shawl. "My last letters."

"I've kept each and every one, but I fear they'll be cold comfort to your son."

Then the screen went black.

Perpetua clung to baby Chaghatai and rocked back and forth, trying to soothe herself while Juliette stroked her back.

Andreas continued. "Very impressive. Letters from jail. The life and times of an early Christian martyr and a woman at that." Then he stood and walked around the table until he was standing directly behind her. He leaned down to whisper in her ear, a stage whisper that the whole room could hear. "But didn't you *ask* the centurion to hasten your death with his swift sword after the lions had their fun with you? What do you call that if not suicide?" He stood up and addressed the group. "I'm not judging, just observing. Believe me. I tried to end my life more than once. But it's tricky."

"Tricky?" Olympe asked. Every face around the table was riveted on him.

Andreas stared into the distance for a moment, before launching into his tale. "The longing for oblivion becomes an obsession, and you think you can't take it for another minute. But then life guts you with a perfect truffle. A smile in the marketplace. Compliments from the Queen. And you find yourself waking up to another day of terror."

He paused and walked to the front of the room.

"Finally, I had no choice. It was the hottest summer in memory. A lump of slightly rotten meat made its way into the stew and His Royal Highness, Louis VI, contracted an epic and ultimately fatal case of dysentery. As the king shit his way through his final days, all fingers pointed toward the kitchen. So, I took the coward's path. Locked myself in the King's cellar and spent a long night sampling his stockpile of the finest wines Bordeaux had to offer. Then I stepped in front of a carriage at dawn."

"I'm reluctant to condone suicide," Gerard said, "but I see your point. The loss of favor at court can be a form of living death."

"You're a pariah," the Fool added. "Worse than a no one, scratching for a way to keep body and soul together."

"But that doesn't explain Frances. She was in her prime." Gerard observed.

"Perhaps that kind of self-destructive impulse lingers in the soul," Olympe said, training her gaze directly on Andreas.

"Don't go pointing the finger at me," he protested. "She had free will and far fewer reasons to end it all." He shoved his hands in his pockets and glared back at her.

"Yes, she seemed to have it all," Smiles observed quietly.

"Emancipation," Olympe said.

"She could write anything she wanted," the Scribe said with a trace of envy.

"In a room of her own," Juliette added. "Imagine."

"I don't understand her," Gwilym confessed.

"I do," Cornelius whispered. "God help me, I do."

Andreas seized the floor once more. "As I was saying, why would anyone want to return to the world? It's run its course. And so have we."

CHAPTER 70

"What about a change of venue?"

All eyes shifted toward the yogi as he emerged from his post at the back of the Committee room.

"Maybe there's another place we can go," he said slowly, as if thinking out loud. "Perhaps higher ground."

"I thought this was higher ground," Perpetua said, looking around in confusion.

"News flash," Andreas announced. "Paradise is closed for renovations."

"I'm thinking...other planets," the yogi replied solemnly.

Andreas snorted. "Like the car guy who wanted to colonize Mars? Don't suppose you have the GPS or contact information?"

"The universe is a grand mystery, but there has to be intelligent life out there," the yogi continued.

"That would be a refreshing change from this group," Andreas sneered.

"Even if there was, who'd want us?" Gwilym asked, extending his rough hands out to the group. Then he shook his head sadly. "We're the Huns of the universe."

The silence in the room was broken by the sound of a match being struck as Andreas lit up. Smiles leaned over to Gerard. "I wonder if he has anything more interesting?"

Andreas blew a perfect smoke ring and said, "Look at it

this way. Maybe this is the last time we have to die. Would that be such a bad thing?"

"He's got a point," Cornelius said. "After all, the longer we survive, the more we have to regret."

"What about a voluntary withdrawal?" Juliette asked, surprising the group with a practical thought. "We go to *Frigus Repono* for a few centuries. Wait and observe. See if humans can turn the situation around. Evolve."

Gerard heaved himself to his feet, unfolding his long limbs like a carpenter's ruler. "More likely we'll be watching the world turn to ash. Have you seen what they've done to the planet? It's scarcely recognizable in some places. Ancient forests that sheltered us for 600 years..." He shook his head as if surveying the devastation. "Plowed under or disfigured by ruthless neglect. The lovely springtime carpets of purple spurge and saxifrage. Gone. Damselfly, bees, and God knows how many species of birds. All gone." He looked as if he wanted to weep but when he continued, his voice had taken on a harsh, accusatory tone. "There's a perpetual unrelenting funeral for nature. The cortege is circling the globe. But does that stop anyone? No! Their rapacity is boundless!"

"*Gotterdammerung*?" Smiles asked.

"The Twilight of the Gods," Olympe said.

"It looks that way," Gerard agreed as he hung his head. "I can't bear it."

"Well, you may be right but there's still money to be made," Cornelius observed, rubbing his hands together.

Gerard straightened his shoulders and trained his full fury on the Dutchman. "That's precisely that kind of thinking that got us into this mess!" Then he lowered his voice, as if delivering an indictment. "We may be the first species to engineer our own extinction." He slumped back into his chair—a study in dejection.

Not a word was spoken as they pondered their collective fate. Finally, the scribe broke the silence. "Maybe they're right."

All heads turned his way and Olympe leapt from her chair. "What?!"

"Maybe our time is over. Everything has to end at some point. Countless civilizations far greater than our own—the Incas and Aztecs, Persians, Mesopotamians, the Greeks, the ancient Chinese, my own people. All gone."

"My point, exactly, dear scribe," Smiles said. "We humans have survived devastating setbacks. History has proven that over and over. Who could have imagined in the depths of the plague-ridden Dark Ages that there would be a Renaissance?"

"Or believe that a mob of women protesting the price of bread could lead a march that would catapult a king off his throne and fuel the French revolution?" Olympe added with a look of pride.

"Or imagine the Beatles while listening to Lawrence Welk?" the Fool said and he hummed the opening bars of *Yesterday*.

"True, we humans do have the ability to make corrections and overcome even the worst of our follies," the yogi agreed and solemnly folded his hands.

Smiles was now in full evangelizing mode, striding back and forth as if addressing a room full of his Victorian shop-keepers. "We must embrace our fate. Return to the world, join the others and carry on. The yogi is right. Life is a gift, and the appropriate response is gratitude, not despair."

Gerard leapt to his feet, overturning his chair as he shouted, "There's no time for another Renaissance! And we had the Enlightenment but what did it get us? The triumph of reason, individualism and skepticism. Our instincts for greed and power dressed up as philosophical notions. We elevated competition and self-interest over the common good, alienating ourselves from nature and each other."

"I give you Exhibit One, Cornelius Beeckman," the Fool said, as he clapped his hands on the Dutchman's shoulders.

"Precisely," Gerard continued. "Exploration became synonymous with exploitation and we never looked back." He smashed his fist on the table top. "I tell you, this time there will be no Phoenix-moment for the planet." He shook his head in despair. "It's too late. And I for one am not eager to witness its destruction."

Undaunted, Smiles mustered his courage and countered, "It's never too late."

"Until it is," Andreas said with finality.

Cornelius stood and solemnly announced, "Time to cast your ballots."

CHAPTER 71

Frances slammed the file shut and fled from the Records Room, but she couldn't escape the black and white evidence that her memory had carefully deleted. Adrenaline to the max left her shaking and sweaty but she fought down her panic. *There must be some way to avert this catastrophe before it's too late.*

She needed a hideout and a shot of something to kickstart her brain. *The subway.* Maybe Antoinette would be on duty, espresso at the ready, and they could conjure up a salvage plan. But no shepherd awaited her. Not even the dog. *Who would come to my rescue after that spectacular demonstration of hubris?*

Words started to flood her head, but there was no time to waste. She had to move or they might find her in the morning, frozen on the spot, transformed into a pillar of salt like Lot's wife. *Just choose. Choose and get moving.*

She set off and immediately found herself in a damp passageway so narrow in places that the rough walls grazed her shoulders. For a panicked moment she wondered if it would close down completely, entombing her in its silence. Then a bit of light announced an intersection up ahead. She squirmed out of the passage and scanned the clearing, but it was identical to the last and no doubt, the next.

Now the fog crept in on all sides, laid siege to the top of

the buildings and filled the courtyard like a rising tide. More than once she lost momentum and wobbled in place but managed to scrape together enough energy to press on, like a wounded animal. Fear and regret seized her.

Amends. Somehow, I must make amends.

A paving stone caught her toe and she fell hard, knees and elbows taking the brunt. Pressing her cheek to the cold stone, she surrendered. *Well done, Daedalus. I'm the minotaur waiting for death.* But a hand reached down and in one smooth motion she was on her feet, staring into the face of Danny, the attendant in Room 13.

"Thank God, I found you," she gasped, clutching his arm with the desperation of a drowning person.

Danny looked puzzled. "I think it was the other way around."

"Whatever. You're just the person I need. I want to try again." She faced him straight on and grabbed both of his shoulders to capture his full attention. "I know I can do it this time!"

"Sorry, Frances. It's too late." Something in his voice told her that the discussion was closed.

"But..."

He raised his hand to dismiss her cry of protest. "Follow me."

Danny deposited her outside her room and departed without a word. As she reached for the knob, she spied the corner of an envelope peeking out from under the door. She grabbed it like an owl plucking its prey from an open field, galvanized by a jolt of hope. But the envelope gave no clue to the sender or contents, so she proceeded warily. The paper inside was stiff and creamy, the message handwritten in the elegant script of a wedding invitation. But the contents were chilling, the language terse.

In the case of Frances Anne Timothy Beacon
The charge of suicide: Upheld

Case #3174: Closed
Transition Specialist: Reassigned
Sentence: Frigus Repono

Frigus Repono. Cold storage. "Florida," she whispered. She stared at the words but they didn't register. She simply couldn't imagine herself not existing. "I'll be gone forever? No!"

It was only a matter of seconds before the full impact of the court order would hit, paralyzing her. So, she dove for the safety of her secret room like a Londoner during the blitz, and braced herself against the door as if trying to foil an intruder. But the room was now a trap. Frances was ambushed by a wildness inside her that was determined to escape, regardless of the wreckage left in its wake. Her chest tightened like a vise, collapsing her lungs. But gasping was out of the question since her pursed lips were holding back an eruption that had been suppressed for years or perhaps centuries.

She glanced at the tiny window and for the first time saw light. Not bright sunshine but a faint rose horizon against a dark green sky. Desperate for air, she rushed over and gave it a shove. "Shit!" She hammered the handle viciously, but to no avail. *Some idiot painted it shut.* She snatched a putty knife from the easel and wedged it in the gap between window and frame, pressing with all her might. A cracking sound confirmed her hunch and she inched her way around the seal, determined to conquer its resistance. With a final thrust the window surrendered and she stuck her head through the frame, like a dog gulping the breeze on a cross-country drive.

In that instant, before she could duck or retreat or refuse delivery, a gust of ocean air smacked her full in the face. The salt was a solvent, breaking down the last barrier. She heard the sound of the sea being sucked away, and then returning to crash and sigh. A gull cried and she was back on the corner of 55th and Madison, wrapped in memories like the fog in a Turner painting. Stunned and inert, she propped her head against the window and closed her eyes. Mac's face waited behind her eyelids.

Once again, she remembered walking on their favorite beach, dodging the incoming tide, picking up the odd shell before going home to make love. Afterward she would sleep with her face buried in his shoulder, his beard still smelling like the sea. Then an avalanche of images tumbled over her. Sharing popcorn in the darkness while watching a French film, then sparring about the plot over dinner at their local bistro. Strolling arm-in-arm through Central Park in winter, when the view through the bare trees extended from the Metropolitan Museum to the high gables of the Dakota. They warmed their hands with chestnuts and scalding coffee while black squirrels foraged in the snow.

"See that tree?" Mac announced one day. "It tried to kill me when I was ten."

"That's impossible," she'd laughed. "Trees are benign, especially a black cherry."

"I don't know a sycamore from an elm," he protested. "All I know is I ended up with a broken collarbone and six weeks in a cast." He reached toward a scar near his left shoulder. "Ruined my whole summer. You call that benign?"

The tumble of memories was relentless. A phone call in the night and the rush to the hospital, then holding hands and sobbing as his father slipped away. And Mac's signature text to check in when she was working or to bid for her attention when she was distracted. Sometimes sitting in a restaurant her phone would beep R U there? She'd look up at his dear face, shocked that her mind could be a million miles away when they were sitting just two feet apart.

On nights when he was gone, she'd crawl over to his side of the bed and press his pillow to her face like an oxygen mask, causing a contraction in her chest so fierce that it made the word soulmate seem like casual acquaintance. Then she'd sleep all night in the impression of his body.

When he was gone.

A tremor like something seismic shook her and she clung to the window for support. Her chest contracted so violently that she was sure she'd vomit, retching the words she couldn't say. She pitched and rocked, unhinged by a single inescapable epiphany.

Paving over my grief didn't kill the pain. It just alienated me from memories of the best thing that ever happened to me.

Then she let out a single piercing cry that seemed to go on for whole minutes. Just when she thought the compression would crush her heart, the howl subsided and waited for her to steal a frantic breath. She tightened her grip on the window and wondered, *Is the human body built for such grief?* Upon the word grief, the howl resumed its tortured aria, determined to wring the last wail out of her sorry self.

When she finally opened her eyes, she saw all her sobs condensed into a cloud on the glass. She drew a heart and wrote their initials: FB+JMP. Then she kissed the pane, leaving her lip prints in the fog. The clock ticked in the silence and for the first time since her arrival, she knew exactly what to do.

She yanked open her door and Gabe nearly tumbled inside. "Take me back to court!"

CHAPTER 72

"You have no right to be here!"

Bailiff Morgan trailed Frances like a bounty hunter to the front of the court room, certain that she was revenge-minded and intent on vandalism. "You had your day in court, Beacon." He pointed toward the door like he was banishing a dog who'd chewed up the new rug. "Now leave!"

Frances spun around and snapped her head left and then right, strafing the empty courtroom with a menacing gleam in her eyes. "Nobody moves, nobody gets hurt." She glanced at Gabe. "That goes for you, too." Without a word, he settled down at a cautious distance to watch the fireworks.

Morgan was accustomed to deference and secretly enjoyed the worried expressions he could evoke simply by shifting in his chair or adjusting his hefty leather belt. Tears, whimpers, pleading. He thought he'd seen it all, but this was definitely new territory. Professional pride kicked in. He wasn't about to be bullied by a woman half his size, so he lunged at Frances.

She ducked and surprised him with a robust shove that sent him spread-eagled into the chair. Before he could recover, she planted one foot on the edge of the seat directly between his legs. With a grunt that reached down to her solar plexus, she sent its dumbfounded passenger flying across the room.

Crash! Thud!

Morgan massaged the back of his head with an expression

that said he might be reconsidering his employment options. Then Frances took up her stance squarely in front of the dark monitor and gave it a sharp smack on the side.

"Or-der!" the bailiff pleaded. "Order in this court!" His voice trailed off to a helpless whimper.

"Save it, Morgan."

With her hands on her hips, she lifted her head, extending her chest like the prow of a ship. One long inhalation and then she fired the first volley. "Now hear this! You're right. I *did* commit suicide."

Suddenly the monitor expanded to wall size and one by one the members of the Committee appeared as holograms. Cornelius took up his stance, front and center. Pierre made room for Perpetua who jiggled Chaghatai to keep him quiet. Without a word the twelve arranged themselves in two rows and gave her their full attention.

Gabriel pricked up both ears. Morgan's mouth fell open like he'd forgotten it was there. Then he gave a short, sharp gasp and jerked to attention. "Say what?"

Frances approached the screen to study one face after another. "That's right. I was a living example of how to be dead because I rejected the most fundamental attribute of being human." She paused and lowered her voice. "The ability to love and be loved. And why?" She planted herself directly in front of Cornelius. "Because I was a coward. Afraid to face the pain of loss."

The bailiff leaned closer. "Go on."

"Not just a coward. I was a hypocrite, an imposter, broadcasting my mantra of *live all you can*, while I anesthetized my heart. In the process, I killed the self I could have been. Should have been."

"Sounds like she's pleading sanity," the Fool said.

"That's tragic," Morgan whispered.

"You have no idea. I had a man who was my true love. Something I didn't dare to hope for, and wasn't sure I could handle. Gentle, funny, caring. My favorite person in the whole world, and he *loved* me." Her voice caught in her throat but she struggled on.

"But I was terrified that if he saw the real me—the flawed fool—he'd turn and run. I didn't trust love. But it was more than that. What if I did love him, really gave it my all, and then he disappeared? I didn't think I could bear it. So, I held back. Gave my inner skeptic free reign, and that tyrant robbed me of the very reason to live."

Andreas hung his head and the scribe put a comforting hand on his shoulder. Gabriel shook his head slowly, and then ambled to the front of the courtroom. "Fascinating confession, Frances. Lots of drama and pathos. But you always were a great performer."

She clenched her right hand into a fist and struck her breast over her heart. "Mea culpa, mea culpa, mea maxima culpa."

"Nice touch. Act of Contrition." Gabriel complimented. "But what have you *learned*?"

She drew in a deep breath. "Here's what I've learned. Too late. That you can't temper love to minimize the pain when it's over. Nor should you want to because the pain is proof of a great love. It's a tribute. I squandered all that because I was... afraid." Her voice rising, she pressed on. "There's one more thing I know to be true. Love requires the courage to be human. To fall and fail and come undone and still love yourself and know you're worthy of love."

She paused and then declared: "I love, therefore I am.

"I told you it's never too late," Smiles whispered to Andreas.

"And I told you tough love works every time."

Bailiff Morgan was on his feet, "You go, girl!" he whooped. Gabriel gave a tiny dog smile but all of this was lost on the penitent. Frances was hunched over, her hands braced on her knees like a sprinter who'd just crossed the finish line of a hundred-yard dash. As she began to sway, Morgan hurried the chair over and clamped a guiding hand firmly on her shoulder.

She collapsed, limp and panting. Her head dropped forward, eyes closed, and she surrendered. Eternal damnation or *Frigus Repono*. Weeping and the gnashing of teeth or oblivion. It no longer mattered. It was as if she'd been picked up by the heels and shaken. There was nothing left. She was a void.

Morgan tapped her gently on the shoulder and pointed toward the screen. Bright blue subtitles crawled below the Committee members with the words, *Brava, Frances. Bene factum.*

"Bravo, Frances. Well done," Gabriel translated.

As she stared at the monitor, the sound of applause filled the court room, slow and muffled at first, and then growing into a roar of clapping and cheers. Frances knew this sound from her seminars. She staggered to her feet and turned to find the formerly vacant gallery packed with boisterous observers. A beekeeper in his gauzy hood stood next to the Oracle, still a brilliant blast of yellow. A fisherman with a net slung over his arm jostled a jailer in French livery. An Ashanti weaver swathed in vibrant Kente cloth linked arms with a nun wearing a wimple the size of a giant kite. A cobbler in a leather apron high-fived a Chinese farmer who tossed his conical straw hat in the air and a young woman raised a new-born infant high above her head in salute.

Frances bowed, then thrust out her arms in a V, as if in a single gesture she could simultaneously embrace and return the sentiment. Finally, her arms curved and crossed in front of her like a ballerina. She wrapped herself in a hug of acceptance and love, her face bathed in tears.

Morgan gave a slight bow as he handed her a sheet of creamy parchment, her Letter of Transit. "Congratulations, Ms. Beacon."

She pressed it to her chest, like a cardiac victim clutching the life-saving paddle that had restarted her heart. Mustering all her courage, she turned to face the monitor where the Committee members were busy congratulating each other on a job well done. Olympe waved her neck scarf in a victory salute. Gerard hurled a bouquet of miniature roses before slapping Smiles on the back in a gesture of mutual triumph. Gwilym clapped his rough hands rhythmically and Juliette inclined forward in a hint of a curtsy. The Mute waved one hand dusted with yellow chalk.

Overwhelmed, Frances closed her eyes and covered her lips with both hands. Then she blew a storm of kisses to her former selves, grateful beyond words for the gift of sharing their saga. When she blinked away the last of her tears, the monitor was small and dark again. All she could see was her own reflection as her lips formed the word *home*.

When she reached the exit, she extended her hand to the smiling bailiff. "Thank you, Morgan." Then she changed her mind and planted a kiss on his cheek.

"Until we meet again," he whispered and handed her Gerard's bouquet.

She stumbled into the hallway, like a triumphant gladiator with nothing more to give. Then she felt a soft nudge.

"Come on, Frances," Gabe said.

Now what? But her mind was blank.

CHAPTER 73

Frances stood in her room clutching the bouquet of roses and her Letter of Transit, but before she could conceive of a next step, she collapsed. All she wanted was her bed. She pulled the covers around her, too spent to appreciate the weight that had been lifted from her spirit and the tangible promise of freedom.

Hours later she heard her phone beep softly through her pillow. She pulled it out and squinted at the screen. R U there? pulsed brightly in the palm of her hand. As she trembled in confusion and joy, her back nudged something solid and familiar. Instantly, she clamped her eyes shut and held her breath, waiting to feel the slight pressure and release of someone breathing. On countless mornings she'd awakened just this way, back-to-back with Mac. Now her only thought was to hold on to this miracle as long as possible.

Don't think. Feel.

Her ecstasy was shattered by a soft knock. "Frances?"

"Go away." At the sound of her voice, her pantomime lover bounded off the bed, gave a low bark and trotted toward the door.

"Don't answer that," she begged.

But moments later she heard soft footsteps entering the room. "I said go away." She pulled the sheet up over her face, like a child who believes that if she can't see the world, it can't see her.

Grayson settled himself on the edge of the bed, cup in one hand, patting Gabe with the other. "So, I wanted to congratulate you on your victory in court. I heard it was quite a scene."

"Please don't say another word," she mumbled through the linens. "I'm a catastrophic loser. A four-star fool."

"Okay. Is this a recent phenomenon or are we heading down memory lane?" He gently pulled the sheet down to her chin and gave her a smile.

She sat up and pulled the covers around her. "I'm serious. I had it all and I threw it away with both hands—because I was a coward."

"You seem pretty fierce to me."

"Nope. Chickenshit to the power of ten."

"That is serious," he said and gave her his full attention.

"I had a great love. The kind you read about in books. But did I give it my all or even let it in?" She paused, still staggered by the magnitude of her folly. "No! And why was that? Because I was afraid of how much it would hurt when it was over." She shook her head in dismay.

"Here. Take a sip." He held out a small, steaming cup.

"Antoinette's?" she asked.

"Who else?" Then he gently prompted, "I'm listening."

"There was this fascinating man. He was smart and kind and loyal. And he got me! Really understood who I was and managed to love me despite that." Then she shook her head. "No. It was even better than that. Loved me *because* of who I was, warts and all. He had such a generous heart and all I could come up with was this miserly self-protective gesture. A bonsai love." She seemed to shrink back into the linens, rubbing her cheek on the sheet for comfort. "I wasted so much time trying not to get hurt, when all I had to do was open my heart and let in the magnificence."

"I guess you never read Dr. Seuss?"

She dropped the sheet and stared at him in disbelief. "I'm

talking about the greatest fuck-up in my life and you're invoking Theodor Geisel? This better be good!"

"It is. The wise old Doctor said: *Don't cry because it's over. Smile because it happened.*"

"Yes, well, it's a little late for that. And what about Mac? He deserved better."

"People make choices, Frances. He must have been getting something out of it." He paused and gave her the slightest wink. "Hot sex?"

Frances chuckled and mopped her face with the corner of the sheet. "He used that trick, too. Said ridiculous things to make me laugh when I was a basket case. Sometimes it even worked. But when I was truly distraught, he'd hold me so tenderly that it felt like I could melt into his body and be safe forever. Life with him was an extraordinary gift for which I have no explanation."

"So that's a *no* on hot sex?'

"Relentless," Frances said, shaking her head.

"It's one of my best features. Never give up." He stood up and held out his hand. "Now, how about if we take Gabe for one last walk? I think this is getting him down."

Grayson patted Gabe's head. "Come on, pal. Lead on! Lead on! The night is waning fast and it is precious time to me."

CHAPTER 74

Gabe shambled down a passage so narrow they were forced to trail behind in single file, like three explorers entering a cave. Before long he lifted his nose, picking up a scent. Then he broke into a trot. Frances hurried to catch up and rounding a corner, she was smacked by a wall of salt air and the glimmer of moonlight on the open sea. With a cry of joy, she grabbed Grayson by the hand and dragged him across the square. They sat side-by-side on a low wall in the semi-darkness with Gabe at their feet.

"It was just as I feared. It ended as suddenly as it began. I was in the Dallas airport, heading home after one of my talks. I was looking for a little gift to thank him for all his help when I got the call. He was on his way to the emergency room. By the time I got there, he was in intensive care." She paused and took a huge breath, gathering enough courage to tell the tale.

"It's okay," Grayson whispered, holding her hand.

"Three years, twenty-five days and it was over. Mac was gone so soon we didn't even have time to talk about what he wanted, so I took his ashes up the coast to our favorite beach. He loved doing photography there. I'd curl up in the shelter of a rock and read. Then we'd go back to the inn and make love."

Frances took a deep breath. Grayson shifted on the wall, reaching down to pat Gabe's head while she composed herself.

"I took him for a last walk and it was just like every other time. Kids playing tag with the waves, birds in a flawless sky. I passed a few other solitary walkers who all said hello the way city walkers never do. Then I headed for a cove filled with dozens of rock cairns, like a Shinto cemetery. I'd planned to scatter his ashes in the tide pools with the starfish and anemones, but I couldn't throw that treasure into the sea. So, I took out just a pinch of ash and offered it to the waves."

Frances paused and closed her eyes tightly, as if trying to gather the courage to go on. A tear leaked out and paused in the hollow below her eye where Grayson intercepted it with his thumb.

"Then I sat on the beach until sunset, holding him in my lap, telling the rocks and waves all the things I'd never had a chance or the courage to say. Just before dark, I drove back to the inn and lay on top of the covers, holding him. I couldn't bear to crawl into that bed where we'd spent so many nights. All the way home I kept thinking that there should be a monument to signal the loss of a great, great man. He was my hero."

She stopped and drew in a long breath. "I'd have given all the years ahead of me to have just one more with him."

"What happened then?"

"I took the coward's path—again! Somehow, I convinced myself that I should just carry on with my life. That's what he'd want me to do. So, I did what I knew best. Worked. Doubled my appearances. Wrote like mad at night until I was nodding at the keyboard. Then I'd take a huge slug of cognac straight out of the bottle to anesthetize myself enough to sleep. That worked for a few hours, then I'd get up and do it all over again. I kept trying to force a positive outcome from my personal nightmare. Work was my armor against grief and I wore it well."

Now she was hunched over, weeping. "I thought I knew him by heart but some days I have trouble remembering his voice. I'm afraid one day his face will disappear and then I'll have nothing."

After a few minutes she took a deep breath and dragged her sleeve under her nose. "God, I'm a mess."

Grayson reached into the breast pocket of his coat. There was a crinkling sound as he pulled out a pack of cigarettes. "Smoke?"

"Got anything more interesting?"

His fingers probed in the pack and he fished out a joint. Not a little twig of a thing but a fatty. More than enough to get the job done.

Frances winced. "I can't."

"Come on. It can't hurt you now."

"It's not that. I'd love to smoke a brick of the stuff!"

"So, what's the problem?" He pulled out his lighter and the flame outlined his profile in gold.

She intercepted his hand. "I never mastered the skill set."

He squinted a question mark.

"I was a 50-year-old pot virgin," she confessed.

"Seriously?" He tried to stifled a laugh.

"Yep. I was a pot snob. More of my misspent youth. I'd watch the stoners giggling for no apparent reason and then eating like they were going to the chair. No thanks. I was uptight and deathly afraid of calories."

"Hey, somebody had to drive," he chuckled.

"Right. Well, when I finally got around to trying it, the only way I could manage was with a water pipe and I still ended up coughing like a two-pack-a-day Marlboro man."

Now he let himself laugh out loud. "It is an acquired skill."

"You're telling me. And there was..." She hesitated but then threw caution to the wind. "Ever heard of Newton's third law?"

"You'll have to remind me."

"You know. Equal and opposite reactions. Well, that's me. For every cough, there was an equal and opposite contraction in my lower hemisphere. PCI—pot-cough incontinence. So, I have a double handicap, remedial skills *and* a failing sphincter. God, I can't believe I said that!"

"Let's try something." He fired up the lighter and touched it to the joint. "Breathe out slowly for as long as you can." Then he took a long drag and the weed glowed in the dark.

Frances exhaled until the hiss of her breath dwindled to a tiny whisper. When she nodded, he took her face between his hands and put his lips over hers. Pure shock trumped the need for oxygen and her mouth flew open. Then he exhaled and the secondhand smoke flowed into her lungs—gently, softly, painlessly. Their lips formed a seal and she found herself sucking on his mouth like a deep-sea diver wedded to a mouthpiece.

Suddenly, it wasn't about the pot anymore. Her tongue began to explore the warm cavern of his mouth and was met with a tenderness that pierced her. He matched her impulse and the boundaries blurred until it was impossible to tell if she was inside his mouth or he in hers. The geography kept expanding until it wasn't a kiss. It was a vast and timeless place where they merged and she never wanted to leave. Without disturbing the moment, she reached under his shirt and found a small lump just below his left collar bone. The imprint of his childhood skirmish with the cherry tree. His body stiffened slightly as she stroked the scar.

"It's you," she whispered. "All along it's been you." She looked up just in time to see his features ripple like a stone had been thrown into a pond and she was staring at Mac.

"It's me." He folded her into an embrace that felt like a huge quilt on a cold night. A plunge into warm water. A return to the womb. She clung to him with all her might and wept.

"Don't cry. It's alright, my darling. You're safe."

They held each other for a long time just listening to the waves as the moon set on the horizon. Then he rose and held out his arms, swaying slightly to the music only he could hear.

Frances rose and joined him. For a moment they stood like two Victorians, their hands touching lightly, eyes locked in a solemn gaze. "Hello, you."

"Hello."

Then J. Macintosh Pfeiffer grabbed Frances Anne Timothy Beacon in a bear hug, whirled around and whispered in her ear, "Shall we?"

It was an unmistakable invitation that froze her on the spot. Her hands slid down his chest, and she heard that crinkling sound again. "Can we?" she ventured, scarcely trusting her voice.

With a smile that said he'd saved the best for last, he reached in his pocket and pulled out a sheet of creamy yellow parchment—his own Letter of Transit. "We can."

Her face lit up momentarily like a thousand candles. Now they could return to the world. Have their reunion. Get it right. There was just one hurdle. The final leap of faith that would allow her to let go of this precious moment and believe.

"Are you absolutely sure?" she implored, nose-diving into a chasm of doubt only moments after tasting euphoria. The descent was so swift that their dance seemed like a mirage, their future together just a rumor. "You're certain that I won't be a hopelessly neurotic fool again, too blind to see what's right in front of me? Or otherwise engaged on the day you're supposed to cross my path? Oversleep and miss my train? What if I turn left instead of right or delete your e-mail unread?" The torrent of fears gushed forth without hesitation or shame, laying her bare. "What if? What if I forget everything I've learned?"

She grabbed him by the lapels and stared into his eyes, fierce and frightened and hopeful in equal measures. Then she weighed each word as if it was her last. "Do you promise I'll look in your eyes and know it's you?"

"Yes, my love. That's how it works."

"Then let's go home."

ACKNOWLEDGEMENTS

 Am I the only one who gets annoyed when Oscar winners rattle off a list of people who 'should' be thanked, or woe be to their careers on Monday morning? It's like listening to a breathless recitation of the phone book. And then, as the music rises to chase them off stage, maybe—just maybe—they squeeze in a hurried *thank you* to a wife, husband or kids.

Well, I never expect to get my hands on an Oscar but I'm determined to turn that practice on its head by starting with my husband, Durnford King, who is my favorite person in the whole world. He's a lover, a goader, a comic, and a profoundly spiritual man. Not perfect, but perfect for me. He's seen me at my most abject, usually just before I text my therapist, and he applauds me for facing my fears. He's also the first one on his feet when I do something well. A brilliant writer, he's an astonishing in-house critic. I can't imagine life without him.

Who else? I have a small group of friends who go way back. They love and trust me despite the fact that I borrow lavishly from their lives for material. I'm not apologizing. All writers do that. So dear friends, if you recognize yourselves in these pages, many thanks. If you don't recognize yourselves, here's to Karen Boiko, Diana Donan, Pat Lem, Marolyn Freedman, Danny Miller, Viki Montera-Heckman, Geri Destefano-Webre and Margaret Maruschak. Also, my cherished brother, Bob Schmidt, my niece Sonya Romero and my sister Sheryl Marmo. And two more beautiful souls, Anthony King and Thalia Ryder. Every one of them has enriched my life and my writing. Thank you for the profound gift of your friendship during this adventure called life. And I hope in the afterlife.

I'll also be forever grateful to my gifted museum colleagues who welcomed me into their world. Thank you, Sharon Vatsky, Lisa Mazzola, Will Crow, Suzanne Isken and Kim Kanatani.

Then there's Anne Isaacs, an amazing therapist who helped me understand what Buddha meant when he said, *You yourself, as much as anybody in the universe, deserve your love and affection.* This may seem like the kind of thing you'd want to grasp a bit earlier in life but as self-realization goes, I've largely confined myself to the remedial group. However, things are looking up.

And what would life be without weekly doses of flamboyant creativity, inspiration and courage from Rob Brezsny, creator of Free Will Astrology? Every Tuesday he delivers a view of the universe that inspires me to hope bigger, love harder and put my best self out into the world. See for yourself at freewillastrology.com.

To my students, in the hundreds, who made me feel like my life has been useful. Many of them are carrying the torch of social justice into the future, including Nicole Chu and Amber Tamblyn, both spectacular poets.

Thanks to Nick Courtright, the publisher of Atmosphere Press, Kyle McCord, my editor, and the entire team of author-centered professionals who made this collaboration an adventure.

And finally, a salute to all the readers who had the courage to pick up a book with *dead* in the title after living through the pandemic. I knew you were out there, my tribe of kindred spirits who have looked for love in all the wrong places, battled personal neuroses like a gladiator, fought for justice against unseen forces and lost hope but found the way. You who love ideas about art, life, friendship and faith, served up with a side of dark humor. The doubters and believers who like to laugh out loud while reading in public and aren't afraid to shed a tear. This one's for you!

ABOUT ATMOSPHERE PRESS

Atmosphere Press is an independent, full-service publisher for excellent books in all genres and for all audiences. Learn more about what we do at atmospherepress.com.

We encourage you to check out some of Atmosphere's latest releases, which are available at Amazon.com and via order from your local bookstore:

The Embers of Tradition, a novel by Chukwudum Okeke

Saints and Martyrs: A Novel, by Aaron Roe

When I Am Ashes, a novel by Amber Rose

Melancholy Vision: A Revolution Series Novel, by L.C. Hamilton

The Recoleta Stories, by Bryon Esmond Butler

Voodoo Hideaway, a novel by Vance Cariaga

Hart Street and Main, a novel by Tabitha Sprunger

The Weed Lady, a novel by Shea R. Embry

A Book of Life, a novel by David Ellis

It Was Called a Home, a novel by Brian Nisun

Grace, a novel by Nancy Allen

Shifted, a novel by KristaLyn A. Vetovich

Because the Sky is a Thousand Soft Hurts, stories by Elizabeth Kirschner

ABOUT THE AUTHOR

Laurel Schmidt is a lifelong educator, art lover and author of four non-fiction books on art, learning and brain development. She taught for decades while working with major museums in Los Angeles and New York. She believes that the secret to longevity is continual growth, so she decided to try her hand at fiction. *How to Be Dead* is her first novel. She lives with her writer husband in Santa Monica, California. Next life—Paris.

Find out more at www.laurelschmidt.com.

CPSIA information can be obtained
at www.ICGtesting.com
Printed in the USA
BVHW081702261021
619923BV00006B/131

9 781639 881239